PRAISE FOR AMANDA PROWSE

'Amanda Prowse is the queen of family drama'

Daily Mail

'A deeply emotional, unputdownable read'

Red

'Heartbreaking and heartwarming in equal measure'

The Lady

'Amanda Prowse is the queen of heartbreak fiction'

The Mail online

'Captivating, heartbreaking and superbly written'

Closer

'Uplifting and positive but you may still need a box of tissues'

Cosmopolitan

'You'll fall in love with this'

Cosmopolitan

'Powerful and emotional drama that packs a real punch'

Heat

'Warmly accessible but subtle . . . moving and inspiring'

Daily Mail

'Magical'

Now

To Love and Be Loved

ALSO BY AMANDA PROWSE

Novels

Poppy Day
What Have I Done?
Clover's Child
A Little Love
Will You Remember Me?
Christmas for One
A Mother's Story
Perfect Daughter
The Second Chance Café
Three and a Half Heartbeats
Another Love
My Husband's Wife
I Won't Be Home for Christmas
The Food of Love
The Idea of You
The Art of Hiding
Anna
Theo
How to Fall in Love Again
The Coordinates of Loss
The Girl in the Corner
The Things I Know
The Light in the Hallway
The Day She Came Back
An Ordinary Life
Waiting To Begin

Novellas

The Game
Something Quite Beautiful
A Christmas Wish
Ten Pound Ticket
Imogen's Baby
Miss Potterton's Birthday Tea
Mr Portobello's Morning Paper

Memoir

The Boy Between: A Mother and Son's Journey From a World Gone Grey
(with Josiah Hartley)

To Love and Be Loved

AMANDA PROWSE

LAKE UNION
PUBLISHING

This is a work of fiction. Names, characters, organizations, places, events, and incidents are either products of the author's imagination or are used fictitiously. Any resemblance to actual persons, living or dead, or actual events is purely coincidental.

Published by Lake Union Publishing, Seattle

www.apub.com

ISBN-13: 9781542024785
ISBN-10: 1542024781

Cover design by Ghost Design

Printed in the United States of America

'I would not wish any companion in the world
but you . . .'

William Shakespeare

PROLOGUE

It was an unseasonably warm May night. Still in the cut-offs and t-shirt she had worn all day, nineteen-year-old Merrin ran up the coastal path that led to Reunion Point, a spit of land around the headland where waves crashed below and gulls nested on the steep cliff face. She inhaled the salt-tinged breeze of this little corner of the wild Cornish coast with its caves and rocky shorelines, before coming to a sudden halt.

The sight of him was enough to do that to her: stop her in her tracks. His broad back hunched inside a navy linen shirt and his freckled arms drawn around his knees. He sat on the cliff edge looking out across the water, flanked by gnarled trees and tumbled-down, rough-hewn rocks, rounded pebbles, bottle-green seaweed and scattered shells. The sun, still fierce at dusk, had for the last fortnight lifted its beautiful golden head to warm the bones of the folk who lived here along the higgledy-piggledy harbourside precariously perched on the rocks, and in the fishing village of Port Charles, where the pub, shop, primary school and church sat facing the sea, sitting firm and proud in the same spots for over two hundred years, give or take a few inches.

Slipping off her trainers, Merrin let them dangle from her fingers as she took a moment, pushing her toes into the spongy grass beneath her feet.

'Hey, you,' he whispered softly, as she dropped by his side and crossed her legs. The flat of her foot lay comfortingly against his thigh. He took her hand and laced his fingers with hers, and there they sat, letting their breath assume a similar satisfied rhythm and quietly staring out over the wild water, where the broad sails of boats littered the horizon.

'That's better.' He raised her hand and kissed it. It didn't matter what the day held for her; knowing this moment of reunion was only ever hours away made anything bearable. Even a day of hard work at her cleaning job.

'I only saw you this morning.' She leant in with her cheek now resting on his shoulder. He turned so his chin lay on the top of her head. So many perfect ways they fitted together.

'I know. It's ridiculous.' He kissed her scalp. 'I want to see you every minute of every day. And when I'm not with you, I'm thinking about you.'

'Really?' She wrinkled her nose, shamelessly fishing for compliments. 'Don't you worry I'll drive you mad?'

'"Love is . . . a madness most discreet." William Shakespeare said that.'

'Did he?' She laughed. 'I'll have to take your word for it.'

'So it's a lost cause, I'm afraid, and far too late to worry about.'

It was not something her family did around the kitchen table: talk about Shakespeare. But that was what he did: he turned her into a different person, a better person. That was the thing about Digby: at twenty-two, he wasn't only handsome – beautiful in fact, with short, dark-red hair, long eyelashes, perfect teeth and wide, cat-like eyes – but he was also smart. Not country-smart, like the boys she knew, but book-smart, and able to quote Thomas Hardy and Shakespeare. For a girl like her, who had hated every second of school, feeling the confinement of the classroom like a weight and preferring to run and jump in and out of rock pools rather than sit with a book in her hand, his learning was impressive. Sometimes, as she stared at his face, she couldn't understand why someone as fabulous as him was interested in someone like her.

They sat in the place where they liked to meet at the end of the day, weather permitting, where the ocean was their television, the clifftop their playground and the cawing gulls the only company they needed. As ever, it felt daring to be on the edge of the grass with the waves smashing against the jagged rocks below, watching the last of the sun sink over the brow of the horizon, covering their world in a fiery glaze.

'I love you, Merrin.' He ran his fingers over the inside of her arm.

It might have been the thousandth time he had said it to her, yet still she loved to hear it; his words lit sparks within her as well as offering much-needed reassurance.

'I love you too.' The acknowledged truth filled her with tiny firecrackers of joy.

'I meant what I said: I want to be with you all the time.' He kissed her and then held her in the way that told her he needed her, his grasp tight, his heartbeat steady and his mouth on the skin of her neck, desperate and seeking.

'Me too.'

'I've been thinking.' He paused and pulled away. 'I don't know how to say it.'

'You can say anything to me; you know that.'

'Okay. I want . . .' he faltered. 'I want us to get married.'

Merrin laughed, loudly and without restraint, throwing her thick, tawny hair back over her shoulder and giggling until she ran out of breath.

'You *are* joking?'

The question leapt from her mouth, his statement catching her completely unawares. Not that she hadn't lain awake in the wee small hours imagining what life might be like if she permanently hitched her wagon to his. Without any grand career ambition, she dreamt of being married to her soulmate, keeping a house and raising children. But it had felt like no more than daydreaming, aware as she was of her tender years and the fact that she and Digby led very different lives and were from two very different families. But, oh, what a sweet dream it was! To marry this boy and live happily ever after, just like her devoted parents. But to admit to a level of love so deep that it might pave the way towards marriage felt like the most enormous risk.

'No, I'm not joking.'

Wriggling free of his grip, she sat up straight, only then noticing the hurt in his eyes. He stared at her with an intensity that was new and searing in its honesty. She realised in that moment that the vulnerability and exposure she felt at being asked must only be magnified if you were the one doing the asking. She ran her palm over the side of his face. To receive a proposal was the most incredible feeling. Intoxicating and an aphrodisiac like no other. Someone wanted to spend the rest of their life with her – and not just someone, but Digby Mortimer, a boy who had been no more than a passing acquaintance until all but twelve months ago! All doubt faded from her mind like early morning mist, eased by the sun's warming rays.

Her life had barely begun, but the simple truth was that eligible men were a little thin on the ground in a small place like Port Charles. She had always thought she'd have to leave the village to find a partner, then drag him back to her beloved Cornwall. The thought of living anywhere other than her home was not something she was prepared to consider, even if it did mean she ended up on the shelf next to the old tea kettle, the family Bible and an old black-and-white photograph of a miserable-looking Granny Ellen and Grandpa Arthur on their wedding day.

'The truth is, Merrin' – he sat up and reached for her hand – 'I'm only happy when I'm with you. Happier than I've ever been. I can be myself for the first time ever. It's like I've shaken off a skin. I don't have to impress you like I do my friends, or pretend everything is hunky-dory when it isn't. And you don't give a shit about the stuff my mother bangs on about all the time – money, status, the *right* thing to do, the *right* place to be seen, the *right* clothes to wear.' He closed his eyes with a sigh, as if even the thought of wearing these masks was exhausting. 'I'm happier sitting here on a patch of grass with this view than at any other time in my life. Whenever we say goodbye, I count down the minutes until I can be next to you again. You make me happy because you love me no matter what.'

'I do.' She crossed her legs and sat forward with her elbows on her knees, her hands inside his. 'I love you no matter what.'

'So let's do it! Why not? Let's get married!'

'Really?'

'Yes. Please don't make me say it again.' He smiled.

'One more time would be nice.' She leant forward and kissed his sweet mouth, feeling a jolt of love deep in her gut for this beautiful man.

'Merrin, will you marry me? Please.'

'Oh, my God! Yes! Yes I will! I'd love to marry you, Digby!' Jumping forward, she lay on top of him, kissing him as he ran his palm over her flat stomach towards her bra so they could celebrate in the only way they knew how.

CHAPTER ONE

MERRIN

Merrin stood outside, barefoot on the uneven cobbles, liking the way they fitted inside the high arch of her instep, anchoring her as she curled her toes around them. No matter the environment, she always felt better without shoes and socks, her feet treading the earth, grass, sea, rocks or shoreline; it seemed to connect her and calm her like nothing else. Especially today and at this early-morning hour when she had woken, climbed from her single bed and trod the narrow wooden stairs, feeling as if a thin cushion of air lay between her and the ground, almost as though she were floating. She was excited mostly, but a little overwhelmed, too. Not that she would show it. It was her knack, keeping herself together when things veered off course – in part because her sister, Ruby, never shied away from high emotion and the chance to display it; her outbursts, mostly unwarranted, were a little draining, no matter how predictable. Merrin's demeanour provided balance.

'Grampa Arthur has collapsed; he's not breathing, Merry! I just seen him in the garden! He's lying on his front on the path!'

'Look at me, Rubes! Look at me! Go and fetch Dr Levington and then go and find Dad in the pub and I'll sit with Gramps. It's all going to be okay.'

Merrin's heart had felt like it might explode and yet she had smiled, kept calm and taken control. Not bad for a nine-year-old. It hadn't all been okay, far from it – Gramps had died – but she knew enough to pretend for as long as she needed to. She missed him still, but it had been a salient lesson that when the shit hit the fan, there might not be anyone else around to take the tiller; sometimes the most responsible person around was you.

She felt a familiar unease at the sight of Lizzie Lick plucking shells from the shoreline and stuffing them into the pockets of her smock, and averted her eyes from the woman most thought of as a weirdo. Merrin glanced back at her surreptitiously with no desire to engage, as Lizzie, who danced to her own tune, mumbled to herself, as per usual.

Breathing long and slow, Merrin closed her eyes briefly, feeling instantly better, calmed. This was the perfect spot with the widest view and she could spend hours here, staring at the waves. Her dad once told her they were the heads of white, foaming horses, cantering up to the break and crashing, before making a sharp turn and petering to nothing on their return. It was now impossible for her to see them in any other way. Looking out over the purple bruise of sky where clouds hung low over the ocean, she offered up a silent prayer.

Please don't rain! Not on my wedding day . . .

The waves roared against the harbour wall in response. The Kellows lived in one of four solid and compact family cottages on the harbourside, although the end two had been sold off a while since as holiday homes. The hands of Kellow men had built them well over two centuries ago, the stones and rocks gathered from the quarry up the coast, each one hefted down to the harbourside. Her dad and the five generations of Kellows before him made their living fishing. And number one Kellow Cottages was where she'd been born and the only place she had lived.

Digby had listened to her reasoning that even when they were married, there was no question of living anywhere other than Port Charles. To try to carve out a life among the crowded streets and throngs of strangers in a city held no interest for her. This village was her home. The buildings along the shoreline were markers, navigational aids and the pillars around which the cottages had sprung. Homes for fishermen and tin miners alike. Nearly all were small and crooked, whitewashed and pretty. Now, with most of the fishermen and the tin miners long gone, the shutters and doors were painted in ice-cream shades and in the summer, scarlet geraniums, crowded into window boxes, danced in the warm breeze, providing visitors with a photo opportunity at every narrow twist of cobbled street and each glance from the windows of their snaking cars, as they navigated the ever-narrowing lanes. Lanes designed for horses, not cars, and for men on foot with fishing nets, not out-of-towners with heavy suitcases full of finery for which there was no venue suitable and no one who either knew or cared about their value. Yes, this was where she belonged and where they would stay and raise their family.

What was it Digby had said? *'I'd live anywhere with you – anywhere. Because where you are is home for me.'* Her heart jumped at the thought.

'Merrin! For the love of God, will you please come in!' her mum called excitedly from the window of the rectangular room with the sloping ceiling that spanned the depth of the house.

'I'm coming!' She let her eyes take one last sweep of the bay before heading inside.

Her mum, Heather, still in her nightclothes, made her way over from the range, which pumped out heat in all weathers, which was why the front and back doors were nearly always open, allowing the odd dog, several neighbourhood cats and sometimes a chicken or two to wander freely from the small backyard into the warm space.

The room had its own particular odour, a welcoming combination of woodsmoke, baking and the wheaty tang of animals. The kitchen-cum-parlour was the heart of the house, and whilst by no means spacious, was still the biggest room, where the family gathered to celebrate or commiserate.

'I've put the curling tongs on and I can do your hair while Dad's in the bathroom, but there's no time for dawdling. You can't be late.'

Her mum, it was fair to say, seemed a whole lot more agitated about the day, the timings and the detail than Merrin was herself. Not that she'd say it out loud, but she'd have been just as happy to have eloped, to have stood on a beach or in a register office or even a little plastic chapel with an Elvis lookalike officiating. How they became man and wife didn't really matter to her, all that mattered was that they be joined in matrimony, in sickness and in health. She loved Digby Mortimer to the point of obsession, fascinated by every aspect of him: the way he looked, the way he sounded, his small unconscious movements, the way he pushed his hair back over his forehead, the flat square of smooth skin at the base of his wrist . . . Just the thought of these jigsaw pieces that made up the whole of him was enough to send a bolt of longing right through to her very core. This feeling was as intoxicating as any liquor.

She reaffirmed her decision to take the day in her stride and not get flustered: confident and unharried in the way that being truly happy had made her. The truth was, no matter the enormous expectation placed on this, her special day, it felt like no more than the final hurdle, and one she and Digby would sail over. After all the calm resistance, questioning, wide-eyed tuts of disapproval and the rationalising of objections raised by both sets of parents – *'You need to live a little first!' 'You're from very different worlds!'* – how hard was it going to be to put on the fanciest frock she had ever worn and waltz up the aisle on the arm of her dad?

'Don't you worry. I've no intention of being late, Ma.'

She reached for the hot mug of tea nestling on top of the Raeburn. Who it belonged to didn't matter. Tea, like most things inside the cramped cottage, was communally shared. 'Lord above! You're heating all of bloody Cornwall!' her gran, Ellen Kellow, was fond of yelling every time she nipped in from her home at number two Kellow Cottages next door, tapping on the door frame with her walking stick and hefting the door shut with her ample bottom.

Pulling her towelling dressing gown around her, Merrin gripped the tea in her palm and took her place at the rickety pine table that had also, for as long as she could recall, lived on the rag rug in the middle of the room. The bathroom, from where her dad now whistled, was at the back of the cottage, once 'outdoors', now 'indoors' by virtue of the lean-to her Grandpa Arthur had put up in the nineteen sixties. The two bedrooms could be found at the top of the steep, wooden stairs.

Port Charles was ever-changing. Restaurants, bars, pop-ups, concessions and businesses with expensive interiors and grinning merchants came and went with the seasons. More often than not, those same merchants who arrived in paradise were, by the end of the summer mere months later, out of pocket and cursing all they had invested, financially and emotionally. Smiles were replaced with tears as they packed up their wares along with their dreams, positioning the large 'For Sale' sign in the window, hoping to attract another dreamer with high hopes and deep pockets. Then they would throw the keys on to the estate agent's desk, before trundling back up-country to wherever it was they had once planned to escape from. She would never understand how they could bear to leave this little slice of heaven.

Her family's cobbled pathway, the deep window seat in the bedroom she shared with Ruby, the tarnished brass door plates, the rusted spear-headed gate with the creaky hinge, even the ancient

Raeburn – in these things she took solace. They were permanent, unchanged and they attached her to the land as surely as if her feet had sprouted roots that went all the way down to the last of the tin that nestled beneath her. It had pretty much been the same for all of Merrin's life and she liked knowing that the wood flooring had felt the touch of her relatives' footsteps, and the soft, knitted blankets on the arms of the chairs the brush of her grandma's fingertips.

She had a glorious life to look forward to – not that she would ever say it, mindful of the feelings of her family and worried that Ruby would rib her about '*acting all high and mighty*' – now she would be living in the grandest house in Port Charles. Her sister, she knew, wouldn't miss the chance to tease her. Not that Merrin would be going far, and she planned on visiting daily, quite unable to imagine a life without the daily banter and cuppa around the range. She pictured her children in this very room and beyond the front door, where the beach had been her playground, and everyone who lived close – neighbours and kin alike – had been her babysitters. But the fact remained that she couldn't wait to climb the stairs to the chauffeur's flat above the garages at the Old Rectory; she just hoped there might be a spot free for her own beloved VW Beetle, christened Vera Wilma Brown.

Digby's parents lived in Bristol for the winter months, a place she had only visited twice. Despite her dad's dire summing-up of the place – '*You wouldn't catch me going there. It's all townies! The same townies that drive us mad all summer – but they're everywhere, all the time! They ain't never going home because they are home! Townies with their fancy restaurants, too many cars and pollution. You don't wanna go anywhere near it, my little maid . . .*' But much to her surprise, she *had* quite liked the city with its noise, traffic, shops, busy streets and harbourside – a bustling place with enough water and boats to make it feel familiar – she hadn't even minded the townies and their coffee shops. Although she had been a little stunned at the opulence of the Mortimers' vast and beautiful Palladian Clifton home, which was fronted with tall stone pillars and wide steps, she knew she wouldn't mind making trips here when necessary.

Both Digby and his father oversaw the biscuit empire that had made the Mortimer family fortune. Like her family's long tradition of fishing, the Mortimers had run their business for five generations. But unlike fishing, the biscuit world seemed a little bit more predictable and a lot more lucrative than the catching and gutting of fish, on account of the fact that, if the catch was a little thin, her dad couldn't whip up a batch on the kitchen table.

Merrin rubbed the damp soles of her feet on the rug, as her mum held her shoulders, bending low to kiss her scalp.

'My little girl, getting married! I honestly can't believe it.'

'Don't cry again,' Merrin instructed. Not only did she find her mum's emotions hard to handle, but she wanted everyone to look their best, and puffy lids with purple dots of distress around her nose was not Heather Kellow's finest look.

'I'm not.' Her mum sniffed through her tears. 'I just can't believe it.' She shook her head.

'So you've said. Do you mean you can't believe someone wants to marry me full stop or you can't believe it's happening today?'

It was most likely the former; Merrin was so very ordinary whereas Digby was . . . he was incredible. A quick shove on the back of her head made her lower her chin to her chest as her mother pinned the top section of her hair into a knot then took up the curling tongs. It was one of the acts that had always bound Heather and her daughters close: ever since they were kids, Merrin and Ruby had sat on the stone wall facing the sea with a towel around their shoulders, while their mum slowly and painstakingly trimmed the ends of their long locks and, on one disastrous occasion, attempted a fringe that made everyone on the school bus laugh and point at them. Merrin had cried while Ruby had punched the chief instigator, Jarvis Cardy, square in the mouth.

Most days, Merrin wore her long, thick hair in a loose braid that twisted to one side at the nape of her neck and sat over her shoulder. But not today. It had been decided that on her wedding day, she would have curls. Digby adored her hair. He loved to run his fingers through it and to have it spread over his broad chest when she lay in his arms, looking up at the big Cornish sky where stars punctuated the inky night. In those moments, Merrin had never known such happiness.

Her mother drew her from her thoughts. 'I *can* believe someone wants to marry you, 'course I can, but you are so young, nineteen . . . just a babby really.'

Here we go again . . .

'You were eighteen when you married Dad. And only a year older than I am now when you had Ruby! And Gran was married to Grandpa Arthur at twenty-two and had Dad soon after.'

'I know all that. It's just that . . . things were different. I suppose . . .' Her mum faltered and the scent of singed hair filled the room.

'I can smell burning!' She tugged her hair from her mother's grip and whipped around to face her.

'It's only a little bit! You've got lots of hair. I'll tuck the burnt bit in, no one will see. Don't worry about it.' Her mum spat on her hair as if any potential flame could be extinguished with such a paltry gob. It did little to erase the stench or restore Merrin's faith in her mum's hairdressing ability.

'Don't worry about what?' Ruby asked as she came down from their bedroom. 'God, what is that smell? It's disgusting!' She wafted the air with both hands towards the open back door. Both she and her mum did a double-take: Ruby's make-up was thick and quite changed the way she looked. Gone was her natural, rosy-cheeked prettiness and in its place . . . Merrin tried to hide her expression, knowing Ruby had gone to a lot of trouble, but her sister looked part pantomime dame and part toddler let loose with her mum's lipstick.

'What you staring at?' Ruby challenged, as was her way, direct and a little defensive.

'Nothing.' Merrin blinked. 'And if you must know, the smell is Mum burning off my hair on the one day I need it to look nice, and *that's* what I don't have to worry about, which is good as, apparently, judging by her sighs and tears, I have a lot of other stuff I should be concerned with.'

'It's my job to worry,' her mum said. 'You are my littlest girl and, if I don't, then who will?'

'Her husband?' Ruby replied, and in one swift move took the mug from her sister's hands, downing the cooling tea before Merrin had a chance to object. 'I'll go put the kettle on.' Ruby made her way to the sink. Her mum once again went to work with the curling tongs. 'I can do your make-up, if you like, Merry?' Ruby called out.

'No!'

'Oh, God no!'

She and her mum laughed in unison.

'Don't know why I even bother trying to be nice!' Ruby mumbled.

Merrin felt her mother jiggle with laughter. Ruby's comical petulance was legendary. As a child, she was the kind of girl who counted the Christmas presents to make sure she and her sister had the exact same number and who used her finger to measure the amount of juice in a glass in case she was being short-changed. Merrin had once asked her mum why her sister was this way.

Heather had shrugged. 'A little bit of theatre and a little bit of the green-eyed monster, I think, but goodness knows, we love you both the same! And never forget she loves *you*. Truly she does. But it's like her pendulum in't quite set right; she swings too far between love and hate – fiery, like Granny Ellen.'

Today Merrin would take her sister's comments in her stride; she was far more concerned with the fact she was off to get herself a husband than her sister's misaligned pendulum.

Husband . . . a grown-up word, heavy with connotation. *Married*. But far from feeling flustered, she let the thought of Digby fill her. *Mrs Mortimer* . . . Her nose wrinkled, as she couldn't help but picture the other Mrs Mortimer. Her mum tugged her scalp with the hairbrush. Merrin winced.

'So where is it you and Digby boy are going to live again?' Ruby asked from the sink, where she was now washing a pair of tights in washing-up liquid.

'In a flat above the garages.' She beamed at the thought of her very own sitting room and tiled bathroom. 'But when his parents are away we'll go into the main house. And don't call him Digby boy!'

'So, if Mum sees you around the big house when she is cleaning, will she have to curtsey? And what if she and Dad are invited to one of her Christmas soirees? Will she be a guest, but also have to carry the canapés on one of them big silver trays?'

Heather had worked for the Mortimers as a cleaner for many years, which meant that Merrin was in the oddly privileged position of having heard her parents' unedited views on her soon-to-be in-laws.

'Ruby!' Heather leapt to the defence of her employer. 'Just stop it. Loretta has always been very kind to me. Truly she has.'

Ruby laughed loudly. 'God, I'm joking! I'm not keen on his mother, but I must admit I quite like old Digby. He told me he'd take me clay-pigeon shooting and I know if we lay bets I can make a fair few quid.'

Merrin laughed, knowing this was probably true. She had seen Ruby's prowess on the pool table at the pub when the townies were there: '*Oh, I use this stick? I mean cue? And I have to do what? Get the balls in the little pocket thing on the sides?*' Merrin would then watch the bets placed before Ruby did what she did best: clear the table with an impressive string of fancy shots.

'And what do you call her, Merry? Mrs Mortimer? Loretta? *Mother?*' Ruby raised her eyebrows.

'Don't be ridiculous!' her mum cut in sharply and predictably. 'She won't be calling her Mother.'

'She hasn't said exactly.' Merrin wished the woman had made her preference clear, but figured this was the kind of detail that would get ironed out after the wedding, when no doubt Digby's mother would say, 'Darling, call me Loretta . . .' probably before giving her a warm hug to properly welcome her into the bosom of the family.

Whilst Mrs Mortimer had only ever been nice to her, Merrin still felt as if she were on trial, under the watchful eye of her future mother-in-law, who often asked her random questions like: 'What do you think about private education, Merrin?'

To which she had stuttered her reply: 'I'm . . . I'm not against it, really, but I think it depends on the child; some kids might like it, but others not, and I'd just want mine to be happy . . .'

'*Kids* . . .' Loretta had repeated, in a manner that made Merrin feel like she had inadvertently failed a test. Mrs Mortimer was also a lot chattier to her when Digby was around, and fell quiet when they were alone. Merrin wasn't used to the silence, not living in this house.

'Morning, all!' Her ebullient best friend came in via the open back door, still in her pyjamas but with her hair neat in curlers.

'Bella!' Merrin jumped up and ran to greet her second bridesmaid, who dumped her holdall, handbag and what looked like her wedding shoes in a pile on the floor. It was typical of Bella, who put very little store in possessions; they were all fairly certain that today would be the first time she would wear a dress, as generally she preferred jeans and old t-shirts.

'How's our little bride doing? Running for the hills or running into his arms?'

Into his arms . . .

'Neither. I'm stuck here while Mum is burning off my hair!'

'She's been moaning all morning!' Ruby called out. Merrin pulled a wide-eyed expression of exasperation at her friend, who winked, well schooled in keeping the peace between the two sisters, who were both her best friends.

'One little tiny bit of hair, that's all! Honestly, no one'll notice a crispy end or two.' Her mum sounded defensive.

'Oh, I don't know, Mrs K, I reckon Loretta might; she has an eye for such detail. "Don't you simply love the early golden glow of summer, rising up from the sea . . ."' Bella had the impression nailed.

Ruby and Bella laughed, but Merrin kept her face straight. It used to be funny, Bella's ability to mimic anyone, but Loretta was Digby's mother and she felt the least she could do was not encourage her.

The house was starting to buzz with activity. Not that the last few days had been calm: her dad had cleaned all the windows of the cottage, as instructed, and had jet-washed the cobbles. Presents had arrived, which her mother had piled up into an elaborate display in the corner, and Merrin had watched surreptitiously from behind her teacup as her sister shook the packages, holding them at arm's length, gauging their weight to guess at their value. She even rattled envelopes against her ear, trying to detect the tell-tale shift of a cheque or a banknote. It had made Merrin laugh. She couldn't give a fig about gifts and suchlike, all she wanted was to be married to

Digby. It felt like days since she'd last seen him as, in keeping with tradition, they had agreed not to see each other the night before the big day. So the previous afternoon they had kissed like it might be their last time, and in truth she loved the promise in their passion.

Heather wiped her hands down her striped nightshirt, then, yanking Merrin's head upright, she gathered the two sides of her hair.

'So, Merry, which is it to be, sides up or sides down?' Her mother stood tall, repeatedly pulling the hair up into a knot at the back of her head and then letting it fall.

'I don't know, either. You choose.'

Her mother tutted. 'You can't say *either*; they are entirely different looks!' Once again she pulled her younger daughter's hair into shape. 'What do you think, girls?'

'Up,' Ruby shouted.

'No, down, hide as much of her mug as possible.' Bella laughed and the girls high-fived.

'You're not helping!' Her mum wiped her forehead and took a breath; she looked close to tears.

'Mum, it's not worth fretting over; it's only hair, who cares?'

'Who cares?' she barked. 'I do, and you certainly should! It is these small things that will make a difference. Look at Cousin Peter's wedding: there was Uncle Peter, a managing director, no less, and I know I've already told you that when Aunty Margaret needed a hysterectomy, she had it done on Bupa.'

'You have!' Bella and Ruby chorused, snickering.

Undeterred, Mrs Kellow continued, 'Money to spare they've got, but no one thinks about the amazing riverside venue or the pre-dinner canapés at Peter's wedding, which I know for a fact cost twenty-nine pounds a head. No, if they think about it at all, the only thing they picture is Aunty Margaret's furry fascinator!'

Merrin pinched her lips together tightly, a trick she employed to stop inappropriate comments popping out of her mouth. It worked. Ruby and Bella were not so practised and sprayed their laughter into the room as they clung to each other, wheezing the words 'furry fascinator!'

'Honestly, Mum, no one will care about whether I have sides up or down. I promise you.'

'I *need* you to care about these things!' Her mother was pleading now.

'But I don't, not really. I don't care so much about the wedding. I just want to be married.'

'For the love of God!' Her mum seemed to fold, and slumped in the old leather wing-back chair by the side of the range. 'I'm getting one of my headaches.'

'Merry's right, Mrs K, you shouldn't worry. Why don't you call your sister and get her to wear that furry fascinator, then that'll be the talk of the town and no one will give a rat's arse about Merrin's hair?'

Heather Kellow pushed her thumbs into her eyes, as if to release some unseen pressure, and sighed. 'I'm trying very hard to make everything perfect for her big day. That's all.'

Merrin sat up straight. 'I wonder why it's called a "big" day? And not a "medium" or a "little" day? I mean, in the scheme of things, compared to what you might go through or achieve in your life, it may turn out to be rather insignificant.'

Her mum gripped the worn arms of the chair and sat up a little. 'Rather insignificant? It's your wedding day! And in a few hours, you shall be getting married, and I'm finding it difficult, Merrin Mercy, to keep my patience. Your dad and I have been working for months to give you the day you deserve, the day that we have always dreamt of for you! And I don't want the likes of

Loretta Mortimer and her lot looking down her nose because I've got your hair wrong or because your dad's got his Truro City tie on!'

'I just don't see why it all matters!' She spoke the truth. The sound of her mum catching her breath, a prelude to tears, sent the room silent. Ruby and Merrin exchanged an awkward look, allies rather than competitors at that moment.

'What have I done now?'

'It's what you haven't done that bothers me, Merrin!' Her mother dabbed at her eyes with three squares of loo roll that she had folded into a little blotter. 'I've had to make all the decisions with Loretta; she insisted I got involved but I felt like I was at work! It wasn't fun for me. I've helped her choose the centrepieces for the table, picked the font for the invites, I even selected the *bloody* hymns.'

Merrin knew her mum was upset if she was using the B word. She hated to see her mother so agitated and knew that Digby's mother could have the same effect on him, remembering the day he had pitched up at the hotel where she was waitressing, his expression downcast as he reached for her and pulled her to him in the car park.

'You all right, love?' She had kissed his cheek as he leant against her.

'I am now. I just needed to be near you.' He had placed his face on her head and breathed her in.

'What's the matter?' It was rare to see him like this.

'Do you ever feel like running away?' He pulled her closer still, as if she were a life force.

She had looked out at the sparkling water and the sun peeking through the light cloud, sending rays down to the sea. Her dad was fixing nets on the harbourside and the door to the cottage was, as ever, propped open.

'No,' she admitted. 'Never.'

'You're lucky.' He had held her eyeline.

'*We*'re lucky,' she corrected.

'Yes.' His expression had changed then, as if in relief. 'We *are* lucky.'

Heather's voice drew Merrin from the memory. 'She's made it quite clear that I don't know the first thing about good taste and, in truth, Merrin, once or twice I felt so cornered I nearly ran away from her, but God only knows the trouble *that* might have caused between you and Digby, so I stayed put.' Her mother took a deep breath, as though trying to calm herself.

'You get married in a few hours and I have done my level best to give you and Digby a special day, one that you will both talk about for years to come, one that will make Aunty Margaret and the Mortimers realise that we are a family to be reckoned with, that Daddy is someone too!'

'Why do you care what Aunty Margaret or the Mortimers think? It's my wedding, not theirs! All I care about is making a home with Digby, looking after him . . . waiting for babies!' She smiled.

Ruby mimed retching and put her two fingers into her mouth. Merrin ignored her.

'I know that, but a wedding is so much more than the event; it's about showing your family and friends how successful you are by how much you spend and by the amount of thought that goes into every little detail' – her mother held up her hands as if in prayer, reciting words that sounded suspiciously like someone else's – 'like whether you should have the bloody sides of your hair up or down!'

There it was, the B word again. Merrin sighed. 'And there was me thinking it was about making a commitment for life.'

'It is! Of course.' Her mum smacked the arm of the chair. 'But that doesn't mean we can't use the opportunity to show off to certain members of the family.'

'Actually' – Merrin walked over and kissed her mum on the top of her head – 'I've had a little think and I think sides up. Definitely.'

''S what I said: sides up,' Ruby confirmed.

Mrs Kellow seemed to soften in the chair, slumping a little and nodding. Her expression was one of relief.

'I just want it to be nice.' She kept her voice and eyes low.

'We all do, Mum.' Ruby spoke softly with only the vaguest hint of sarcasm.

The air crackled with nervous tension.

Merrin looked out of the window at the thickening cloud and wondered if it were too late to elope? The thought of her and Digby alone without Ruby offering cutting asides and with an Elvis impersonator who had no desire to impress Aunty Margaret had never been so appealing.

CHAPTER TWO

Merrin

'I can't do this!' His voice was loud and warbling. The sound of someone on the edge.

Merrin looked towards the narrow corridor as her dad came from the bathroom, racing into the kitchen in his boxers, socks and shirt with the collar poking up under his chin and the cuffs flapping over his hands. 'I feel like a trussed-up turkey!' he moaned. 'I can't get the collar stick things in the little holes and I can't do the cufflinks by myself. I don't know how people put a suit on every day. It'd kill me! Why in the name of God do we have to get dressed up like this? As if today wasn't going to be stressful enough; I don't see why I can't go in my best trousers and—'

'Sports jacket!' Merrin and Ruby finished his sentence, laughing and pointing at each other on cue. He had been moaning about his hired attire since they had collected it from the shop in Truro two days ago, keen to point out he had a perfectly serviceable navy sports jacket that had only been worn a handful of times in the decade he had owned it.

Merrin watched as her mum stood, arms outstretched, willing as ever to help the man she loved, walking over to him with her head on a tilt, as if he were a child that needed placating. She loved how they interacted and relied on each other, knowing it was something she and Digby would build for themselves too.

'Come here, love, and don't go getting in a tizz.' Her voice bore the soothing tone she reserved solely for him and her girls when they were a little under the weather. Ruby and Bella smiled as they looked on. Ben getting in a tizz and his wife having to calm him down was a standard occurrence. They seemed to thrive on it.

By the flustered look on her dad's florid face, Merrin knew her mum's work was not yet done. With deft movements, Heather plucked the collar stiffeners from her husband's palm and inserted them into the little slots, while he raised his neck and poked out his chin. Next, she carefully folded his cuffs and placed the fiddly cufflinks into the holes. Finally, she patted his arm.

'There.' She kissed his nose. 'Look at you, Mr Kellow, you look very handsome.'

'You are only saying that because it's true!' He bent and kissed her cheek in return. 'Thanks, my lovely.'

'It's true, Ben, you'd give that George Clooney a run for his money today,' Bella enthused.

'What do you mean, *today*, Bells? I might be dressed up like him, but he made that whole movie where he dressed up like me, what was it called, Heather?'

'*Perfect Storm*, and how I truly hate that film.' Her mother's tone was clipped. No one needed to ask her why.

Merrin decided to change tack. 'We've got ages yet, Dad. We don't have to be at St Michael's until three.' Merrin knew loitering around in his uncomfortable borrowed clothes would do nothing to aid his stress levels, or anyone else's, for that matter. In a small space, moods were infectious. And she understood; her dad was either in his fishing gear or jeans and a holey old sweatshirt with a soft shirt underneath. She had only seen him in a suit once before and that was for Gramps's funeral.

'I know that, love, but I have something I need to do first.' He winked at her.

'Oh no, not work! I thought Robin and Jarvis were taking care of things today; you'll get filthy! I don't want you walking me up the aisle covered in stinking fish guts!'

'I'll remind you that it's stinking fish guts that has paid for the roof over our head and the food we put on the table.' He pointed at her. 'But actually, no, I'm not working. But I do need to go out for a bit.'

'Don't be late, Ben! Please!' her mother pleaded.

'I won't.' He made his way to the door before turning to look back at his family. 'Think I'd better go and put my trousers on first!'

They all howled with laughter and Merrin savoured the moment. Despite her eagerness to go and grab the next chapter of her life, she felt an ache deep in her gut at the fact that her side of the bedroom was packed up and her clothes and bits and bobs had been stuffed into bags, ready to move to the chauffeur's flat. She wanted to be married to Digby more than anything, but this was her last morning as a single girl in this little house with all its comings and goings, and it felt strange. There was a faint echo of loss edging her thoughts, as the realisation hit that she was going to miss moments like this when she was up at the big house. Silly, inconsequential exchanges, but it was just this silliness, this shared ordinariness, that made up her whole life, as the Kellows wrapped each other tightly with a web of love.

'I can't believe that this time tomorrow I'll wake up and you'll be sleeping somewhere else, Merry.' As if reading her thoughts, her mum barely got the words out before the next bout of tears.

'For the love of God, she's only going up the road!' Ruby pointed out.

'Ruby's right. I won't be that far away, Mum.'

'Up the road or halfway round the world, you still won't be at my breakfast table.' Her mum pushed the wad of loo roll up under her nose as her husband appeared from the bathroom, newly trousered.

'What you crying for now?' He placed his fingers inside his collar and pulled. 'Don't tell me you've got to wear a get-up like this too? Cos if you have, then I understand completely, I feel like bloody crying as well!'

'Dad, it's for one day! Less than that, half a day! You always said you'd do anything for your girls and so today I am asking you to get trussed up like a turkey . . . and if you could do it without moaning every five minutes, that would be marvellous.'

'I'll try, my littlest maid.' He beamed at her. 'I will try.' He, too, reached for the handkerchief in his trouser pocket and wiped his eyes.

'Flippin' 'eck, am I the only one not crying?' Ruby yelled. 'She's getting wed, not going to the gallows. This is a time for celebration! If it was me leaving home, you'd be dancing a jig and roasting a whole hog!'

Her sister did this, too, joked about petty rivalry and smarted if ever Merrin was shown any advantage. Ruby's envy was sometimes funny, but just as often it was upsetting and misplaced, and Merrin was unsure from where it had sprung.

'That's not true, Rubes,' her dad placated. 'I've never had fancy for a whole hog; reckon we'd go for a couple of pheasant.'

'Very funny.' Her sister huffed. 'Well, be in no doubt, *I'm* not sad. I *finally* get the whole bedroom! It's a good, good day. I'm opening the gin!'

'Atta girl!' Bella clapped.

Her sister rummaged in the cupboard, pulling out four mismatched glasses of varying shapes and sizes, into which she sloshed generous amounts of gin, topped up with slightly flat tonic. 'Here we go!' She handed a glass each to her mum, Bella and Merrin, before taking one herself. 'To the bride!'

'To the bride!' they chorused.

Merrin sipped the strong drink and set it to one side. Drinking wasn't really her thing. It wasn't that she didn't like it; she just wasn't very good at it. Digby ribbed her over the fact that after one small glass of wine she was what he described as tipsy.

'Don't I get one?' Her dad had no such issue – he'd certainly had enough practice. 'It's thirsty work putting a shirt and bloody tie on.'

'No, you've got to pace yourself, Dad. We can't have you turning up at St Michael's half cut. Can you imagine Ma Mortimer's face if you started slurring your words or tripped up the aisle, or worse, farted during the vows? She'd never forgive you!' Ruby pulled a wide-eyed expression at their dad, who nodded at the truth.

'Don't think she likes me much as it is, can't see a fart making that much difference. I recall the great Sunday lunch when we were summoned and old Guthrie was as pickled as a herring at the top of the table, and she was swanning around like it was normal to have her husband snoring in the chair before they'd even served the pud. Nuts, they are. And she had the nerve to tut when I licked my finger, having pushed up the drip on the gravy jug. Bloody woman.' He mumbled, then left the cottage, whistling.

'How you feeling, Merry?' Bella, always able to read her friend's mood, asked softly.

Merrin found a neutral expression and sat back down, not keen to be reminded of the awkward lunch and how she and Digby had stared at each other, wishing they were anywhere but refereeing at the table while their parents tried to slice through the atmosphere with small talk and Guthrie mumbled in his sleep. Bella eased her wide bum into the chair opposite hers.

'Calmer than I thought. Excited.' She raised her shoulders as her mum once again set to work with the curling tongs, pulling her hair this way and that. 'I can't wait for it all to begin . . .'

'Now' – Bella sipped her gin – 'there *is* something we need to talk about.'

'What's that then?' She was curious.

'When you're married, which you will be in a few hours' – she looked at her watch – 'Digby may . . . and don't be scared, but he may want to have sexy time with you.'

'Oh, for the love of God!' her mum tutted, but her shoulders shook with laughter.

'Sorry to have to mention it in front of you, Mrs K, but it's a fact. And someone needs to set this poor, innocent girl straight.' Bella held up her hands authoritatively.

Ruby threw her head back and howled her joy. This was Bella's skill; her words and humour provided a glue of neutrality that bound her to her sister. Merrin felt her face colour, glad she was leaning forward with her eyes on her bare feet, which, she could see, needed a good scrub.

Bella continued, undeterred. 'Sexy time can be a wonderful thing.' Her voice was solemn and flat, like she was giving a sermon.

'Well, you should know, you do it often enough,' Ruby put in.

'Ruby Mae!' her mum shouted.

'What? It's true. And please don't interrupt her, Ma, this could be the most important advice our Merrin gets today.'

'I very much doubt that,' her mum added.

Bella coughed; she loved an audience. 'Miss Merrin Mercy Kellow, I'm going to give you the advice my dear, sweet old mother gave me.'

'Your mum is not dear or sweet and she'd cuss the hide off you if she heard you call her old,' Heather interjected.

'I'm ignoring you, Mrs K.' Bella cleared her throat. 'Now, I'm going to give you the basics. And it's all to do with his wiggle and your tuppence.' Even Bella struggled to contain her laughter.

'Tuppence!' Merrin clutched her stomach, as laughter erupted from her. 'I haven't called it "tuppence" since we were at primary school!'

'Well, I don't know what else to call it.' Bella seemed to consider her options. 'I quite like "lady garden".'

'Lady garden!' Ruby shrieked. Merrin was becoming increasingly glad her dad had left the house.

'My mother prefers the word "privates",' Bella added.

'Privates!'

The girls laughed loudly, and even her mum joined in. This was more like the mirth and joy she had envisaged for her wedding day.

'Knock knock!' came the sound of a male voice.

Merrin whipped her head towards the back door, where Jarvis Cardy – the same Jarvis whom Ruby had punched in the mouth over a decade ago – stood, wearing the jeans and a sweatshirt he wore to fish and holding an envelope.

The sight of him, and all he had possibly witnessed, was enough to send the ensemble into the next level of hysterics.

'Jarvis!' Merrin jumped up, trying to contain her giggles. 'How long have you been standing there?'

'Long enough, Merry.' He looked away and shifted his feet awkwardly. 'I just brought you a card.' He walked forward hesitantly with the card in his outstretched hand.

'Oh, Jarvis, thanks! That's lovely.' She held her dressing gown closed at the neck and took the shiny gold envelope from her friend.

'It's a fancy one; I got it in town. It's not one from the shop.'

It meant the world that he had gone to so much trouble. Mrs Everit's selection of cards in the village store was no more than a yellowing assortment of faded tat, covering children's birthdays and one or two 'In Sympathy', but certainly nothing that would be suitable for the Port Charles wedding of the year.

'I'll save it and open it later with Digby, if that's okay.'

''Course it is.' Jarvis coughed and his cheeks blushed crimson.

The room fell quiet, as if all were equally embarrassed, not only by what he might have overheard, but also by the fact that he had briefly been Merrin's boyfriend before Digby. Merrin felt acutely aware that in a parallel universe it could have been him at home right now, looking for cufflinks and ironing his good shirt, him waiting for her at the end of the aisle.

'I'd best let you get on. Good luck, Merry. Enjoy your day.'

'I will, and thanks for the card.' She held it aloft as he turned slowly, as if reluctant to leave. He hovered in the doorway, taking her in, head to toe.

'And Merry.' He swallowed.

'Yes?'

'I just wanted to say . . .' Again he faltered, and licked his lips.

'Spit it out, lad!' Bella encouraged.

'Leave him alone, Bells! You take your time, Jarv.' Ruby came to his defence, as she often did, as if trying to make amends for the great mouth smack he had received when they were kids.

He looked up and smiled at her, grateful, it seemed, for the ally. Then he appeared to lose his nerve and looked again at his feet. 'Nothing.' He shook his head and made his retreat. 'It don't matter.'

Merrin watched him go, glad he had not said or done anything that might have embarrassed them all. She turned to face her bridesmaids and mother, who all stared at her.

'What?' she asked, knowing full well that their thoughts probably matched her own.

'Here we are then!' Her gran, Ellen Kellow, announced her arrival, breaking the silent impasse and slamming the back door shut with her bottom. 'A fisherman's daughter marrying a

Mortimer, did we ever think we'd see the day?' She chortled and shook her head. 'I know I never did, that's for sure. What would old Ma Mortimer say?'

'Loretta?' Heather asked, her eyes crinkled in confusion.

'Loretta, pah. No!' her gran yelled. 'Not Loretta, *his* mother, Guthrie's mother, Eunice. A meddler, that's what she was. A rotten stinking meddler!'

Ruby locked eyes with Merrin, who shook her head almost imperceptibly to let her sister know that she didn't have the faintest idea what her gran was wittering on about either.

'Tell me you're not having your hair like that?' the old lady commented tartly as she sat down in the wing-backed chair her daughter-in-law had only recently vacated.

'It's not finished.' Merrin touched her fingers to her curls.

'Well, I can see that!' Her gran, as usual, didn't pull any punches. 'Ruby, go make your gran a cup of tea!'

Ruby idled to the stove to once again set the kettle on the hot plate.

'I've just passed Jarvis on the path with a face like a smacked arse. Reckon he regrets not popping the question himself.'

'Don't be daft, they were only little 'uns when they were courting, playing at it more than anything,' her mum cut in.

'Exactly! Jarvis has no interest in Merrin, he's far too smart for that,' Ruby fired with her usual lack of charm.

'I know all that, Rubes, but someone should tell it to Jarvis's face; it looked close to tears.'

'Jarvis is a good lad. Reckon you've broke his little heart!' Bella joined in. 'It's not too late, Merry. Until that ring is on your finger you can still change your mind!'

'You're not funny, Bella. I don't love Jarvis. I *never* loved Jarvis, not even a bit. He was just a mate who I practised kissing with, really. I love Digby, and Mum's right, we were only playing at it.' It was the truth. She and Jarvis had embarked on a childish love affair, no more than a juvenile fling that lasted mere months, and they'd certainly got nowhere near the wiggle-and-tuppence stage, but he was her last and only previous significant other, the boy who now worked for her dad and had laughed at her fringe. 'What I feel for Digby is the real deal . . .'

'How do you know, Merry?' Bella's question was genuine, with no hint of her comedic tone.

Merrin took a breath. 'It's hard to put into words, but I just do.'

'She's right,' her gran chimed. 'It's a feeling in the pit of your stomach and a confidence that comes with it. It's so strong you'd ditch your whole family and all you know just for the feel of their arms around you.'

Merrin smiled warmly at her gran, knowing she could not have put it better herself.

'Was it like that for you and Arthur, Ellen?' Heather asked softly.

'No, 'twas not!' Ellen Kellow spat, and everyone laughed.

Merrin took her time. 'I *know* Digby's the one, and I've known it since that first date, that first contact.'

'That first sexy time?' Bella yelled, and even Ellen laughed.

Merrin tutted, but the truth was yes, especially then. She closed her eyes briefly, picturing the face of the man who today would become her husband.

CHAPTER THREE

Jarvis

Jarvis Cardy had woken early. No matter the day, week or month, rain or shine, hail, thunder, snow or a summer's morn, he always woke a little before five a.m. It was the fisherman's curse and he was unable to adjust his body clock when on land; his mind alert and ready to work at the ungodly hour. He had gripped the side of the bed and taken a second to establish whether he was rolling on a wave or on solid ground, thankful for the soft resistance of his mattress.

Not that he'd slept very well. It had been a fretful night of discomfort, as his body twitched and his thoughts raced. He'd climbed from his single bed and pushed open the double doors that led to the flat iron railing of the Juliet balcony. This room at the top of his mother's house on the corner of Lamp Hill was his haven. Ben, Robin and he had renovated it some five years ago when his dad had packed a bag and left. Jarvis, then aged sixteen, had been lost, bereft.

Now, with that particular sadness behind him, he could see that smashing up through the plaster board and turning the attic space into his own private floor had not only been good for him, giving him physical separation from the rest of the house, but it was also vital for his mental health. And not to mention the perfect distraction, as thoughts of his absent dad were buried under the hauling of lumber, the sawing of wood, the hammering of nails, the laying of the floor and the painting of walls. His anger was taken out on joists, lumps of metal and vigorously mixed buckets of plaster. When he'd woken after that first night in his new room and stood at this window, looking out through the gap between the church spire of St Michael's and the tall houses of Fore Street, he could see the cove, the sea and the bend of Kellow Cottages, where Merrin lived. He felt then pretty much as he did now, relieved that no matter what turmoil might come along and rob him of decent sleep, the world outside his window was unchanged.

'Tea, love.' His mum spoke as she knocked and entered his room, the creak of the floor overhead the indicator that her son was awake.

'Thanks.' He took the mug into his palms, grateful.

'How you feeling?' She studied his face in the way that irritated him, made him feel like a child.

'I'm fine.'

'You don't look fine.' Nancy let her eyes crinkle empathetically. 'You look sad, and that's okay. When your heart hurts, it's okay to say so. You don't have to be the big man all the time.'

'I don't think I am a big man.' He held her gaze, as if her words were accusations.

'But that's just it, Jarvis, you *are*. You have the biggest heart and the kindest nature of any man I know. I'm so proud of you. But it's still okay to feel sad. It only makes you human, and your humanity is one of the things I admire most about you. You're smashing. Don't ever forget that. And' – she took a breath, a clue that what came next might be more important than the usual small talk she liked to fill the air with – 'when you give your heart to someone, not that I want you to be in a hurry to do *that*,' she emphasised, 'make sure you give it to someone worthy. Someone who thinks you're as lovely and as special as I do. I think anything less would be a great shame.'

'Thanks, Mum.' He sipped his tea, feeling guilty that he had sniped.

'Is there anything you want to talk about right now?' she asked, turning on her heel, as if second-guessing his response.

'Nope.' He turned back to the view.

'You know, love, no matter how bad a day seems or how much you feel stuck, the sun always rises and with it comes a brand-new day with brand-new possibilities. Things can change in a heartbeat.' She clicked her fingers.

'Yep.'

'It's true. When . . . when your dad left, I felt like my heart had been shredded; I didn't know how to stand up, how to breathe. I fell down.'

He nodded. He remembered every single second of it. Her distress floating from beneath her bedroom door and how helpless he had been to fix things, and how that helplessness had balled in his gut and made him feel both empty and full at the same time.

'And then, last year when he came back, wanting to give things another go, saying he'd had a change of heart, *again*, and that he would like to come home.' Her voice cracked. 'Do you remember what I did? What I said?'

'Yep,' he whispered. Knowing she was going to remind him anyway.

'I cried. I had always planned how mad I would get if I saw him. I had planned all the things I would scream at him!' She spoke through gritted teeth. 'But I didn't. I cried and I very calmly told him how he had spoilt so much; he had given up our lovely life, for what? A thrill. A buzz. Walking away from his family, his home and from Port Charles for something unknown, the promise of a happier, better life that came packaged in a face that was younger and prettier than mine. But it was good, Jarvis, because it was closure. And you now have closure because she is gettin' wed. You will heal and you will feel better. Maybe not today or tomorrow or next week, but one day.'

Again he fixed his eyes on the cove and nodded.

'I'll leave you to it then. Remember, Jarvis, love can be fickle and your feelings for the object of your desire can turn on a sixpence into something a lot like loathing. They don't tell you that.' She tapped the wedding ring that still adorned her finger on the doorframe as she left.

Jarvis closed his eyes, and when he was certain she had gone, gave in to the feeling that had been building at the back of his throat and stinging his nose, as he cried great, gulping tears that fell down his ruddy cheeks and dripped from his chin.

'I love her!' he whispered out into the morning sky. 'I've lost her for good. And that ain't ever going to feel better.'

Jarvis turned on the path after delivering his card and walked across the cobbles in front of Merrin's house. He could hear the guffaws of laughter, mainly coming from Bella's big gob, and knew they were probably laughing at him, but what did it matter? It wasn't as if he could hurt any more than he already did. He curled his fingers into his palm, capturing the point where her fingers had briefly touched his when he handed over the card. Try as he might, he couldn't remember exactly what he had written, and a cold knife of fear cut his confidence at the very thought that in his distracted state, he might have accidently written something soppy or inappropriate on her wedding day – something which she would now reveal in front of Digby the dickhead. He closed his eyes briefly and prayed this was not the case, fearful that the words on the card, sent with the very best of intentions, might at some point come back to haunt him. His stomach leapt with the threat of nausea. She had looked happy, smiley. But what had he expected? It was this fact alone that had prevented him from saying the words cued up on his tongue. The words he had practised as he had showered and walked down the hill with the big gold envelope in his palm.

'It's you, Merry. You are my one. My person. You are kind and calm and sweet, at least you always have been to me, not like some of the other gobby girls around here. And I can't stop thinking about you and I can't sleep for thinking about you. And if ever things don't work out with Digby you know where to find me. I'll be waiting. I'll wait for ever. Because I love you, and whatever it was I did or didn't do that stopped you holding my hand and kissing me, then I'm sorry, and I wish I could go back and do things differently. I had been about to tell you we needed to make more effort, really get to know each other, when you met Digby, and that's when my world fell apart.'

'All right there, Jarv!' Mac from the pub called out from the dock. He raised his hand. 'Cheer up, lad, it might never 'appen!' Mac chortled, but Jarvis could only smile briefly. The fact was, it had already happened. And he had never felt so low, not ever.

He kept his eyes on the coast path he had been walking his whole life. He knew every square inch of the rocks, stones and earth; in all lights and in all weathers, he could find his way with no more than his footfall, but this morning he needed to concentrate on every step. Not only because it stopped him having to interact with Mac, whose words of ribbing or solace were more than he could cope with, but because it also stopped him or anyone else in Port Charles spotting the fact that he had been crying. Mainly, though, he had to concentrate because he felt as if there had been a shift in the world and he didn't entirely trust the ground beneath his feet, fearing he might topple or fall into a crevice at any moment.

He had come to realise in recent weeks that it wasn't only the loss of Merrin that was hard to take, but the fact that the comfortable place he held in the bosom of the Kellow family might also be in jeopardy. And the idea of being usurped by Digby Mortimer was just as unthinkable. Ben Kellow had been like a father to him, especially in recent years, when his own had been absent. He had plucked him from the school life he hated and given him a spot on the *Sally-Mae*, and when funds allowed, he gave his mother money – not that Jarvis was supposed to know about that. And Heather had welcomed Jarvis to their table for many a roast dinner, and when they were out at sea she packed him lunches and suppers. Doorstep sandwiches made of crusty white bread, stuffed with ham and cheese, pickles and mayonnaise. Slabs of fruit cake thickly spread with butter, a punnet of soft, sweet nectarines and squares of clotted-cream fudge in their own muslin bag – a sweet treat to swallow with a warm drink when the night felt long. It was one thing for Merrin to have Digby as her boyfriend, but for Ben and Heather to have him as a son-in-law? The thought of not being welcome in that little cottage where he had known only love and laughter sent cold bolts of fear through his gut.

He walked along the path and dropped down towards the slipway, turning sharply left into the Old Boat Shed.

'Anyone home?' he called out as he pushed the lower door open and stepped inside.

'Up here, lad!' Ben called from the loft above.

Jarvis painted on a smile and trod the rickety stairs that ran up the side of the internal brick wall. He looked down at the three boats that lived in the shed and the cart next to them, which gleamed.

''Bout bloody time!' the stockily built Robin called out, laughing as he threw Jarvis a can of beer, which Jarvis caught, just. 'We've missed you, Jarv!'

'Well, I'm here now.'

He sank down into one of the two battered leather armchairs that took pride of place in the loft. Ben, he noted, was dressed up to the nines; he looked quite comical, but also like someone else entirely. He was sitting up straight with the shiny toe of his lace-up resting on the knee of his pressed slacks. It was rare to see him in anything other than clothing full of holes or with wood glue or patches dotting his jumpers and fleeces. Jarvis thought how odd it was that a shave, a smart shirt and a pair of brogues changed the demeanour of a man. Again he thought of Digby, with his soft hands and his well-spoken drawl, who he had seen in the pub on occasion with his la-di-da mates, his expensive shirts hanging outside of his trousers by design. The cold beer felt good as he hurled it down his neck.

'You might be medicating with that, son, but go easy. I've had me own reminder this morning to pace meself. We need you in fine form to drive that carriage and get us to St Michael's in one piece.'

Ben was right. Jarvis put the can on the rough wooden floor.

'You sure you're up to it, Jarv? We can always find someone else to drive if you don't feel like . . . if it's too much . . .' Ben's tone softened.

Jarvis shook his head firmly. 'No, there's no one Mum trusts with Daisy except me. She can be a bit of a temperamental old mare.'

'Now that's no way to talk about your mother!' Ben interrupted, and all three laughed.

'I'm talking about Daisy the horse, of course!' Jarvis shook his head.

'Reckon my girl's going to like our surprise?' Ben beamed in excited anticipation.

'I think she'll love it.' Jarvis smiled at the thought of doing one thing to make Merrin happy on her special day.

'She'd better! We've gone to enough trouble!' Robin shouted, his voice seeming even louder today. 'But it certainly looks beautiful. I take full credit for the flowers.'

'You did a good job,' Ben acknowledged. 'I'd do anything for that little 'un.' He sniffed. 'And it wasn't as if I was going to pick something off their bloody wedding list. Can you see me giving her a set of pans or a bloody duvet and pillowcases?' He laughed. 'No, this is a far more fitting gift from her old dad.'

'I know she'll love it.' Jarvis spoke with confidence.

'What do you reckon to this get-up, then?' Ben tugged at his collar. His words invited mockery, but his expression suggested he was actually looking for a compliment.

'You look like a proper gent, Ben.'

'I do, don't I?' He nodded, seemingly satisfied, as he shot his cuffs. 'Think I'll fit in with the Mortimers?' He lifted his nose.

'Don't know why you'd want to,' Robin shouted, and this time Jarvis didn't mind, agreeing with the sentiment.

'You know, lads . . .' Ben took his time, choosing his words carefully. 'This is Merry's choice.' He sat forward, resting his forearms on his knees. 'We know she's a smart girl, a good girl, and so we have to trust she knows what she's doing.'

'Do you like the boy?' Robin asked the question Jarvis would not have dared to.

Ben ran his hand over his newly shaved chin. '*Like* is a strong word.' The boys laughed. 'I thought it'd be a flash in the pan when it first started, but look at us all.' He ran the flat of his palm over his lapel. 'One year on, and they've hardly been apart. I've got to know the boy this last year, and I have to say he's always polite, compliments the wife's cooking and brings me a decent bottle of red now and then, so I can't grumble. Plus, I trust Merry's judgement; she's got her head screwed on and she's been raised right and so I'm willing to welcome him into my family with open arms if he makes her happy.'

'And if he doesn't?' Jarvis blinked.

This time his words needed no such consideration. 'Then I'll throttle the little bastard! Or take him for a ride on *Sally-Mae* in a pair of concrete boots.'

They all chortled.

'I'm joking, of course. He seems like a nice enough lad. You seen our Merry today, Jarv?'

Jarvis shifted in the chair. 'I dropped a card in. She was getting ready. All the girls were there.'

'Why do you think I'm here?' Ben chuckled. 'I'm hiding out.'

'There's worse places.' He took in the view.

As he often did on a day like this, Ben had opened the wide wooden hatch, which was effectively one whole side of the room, and lowered it on its chains. It was as if the loft was in the sky itself, as sunshine and warmth touched it and dust particles danced in the rays of light. It was at moments like this that Jarvis found it even harder to fathom his father's actions. The man had given up a place on Ben's boat, a seat at his mother's dinner table and a view like this on idling days. What was it his mum had said? 'Love can be fickle . . .' And in some ways he understood, knowing he would have done anything, gone anywhere and given up everything to have Merrin feel about him as he did her.

'Beautiful day.' He stared at the water, trying to divert his sadness, and inhaled the warm, salt-tinged breeze that filled the space.

'Yep. He's already been asked if the Boat Shed's for sale twice this morning by a couple of blokes with good shoes, empty heads and full wallets.' Robin shook his head and ran his callused palm over his face. 'Mind you, the thought of getting up at the crack of dawn to go out fishing in the dead of winter.' He sucked air through his teeth. 'A big fat wallet of cash from a townie might be a lot more attractive, eh, Ben?'

'You can't sell it!' Jarvis's heart beat a little too fast at the prospect. His interest was selfish: this loft was his haven, his social life and the place he felt closest to his dad, who used to sit on this very chair and while away the hours with Ben. He ran his fingers over the cracked leather arm of the chair, as if feeling the warmth of his useless dad's lingering touch.

'Ignore Robin.' Ben shook his head at the man. 'I'd never sell it. It's a little piece of heaven right here in Port Charles. The memories I have line the walls and fill all the gaps. Courting my missus, mucking about with your dad' – he nodded at Jarvis – 'even sitting here on days like this with you two hooligans.' He grinned. 'This loft is my place and it ain't for sale, not now, not never!'

Jarvis took a deep breath and felt his pulse settle. It was one less thing to worry about and small fry compared to the hollowed-out sensation in his gut and the way his heart felt like it had dropped down into his boots. It was in fact quite similar to the way he had felt when his dad left. He was empty and yet full of loss.

He pictured Merrin's eyes as he had handed her the card. She looked happy, excited, and he was certain it was the first time he had seen her look that way. He picked up the can of beer. No harm in finishing it, he thought, chugging it down, relishing the cold bubbles as they hit his throat.

CHAPTER FOUR

Merrin

Merrin stood in front of the narrow full-length mirror on the back of the bedroom door and stared at her reflection, unable to believe the transformation from her usual scruffy self into this person she barely recognised. She felt a flutter of joy in her stomach: *this* was how Digby was going to see her! She couldn't wait. There had been times when, introduced to the double-barrelled girls from his old school or university who were passing through or here for the weekend, plain old Merrin Mercy Kellow had felt the punch of inadequacy in her gut. How Digby felt about her had never been in doubt, nor did she have the slightest misgiving over her decision to marry him, but she'd be lying if she said the polished Penelopes and vivacious Veritys who had skied with him, sailed with him and played tennis with him didn't leave her feeling a tiny bit like an outsider. There was one notable supper at his parents' kitchen table when all, bar Merrin, had been apoplectic with laughter over an incident she had not seen at an event she had not attended.

'Sorry, Merry, are we being a little rude?' The girl, Phoebe, had placed her hand on her arm. 'Don't worry, it was before your time.'

'I'm not worried.' She had sipped her gin. 'And Phoebe, you're not being a *little* rude.' Her words, offered sharply yet calmly, had given her confidence that she could, when and if required, stand up to these girls of Digby's inner circle.

The room had fallen silent and Mrs Mortimer had stared at her with an expression that Merrin found hard to fathom; she couldn't decide if it was admiration that the quiet girl had found her voice, or fury. Not that Merrin had ever mentioned this to Digby, knowing they had a lifetime to catch up on activities and make their own set of memories, and also not wanting him to think she was one of *those* girls: clingy and insecure, even though she did on occasion let self-doubt infiltrate her thoughts and feel the sharp beginnings of becoming both.

In these moments, it was as if he had a sixth sense. He would come close to her and reassuringly hold her hand, run his fingers over her back or just look her in the eye. The hours they had spent up at Reunion Point, revealing their inner selves, confessing to their fears and sharing their dreams, meant they were in tune and could gauge when what might be an innocuous remark to anyone else was actually cutting the other quite deep. He seemed to know just what she needed and when. She had said as much to Ruby, who had lifted her top lip. 'Wow, what a catch! He sounds wonderful!' Her tone had been mocking and Merrin had resolved not to share such insights with her again. It saddened her that she needed to censor what she revealed to her sister, but there was precious little she could do about that. Bella reasoned it was because Ruby craved the stable relationship Merrin boasted of, but this understanding didn't do much to make her barbs more palatable.

Over the last few weeks, before sleep, she had imagined walking up the aisle on her dad's arm, picturing the moment her fiancé turned his face towards her and his expression as he first glimpsed her in this wedding dress. The thought of it had been almost as exciting as the reality of this moment. Taking a step closer, she scrutinised the frock. It was beautiful, breathtakingly gorgeous, and it was hers. The slim-waisted, full-skirted affair did indeed fit her like a glove, just as Mrs Mort— Lor— Digby's mother had said.

They had gone dress shopping in Truro. She and her mum had been towed along as Digby's mother had either shaken her head or beamed her approval at each fabric suggestion, accessory tried on and every one of the thousands of dresses that had been lowered over her head by willing staff keen for the big sale. It had felt weirdly exciting yet at the same time mildly unpleasant to be trying on a frock that cost more than Vera Wilma Brown.

Her future mother-in-law had told her to enjoy it, but her own mum had remained a little subdued, adopting the same quiet manner as she did when cleaning up at the Mortimers' house. This, she was in no doubt, was due to the fact that Loretta was paying and made the fact known at every opportunity. It had taken the gloss off what should have been an extraordinary day.

Merrin had put it down to the woman's enthusiasm and confidence when it came to matters of taste. But right now, no matter how she had come by the dress, Merrin felt like a princess, as she had always secretly hoped she might, and she was aware that she should catalogue each second and every emotion so that, one day, she could tell their children about how she had looked and, more importantly, how she had felt in these, her final moments as a single girl on her wedding day.

The photographer was downstairs, ready to capture her as she came down the narrow wooden stairs and waltzed out of the house to start the next chapter of her life, so she pulled her full ivory taffeta skirt out before running her fingers over the flat diamanté band across her stomach. Her shoulders were bare, dusted with bronzer. The wide collar of the dress sat snugly over her décolletage. Her mum, she had to admit, hadn't done a bad job with her hair and loose curls grazed her neck while the sides were artfully pinned in a messy half-bun on top. And Heather was right: you couldn't see the crispy burnt bit now it was tucked in.

'So what do you think, Rubes?' she said to her sister, who was sitting on her bed in a floaty, lilac-coloured bridesmaid's frock, her make-up, thankfully, toned down a bit at Bella's suggestion, and with her knees bunched up under her chin. 'Rubes?' She turned, alarmed by the silence, wondering if it was because maybe she didn't look quite as fabulous as she had thought; was something amiss with her hair? Merrin braced herself for a cutting insight from her sister's sassy mouth. To her astonishment, her big sister, who had once pulled out her own rear tooth rather than make a trip to the dentist, who always captained the winning team in the annual Port Charles rowing regatta, and who had a certain reputation for being as tough as old boots, looked very close to tears.

'Oh, Rubes! What's the matter?' As Merrin bent down and rested her knees on the side of her sister's bed, her dress rose up around her like a giant, shiny puffball.

'You look . . . you look incredible! And I'm . . . I'm really going to miss you! Even if I say I won't.' She stuttered her admission, this girl who loved fiercely.

Merrin pushed her finger up under her nose, a little overwhelmed by the rare sentiment so openly expressed, but at the same time not wanting the tears that threatened to smudge the neat slick of mascara she had applied to her top lashes.

'I'm going to miss you too,' she managed, unable to disguise the croak to her voice.

'He'd better be good to you . . .' Ruby spoke through gritted teeth.

'He will be.' She smiled with confidence at the thought of her beloved. 'I *know* he will. I feel like the luckiest girl in the world. I just love him!' She shrugged, as if there were nothing more to say.

Ruby climbed from the bed. 'Come on, then, let's get you buttoned up at the back; you can't be walking into church with your arse hanging out, and you don't want to keep your boy waiting.'

'I've only ever slept in a room with you, Ruby.' Standing, she turned and lifted her hair as Ruby slipped the covered buttons into the fiddly loops.

'Well, if you want me to come and crash on the floor of your fancy hotel . . .'

'Thanks, but that won't be necessary.' Merrin again felt the rumble of excitement in her gut at the prospect of walking into the honeymoon suite at Pencleven Court with a wedding ring on her finger. She imagined floating into the reception. '*Hello, can I get the key for the honeymoon suite – it's Mr and Mrs Mortimer . . .*'

The hotel rooms had heavily influenced their choice of wedding venue. She had been reticent at first, suggesting they keep things small and within a tight budget, knowing her parents wanted to contribute, but Digby had told her that the sky was the limit, that they would gratefully accept her mum and dad's offer, but his parents were happy to pick up the tab. He was, after all, their only child.

'We are only going to do this once, Merry. Once! And so it's roast beef, vintage cars and five star all the way. This isn't some budget get-together, it's our wedding!' He had jumped up and down on the bed in the chauffeur's flat above the garages, which was in the process of undergoing minor renovations, and she had laughed, kissing him hard on the mouth, as he promised her champagne on ice and a real fire on their wedding night, no matter the weather. To be able to spend freely had been a thrilling novelty. In truth, she was looking forward to that time alone with him more than the service and three-course meal and disco that preceded it.

'Not that I don't appreciate the offer, Rubes, but I won't be missing you tonight. We're planning on making the most of the four-poster bed!'

'Wiggle and tuppence!' they chorused, and hugged each other tight for a beat longer than was usual, sharing the moment, both aware that this was the end of an era and neither entirely sure how they would navigate the next.

'What in God's name are you two doing up there? You're making one hell of a racket!' Bella yelled up to their bedroom.

Ruby ran down the stairs, humming and tooting the chorus of 'Here Comes the Bride', while Merrin followed more sedately. She paused as she neared the bottom, knowing that she would never forget the sight of her mum, dad, sister, gran and bridesmaids gathered in the little hallway at the bottom of the stairs, all looking incredibly smart in their finery. They scrubbed up well. The girls' lilac dresses and her dad's gold paisley tie matched her mum's silk dupion coat, which sat neatly over her knee-length tunic dress. Excitement came off them in waves. Their expressions were of love and it was all directed at her. She drank it in, appreciating all that they had ever done and the fact that their unfailing support and sacrifice had given her the most amazing life of warmth and safety, right up until this moment. She might have thought she looked nice enough, but the way her dad's mouth fell open and her mum's tears gathered, the sharp intake of breath from Granny Ellen and the sight of Bella placing her hand over her lips as she shook her head left her in no doubt that Digby would be impressed.

'You look so beautiful!' her dad managed, as emotion spilled from him.

'You really do, Merry!' her mum echoed. 'Like something from a magazine, but prettier.' Then she reached up her sleeve for her handkerchief and blew her nose.

'Where's the photographer?' Merrin looked into the parlour to see if she could spot the man Digby's mother had insisted on booking.

'I shoved him outside.' Bella spoke around a mouthful of food. 'He wanted to push and pull us this way and that, so I told him he could wait for you out there.'

'What *are* you eating, Bells?' Merry noticed the large sandwich in her hand.

'Bacon sandwich.' Her best friend lifted the offending article high. 'So, you remember when Mac from the pub got married and we didn't get any grub until the evening? I was bloody starving; not making that mistake again, no siree.' She took a large bite and wiped ketchup from her bottom lip. 'Plus, I find a chunky bacon sandwich makes a decent beer cushion.'

Her dad chuckled. He loved the girl and her manner.

'Just don't drip grease on to your dress!' Merrin caught the twisted-mouthed look Bella and her mum exchanged, suggesting it might be a bit too late for that particular warning. 'You'll all have to move outside; I'll never get past in this meringue!'

The huddled group did just that, apart from her dad, who held back as the troupe made their way out on to the cobbles at the front of the cottage. She could hear the photographer clicking away and smiled at the thought of Bella's bacon sandwich featuring in her wedding pictures. God only knew what Ma Mortimer would make of that!

Her dad took his time, savouring the moment, but finally he reached up and took her hand in his, leading her down the last couple of stairs.

'I don't think I've ever been prouder of anything in my whole life.' He pushed out his chest and looked her over from head to toe. She saw pride swimming behind his eyes. 'Look at my little girlie. Proper job. Beautiful!'

'Thank you, Dad.' Merrin was careful not to tread on the hem of her frock. 'Don't be too nice to me or you'll set me off!' She walked into his arms and closed her eyes briefly, knowing the next man who held her would be her husband and that her life would be forever changed. 'I wish Gramps was here.'

'He's here, love.' Her dad wiped his nose. 'Don't you ever doubt that he's here.' They were silent for a second. 'Anyway, I have a rather unusual gift for you, Merry. Something appropriate for my daughter on her wedding day.'

'You didn't have to get me a present, Dad.' She knew they had scrimped and saved to give her this very perfect day, meeting some of the cost for the wedding, with the Mortimers picking up the slack.

'Well, it's something I wanted to do and something I hope you won't ever forget. The lads and I have been working on it for months.'

He opened the front door and stepped out, turning back to watch her face, his arm out ready to take her hand and guide her over the cobbles.

'Oh, Dad!' Merrin felt her heart swell and her stomach fold with love for this man. The old open-top horse cart that lived in the boat shed, the one with the horse-hair-stuffed seats and the dodgy cracked paintwork that she and the girls had clambered over, camped on and climbed up when they were small, had been repainted, polished, restored and now stood in front of their home, covered in flowers! Nancy Cardy's old carthorse Daisy, who lived up on Grange Farm, was harnessed in place, and none other than Jarvis himself sat on the leather-mounted seat with the reins in his hand, ready to drive her to the church.

'Jarvis! This is amazing! I can't believe it! Thank you!'

He gave a small nod and kept his eyes on Daisy. She understood his slight awkwardness, having been enlightened by the gang earlier that he might still have feelings for her. Not that Jarvis or his feelings could concern her today of all days.

'Dad! Oh, my goodness, it looks beautiful!' She walked forward in her kitten-heeled shoes, holding the hem of her skirt up with one hand and gripping her simple lily-of-the-valley bouquet in the other, before letting her dress go and running her hands over the multicoloured wild flowers. Long lengths of variegated ivy and snaking leaf garlands had been braided and affixed to the sides of the carriage, the harness, the spokes of the wide wheels and anywhere they could be attached. Even the old clodhopper Daisy had flowers painted on her bridle – the work, she suspected, of the artistic Nancy.

'We can't have our girl walking to the church; you will travel in style!' Her mum clapped.

'I really will! I love you all so much!' Happiness spun her in a cloud of joy that was sweet, perfumed and glorious. She breathed it in, knowing there would rarely be moments like this in her life, when everything was perfect.

'And we love you,' her mother called in response.

Bella fetched the small, rickety wooden stepladder from the side alleyway and the photographer continued to snap as Merrin hitched up her skirt and used the ladder to climb up on to the fat pillows that had been placed on the bed of the wooden cart. Sitting up straight with her legs now dangling over the edge, she looked at the view out over the bay where the sun, high in the sky, sent diamonds to dapple the sea.

'Are you coming up, Dad?' She patted the pillow by her side.

''Course, but I thought I'd sit up with Jarv.' He made his way to the front and climbed up. Adept as he was at stepping on and off ladders on boats whilst rolling on the sea, this short hoick up to the driver's bench was a doddle, even for a man trussed up like a turkey.

'Don't worry, Merry!' Bella climbed the ladder next and took up a spot at the back of the cart. 'We won't let you take your trip to the gallows alone!'

Before Merrin had a chance to question the plan, her gran was being shoved, bottom first, up on to the cart by Ruby. Next came her mum and, finally, her sister, until all the women were settled on pillows, sitting in a sea of floaty lilac silk, the soft reams of her ivory taffeta gown, all set off with the abundance of flowers in their hair, held in their hands and looped around the cart itself.

Their laughter was loud and drawn from the deep wells of happiness inside them. This was some day! The photographer stood on the lane and clicked like crazy, capturing the sight of the cart in all its glory, trundling down the lane with its raucous, floral-framed crew.

Locals and tourists alike – one of whom looked a lot like Aunty Margaret, sporting a rather dazzling fascinator as she made her way to the church – stopped to wave or stare.

'I'm getting married!' Merrin shouted out before falling backwards into her bridesmaids and kin, who captured her arms and kissed her face. She lay looking up at the blue sky with nary a cloud to spoil the view and knew that she had never been happier than she was at that precise moment.

Word seemed to travel ahead that the bride was en route and the residents of Port Charles who were not already in the pretty church at the top of the hill awaiting her arrival came out on to the streets to call her name or wave. It was big news in their little village that one of their own, a Kellow girl no less, was marrying the boy from the big house.

'Look, Merry!' Bella pointed as she pushed her friend up into a sitting position. The side of the Old Boat Shed by the slipway had been decked with a large banner that read 'Merry & Digby' and had a large love heart painted beside the words. She bit her lip; the love, gestures and supreme effort, all for her, were almost overwhelming. She let her head hang down and breathed slowly through her nose, feeling a little light-headed and wishing that she, too, had necked a hefty bacon sandwich before leaving.

'I . . . I don't know what to say,' she mumbled.

'You don't have to say anything, love, just you enjoy it!' Her gran beamed and waved to some of the onlookers as though she were the bride. Her mum wiped her eyes and nose with her lace-edged handkerchief.

The troupe inelegantly alighted at the bottom of the hill to spare Daisy the effort of travelling up it with a heavy load, and walked en masse up the street to the entrance of the church. The bells rang out loudly and strangers gathered on the kerbside to watch Merrin and her entourage, each holding up a section of her skirt, pass. The situation was as ridiculous as it looked and Merrin found the whole charade amusing.

'I feel like a queen!' she giggled.

'Today you are a queen!' Ruby replied.

With all the fun and their unusual arrival at the church most of her nerves had disappeared and, if anything, she felt more eager than ever to get on with it.

'He's in there! I haven't seen him for twenty-four hours and he's in that building!' She clamped her teeth and jumped on the spot, making her heels click clack on the tarmac, knowing that in mere minutes Digby would turn and she would smile at him, just as she had imagined.

'Calm down, love! We don't want him to think you're too keen!' Ruby advised.

'She's marrying him, you daft cow, how much keener can she be?' Bella tutted. 'Look at her! She's beaming. If I, on the other hand, was about to make a lifelong commitment, I would be shit scared.'

'All right, you two, settle down!' Heather Kellow kept the peace the way she had since they'd all been at playschool, when regular fights would break out between them, usually over Play-Doh or whose turn it was to go on the trike. 'Right, this is where we leave you, my darling.' Her mum kissed Merrin softly on the cheek and ran her fingertips under her chin. 'My amazing girl. May you and Digby be as happy as your daddy and me. That's all I want for you. All I've ever wanted for you.'

'And walk carefully up the aisle – don't bloody fall over!' Her gran offered the sage advice as she linked arms with her daughter-in-law, and the two women disappeared inside the wide oak door. Merrin watched them walk away slowly, with a small reluctance to their gait and leaving a kind of sorrow in their wake. And she understood.

The girls fell silent and took up their place behind Merrin as her dad stood by her side. She brought her bouquet to her nose and inhaled the sweet scent of lily of the valley.

'I'm going to keep this for ever, preserve it. It's beautiful, isn't it, Dad?' She held it out so they could both admire it.

'It is, my love, but no flower can match you today, none. Digby is a lucky man and if he treats you right, he'll be my son.'

'Oh, Dad!' She slipped her arm through his and, with her heart full, waited patiently, as instructed by the vicar, for her musical cue: the opening bars of Beethoven's 'Ode to Joy' – Digby's mother had insisted on the tune.

Her dad patted her hand and rocked on his heels nervously as the vicar appeared on the front step.

'Flippin' 'eck,' she heard Bella say softly. 'Oh Lord above, help me. I think I might fancy the vicar!'

'Well, you would, Bells, he's wearing trousers,' Ruby whispered back.

'He's wearing a frock, actually,' Bella corrected.

'Not that that'd stop you,' Ruby whispered. 'We all remember the incident in The Loft nightclub.'

'It was dark!' Bella hissed. 'And she was very persuasive.'

Merrin swallowed her laughter; this was not the time or place for such discussions. Yes, she liked a laugh with her girls, but this was her wedding day and she felt the full, glorious weight of it.

The Reverend Pimm walked slowly towards her, stopping once and clasping his hands in front of him. She smiled at the man who had given her and Digby lessons in married life once a week over six weeks. They had sat side by side in his study and he had asked questions she knew they couldn't get wrong, because she loved the boy and only had to tell the truth. His words were fresh in her thoughts.

'Communication is key to everything. It's vital you are able to speak your mind and say how you feel. Not every day will feel like your honeymoon; there will be days when compromise will be the order of the day.'

Digby had laughed, reached over and squeezed her hand.

'Hi!' she mouthed, and pulled an excited face at the vicar.

It was only as he drew closer that she could see he wasn't smiling. He looked, to steal a phrase from Ruby, shit scared . . . Merrin wondered if he might be feeling ill.

'You all right, Vicar?' she asked brightly. 'You're a bit pale.'

'Am I . . . ? Oh yes, yes, I'm quite well, almost. I mean, I'm not ill, no.' His flustered response caused snickers from her bridesmaids.

'Good luck, Merry!' came a call from the church gates. 'Ooh, we're running late, had to wait for the post van! Sorry, Vicar! But as long as we're in before you, that's all that matters, love, isn't it?' Mrs Everit from the village shop called out as she hurried up the path to the church wearing a large straw hat and her Sunday-best dress; behind her, her husband tripped as he tried to keep up while also tying his navy-blue tie.

'Thank you, Mrs Everit, Mr Everit, and no worries. See you both later!' Merrin waved.

'Have you got the nerves, Vicar? Must be quite an occasion for you – not every day we get a wedding like this in Port Charles, eh?' Merrin's dad stood tall, smoothing the lapels of his morning coat and pushing out his chin, shining with pride and giving no hint of the discomfort he had complained of earlier in the day.

The Reverend Pimm stepped forward and placed his hand on her arm. 'Merrin, I need you to come with me.' His eyes held hers and his tone was kindly.

'Oh, I thought I waited here with my dad and the girls until I heard the music and then walked in, like we practised.'

The vicar swallowed and nodded slowly. 'There's been . . .' He looked skyward, as if this was where the inspiration, divine or otherwise, might lurk. 'There's been a change of plan.'

'Oh, okay. Do I need to wait somewhere else?' She was a little confused, and felt her spit thicken at the prospect that something had gone wrong, but one look at the vicar's quiet smile and her worry fled. What was it he had said during their practice? *'Don't aim for perfection on your day, there is always some unforeseen hiccup – think about the bigger meaning and embrace all that it brings you . . .'* She nodded, deciding to do just that and embrace all that was coming her way.

'Yes.' He smiled at her again. 'If you could come with me. And you, too, Mr Kellow. The rest of the wedding party – you can wait here.'

'Don't be long, Merry!' Bella called out. 'It's bloody hot and my bra's digging in!' She fanned herself with her flowers and Merrin cringed at the fact that her friend had announced this to Reverend Pimm.

The vicar walked at pace around to the back of the church. With her dad by her side, Merrin did her best to keep up, her kitten heels clattering on the path. Finally, they followed the vicar into the gabled porch that led to the vestry. The large square room with flagstone floors and wood-panelled walls smelt dusty, but it was cool and she was thankful for a respite from the heat. The vicar pushed a red velvet chair into the middle of the room.

'Please sit down, Merrin.'

Quite bewildered as to what part of the ceremony she might have misunderstood, she did as Reverend Pimm requested, spreading her dress around her on the floor so as not to crease the bodice. Her dad stood behind her, his hand on the back of the chair.

'I'm not sure what's going on!' She giggled.

The vicar dropped down on to his haunches and balanced on the balls of his feet in front of her. Then his smile disappeared and, looking her in the eye, he started to speak slowly.

'I have only just this minute received a telephone call,' he began, his words issued from a mouth sticky with nerves.

'Is everything okay?' she asked quietly, with a creeping dread that made her bones feel brittle.

He shook his head. 'I'm sorry to say, Merrin, that everything is not okay.'

'Oh?' She took a deep breath and gripped her bouquet tightly.

'It was Digby. The call was from Digby.'

Merrin was glad she had taken up the offer of a chair as the room seemed to spin and her knees went a little weak. 'He called you from the church?' She looked towards the wall beyond which her love stood, her thoughts jumbled. 'Is he all right?'

'He is all right, I think. Yes.'

'Well, good.' She exhaled with relief, because as long as he was all right, everything would be fine . . .

'But he did give me a message – some news, if you will.' Again he swallowed and exchanged a brief anxious look with her dad.

'What news? Has something happened?' Her thoughts raced as she pictured her beloved. *Had he lost the ring? Fallen out with his mother?* She knew things between them could sometimes be a little fraught and worried that in the heat of the moment, with so much going on, maybe they had had a tiff? She thought of all the possibilities and all the solutions, deciding not to let anything spoil her day.

'He is fine.' The vicar paused and licked his dry lips. 'But . . . but he is not coming.'

She shook her head; it was as if the vicar were speaking another language. 'Not coming where? He's what? Isn't he . . .' She turned in the chair and this time pointed towards the main church.

'Merrin.' He sounded her name with conviction and it drew her attention. 'Digby is not coming here today to get married. He told me he's going away and that there will not be a wedding today.'

'What are you talking about? Don't be so daft.' She studied the vicar's face, waiting for the punchline. 'Of course there's going to be a wedding; I've got my dress on! My . . . my mum's in the church and the girls are . . . the girls are outside and . . . and we've booked the honeymoon suite . . .' Suddenly it was as if the air had been sucked from the room. 'I can't breathe!' She scrabbled to reach the buttons at the back of her frock and tore at the shawl collar across her chest, as if it were suffocating her.

'I'll fucking kill him!' her dad yelled. 'I will fucking kill the stuck-up little shit! Thinks he can butter me up with a few fancy bottles of red plonk and a kind word, and then he does this!'

To her surprise, the Reverend Pimm didn't offer any words of defence on Digby's behalf or try to calm her dad. Instead he poured a glass of water from a jug and handed it to her.

'Take deep breaths, Merrin. Take deep breaths and sip some water.'

'I want to . . . I want . . .'

'Yes?' He bent low and looked into her face, as if he might be able to help with her request. But the truth was she didn't know what she wanted.

'So what do we do now, Vicar?' her dad asked, as he pulled the tie from around his neck and yanked at the collar until it was loose, the buttons undone.

'Would you like me to talk to the congregation? I can keep it vague, thank them all for coming and send them home?' He spoke slowly and softly in the voice he had used when they had buried Gramps.

This can't be happening . . . it can't be happening . . . Merrin leant forward in the chair. She felt weakened, her body quite limp, as she stared at the silk toes of her shoes sticking out from beneath the voluminous skirt of her wedding dress. *There must have been a mistake . . . he wouldn't do this to me, he loves me! And I love him! There's been a mix-up . . . we'll sort it out . . . it will all get sorted out . . .*

'Yes, thank you. I don't think I'd know what to say,' her dad replied.

'No, wait!' she called out. 'Don't you think we should call him back? I mean, he might be coming after all; the whole thing might just be a terrible mix-up, and then what would everyone say if you've sent them home? Don't you think we should call him? I want to speak to him!' She was suddenly certain that a phone call could fix this. 'I do. I want to speak to him.'

'Of course.'

The vicar moved with some reluctance to the telephone on the oak trestle table and picked up the phone. He ran his finger over the notepad next to it and dialled the number before holding out the phone. She stood and gripped the receiver in her shaking hands, keeping it close to her face.

'Hello?' It was the distinct voice of Digby's mother.

'It's me,' Merrin began without pre-planning or forethought. 'It's Merrin.'

'Merrin.' There was an uncomfortable moment of silence. 'I've been waiting for you to call.'

'I'm . . . I'm at the church and I don't know what's going on. I . . . I need to speak to Digby.' She heard the crack in her voice.

'Merrin, dear.' Mrs Mortimer took a deep breath and her words when they came were issued slowly, as if rehearsed. 'Now, I'm sure this is a rotten day, but you will look back on it and breathe a sigh of relief.'

'What are you talking about? I just want to speak to Digby, please.' She was in no mood to listen to his mother; she needed to speak to her fiancé. 'Please, can you just put him on the phone?' She was aware of her tone of desperation.

'I'm afraid he's not here.'

'Not there? Where is he then?'

'I don't know where he is.' It sounded like a lie. 'Probably packing and then heading to the airport. I told him I thought the South of France was a good idea, but I'm not entirely sure.' Her tone was a little clipped, and whilst it wasn't lacking in kindness, it suggested it was a done deal. He had bolted.

'What do you mean, you suggested the South of France? What's going on?' Merrin could only repeat. 'We are getting *married* today! Right now! We are getting married! I'm here in my dress and there's a church full of people!' Her voice rose.

'Well, that won't be happening.' Merrin let the woman's words sink in. 'And as I said, in time, you will come to see that it really is for the very best. I think he may have had a change of heart.'

'A change of . . . I don't . . .' She didn't know what to say, didn't know how she should feel or what she should do. The whole thing felt surreal, dream-like. Once or twice she looked towards the door, expecting Digby to burst in and point at her. *'Got you! Come on, Merry, let's get hitched!'* But he didn't, of course. Her head swam and her thoughts were foggy. Her legs shook so badly she thought she might tumble. She was aware of her dad and the vicar staring at her.

'Trust me. Go home, dear. Go home to your family. And one day you will be able to look at this day without pain. Let yourself live, Merrin. Grab life and run with it, because it's short.'

The woman's advice landed in her ear like salt in a wound. She put the phone down sharply.

'Merrin, love? What did she say?' Her dad stared at her, his arms wide, as if he, too, were at a loss as to what came next.

She looked up and spoke calmly, belying the desire that was building inside her to scream the place down or smash something, possibly both. Her heart hurt, like it was speared, and each beat caused the tip of the spear to pierce her skin.

'Go and talk to everyone, please, Vicar. Tell them . . . tell them thank you for coming, but that there won't be any wedding today.'

Her dad swallowed and the vicar nodded, his cassock swishing as he walked through a back door into the church. Merrin could hear the faint strains of music, the music she should be walking down the aisle to. It came to an abrupt halt. And next she heard the sharp collective burble of surprise and the odd shout and cry. Sinking back down into the chair, she decided to wait until the place had emptied before making her exit, wanting to see as few people as possible. A girdle of shame made breathing difficult.

Only a minute later, the vestry door smashed open against the wall. It was her mum and her gran.

'Ben!' Her mum searched her husband's face, the man who fixed everything for his family, as if he might have the answers. 'What in the name of Judas?' She put her hand to her throat.

'He's not coming.' Her dad shook his head and breathed through his nose.

'Not coming? What are you talking about?' Her mum parroted her own disbelief.

'He's not coming, Heather. He left a message with the vicar. The cowardly little shit.' He spoke through gritted teeth. 'Wait till I get hold of him!'

Her mum rushed to where Merrin sat in the middle of the room, and she, too, dropped low in front of her, and smoothed her hair from her face. 'Merry, my little darlin', what's happening?'

'I . . . d-don't know.' She spoke the truth. The voices in the room seemed to echo as debate and questions flew back and forth. 'I don't know anything . . . I don't know what's happening.'

'It's a bloody disgrace is what it is! Them Mortimers are more trouble than they are worth, always were, always will be!' Merrin's gran shouted, loud enough to show that she didn't care who heard. 'There are ways to stop things. There are ways! But to let you come to the bloody church? Wicked is what it is! Wicked!'

'Not now, Mother!' Ben quieted his mum and the room fell silent, eerily so.

After such an upset, an event so surprising and curious, Merrin might have assumed that tempers would fray, questions would be fired thick and furious and that each one of them there would try to verbally work out just how they had arrived at this point? But no, her dad stood with one arm across his waist and the other hand up over his mouth and chin, as if holding himself together, her gran cooed, as if Merrin might be sleeping, and her mum, with the tip of her tongue resting on her lower lip, shook her head repeatedly in short, sharp movements, as if trying to clear a fog. But all were quiet, as were she and the Reverend Pimm, who darted in and out of the room. Once or twice he placed his hand on Merrin's shoulder and pressed down, as if he wished to transfer some of his strength, his calm belief, to get her through the day. She wished it too.

They stayed this way for some minutes – how many she couldn't be sure, five, ten, thirty? Everything, including her grasp on time, was skewed. Waves of nausea flickered in her gut and she had to remind herself to take a breath, to stay present. Her thoughts were watery and once or twice she forgot where she was. It was only the sight of the frock bunched up on her lap and the flowers in her hand that reminded her, and the realisation gave her a start, as if she had hit the floor.

'Jarvis's brought the cart round,' Ben whispered to his wife.

With her mum at her elbow, Merrin stood on wobbly legs, her feet feeling strangely disjointed, as if she had no control of them. With her parents either side of her, each holding an arm, keeping her upright, and her lily-of-the-valley bouquet now abandoned on the vestry floor, she stepped into the porch and out into the light of day. Her two beautiful bridesmaids were standing where she had left them. Their expressions of sorrow were at odds with their pretty lilac dresses. The cart, too, looked a little sorrowful, stripped of its beautiful flowers, but she thought it fitting. Word had obviously spread and with this realisation came a flush of hot shame that coloured her face.

The vicar flapped up and down the path, his long black cassock billowing as he moved. He seemed to be doing a good job of clearing the church grounds, waving off friends and neighbours, all of whom were staring at the floor or each other, seemingly at a loss as to what to do next. Embarrassed on her behalf. This she understood: they, like her, had expected a day of celebration, of fine food, good wine and a night of dancing, but instead they were being asked to go home without so much as a slice of wedding cake. Her dad checked the coast was clear as he guided her out along the path. She leant on him, unable to trust her body to stay upright without such a prop. Ruby and Bella ran forward, their tears loud and their distress raw. They held her, touched her hair and kissed her face, placing their arms around her shoulders as they murmured gently to her.

Little baby, it'll all be okay . . . We've got you, Merry, we are right here . . . Let's get you home . . . It will all be okay . . . Are you cold, doll?

Their words sounded to her like they were being spoken underwater, her breathing was loud in her ears and she could hardly remember how to take a step. She kicked off her shoes and left them on the path, barefoot now on the tarmac, just how she preferred it, grounded and able to feel the earth, warm beneath her feet.

Are you? Are you cold, doll?

It was only this repeated question that made her realise her limbs were trembling and her teeth chattering, but no, she wasn't cold, more . . . in pain. She felt broken. Her chest hurt. Raising her fingertips, she ran them over the front of her dress and up to her throat, just to check that nothing was actually lodged there and no one had noticed; she would have been quite unsurprised to find a dagger, hilt-deep, sitting squarely in her breast.

'Where's the ladder?' her gran called, drawing their attention to the fact that it was quite a step up for an old girl like her.

'Where's the ladder?' Ruby asked the group, even though it was evident no one had thought about the return journey because they didn't expect there to be one. The plan had been that Guthrie Mortimer's chauffeur would drive them in his vintage Rolls to Pencleven Court, where they would celebrate with dancing and champagne.

Her dad scanned the floor to see if there was something that might suffice as a step. Merrin felt her legs sway a little.

I just want to go home . . . someone, please take me home . . . I don't want people to see me dressed up like this . . . like a bride, but not a bride . . . The dress that had earlier filled her with confidence now painted her as a fool. The clingy bodice was constricting and the diamanté waistband sparkled more brightly than ever, catching the sunlight and calling to be admired. She wished it would be quiet. Wanting nothing more than to blend into the surroundings or, better still, disappear altogether.

Her mum leant into her, propping her up. 'It's all right, love. Hang on, my darling. We'll have you home before you know it.'

Merrin felt an arm beneath her shoulder blades and another around the back of her thighs, and suddenly she was being lifted from the ground, grateful to be in Jarvis's arms. He walked to the cart and she buried her face in his neck. He stood tall and laid her on the pillows, before shrugging his arms from his jacket and laying it over her. Bella and Ruby clambered up, giving each other a leg up and scrambling on the wood. They were, she noted, still holding their redundant flowers, but were clearly no longer concerned about keeping their floaty lilac frocks pristine.

'I'll walk down the hill with your mother, Ben.' Heather spoke softly. 'You travel back next to Jarvis and get the big kettle on. We'll be with you soon enough and I think the fresh air'll do us both good.'

'Okay, love. Sure you don't you want me to come back with the truck?'

'No, it's only five minutes. I'll see you there as soon as. It'll be nice to have a little walk, won't it, Ellen?'

'Wait till I get my hands on that boy! How dare he?' Mrs Kellow senior raised her cane as if it were a sword. 'That family is poison! Pure poison! This is what they do!'

Merrin was aware of the conversations taking place around her, and of her girls, who gathered close. Both of them were crying, and she envied them that, as not one tear had left her eyes; she could barely blink.

As the cart moved away, she was lulled and what little remained of her strength left her core. Weakened, she fell further back into the pillows as her girls held her fast. They captured her arms and legs, huddling forward, anchoring her, as they kissed her face.

She lay looking up at the gap between their bowed heads as they shielded her from the sight of tourists and those in their wedding finery, who were heading back to their cars and homes.

Merrin stared into the sky, where storm clouds now gathered, not that she minded, wanting to experience the full force of thunder and lightning. She felt as if she were sinking, down and down into a dark place beneath the cart, beneath the earth, and all her hopes and dreams, now cloaked in sorrow and loss, were sinking with her. She knew that she had never felt such deep sadness as she did at that precise moment. Her life, her plans and her dreams had been shredded and she was blank, raw and floundering, gasping for air like a fish in the net. Exposed and to be pitied, an almost bride. It felt like a nightmare and one she wanted to end. She hoped she might wake and find it was the start of the day, when she would once again stand on the cobbles in her bare feet and embrace all that was coming her way, knowing that her beloved Digby was waiting for her.

'Let it out . . .' Bella urged.

'She's right, let it all out, babby,' Ruby added.

'No one can see you, Merry, you can have a good old cry.' Bella smoothed the hair from her forehead.

But Merrin stayed silent. She couldn't cry because it didn't seem real, any of it.

CHAPTER FIVE

Jarvis

Knowing the wedding service would now be in full swing, Jarvis had parked the cart up on the flat and was giving Daisy a drink and a good rub behind the ears when Robin came haring around the corner with some urgency, his suit jacket flying behind him, eyes wide and the smooth soles of his lace-up shoes slipping on the warm pavement.

'You're not going to believe it, Jarv!' He bent over, one arm leaning on the cart, as he caught his breath. 'He's only gone and done a runner, left her standing at the altar! He stood her up, he bloody stood her up!' He was breathless, but agitated too, excited almost, by the turn of events.

'Is this a wind-up? Are you joking? Because it's not funny.'

There hadn't been much amusing about the whole day. It had been painful for Jarvis to be the one who drove Merrin to the church where she was to marry a man who was taller, richer and luckier than him. Luckier because it was Merrin who would walk up the aisle and take his hand, Merrin who he would wake up to the very next day . . . but there it was. Jarvis knew he was the only one able to confidently navigate the lanes with the cart and keep control of old Daisy, who trusted him. It was a favour for Ben and for Merrin: a gift of goodbye.

He had been aware of Ben taking his seat next to him on the leather bench at the helm of the cart and had felt his arm across his back, giving him a brief hug. The contact and kindness had been enough to cause his tears to bloom once again. Sniffing, he had kept his eyes down to hide his distress, keen that no one saw the state of him, and with the girls in position, he had gently clicked his tongue, uttered commands and pulled the soft leather reins, steering Daisy to the left and right along the cobbled streets of Port Charles. With the laughing women on the flower-filled cart, the horse plodded slowly on, as if she, like he, was reluctant to arrive, knowing that after this long-planned-for trip, nothing would ever be quite the same again.

'You're doing great, Jarv,' Ben had encouraged. 'You're doing great.'

He had got the impression the man meant more than just his ability to steer Daisy along the path. He hadn't watched them alight, but had taken his time, wanting to put distance between himself and the bridal party on this fine, sun-filled day.

'Seriously, Robin, are you winding me up?' Sweating and with his heart racing, he felt the stir of drama in his veins and knew that if this were true he should act, do something!

'I'm not! I swear on my life!' The man put his hand on his heart. 'He never showed. Everyone's going home or going nuts! I can't believe it!'

'Me neither,' Jarvis concurred, trying to take it in. 'Why? Why would he do that?'

'Who knows?' Robin caught his breath. 'Christ, Jarv, what do you think Ben'll do when he gets hold of him? I almost fear for the lad.'

'I wouldn't like to say, and never mind Ben, wait till Ruby gets hold of him.' She had a certain reputation for being lively. He felt something spark inside him that felt a lot like relief – not at the sadness Merrin might be feeling or for the humiliation she had endured, but simply at the thought that the girl he loved was not taking the name of or spending the night with Digby Mortimer. He decided to keep his relief to himself. 'Did you see Merry? How is she?' The enormity of the situation started to sink in, and one thing was for sure, this was no time for celebration, not if Merrin was hurting. He would never want that.

'No, I didn't see her. The vicar gave a short speech and all hell broke loose. Some of the women in the church started crying and Heather and Granny Kellow went roaring up the aisle like they were on a mission! I've never seen the old girl move so fast.'

'I'd best get the cart back round; they are going to need a lift home.'

'They could walk?' Robin suggested. 'It's not like they have much to celebrate.'

Robin was right about that.

'Help me get the flowers off!' Jarvis set to, removing the pretty braids that had been so admired not an hour since. He figured Merrin would need no reminder of the journey she had taken, laughing among the flowers . . . Robin tugged on a plait of ivy and tossed it to the floor along with the bunches of lavender that had been tied into the corners. By the time they had finished, the cart, whilst still in better condition than it had been for years, was a lot less ostentatious.

'Come on, Daisy. Come on, old girl!' Jarvis climbed up into the seat and, with a soft click to the roof of his mouth, set off towards the church to collect the girl he quietly and discreetly loved.

Her face . . . he knew he would never forget it. Flanked by her parents, she had a look of utter confusion, as if she didn't know which way to turn. Her mouth open, she was gasping for breath and without the words to convey her sorrow that her eyes had no such trouble relaying.

He wanted to run to her, take her in his arms and drag her away from the bloody church; he wanted to hide her, protect her and help her heal, and if it wouldn't have been so ridiculous and misplaced, he wanted to place her beautiful head against his chest and cradle her better. He wanted her to know that Digby was a fool, an idiot, a madman to let her slip through his fingers! And that he, Jarvis Cardy, would never hurt a hair on her head or let her down. He would make sure she understood that what he felt for her was a heart-thumping, soul-sparkling love that filled him up. And he knew he would die a happy man if he could wake and look at her face across the table each morning; happy because he knew there was nowhere else he would want to be and no one else he would want to be with. She could rely on him. He would give her the fairy story, friendship, respect and deep, deep love. He wanted to put down strong roots with her that entwined and grew deep, going all the way to the mines, where their ancestors had dug in the dark for tin.

But of course he would do and say no such thing. Because today was supposed to be her wedding day. Instead he would go gently, slowly, and be there for her as her friend.

CHAPTER SIX

MERRIN

Merrin kept her eyes closed, trusting Jarvis to lift her down from the cart. The girls, again with arms wrapped tightly around her, spirited her into number one Kellow Cottages. If a close hold and whispered words of love and reassurance were enough to heal, Merrin would have skipped into the kitchen, whacked the radio on and danced her way back to happiness. If only.

Like a wobbly-legged survivor in the aftermath of an atrocity that had left the room darkened, changed, she tentatively felt her way to the window seat in the parlour and sat down, running her hand over the brightly embroidered cushion that had been there for as long as she could remember. Her dad filled the broad-based kettle and set it on the range. His morning coat lay discarded over the footstool in front of the fire. Scanning the room where she had spent the morning, Merrin felt the creep of cold over her skin, despite the warmth of the summer day. The curling tongs, her make-up mirror and the abandoned glass of gin were where she had left them. Bella picked it up and necked it. It seemed that gin, like tea, was communal in this house.

'Merrin?' Ruby spoke loudly enough to make her jump.

'What?' Merrin stared at her sister.

'I've been asking what you want to do, love.' Her sister spoke softly, kindly, her eyes mournful and her touch light as she reached for Merrin's arm. 'Do you want to go and lie down, or go for a walk, or just sit and have a cup of tea? What do you want to do, babby?'

Merrin shook her head; she hadn't heard a thing, tuned out as she was to the awful reality of her situation. 'I don't . . . I don't know. I think I'd, erm . . . I think I'd like to talk to Digby.'

'You are *joking* right now?' Bella suddenly stood tall and folded her arms as if she were a human shield.

'I just want to check he's okay—'

'Check *he's* okay?' Ruby riled, interrupting her. 'Why isn't he calling you to see if *you're* okay? It's his fault, all of it! The bloke has got some bloody nerve, and when I get hold of him—' She balled a fist and smacked the flat of her other hand.

Merrin shook her head, hating the rising tension and noise. 'He . . . he wouldn't have done this on purpose. There has to be a reason.' Of this she was certain.

'The reason is he's a coward and a knob!' Bella added.

Merrin chose to say nothing rather than invite more of their commentary. It wasn't that she didn't appreciate their concern, expressed in so many variants, but they didn't know what she and Digby shared; how could they? What connected them was a deep and unshakeable love. He had said so only yesterday, and her instinct told her that nothing could have changed in such a short time. Maybe he had got cold feet over such a fancy affair? Maybe his nerves had proved too much and he, like her, would be happy to go to Vegas and let Elvis do the job? She wanted to talk to him, *needed* to talk to him, knowing that until she had heard the words from his mouth she would not believe that he had simply had a 'change of heart' and was popping off to the South of France. It didn't make any sense. Not to her.

Her mum and gran walked in.

'I just seen him,' her gran blurted when she was barely over the threshold, the words desperate to escape.

'Seen who?' Ben called from the stove.

'The Mortimer boy! Guthrie's son, Digby!' She spat his name like she was ridding her mouth of something nasty.

Merrin sat forward in the seat with difficulty; the frothy reams of material made free movement a little tricky as energy surged in her veins.

'Where was he? Where did you see him, Gran?' she asked, and for the first time since sitting in the vestry, hope spiked inside her. He hadn't rushed off to the airport! He was still in Port Charles! Her instinct was to run out of the door and go to him.

'Round the back of the pub, standing by the wall; looked like he might be hiding.'

'I bet he bloody is!' Ruby snarled.

Despite the situation, Merrin felt protective of Digby and didn't want her sister to talk about him like that. 'I need to go and get changed.' She scrambled clumsily from the window seat and up the stairs.

'I don't think you should go and find him, Merry, I really don't.' Ben spoke softly, but his eyes belied his words, as if a deep fury simmered behind his kind tone.

'Surely you're not going to go? That's a bad idea!' her gran hollered. 'You need to let it be, girl. I know you're hurting and I know how bad, but life isn't always about love – sometimes it's about doing what your father tells you and making the best of it and hoping it all works out, or at least it was in my case. And if you can have great love once, you can have it again, my little maid.'

Merrin ignored her, not willing to have the same conversation she'd had with the girls again. 'Can you come up, Bells? I need you to undo my frock.'

She heard Bella's footsteps thump upstairs and at the same time the slam of the front door.

'Has someone gone out?' she asked her best friend, worried for Digby and hoping that nothing damaging would be said to his face, knowing how awkward that would be when all of this was over and they sat down here to a family Sunday lunch, as they did every other Sunday, taking it in turns to eat with each set of parents.

'Ruby might have nipped out.' Bella turned her by the shoulders until she was facing the small back window between their beds and began to undo the fiddly little buttons. Merrin stared out at the yard, which adjoined her gran's yard next door via a rickety wooden gate. She pictured her and Digby kissing right there on the back step before saying goodbye only a day ago.

'*One more sleep . . .*' His words full of promise as he had pulled her towards him, running his fingers through her hair, as flames of desire warmed her from the inside out. '*I can't wait, Merrin Mercy Kellow!*'

'Has she gone to find him?' Concern dripped from the question.

'I don't know.' Bella kept her voice small and withering, rubbing furiously under her nose with her finger, as she did whenever she had to tell a lie.

'Why does she have to stick her oar in? I just want to go and talk to him and figure this out without all the bloody drama!' Merrin yanked at the bodice quicker than Bella could undo the buttons.

'Keep still! Every time you pull forward I drop the little loops and have to start again. I think it's too late for anything to be done without drama today. And the reason your sister is sticking her oar in is because he's done a shitty thing to you and she loves you. We all do.'

'I know that, Bells, and I love you all, but he's my fiancé and I know there will be more to it; he's not a bad person, something must have happened.'

'Or maybe he is just as I described him: a coward and a knob.'

Merrin shook her head. 'He's not. He's lovely and I love him and I know he loves me.' Her mouth twitched into the beginning of a smile at the thought of him and she prayed she spoke the truth. She *knew* Digby, knew him better than anyone else, and could so easily recall the words whispered in the darkness as they lay together on a mattress, her head on his chest, their fingers entwined. *'I can't wait to grow old with you, can't wait to have decades behind us as an old married couple. It'll mean we have memories, history . . .'*

Bella undid the last of the fiddly buttons and the voluminous dress dropped to the floor, filling the space between the two single beds with reams of frothy material, which Merrin had to clamber over, kicking to free her feet, which got caught in the fabric.

'Well, if he's as lovely as you say, then maybe you two will sort everything out, but no person on this earth is worth sacrificing yourself for. Don't ever stop being you and don't ever bend so far to accommodate someone that you break. Do you know what I'm saying?'

Merrin pulled on the long-sleeved t-shirt that she had slept in the night before and stepped into her jeans, which were soft with too much wear and in need of a wash, both retrieved from a pile at the end of her bed.

'I do know what you are saying, and I love how much you all love me, but you have to trust me.'

'I do, but . . .'

Merrin wished her friend would hurry up; she wanted to go and find Digby. Impatience made her jumpy.

'Don't you feel a bit angry at being left in the church like that? The vicar had to send everyone home, Merry! The whole bloody thing is awful!' Bella let her shoulders rise and fall, as if knowing her words were inadequate.

'I'm aware the vicar had to send everyone home, and no, I'm not a bit angry.' She shook her head, speaking softly. Her words, despite her urgent need to leave, were slowly found and delivered. 'I'm totally destroyed. Totally. It's like I'm dreaming. I'm hollow and gasping for air, desperate to find out the truth, to understand the *reason*, and I can only do that by looking him in the eye and hearing it from him, and only then might I be able to process it, because if I don't' – she put her fingers in her hair – 'I just might lose my fucking mind!' Her voice was reed thin. Without warning, her gut bunched and her throat tightened, and she bent forward and retched, aiming her mouth over the wastepaper bin that was full of tissues covered in the make-up Ruby had wiped from her face, heaving until a thin and inadequate bile dribbled from her.

'You've nothing to bring up, love. Should have had a bacon sandwich.'

Merrin straightened and wiped her mouth on her sleeve. 'I'm clinging on, Bells. But only just.' Her voice quavered.

Bella placed her hand on her friend's shoulder. 'I understand, Merry. I do understand.'

Merrin took a moment to steel herself before rushing down the stairs, where she stopped in the parlour to shove on her trainers.

'Where are you heading off to, lovey?' her mum asked, as she, her dad and her gran sat around the table, their wedding outfits quite incongruous to the moment. They all stared at her, transformed now from bride to their ordinary daughter in her jeans and t-shirt as if it was any other day, which is exactly what it had become.

'Just think, I should be tucking into my roast beef about now,' her gran lamented, sidetracking the conversation. Her comment didn't help and again Merrin felt the bite of nausea.

'I'll go make you a sandwich, Ellen.' Her mum stood and rolled her eyes.

'I'll have a sandwich, if you're making, Heather.' Her dad rubbed his stomach.

'I shan't be long, I'm going to see if I can find him and then I'll come straight home.'

'I wish I knew what to do, Merrin, what to say.' Her mum voiced her thoughts. 'But I really don't. I don't know whether I should be telling you to stay home or trying to make it better or getting mad on your behalf, or going up to the house to have it out with Loretta; I just don't know what I'm supposed to do.' She unpinned the elegant lavender-and-heather corsage from her coat; it had started to wilt.

'That makes two of us.' It hurt to see her mum flustered and concerned on a day that had held so much promise.

'You want me to come with you?' Her dad swivelled round on his chair.

'No, Dad, but thank you. I love you.' She let her eyes sweep her family, whose sadness slipped from them and pooled on the floor. They all looked a little slumped, weighed down by a mixture of disappointment and impotence. 'And I'm sorry.'

'You have nothing to be sorry for! Nothing!' Her dad's voice caught.

The money! You have worked hard and saved hard and spent money, and now this . . . and Mum works for Loretta and I've caused all of this! I feel sick . . . Shock and grief rendered her unable to express this.

'And we love you,' he continued, 'more than you'll ever know.'

Merrin shut the front door behind her and ran across the cobbles. It felt good to be exerting her body, as if a little of the tightly packed grief in her system was released. She looked out towards the cove and spied Jarvis holding the bottom of a tall aluminium ladder and Robin leaning out with his arms outstretched, removing the sign from the side of the Old Boat Shed. She was thankful to them both, but especially her mate Jarvis, who had been so wonderful when she needed him most. It was as she made her way towards the back of the pub that she spied Ruby walking along Fore Street, coming up towards the slipway.

'Hey!' she called, and waved. Her sister, she noted, had tucked the long skirt of her dress into her knickers, probably so she could run more easily. She was also, rather ominously, holding one hand inside the other. Merrin broke into a run until she caught up with her.

'Did you find him? Where is he?' She spoke quickly, her stomach bunched at the thought of facing him and her breath coming in nervous pants.

Ruby couldn't look her in the eye and kicked at the ground. 'Yeah, I found him.'

'Did you talk to him? What did he say?' Her chest heaved with urgency.

'Not much. He wanted to know where you were,' Ruby explained, and just to know that he had asked after her was enough to send a jolt of positivity through Merrin. Maybe all was not lost.

'What did you say? Is he waiting for me?' Merrin's voice had gone up an octave.

'Not exactly, and yes, he *did* ask where you were, but I don't know if it was because he wanted to find you or wanted to avoid you,' Ruby levelled.

'So where is he now? Tell me!' Merrin's tone was that of someone whose desperation was not matched by the person she was talking to. Her fingers splayed and twitched; time was of the essence.

'I think he was heading out on the coast path.' Her sister offered this quietly.

The coast path, out towards Reunion Point, the place he proposed . . .

'What have you done to your hand?'

'Nothing.' Ruby hid it behind her back.

'Did . . . did you hurt him?' Merrin hated her level of concern after what Digby had done, her humiliation still raw.

'Only his nose.' Her sister smiled and flexed her knuckles.

'God, Ruby, why? You just can't leave things alone, can you!'

'Calm down! I'm joking. I didn't hit him, but I might have smacked a wall and pretended it was him. And you should be thanking me for having your back, not worrying about that arse-hole! That's typical of you.'

The fact that Ruby had hurt herself on her account added another fine layer of guilt to dust Merrin's bones, atop the horrible sinking feeling in her gut because her parents were out of pocket, and at the thought of her mum's awkwardness when she next went to work. Her lovely mum, who only wanted to go into a house, scrub it and leave, *cleaning ninjas . . .*

'You can't punch your way through life!' Merrin paced back and forth. 'Hitting him or a wall or anything else does nothing to help me, nothing at all, it's just another shit thing to deal with. I give up!'

Leaving her sister standing near the slipway, she raced along the road that met up with the coast path, her heart beating faster and faster as she climbed higher and higher.

'Oh, and you're very welcome! As I said, you're lucky I care enough to want to sort him out! Thank you, *Ruby*!' her sister yelled after her.

Merrin ignored her, without the energy for anything other than finding and speaking to Digby. There was only one way into and out of the spit of land so if he was heading back to town, she would see him. Inside, she felt a strange mixture of joy and trepidation at the thought of coming face to face with the man she should by now be married to. *My husband* . . . It was a thought that had sustained her since he had proposed. In fact, from their first conversation, he had filled her thoughts and crowded out any suggestions of a future without him. Because it was love, pure and simple. A deep, deep, all-consuming love. Not that she had believed in such things until it happened to her.

Merrin's life had changed in a minute on the day she met him. She had woken on a 'couldn't be bothered' day. With her hair unwashed and half tied up on top of her head, her clothes plucked from a pile on the bedroom floor and her less than fragrant trainers shoved on to her feet, she had set off up the coastal path in her mother's shadow to help her clean the Mortimers' house. It was only hindsight that would leave her wishing she had scrubbed, fussed and groomed until she sparkled.

Having helped her mum vacuum and mop the tiled hallway of the Old Rectory, she had taken the bucket outside to empty it on the flowerbeds, taking a moment to look down over the valley at the wide sweep of the fields that led all the way down to the cove. The garden, and the view for that matter, was one of the most beautiful she had seen.

'Ah, Merrin, dear!' Mrs Mortimer had called from the lower slope, in the way that she did, sounding and looking very much as Merrin imagined a head teacher might, if the head teacher were loud and had a fondness for floral fabrics, suede gardening gauntlets, pearls and velvet headbands. '*Such* a lovely day!' She approached with a wide wicker pannier on her arm in which nestled a glorious combination of lavender and roses with a heady bouquet. The woman looked like something from a perfect-house magazine. Even in the heat of the mid-morning sun, her lipstick was pristine and her skin without a bead of perspiration.

'It really is.' She turned to face the sea. Mrs Mortimer made Merrin nervous, despite being so very nice. The Mortimers had been in residence at the Old Rectory for generations. Loretta and her elderly husband had, some years ago now, filled it with antiques, squidgy sofas, potted plants and large, heavy mirrors. Merrin knew the house well. She had on more than one occasion tagged along when her mum cleaned it, running her hands over the broad bend of the dark wooden bannister rail and the old iron locks that led to more rooms than two people could possibly need. The view today from the brow of the manicured garden was beautiful. The sun was high and sea diamonds danced on the water's surface. From a distance, Merrin thought she saw shapes: seals, swimmers and boats, which always, upon closer scrutiny, turned out to be no more than the dart of a silvery fish or the swirl of water as it navigated a rock. She was, as ever, gripped by the moving images of the ocean.

'How much do I owe for today, dear? I'm sure it's more than usual, as your mother has had help.' Mrs Mortimer walked towards her, removing her gauntlets as she did so.

'Erm . . .' Merrin wasn't sure what to say. 'Mum'll be out in a minute. She's just finishing off.' She thumbed in the direction of the house.

'Yes, of course. Would you like a drink? It's jolly hot.'

'No, no, I'm fine, thank you.'

Her mum had reminded her in no uncertain terms of the protocol when in a client's house: 'No break and no slacking. They might offer a drink or snack, but won't be thankful if you accept. We go in and out as quickly as we can with the least fuss, noise and interruption, and we do the very best job.'

'Like cleaning ninjas.'

'Exactly. Like cleaning ninjas.' Heather had smiled.

As Mrs Mortimer opened the wide front door that led to the grand hallway with the newly cleaned floor, Merrin felt her heart boom in her chest as she stared at his face.

'Mum! I've been looking for you – fancy a game of tennis? It'll be quick – I'll thrash you and then you can get back to your roses or whatever it is you're doing.'

'You are so mean to your poor, aged mother!' Mrs Mortimer gave a soft laugh.

Merrin watched as the woman put the pannier on the low front wall, next to a vast stone urn full of blue hydrangeas, and placed her gauntlets neatly next to the vase.

'Forgot to say, my son is home for the holibobs. He is frightfully noisy, and very rude about my tennis ability, but jolly good fun!'

Merrin watched the boy walk slowly from the house. He was tall and broad and, in his pyjama bottoms and a crumpled navy linen shirt, didn't exactly look ready for tennis, despite the wooden racket that rested over his shoulder. He had short, auburn hair and beautiful pale skin, which looked as though it had never been kissed by the sun or felt the sting of the sea. Very unlike the weather-beaten, leathery tan that graced the faces of her dad or Jarvis and Robin, who spent their time on the water or the shoreline in all seasons.

He stopped short and stared at Merrin, and she felt her face colour under his scrutiny.

'Hi!' He lifted his free hand in a wave, even though he was standing close.

'Hi.' She held his gaze, fascinated and drawn by this man, who was, she knew, a little older than her, but not much. His shirt hung from his slender frame to reveal the sharp bite of his pale shoulder blade; the small shadow beneath his clavicle held a particular fascination for her. She wanted nothing more than to reach out and run her finger over it, and curled her fingers into bunched fists to stop herself from doing just this. He blinked under her intense gaze and smiled. Mrs Mortimer made her way into the house. Not that she saw her go, but she was glad nonetheless for the chance to be alone with this boy.

Merrin felt an awakening inside her like a deep, low hum in the base of her gut that sent ripples out along her limbs. She wanted to stare at him and the urge to touch him didn't lessen. It had been the longest time since she had found anyone of interest. But this . . . the way standing in front of this stranger made her feel was something else entirely. Excitement fizzed in her veins and her mouth felt dry with nerves. He was sophisticated, worldly and posh – all things that drew her. Merrin knew she needed to work hard to carve out a successful life, but wanted more than to wake each morning wondering where the money was coming from to put coal on the fire.

The boy stared back and she didn't look away. His eyes were of the palest blue and there was something in the way he looked at her that felt familiar, as if he knew her. Yes, it sounded ridiculous, improbable, and yet the pull of him was strong. It was all she could do not to reach out and touch his face, wanting to confirm that he was real.

'I was hoping for a game of tennis, but they say there's a storm coming in and I'm not keen enough to play in a downpour.'

'They say a lot of things, these weather people, mostly rubbish. If you want to know the weather, look out of the window, that's what my dad says.' She took in his profile as he stared out over the skyline.

'Is he a meteorologist?'

'No. A fisherman.'

'I see. And what do you say? Do you think it's possible to go from warm sunshine on a day like this to a raging storm?'

'Yes, I think anything's possible in Port Charles.'

'Is that right?' Those eyes and that smile were enough to make her feel quite heady. 'You're Heather's daughter.'

'Yep, one of them.' She raised her left shoulder slightly and tilted her head the way she had practised in the mirror, knowing it made her look slimmer and, she thought, a little prettier too. 'I've not seen you for a long time. I remember you playing here in the garden when I came up once with Mum when I was small.' She wished she had something better to say, something witty or interesting.

'I've been away at boarding school in Bristol since I was seven and we have a place there, so I've tended to stay where my mates are or I go abroad during the holidays. I've been here at Christmas time, but I haven't seen you in the pub or anything.'

'Don't really go to the pub,' she admitted, wishing she *had* gone to the pub if it might have meant bumping into him, and wishing she could give him details of *her* fabulous life and where she *did* go. '*Oh, I'm usually in a wine bar somewhere!*' or '*My family has a yacht!*' The wine bar was in fact Bella's dad's shed, where they sipped and grimaced as they swigged his home-made blackberry wine from a murky, sticky-rimmed bottle, and the family yacht was the stinky little trawler *Sally-Mae*, named in part after her great-gran, whose portrait hung over her mum and dad's fireplace.

'I'm Digby.' He gave the name she already knew and looked at her as if taking her in, smiling, seemingly liking what he saw. It made her heart give a little skip.

'Digby,' she repeated with a small nod, holding his eyeline.

'Well, that's going to be tricky!'

'What is?' She wondered what she had missed, lost in listening to the perfect roundness of his vowels and his accent, which placed him beyond the county boundary.

'If you're called Digby, too, it could be a tad confusing.'

'Oh!' She laughed. 'No, I just wanted to say your name. I'm Merrin.'

'Merrin, yes, I knew that. It's a great name; it reminds me of the sea. Merrin . . .' He sounded it out perfectly. 'Why did you?' He took a step closer.

'Why did I what?' She shook her head and swallowed, her heart clattered in her chest and her words stuck on her tongue.

'Want to say my name?' He moved closer still and leant forward, resting his forearms on the wall. The closeness of him was almost dizzying.

'I don't know.' She stared at her feet, wishing she weren't wearing her tatty daps and wanting to rewind and be a little cooler, a little less open and a whole lot cleaner.

'Well, for what it's worth, I like you saying my name. And I like saying yours, Merrin.'

'Digby.' She looked up as he turned to face her and, with the sun behind his head, lighting up the space behind him like a halo, she thought he might be the most beautiful person she had ever seen.

'So, what is there to do here? My mum and dad love it, but I always find it so quiet!'

'There's not much to do; we kind of make our own busy, but I think that's what people love – the quiet.' She kept her voice low. It was the truth, and yet thousands of people flocked there every summer, as if wanting to confirm this for themselves; thousands of people who wanted to escape the cities and spend a fortnight making their own busy too. 'Unless you like the sea and boats and fish.'

'I don't. Not particularly. Much to the annoyance of my dad, who is a bit boat crazy, always talking about his adventures on the high seas.'

'So what *do* you like?' She shook her head, trying to make her hair fall alluringly over her shoulder. This, too, she had practised in front of the mirror in the bathroom.

'In no particular order, I like fast cars, ice cream and tennis' – he held the racket up – 'and sleeping and the works of Thomas Hardy, not his novels, although yes, those too, but his poetry.' He closed his eyes and breathed in through his nose, as if inhaling the words in his memory, as if they were soft cake or a good soup. 'Do you read Hardy?'

Digby Mortimer thought she was a girl who might read Hardy! She felt like his equal, this rich boy who had all of life's advantages.

'I don't really read much at all. Or play tennis, and I've never been in a fast car. But I *do* like ice cream.' She latched on to the one thing she could relate to.

'Then we should eat ice cream together. For sure. Let's do that today . . . let's find a place and sit and eat ice cream, even if it rains. We can find a spot to shelter and wait for the sunshine. If you'd like?'

Merrin squeaked and nodded, like a compliant mouse, but one who wanted nothing more than to sit with him and wait for the sunshine. 'Merrin?' her mum called from inside the house. 'You cleaned that downstairs lav yet?'

Again she shook her head, as if her shimmering locks could distract him from her mother's shout.

Even now the memory of that spark, that attraction, was enough to ripple through her loss like warmth, like happiness. With a muddle of thoughts and her blood sugar low, she pushed on up the path towards Reunion Point and . . . and there he was . . .

Her brain, it seemed, had not caught up with the disastrous events of the day, and the sight of his broad back hunched inside his linen shirt sent a shiver of longing deep into her core, which was at once both harrowing and confusing. Her shoulders sagged with the familiar feeling of relief at seeing him.

Slipping off her trainers, she let them dangle from her fingers as she took a moment to push her toes into the spongy grass beneath her feet, instantly anchoring her, allowing her to feel connected to something bigger than what was happening between her and Digby. The perfect distraction from the fact that a few dozen mini trifles were at that very moment probably spoiling, and the dainty hand-made chocolates with their piped initials had no doubt been abandoned on the edge of warming saucers.

'We are doing this once, Merry, and if Mademoiselle wants hand-crafted chocolat, *then Mademoiselle shall have it!'*

Not that the detail mattered; none of it did. Her only preoccupation was sorting things out with the man she loved and figuring out what forces had been at play to bring them to this point. There was one thing of which she was certain: what they shared was recoverable, it had to be; it was her whole future. The strength of their love was enough to overcome just about anything. The way she felt at the sight of him enough to confirm this.

Ridiculously, she felt shy about calling out his name, this man with whom she had shared her body, her love and her dreams for her future. The man with whom she had run through a list of possible baby names and then giggled with delight at the absurdity that it was even under contemplation.

'Horatio? You have got to be kidding me!' she had howled.

Digby Mortimer, who she loved with a strength that made the consideration of a life without him a painful thing. Her stomach bunched and the breath caught in her throat. She did her best to swallow the sickness that again threatened.

As she drew closer he seemed to sense her presence and turned his head. His expression was hard to fathom: nervous, certainly; upset, possibly. Either way, he carried the air of a stranger and this fact alone was enough to cleave her heart in two. His face didn't break into a smile at the sight of her and his eyes didn't glaze with longing. The biggest shock was how quickly this change had occurred.

Instead of reaching out for him – Merrin felt, even in such a short amount of time, as if she had lost that privilege – she sat down next to him awkwardly, wearing a cloak of embarrassment, buttoned with grief, and folded her hands in her lap. Close enough that he could reach out and touch her if he so desired, but not so close that they were automatically touching, which had always been their default position, arm to arm, thigh to thigh, hand in hand, her head resting on his shoulder, her foot on his leg, her mouth seeking his. She missed him already, missed what had slipped through their fingers.

It was easier to talk to him if she kept her eyes trained over the water, concentrating on the breaking waves, the shifting clouds, the boats bobbing on the horizon – anything other than his face and the suggestion of betrayal that glinted in his eyes. Her loss was complete, her pain physical and her spirits sank lower than she knew was possible. There was one fleeting second when she peered at the waves cavorting over the jagged rocks and recognised the unpalatable, brief thought that to jump and land among them might bring an end to this misery.

'I don't know what to say to you.' Her words coasted out on a burble of nervous laughter.

'I don't know what to say to you.' His tone was short, alienating her further still.

She waited, hoping he might say more, and when he didn't, she drew on every bit of strength she could muster and took the lead. 'It's been the most terrible day . . .' She whispered the understatement.

'Yes.'

'Did you, erm . . . did you get nervous?' She'd hoped he'd speak freely, and she resented the fact that she was having to prise answers from him. 'Was that it?' She hated the note of hope in her question, knowing that she needed answers, no matter how painful.

She didn't have to be looking at him to see him shaking his head in her peripheral vision, and awareness of this slowly pulled the plug of hope from her gut.

'I . . . I just don't understand,' she began.

'It's complicated.' He swallowed.

'It's not really, though, is it? Or at least it shouldn't be.' She cleared her throat, her spit thickened with nerves. 'You asked me to marry you. You told me you loved me. We planned the wedding. I put on a massive frock and you didn't show up.'

He sighed and ran his fingers through his hair. 'I don't know if I can deal with this.'

'You don't know if you can *deal* with it?' She felt the first flash of anger and it cracked open her kindness and her desire to figure this out civilly. Maybe Bella was right: the reason he hadn't shown was because he was a coward and a knob. But if this were true, she felt diminished by the fact, knowing he was her great love and that she had picked him to marry. 'You don't have a choice, Digby! You can't do something so bloody awful to me and hope it all just goes away! You have to deal with it. This is Port Charles, not London – I can't hide away or lie low until it blows over! This is a tiny place and what you have done to me is big news.' Her chest heaved at this truth. *Everyone would be talking . . . everyone . . .* It was a thought as monstrous as it was unbearable.

'I know, I know.' He covered his eyes briefly; she suspected that like a child he hoped that when he looked again she might have disappeared entirely. No such luck. 'I've had my mother going at me all night and again this morning and I'm exhausted with trying to get everything straight in my head!' he levelled.

'Going at you *how*?' She wasn't sympathetic, but she was certainly interested. She had always felt his mother might in some way view her as a little inadequate, not quite the type of girl he usually dated. An image of Phoebe came to her mind, the girl who had placed her hand on Merrin's arm. *'Sorry, Merry, are we being a little rude?'*

'She kept telling me how this might be the biggest mistake I would ever make, how she thought at first it was a summer fling that would run its course and how she's had reservations since that first night we told them we wanted to get married.'

'She never thought I was good enough for you. I knew it. Her niceness is a thin veneer. But I never thought she'd have this much influence.' She let this hang. To hear confirmation that Mrs Mortimer did not think she was good enough for her son chipped away at the fragile veil of confidence in which Merrin was wrapped. It felt horrible. 'But so what if your mother doesn't like me? It wouldn't be the first marriage where that was the case!' She hated how much it sounded like she was pleading, shovelling away the hurt, still shamefully trying to find a way in which she might be wed to this boy she so loved.

'Apparently, she's tried hard to put her worries to bed because all she wants is for me to be happy.' He spoke the words her parents, too, held as their mantra. 'But all her words have fallen on deaf ears, because I didn't want to hear it, Merrin. I wanted to marry you!'

She heard the emotion in his voice and felt the first sting of the tears she had managed to keep at bay all day. Mainly in response to the tense he had chosen: *wanted to marry you . . .* Without him saying another word, she knew this was no longer the case. They were words that cut her loose, dissolved their bonds and left her wondering how she was going to go on. Her mouth twisted and her eyes crinkled in an ugly cry that gave no credence to aesthetics

– her hurt went far, far deeper than that. It was no real surprise to hear how much his mother disapproved, but no less upsetting for that. She pictured the woman making her try on one wedding dress and then another and another . . . a ridiculous and cruel pantomime while she poured words of doubt into her son's ear. It was the most horrible thought. And one that was impossible for Merrin to understand: how, *how* could a woman do that to another?

'It . . . it hurts,' she stuttered. 'I haven't cried all day because it didn't feel real, but now . . .' She felt the warm, constant trickle across her cheeks. 'You've broken my heart, Digby.' Her voice faltered. 'You've absolutely broken my heart. You're listening to your mother over me and I guess that's the point at which we fall apart. You choose her. I get it.' She let this sink in, her sadness pulling her down and rendering her weak. 'But in the process, you sold me a dream . . . and now you've humiliated me in front of my family, my neighbours, all the people I care about. All my life I've tried to live well, live quietly, knowing how reputations can be made or broken in a small place. It was important to me; I am a Kellow and we built Port Charles. This is my *home*, I'm part of it and it's part of me and now I'm marked: I have a story, a scandal that will follow me like a bad smell.' Her voice was now no more than a rasp. 'This is the day people will talk about. The day I put on a wedding dress and everyone in the village turned out in their finest clothes and you didn't show.' Her tears fell and her eyes felt sore, as hysteria reached for her and held her fast. 'I shan't shake that off, not ever. I'll be the new Lizzie Lick.' Her voice croaked at this truth.

Digby shook his head, as if this very thought was absurd.

'And I could never have imagined that you would do something like this to me, not ever. I would have thought you'd be the last person to do something like this.' She swiped at her nose with her fingertips, caring little how she looked or that she had smudged the artfully applied slick of mascara or that her eyes might be bloodshot and her nose running.

It was not the fairy-tale beginning she had been planning and picturing for months. It was in fact their ending. This was happening. It was real. They were done. Her body felt hollowed out, scooped of all substance, and she was no more than a shell of her former self, frail and pulled eggshell thin with disappointment.

'I can't believe it.' She whispered the truth.

'You are the most amaz—'

'Shut the fuck up, Digby!' she snapped. 'Don't you dare give me that bullshit about how fantastic I am and how someone will be lucky to have me, or whatever other crap you are about to spout.'

He closed his mouth.

Her breath came in gulps and it was hard to get words out through a throat so narrowed with distress. 'I don't know how to get over this, not right now. I honestly can't see what happens next.' She bit her lip. 'So many people hurt, embarrassed, involved' – she pictured the girls shielding her on the cart – 'and they're all waiting to give you a piece of their mind.'

'I've already had a run-in with Ruby.'

She ignored him. 'I feel so stupid. I thought you were someone different, someone I could open up to. I've told you everything, painted a picture of the life I wanted, and now I wish I hadn't. I thought I could *trust* you. I *believed* you, I thought we were on the same page, but turns out we weren't even reading the same book.' A fresh batch of tears gathered and she did nothing to stem them.

He looked at her and again his mouth flapped as he tried to form the words that might make everything a bit better. Had such words existed.

'I never wanted to hurt you, Merrin. You *are* fantastic and I don't deserve you.'

'Damn right you don't.' Her voice was reedy.

'My mother, she's . . .'

'Don't embarrass yourself by laying this at your mother's door!' She faced him fully, allowing him for the first time to see her face and the distress seeping from her. She saw his eyes momentarily crinkle, as if he were disturbed by the sight. 'You're not a child. You are a grown-up, able to make your own decisions.'

'I wish it were that simple.' He gave an ironic snort of laughter. 'But it isn't. My parents pay my salary, insure my car, *own* my car, pay my credit card.' He bit his lip. 'She asked me what I would do if they withdrew their support and' – he shook his head – 'it threw me. I mean . . . what would I do?'

His words landed like a punch to her stomach. He had chosen money over her. 'The fact that you even have to ask that question and are so clueless makes me cringe. I knew you were gifted so much, but I actually admired how hard you worked and how determined you were to make your own mark, but I was wrong.' She thought of the times when money had been tight and her mum and dad had pulled together to paper over the cracks, fill the gaps, plug the shortfall – but always, always, together. The fact that Digby had seemingly fallen apart at the mere suggestion of a lack of funding was proof that Digby and she had never been on the strong foundation she had imagined. It was a lie – all of it was a lie. 'If you loved me in the way that you need to when you marry someone, then none of what your parents threatened would be an issue.'

'I guess you're right.' He answered quickly enough to launch a dagger of rejection that this time landed squarely in her breast. She looked down, not for the first time that day, to see if she could see any injury. Her chest heaved as sobs continued to build inside her. Her distress was evident and she wished she had better control of it, wanting to talk calmly, but with her hurt causing pain to every fibre of her being, there was very little she could do about it.

'Why . . . why did you wait until today to change your mind? All the weeks leading up to this, all the times we talked about our future and you had a chance to say you weren't happy, or that you'd changed your mind. We sat there with Reverend Pimm and agreed to always communicate! There were so many opportunities for us to figure stuff out, or at least for you to let me down with my dignity intact. Why let me get ready and arrive at the church like . . . like an idiot?' The situation became more monstrous as she voiced it. And with the protective layer of doubt, the cushion of hope that had meant it might not be the end fully slipped from her mind and, finally, shock subsided, nudged out by the beginnings of fury.

'I didn't know quite how strongly she felt and I never thought they'd cut me off.' His answer was vanilla, weak and irritating because of it. She had been put aside for the promise of money and in that moment she despised him for his lack of backbone, hating his voice, everything about him.

'You really are the worst kind of human being,' she fired.

'I feel it!'

'Good! I've put everything on hold for so long, working part-time jobs and waiting for my life to start because of all we planned, all your promises. You told me not to go full-time in any one job where I might have a chance of working my way up the ladder, you said it was because we'd make plans together, that we might travel, that there might be a place for me at Mortimer's, that we'd have a baby, build a life, a home! God, I *am* an idiot!'

She pushed her palms into her face and rubbed away the never-ending stream of tears. 'I actually feel sorry for you, Digby.' She stood and wiped the grass from her legs, before slipping the narrow engagement ring from her finger, the ring given to her in lieu of *the* engagement ring he had promised her: his grandmother's ring, which had never materialised. 'Here's the ring you decided was better because your gran's ring was "old-fashioned". Was that the truth or another lie? Did you simply not want me to have it? Maybe your mother decided I wasn't worthy of it?'

The way he blinked told her this was in fact the case and she wanted to hurl the meaningless band of gold into the ocean. Not that she had cared, not really, but now it was just another clue to the sorry ending to their story. As she gave it back to him, his hand, she noted, was shaking as much as hers.

'I do,' she pressed. 'I feel sorry for you, Digby, because I would have been wonderful to you. I meant every word I said, even if you didn't, and I would have worked hard to make you happy. But now I can't even stand to look at you, and that's a shame for you, I think, to have fallen so far in my view.'

His expression was one of anguish; it seemed that her words had hit home and this brought her an ounce of satisfaction.

'Merrin, look, we need to talk about what happens now; we could bump into each other when I'm home and—'

'This is not your home!' She cut him short. 'It's mine! *My* home! And as to what happens *now*?' She balled her shaking fingers into fists as she stared at him. 'What happens now is that I pick myself up and get on with my life and you jump back into your mother's apron pocket and catch the crumbs she throws you. And every day you live like that, know that you are not good enough – not for me, anyway.'

'I thought you loved me!' he called as his eyes misted.

'I do.' She whispered the saddest fact, then whimpered, a wounded sound over which she had little control. 'And that's the hardest part. But I will learn not to.'

Making her way back along the coastal path towards Port Charles, she knew without a doubt that his eyes would stay glued to the horizon and he would not do her the courtesy of watching her walk away.

She nodded to herself. *I will. I will learn not to love you.*

And then a thought struck her that was so obvious it brought some small amount of relief. *I will learn not to love anyone in this way ever again and I will not trust anyone in the way I have trusted you, because this feeling – like I might break, like I couldn't care less right now if I live or die – this is not worth it, not worth it at all.*

CHAPTER SEVEN

Merrin

Merrin concentrated on putting one foot in front of the other. Ignoring the physical pain in her chest, her narrowed throat and her eyes now bitterly sore from sobbing, she gripped her trainers in her fingers and stumbled her way along the harbour wall, counting the steps and the moments until she could fall through the front door of the little cottage and into her mother's arms.

'I want to disappear . . .' she whispered.

'Ah, there she is!' came the shout.

She looked up in time to see Mr and Mrs Everit walking briskly towards her, still in their Sunday best and clearly making the most of the effort they had gone to, parading around the harbour. Her heart sank, wanting nothing less than this interaction in her current state of distress.

'Merrin, you poor little lamb,' the woman called, and waved as she drew close. 'What can we say?' Mrs Everit reached out and pulled her into an awkward hug. 'If I've said it once today, I've said it a thousand times, you were the prettiest bride I ever did see.'

Her stomach bunched with something close to shame to hear the words of falsehood, because she might have looked pretty, but she was no bride. Shrugging herself free, she took a step backwards, hopefully out of reach, whilst trying to acknowledge, as best as she was able, the misplaced compliment.

'Thank you,' she whispered, rubbing her thumb on the underside of her finger, where she used to feel the bump of a gold band; just another thing that had been taken away from her today and that she would have to get used to.

'Not that it makes what happened any easier for you, I'm sure.' The woman tutted and shook her head with a look of abject pity. 'Now will you look at the state of your face, what a thing! Of course, I can't imagine what you are going through. Mr Everit was as keen as a puppy offered sausage on our wedding day, couldn't get me up the aisle quick enough.'

Merrin glanced at Mr Everit, who gave a salient nod in confirmation.

'But you listen to me, girl, I'll tell you what I've told *everyone* I've seen: you are only young and there's plenty of time to find someone who will take you on. Didn't I say that, Walt?' She nudged her husband, who again nodded his confirmation. 'People will stop talking about it in time.'

People are talking? Of course they are! They all are! Merrin felt her face colour at the confirmation of her worst nightmare.

'And then you can get back on the horse!' Mrs Everit exclaimed. 'Don't you worry, Merrin, someone will want you!'

'I . . .' Words of goodbye failed her.

'Merrin! Merrin!' She heard the voice calling behind her and turned to see the Reverend Pimm, who, in his jeans and shirt, took a second longer for her to place than was comfortable. He signalled from the pavement in front of the pub and beckoned to her.

'We'll no doubt see you very soon, dear,' Mrs Everit said with her head cocked to one side and a half-smile of pity on her mouth. It made Merrin feel worthless, like a thing to be comforted, and she hated it.

The vicar jogged up over the stones and along the slipway. Pulling the sleeves of her t-shirt over her shaky hands, she walked down to meet him.

'Sit! Before you fall; you're very pale.' He patted the wide, low wall and she did as he instructed. 'I thought you looked like you might need rescuing.' He pulled a comic face and she raised the smallest hint of a smile.

'Mrs Everit means well.' She had known the woman with her unfiltered observations and warm heart all of her life.

'No doubt.' He took the spot next to her and rested his foot on an old lobster pot. 'Stupid question, I know, but how are you feeling?'

She coughed to clear her throat, but even so her voice was still little more than a rasp. 'I don't know really. Like I'm falling . . .'

'I bet.' He took his time. 'It might feel like the end of the world, but it isn't. I see people all the time who are torn with grief and they can't imagine a day when they'll be glad to see the dawn, but that day comes. It's a surprise to them, always, but not to me because I see it often. It'll be the same for you, Merry. I'm sure of it.'

'I hope so. I don't know what to do now. I don't know what happens . . .' She stared at the water and tried to sort through her jumble of thoughts. 'I feel . . .' Again the right words were not readily forthcoming. 'Like I've run into a wall and I am in pieces and I don't know how I'll get put back together.'

'You'll put *yourself* back together and that'll be your job for a while; take time to do it, let it be your preoccupation. It's necessary. Hindsight will show you that this is a great opportunity. You'll be like a house flattened by a flood or a tornado – rebuilt stronger than before, able to withstand whatever life throws at you, because you will have come through the storm.'

His words offered little comfort, and she wiped her nose and spoke with her eyes lowered. 'Did you ever get the feeling, Vicar, you know, when we were having our classes and stuff, did you ever think, "Oh, this won't last", or that he might not have loved me or anything?' Her question was draped with a tone of desperation; she wanted to understand, to see if there was something she'd missed.

He shook his head. 'I've been thinking about those sessions, and no.' He sighed. 'I often get an inkling when people are going through the motions or when one half of the couple appears to be under duress, and I tailor my advice accordingly. Trust me, I've seen it all.' He paused and looked up. 'But with you and Digby? I was happy to give you my blessing. Excited for your future.'

'Me too.' Her tears clouded her vision.

'You're no doubt in shock, as are we all, and I really just wanted to remind you that the doors of St Michael's are always open if you want a quiet place to sit and think, or if you want to talk.'

She nodded her thanks, knowing in that moment she wanted only to talk to her family, safe and sound at home in front of the range. She looked towards the cottage as if to express that longing.

'I'll let you get on, Merrin. But remember what I said: however much pain you are in, it will pass. It will all pass; everything does. I've said as much to everyone who has cornered me this afternoon.' He rubbed his face and looked out towards the sea, speaking freely, as if forgetting momentarily who he was talking to. 'I feel like I've been inundated, just about everyone in Port Charles, and even people I've never met before, all with idle hands and busy tongues, wanting to give their opinion on what happened or find out the gossip.'

Her stomach shrank. It was happening . . . In a matter of hours she had become an object of ridicule, wiping away her good, solid reputation and marking her as someone to be pitied: the Kellow girl with ideas above her station, who thought, laughably, for a minute she might snare the boy from the big house and waltz off into the sunset. What a born fool!

'Take care, Merrin. Take good care.' He smiled at her kindly as he loped back up the road.

Merrin stared at the sandy ground, wishing she could fall into it, away from prying eyes and tattling tongues. She felt small.

'The tide will change!' The words boomed loudly, coming from behind her.

She looked around and into the face of the sad, scuttling form of Lizzie Lick – not her real name, but how all the locals knew her – coming up from the foreshore. Her hand was wedged in her mouth as if it were a shock to her that she had spoken out of turn or too loudly.

'She licks the windows of parked cars, no one knows why . . .'

'She used to be a lawyer who went mad and now lives in a cave.'

'I heard she went to prison . . . why would they send an innocent woman to prison? They wouldn't, would they?'

'I heard it was murder . . .'

The rumours surrounding Lizzie were as fanciful as they were numerous. But Merrin knew the sad truth.

And now as she rushed home to stand by the front door with her wedding day in tatters, she realised they were right, all of them. Her dad in his assumption that Digby was an idiot, her mum with all her reservations about the boy, and even Ruby, who had quite rightly seen that Digby didn't have it in him.

'How stupid are you, Merrin?' she whispered. 'You should have listened to them.'

Walking slowly into the cottage, she found her mum and dad sitting on the little sofa in front of the fireplace. Her mum was already in her nightclothes and her dad had changed out of the suit he hated and had wasted money on, the suit Mrs Mortimer had insisted on the whole wedding party wearing.

'We can't have a mismatched wedding party, that would simply not do!' Her voice was more like nails on a chalkboard in the remembering.

'We were just starting to get a bit worried. I was going to come looking for you,' her dad breathed. He had dark circles under his eyes and furrows of anxiety on his brow.

'I'm okay,' she lied. 'Well, not okay exactly, but home.'

'I can imagine your head is all of a dither.' Her dad looked close to tears for all she had had to experience.

'Just a bit.' She swallowed at the understatement. 'Mum always said that when it came to love I would just know when it was right . . . and I *knew*, or at least I thought I did.'

Ben looked at his wife sharply, seemingly lost for answers, and Merrin saw the frustration in it. Her mum looked at the floor.

'Yes, I did say that.' Heather raised her gaze. 'And I meant it. But I should have also said that love is no more than a glimpse of a heart in time. It's a moment captured when the words that leave your lips, the thoughts in your head and the desire in your body are in sync. It causes a rush of good feeling high enough to reach the sky. But sometimes, you can glimpse that same heart a month on, one decade on, one lifetime on, and you see something very different.' She took a deep breath. 'For some people the strength of feeling is the same: a tower standing strong and true.' She smiled at her husband and Merrin knew she spoke for herself. 'But for others it might have shrunk a little and for some it has plummeted and lies on the ocean floor, shrivelled to nothing, waiting for the tide to wrap it in its watery arms and carry it far away from memory.'

'Only hours ago I would have sworn that would never have happened to Digby and me, Mum. He said he loved me with a madness. William Shakespeare said something similar.'

'Why would we give a rat's arse what some old dead bloke might think? Or what bloody Digby thinks, for that matter!' her dad harrumphed.

'What I'm trying to say, Merry' – her mum stood and shot her dad a withering look, doing what she did best, smothering any flame of discord before it took hold – 'is that your life is still waiting to be lived, girl, and you have to wring every drop of joy from it! And when you do find that proper, forever kind of love, treasure it, don't be reckless with it and never take it for granted. It will come to you, I'm sure of it.'

Her mother's words were well meant but Merrin could not see herself ever loving again. Not ever.

'Anyway, enough words about love, Merrin.' Heather sat forward and twisted the fabric of her nightdress in her hands. 'Did you see him?'

'I did.' Merrin felt the strength leave her legs and sank down on to the rug in a heap. 'Oh, Mum! I hear what you say about love, but how can I have got it so wrong? How can it be that he doesn't love me? Doesn't want me? I don't understand! I know it's true, but I can't believe it's true!'

'Oh, little love, I wish I could take all of your hurt away.' Her mum knelt next to her and stroked her hair while her dad paced and murmured with murderous intent.

'Why,' she hiccupped, 'why did this happen to me?'

'Because you picked the wrong boy, Merry, that's all. It's his loss, his bloody loss.' Her mum spoke convincingly.

'It hurts.' Merrin screwed her eyes shut, finding momentary relief from the salty sting of tears.

'And it will. For a while, but not for ever.'

She remembered the vicar's similar words. 'I feel so stupid. Everyone is talking about me.'

'Probably.' Hard as it was to hear, she liked that her mother didn't offer any dishonest platitude to ease her thoughts. 'But that, too, won't last for ever. And I expect more people are talking about him and what a big mistake he has made. There's many who will have judgemental thoughts about what he's done to you, sweet girl.'

She felt an irritating flash of concern over his safety, burying it quickly under the memory of handing the ring back to him.

'Do you want something to eat? A hot drink?' Her mum offered familiar solace in the way she knew how.

Merrin shook her head. 'I just want to go to bed.'

Heather kissed her forehead and Merrin let her dad hold her close before slowly climbing the creaky stairs on legs that felt like lead and with a weakness born of fatigue that made the task feel almost impossible. She paused at the top. The bedroom door was open and the first thing she noticed was that Ruby had tidied up. Merrin's bed was neatly made with fresh bed linen and the cover turned down invitingly. The make-up, the plates littered with toast crumbs and the dirty laundry had disappeared. The narrow strip of carpet had been vacuumed and the window opened to let in a fresh breeze. Three pink roses had been placed in a bud vase on the table between their beds. Ruby stood in the doorway of her parents' room to allow Merrin space. It was an act of kindness so moving and it meant all the more that it was Ruby who had performed it.

'It looks lovely. Thank you,' she managed, as another batch of tears fell.

'You look so sad.' Her sister reached out and let the burnt lock of her hair fall through her fingers.

'I am.'

'Go to bed. I'll stay right here with you.'

Merrin nodded, glad of the fact that she was not going to be alone. She climbed under the cotton counterpane they favoured in the summer months. The pillow was soft and welcoming and the smell of fabric conditioner pleasant. She found that by concentrating on these small things she could subdue her pain.

'Where's my dress?' She remembered abandoning the voluminous frock.

'I packed it away and put it back in the box it came in. It's under Mum and Dad's bed. It can stay there till you decide what to do with it. Sell it? Burn it?'

Merrin let out a small murmur of acknowledgement, unable to think about the best course of action right now, unable to think about much coherently; her thoughts were erratic, jumbled and edged with sadness.

'I thought I'd got rid of you; I was looking forward to having this room to myself.' Ruby tried to lighten the mood.

Merrin stared at the ceiling, trying not to picture the four-poster bed at Pencleven Court and the real fire she had been promised. She blinked, wondering when the longing for Digby might stop and how she could reconcile this feeling with the knowledge that they were over.

'It's like I'm dreaming, Rubes.' Rolling on to her side, Merrin pulled the cover over her shoulder. 'I can't believe how in such a short space of time everything changed.'

'I'll never forget your face coming out of the vestry with Mum and Dad supporting you.'

Merrin watched her sister's face crumple.

'I'm sorry I went to look for him. I didn't want to upset you, but I was angry.'

'Don't worry about it, Ruby. I'm lucky I've got people who care about me.'

'And you have, lots of us. And we'll help you get over this. I promise you, Merrin.'

These warming words were lovely, but not enough to thaw the icy kernel of hurt that had taken root in her stomach.

'Mrs Everit said everyone is talking about me. The vicar said as much too.' She felt her muscles tense, shivering despite the warmth. 'How do I go back to being the old Merrin Kellow without everyone pointing and looking, everyone knowing what's happened to me, feeling sorry for me?' Her voice was muted.

'Time, I guess. Time and waiting for the next person to spectacularly screw up in Port Charles and steal your thunder.'

'You think I screwed up?' Her fragile state meant she took the words that had been spoken as a balm and translated them into an accusation; her heart beat a little faster and her sorrow magnified.

'Only by making the wrong choice, and to be fair, he played it well; even I thought he was half decent.'

She was glad of Ruby's kindness.

'What did he have to say for himself? I'm assuming you found him?'

Merrin nodded. 'It was awful. He was very cool, already a stranger, and it was odd not to touch him or hold his hand.' Again those darned tears kept coming. With a pain now pounding in her temples, she wished they would stop.

Ruby lay on her own bed and mirrored her sister's pose. The two stared at each other across the narrow gap, as they had been doing all their lives.

'He doesn't deserve you, and no one deserves what happened to you. It was a shit trick.'

'Yep. It's funny, Rubes, you know I was never that smart at school, I knew I'd always have to work hard.'

'That's always been the Kellow way,' her sister interjected.

'I know. And I'm fine with that. I just wanted to be happy. I've never been that fussed about a fancy career or money, I know that doesn't mean success.'

'For some it does. Like old Ma Mortimer.'

'Yes, but not me. And when Digby proposed, it was like something opened up inside me, it brought me peace. As though I'd been worrying about my future without really knowing it and then I didn't have to worry any more, because it was laid out in front of me, and it felt wonderful. All I've ever wanted was enough of a wage coming in for the odd luxury, to be able to put food on the table, and a family.' She felt her gut fold at the image she conjured of her babies, picturing herself in the matriarchal role her mother performed so well. 'That's it, really: domestic bliss. I know it's not always the most fashionable ambition, but I can't help that.' She wiped her eyes on the corner of the pillow slip. 'I felt grateful he'd asked me. He talked of places I'd yet to see and fancy holidays, swish restaurants, travel. All the things that "other people" did. And I nearly became "other people". I loved him, Ruby – I love him.' The admission made her voice catch. 'Marrying him felt a bit like taking a short cut into the life I wanted: a comfortable life that meant I could make a wonderful home and raise my children. And we would have done it right here in Port Charles.'

'You'll build a different future. You can still have all of that, just not with that prick.'

'Maybe.' She felt the dream slip from her, knowing that to give in to that kind of love, that kind of promise, was too risky. She would never put herself in this position again. Never.

'Go to sleep. Close your eyes and go to sleep. I'll sit right here and I won't leave until you wake. Try and rest, Merrin Mercy.'

'Thank you, Ruby. I do love you.' She closed her eyes, which felt full of grit, and wished she could sleep for a hundred years.

'I love you too.' Despite her whirring thoughts and broken spirit, it was the last thing Merrin heard before sleep claimed her.

◆ ◆ ◆

Merrin woke the next morning and lay still in the bed. Her night had been fretful with regular wakeful interruptions to sob into her pillow or stare out of the window, where every corner, every wall, every patch of grass and every lane held an image of her and Digby together. It was almost more than she could stand. With her head still pounding and her eyes swollen, she looked over at her sister.

'Morning.' Ruby stretched. 'Tea?'

She nodded. 'I'll go make it and bring it back up.' It felt like the least she could do after her sister's wonderful support the previous evening.

'Well, I don't feel so bad about still having to share a room with you if this is the service I can now expect.'

Merrin, still in her jeans and t-shirt, pulled her hair into a ponytail and rubbed her eyes before slowly treading the stairs. Pausing in the little hallway, where the front door was, as ever, thrown wide, she looked through the crack in the parlour door, steeling herself to face her parents, who were no doubt still wanting to ask questions and offer solutions, neither of which she felt strong enough to address. Merrin laid the flat of her palm on the cool, wide stone wall and couldn't help but think of this time yesterday – the air of excitement, the anticipation of a new life about to begin – and yet here she was, back to square one, but with her heart and faith bruised. Once again this fact hit her squarely in her chest like a flying object.

Her dad was, she noticed, sitting on the battered narrow sofa in front of the fireplace.

'Come here, my beauty.' He patted the space next to him and her mother rushed over and dropped next to him on the floor, her head resting on his legs. It felt invasive to watch the moment of intimacy, but what came next caught her attention.

'What we going to do, Ben?'

'What can we do? Be there for her, put our arms around her. It was all anyone could talk about in the pub last night. I left early, sick of hearing the guesswork, I was. Everyone has an opinion on it! We need to try and keep the gossip from our door. It'll do her no good to hear it.'

Merrin's heart boomed in her chest and again she felt sick. Her dad was right, it did her no good to hear it . . .

'Easier said than done in Port Charles,' her mum confirmed, and again Merrin's nerve faltered.

'She ain't as strong as Ruby. I worry it'll bring her right down.' Her dad sighed and Merrin's thoughts swam; this was hard to hear.

'All she wanted was to be wed. But I had a bad feeling about it.'

'We both did, but what could we do? We told her what we thought, but when the heart's leading, it's hard to navigate any other course.'

She remembered their somewhat subdued reaction to the news of her engagement. What was it they had seen that she had missed? Had everyone in the village seen it? She felt so foolish, so embarrassed.

Her dad bent low and kissed his wife's head. 'I know I couldn't have walked away from you, no matter what anyone said. I loved you from the very first. Even now, after all these years wed, I can't get used to being away from you. It will never feel right to me.'

'I hate it too.' Her mum laced her fingers with his as he raked her thick, dark curls and let his fingertips graze her cheek. 'I sleep differently when you're away at sea, Ben. The absence of you is a physical thing for me; I can't quite take a full breath or concentrate, not while the man I love is away and in possible danger, it's like my spirit can't rest.' Heather leant up and kissed his face.

Quite trapped, Merrin was loath to make her presence known, feeling it an invasion of the beautiful moment whether she interrupted or stayed quiet.

'Still.' Her mum smiled. 'Fourteen whole days until you set off again. That means fourteen nights of you next to me in our rickety old brass bed. And there ain't nowhere on the whole planet I'd rather wake than by your side in our little bedroom with the sloping walls, floor and ceiling. And with Merrin knocked sideways, I'm glad you're home.'

Her dad sat back in the chair. 'You know, I hear some of the lads on the bigger boats saying how glad they are to be away from their missus and her nagging, but I never say that and I never think it. I love you as much today, Heather, as I did when I first saw you and on our wedding day, when I put that ring on your finger. It's important you know it. We can get through anything. And we can help Merrin get through anything.'

Merrin felt the swell of loss in her veins for all she had lost.

Letting the front door bang against the wall to herald her arrival, Merrin walked into the parlour, aware that her cheeks were flushed.

'Morning, darlin'.' Her mum sprang up from the floor and ran to her. 'You been out for a wander?'

'Yes.' She kept her eyes on the floor and lied.

'Let's get you tea and toast – ain't nothing that can't cure.' She rubbed the top of Merrin's arms en route to the stove.

There was a loud knock on the door frame and her dad walked briskly to the front of the house.

'Now then, Mac, what can I do for you?'

'How's young Merrin doing?'

'Not too bad.' Her dad spoke with as much jollity as he could muster.

'She's quite the celebrity!' Mac, the pub landlord, bellowed. Her mum shot Merrin a look and hesitated to close the door, clearly unsure of the convention.

'Is that right?' Ben's tone now a lot less jolly.

'She's the talk of the town, all right!'

His words were like daggers, sharp and wounding. Merrin felt a quake in her stomach.

'What is it you want exactly, Mac?' Her dad was now short with the pub landlord and she knew this was for her benefit.

'You left your wallet on the bar last night. I said to Robin and Jarv, not like he can afford to be throwing money away. I bet it cost you a pretty packet for the wedding and all – I saw your fancy suit and Merrin's dress! Thought I'd better bring this back to you, can't have you any more out of pocket!'

Merrin heard the door slam and saw Mac slope off across the cobbles.

'What the bloody hell is going on? I'm still waiting on a cup of tea!' Ruby shouted as she hurtled down the stairs.

Merrin collapsed on to the rug in front of the sofa.

'All I did was fall in love and all I wanted was to take care of a family, be a mum and make a home, and now this; my whole life has fallen apart! I'm a bloody laughing stock!'

'Ignore them.' Her mum sank down to the floor with her and held her tight. 'Ignore them all.'

'How can I? I wanted to live quietly.' She looked up towards Reunion Point and wondered how long Digby had sat there, wallowing in self-pity. 'And now I'm something different. Someone different. How can I live a quiet life in the place I love when I am marked as *that* girl?'

'It'll pass, Merry. It will.' Her sister looked anguished.

She shook her head. 'I can't, I can't stay here, not with everyone talking about me and about yesterday; I can't stand the thought of it. I don't want to see anyone, don't want to go outside. Staying here with reminders on every corner and people wanting to bring it up would make it hard for me to get over it, hard for me to rebuild myself.'

'Don't be daft, my love.' Her dad's expression was fearful. 'You are just very tired and things will seem different in a day or two. You need to be right here among the people who love you. We'll have no more talk of not staying here. Port Charles is where you belong. It's where we all belong!'

She tried to sit up, tried to find a way through the waves of distress that had knocked her from her feet, but her sadness was too all-consuming. Merrin didn't know how to stop crying, didn't know how to flick the switch that would make her instantly stop loving Digby Mortimer, but the one thing she did know: her dad was wrong, she did not belong here in Port Charles, where being left at the church and how she had been jilted would live on in the mouths and minds of all those present and even those who weren't. She would not be *that* girl. She would not give old Ma Mortimer the satisfaction. No.

Heaving herself into a sitting position, she looked at her wonderful parents and sister and knew that she would miss them and all the chaos of this little cottage, because she *would* leave. She would go away and build a life; not the life she had dreamed of, but a life away from this noise and the stain of her 'almost' wedding day. And she would do it alone. Forgetting these had been her thoughts and not rational conversation, she stared at her family through her tears.

'I'm going to miss you all so much,' she whimpered.

Her dad sank down into the chair and her mum wrapped her tightly in her arms, as if this could prevent the inevitable. The sound of their tears echoed around the bay, before the wind whipped up the saddest noise and carried it far, far out to sea.

CHAPTER EIGHT

Ben

It was a cold winter's day and, even before he left home for the day, Ben was looking forward to returning, kicking off his boots, a hot bath and an evening in front of the fire. He would never admit it to his wife, but a small part of his joy at coming home after being out at sea on the *Sally-Mae* had been missing since Merrin had left Port Charles. Ruby was an ever-present source of happiness with her spiky manner and lack of filter and he loved nothing more than to hear about her day spent working at the fishmonger's in town. It was, and always had been, interesting to him how much folk were willing to pay for what he hauled from the sea. He used to joke with the girls when they were little, explaining the role of a fisherman and how his catch went from his boat to tables far and wide.

''Magine that, liddle ones?' he'd laugh. 'One minute you're swimming about in the briny, a happy little lobster, and the next you are facing a boiling pot while a fat man in an expensive suit sits on a velvet chair with his napkin tucked into his shirt collar, willing to pay over the odds for nothing more than a bite of your bum!' The girls had found this hilarious, but there was, as ever, truth in his joke. He smiled now at the memory of them at such a young age.

Not that there was anywhere on God's planet he would rather be than in this small plot of land that was his home, but he would be lying if he said he didn't mind the fact that one of his daughters was so far away. It was a dilemma. He of course wanted his girls to find their feet and fly. Doing whatever it was that made them happy, but if he had his wish, no matter that it might be a selfish one, he wanted them close. His little family, his greatest achievement, within reach for a shared cup of tea, a glass of blackberry wine or a good old chat in front of the fire.

He knew, too, that Heather, as much as she tried to hide it, now carried a certain sadness about her. He understood; it was as if all was not quite right in the world with their littlest so far away. She might only have been on the outskirts of Bristol, three hours away on a good run, but it felt like she was on the other side of the world when she wasn't under their roof. They had raised two strong women and yet the thought he kept to himself was that at some level he felt it was his job to be there if and when anything went wrong. Not that there had been much he could do when things had gone so horribly wrong last summer. His impotence surrounding it was like a paper cut in his mind that just wouldn't heal.

Those damned Mortimers . . .

Climbing down the rickety stairs, he felt his fingers flex and form a fist as they did when he pictured Merrin's face in the vestry, as she sat upright in the chair with her dress puffed up all around her, looking at once like a child and yet somehow older, as if the reality of life, something truly terrible she had not known existed, had been revealed to her. He exhaled deeply and tried to settle his pulse, which always raced when he pictured the face of the boy he had welcomed into his home for cosy suppers and anecdotes recounted around the table.

'I could still bloody kill him!' he muttered under his breath, wondering if this feeling would ever subside. He rubbed at the top of his arm, where a shooting pain had a tendency to spark, due to the cold, no doubt, and the effect of hauling heavy nets and crates of fish at his age in all weathers.

As he rolled his shoulder and walked into the parlour, Heather called from the stove, where she stirred a lamb stew, the rich, peppery aroma filling the air.

'Where you going, Ben?'

'Old Boat Shed.' He grabbed his old oilskin jacket and pulled on his sturdy boots.

'That'll make a change.' She sighed.

'Where else am I to go? This is Port Charles! There in't that much choice!'

'I know where we are. And well *you* know that my point is that you can't keep hiding up there. It won't bring her back. It's been nearly six months.' She spoke over her shoulder.

'You think I don't know that? I just need to sit and think and look at the sea. Ain't too much to ask, is it?'

'If that's what you need to do, love, but as far as I can see, you're in danger of growing gills: you're either on the sea, in the sea or looking at the bloody sea.' Heather turned her attention to the salting of her stew.

'That's about right. I'm a Cornishman.' He chuckled.

'Yes, you are. A proud Cornishman, but you used to be a proud and happy Cornishman. You can't live sad. You have to live happy!'

He gave a wry smile; this from the woman who wept behind closed doors when she thought no one was listening.

'Is that right?'

'Yes! Merrin seems okay, she really does, so it makes no sense to brood. You've heard her on the phone and read her letters: she's working hard and has found her feet. She seems settled.'

'Didn't even come home for Christmas.' He remembered what it had felt like to wake for the first time on a Christmas Day without both his daughters under his roof, and the rather subdued celebrations that had occurred in light of the year they had had.

'For the love of God, let it go, Ben! That's her busiest time, she couldn't get away.'

He snorted, not fully believing this and suspecting that Merrin would use any excuse not to come back to the place that now held such negative associations.

'That Mortimer boy,' Heather began. The mention of him enough to make his pulse race.

'You think I'm sad because of the Mortimer boy?' He stared at her. 'No, no, Heather!' He shook his head. 'I'm *furious* because of him, bloody furious at him and his bloody mother with her airs and graces, but I'm *sad* because my little girl is far away. And I don't like it one bit! It don't feel right to me and it never will. She belongs here, at home in Port Charles. And I wouldn't mind if she'd gone off to pursue something wonderful or because she'd fallen in love or was travelling the world, or for a million other reasons' – he slipped his arms into his old yellow oilskin jacket – 'but it's none of those things. It's like she was chased out by what he did to her. He made her feel stupid and like she couldn't hold her head up, and *that's* what I can't get over, that's what I'm furious about! She felt like she had no choice! All because he led her in a deceitful dance and folk can't keep their tongues still in their empty heads. Who does she know over that way? No one!'

He chose not to voice the destructive thoughts that disturbed his sleep, nightmares of his little girl living an unhappy life, painting on a smile while wondering what her family were up to in the place she loved. He thought of his loneliness sometimes when he was at sea. It often felt like there was a party going on at home to which he wasn't invited, like he was forgotten, and it tore him up inside. He hated to think of Merrin suffering similarly.

'You think I like it?' Heather's bottom lip trembled and his heart sank; how he hated causing her a moment of upset. Instantly, he regretted speaking so freely. 'You think I *like* living with the heart ripped out of my home? And with you skulking off every five minutes to that damned boat shed to sit with Jarv and Robin like three daft idiots all staring at the water, brooding over what they can't bloody have?'

'What can't Robin have?' He scratched his scalp; Robin the confirmed bachelor had it all, as far as he could tell. He lived a carefree life, the money in his pocket was his to do with as he pleased, he had a decent roof over his head, friends aplenty and a regular seat at the bar of their local.

'Nothing. I don't know.' She coughed and her face coloured, suggesting to him she *might* know, but would rather not say. 'But what I do know is that I'm a bit sick of it. All of it! Lord knows I want her home; I wish I could wave a wand and have her back here with the life she had before she met the bloody boy! Or better still, back to the day I asked her to come cleaning with me up at the Old Rectory and I would instead let her sleep. I'd let her sleep all day and night rather than let their paths cross. But it's Merrin's choice and while she's not here we have to make the best of it.' His wife bashed the lid on to the casserole pot and abandoned her cooking, before rushing up the stairs.

Ben was about to slam the front door in a matching protest when he looked to the chair in front of the fire and did a double take. Ruby was sitting with a plate of toast on her lap and a magazine open.

'Sometimes I actually wonder if I'm invisible!' she yelled.

'Who said that?' Ben looked over her head, hoping to make her laugh, before jamming his woolly hat on to his head and leaving.

'Very funny,' Ruby smarted.

CHAPTER NINE

Merrin

Merrin straightened her ponytail and swallowed her nerves before knocking on the door of the wood-panelled study with the fancy coat of arms on the wall and walking in. A real fire roared in the grate. This room was indicative of the whole hotel: warm and cosy. The irony wasn't lost on her that instead of staying in a place like this on her wedding night and embarking on married life, she was now *working* in a place like this with marriage something she had dismissed from her mind. Never again would she put on the fanciest frock she had ever worn and head to church. The thought made her shiver. She had learnt the hard way that being asked to marry and actually getting married were two completely different things.

Lionel Milbury Fortescue, the current custodian of Milbury Court, was seated behind his wide oak desk with the leather-inlaid top. His smile was, as ever, broad and his welcome warm.

'Merrin! Yes, do come in and take a seat.'

She liked how he knew the name of every staff member and took an interest in him or her. It made the place feel like home for people like her who lived in, or at least as home-like as it could be for someone whose heart lived in a wild Cornish cove, one hundred and sixty-odd miles away.

'How was the golf club dinner? I've heard great feedback.' He clasped his hands on the desktop, his chunky gold signet ring sitting snugly on his little finger.

'Good, I think,' she said as she sat down. 'Got a bit rowdy at the end, but I suppose that's the sign of a great evening. And by rowdy, I mean loud singing in the bar, not a scrap or anything like that. There was no need to call the police, which is always a plus,' she clarified.

He laughed. 'The thought of a scrap breaking out among the octogenarians and great and good of the local golfing community is quite amusing to me.'

'Well, maybe next year.' She smiled.

'Yes.' He took a deep breath and she shifted in her chair as his expression changed to one of seriousness. She steeled herself for what might come next, suspecting it to be bad news. She had, after all, been called from her shift to his study. 'It has been quite an unsettled time since you arrived. As sometimes happens, we have been a little topsy turvy in terms of staff and I'm glad to say that we have now found our new restaurant manager, which means that Alison, who as you know has been covering the role, can go back to her job as head waitress, and we have adequate numbers to cover the restaurant, as Maxine is due back from maternity leave.'

'I see.' Her spirits sank. She'd heard the chat in the staff canteen and knew change was afoot, but she liked it here, was thankful to have found employment when she needed it most, and tried now to think of where she might head next and whether Lionel, as he liked to be called, might be kind enough to give her a reference. A recommendation from an establishment like this could do no harm.

'Yep, all change!' He chuckled. 'I can't tell you how impressed everyone has been by your attitude and your work ethic. It hasn't gone unnoticed. You're always punctual, friendly and as neat as a pin.' Happy at this compliment, she smoothed her hair behind her ears. Having taken the nail scissors and hacked off her locks soon after arriving, her short bob was not only a way of shaking off her past, it also reshaped her for the future. 'In all honesty, Merrin, you have sailed through your probation. It feels like you've been here for years.'

'Thank you.' She smiled into her lap; maybe a good reference would be forthcoming. Fidgeting with her fingers, she waited for the 'but'.

'But . . .'

Here we go.

'With the restaurant at full staff capacity now . . .' He paused and she waited for the axe to fall, wondered what wording he might choose to soften the blow. 'We were wondering if you might like to try a different role in another department?'

'Another department?' She sat up straight; this was great news!

'Yes, we were thinking you might like to try your hand at working on reception?'

'Reception? Yes!' Her enthusiasm and relief were evident. When Merrin had worked as a cleaner or behind the bar at the Port Charles Hotel, she had itched to have a go at working on reception, wanting to do things differently, better. Having pored through enough glossy magazines, usually left behind by residents, she knew that it was the small touches that could make a difference to a place: bowls of sweets on the countertop; fresh, not fake, flowers on tables; and never, ever letting a stinky old dog like Ernie, who lived at the Port Charles, wander the restaurant floor, shedding his coat and farting while people were trying to enjoy their morning coffee . . . 'I would really like that. It's something I've thought about before.'

'Well, that's marvellous news. So all that remains is for HR to switch your department codes for payroll and to get you trained on the computer system, which, to be honest, Merrin' – he spoke from the side of his mouth – 'if I can master it, then anyone can.' He stood to indicate the meeting was over.

'Thank you, Lionel, for the opportunity. I hope I don't let you down.'

'I have no doubt you'll do a sterling job.' He clapped.

'I'll do my best.'

She left the room walking a little straighter than she had in a while. It was wins like this that helped dilute the thick, gloopy feeling of inadequacy in her veins. It wasn't only that Digby didn't love her and that their whole relationship had probably been some kind of elaborate game to him, but also that her judgement had been so off. It was, even now, a surprise that he had done such a thing, been *capable* of doing such a thing.

During the day when she was busy, her time filled and her thoughts occupied, it was easy not to dwell on it. However, when she kicked off her shoes at the end of her shift and climbed between the freshly laundered sheets of her bed, settling down in a room that was not where she longed to be, her mind would conjure images of looking over the gap towards her sister with the sound of stays knocking on the masts in the breeze . . . that was when loneliness bit and she gave in to tears. No matter that in her head she could tell herself she was better off, it seemed that her broken heart had not quite got the message. Not yet.

She missed her family and friends with a depth that mirrored her pain; thinking of them before she fell asleep, sending silent apologies out into the night sky and hoping her words might fall into their ears as they slept. Trying and failing to bury the guilt of what she had put them through, the money they had needlessly spent and their hurt that she had all but abandoned them. But abandon them she must if she had any hope of recovering the pieces of her heart and her dignity.

In these quieter moments before sleep, she was reminded that her world had been cleaved open and her dream of building a life in Port Charles with her very own family, hand in hand with the man she loved, was no more than just that: a dream. Unbidden, she replayed the day of her 'almost' wedding over and over, knowing that if things had been different, she would right now be a newly-wed, making food for her husband, learning the lie of her new home, sitting in front of a fire with him of an evening. Nipping back to Kellow Cottages each day to catch up on the gossip with the women who had shaped her and happy, so happy, to know that each night she got to sleep in the arms of Digby. She missed him with a physical ache. This new life at Milbury Court felt very much like starting from scratch.

But, oh, how her bones mourned for home! Equally, she missed the crisp Cornish air, the view out over the cove, sitting on the harbour wall with her bare legs dangling in the sun, the rickety wooden stairs of Kellow Cottages, a cup of tea in front of the range and bickering with Ruby. She missed all of it – not that she would ever confess as much to her parents, knowing this information would only make them fret.

'Hey, Mum.' Merrin lay back on her bed and held her phone to her ear. Closing her eyes, she pictured falling into one of her mother's enveloping hugs and felt the chill of loneliness shiver through her.

'Hello, my darlin'! How lovely to hear your voice!'

'And yours. I've got some news,' she began.

'You're coming home?' her mum interjected with such excitement it was enough to fold Merrin's gut with longing and guilt.

'No, Mum, I can't.'

'I know.' There was a drawn-out pause. 'It feels a shame that you let the likes of the Mortimers or some petty gossip keep you away.'

Merrin rubbed her temples, unwilling to have the conversation yet again. 'I can't face it. I'm not ready.' She closed her eyes again, feeling her heart beat a little too fast. 'What's it like when you see the Mortimers? How has it been between you and Loretta?' She managed to say the woman's name now with ease; gone was any consideration of what might be polite or prudent.

Heather drew breath. 'I don't really see her too much, love. I mean, no more than to wave at or nod good morning to. And it's a little awkward, but it's fine. We always got on well, really. Friends in our own way. And we live in a small place, so . . .' Merrin refrained from adding that she didn't have to tell *her* that. 'Plus, I don't work for her any more. I handed in my notice.'

'You gave up your job? Oh, Mum.' She hung her head, knowing this had been kept from her and smarting with the realisation that her mum and dad had lost a large chunk of income. 'It's all my fault.'

'No, it isn't, it's Digby's fault.'

'And hers. His mother. It's her fault too.'

'Maybe, but as I say, he's a grown man, not a child, and he should have found his balls and spoken up earlier or stood up to her, either way.'

Merrin laughed. Her mum's sentiments pretty much echoed her own. 'You said "balls".'

'Yes, I did.' Heather was smiling now, she could tell. 'I've taken a couple of your old shifts at the Port Charles Hotel and it tides us over. Don't you go worrying about us, we are right as ninepence.'

Merrin wanted to believe this. 'I want to pay you back, Mum. I'm going to set up a monthly transfer; it's not much, but it'll make me feel less rubbish.'

'You don't have to do that.'

Merrin read between the lines that the money might be useful. It was the least she could do.

'And have you met anyone nice?'

'You mean like a potential boyfriend?' Her lip curled and her stomach dropped at the thought.

'Yes.'

'No.' She didn't socialise at all, preferring to keep herself to herself, and had not allowed herself to make a friend, let alone find a boyfriend. 'Definitely not. I can't see me ever committing to anyone like I did with him. I don't think it's worth the risk. It hurts too much, Mum. Even now. It changed me.'

'Oh, it is, Merry!' Her mum's tone was urgent. 'Don't ever think that. It is worth the risk. It would be the greatest shame if you didn't let yourself love and be loved, it really would. I can't think of a life without your dad in it, no matter he drives me crackers! Or my girls.'

'We'll see. But at the moment I try not to think too far ahead. Anyway, the reason I called was to give you my news.'

'Yes! What is it?'

'I got a permanent job, a promotion, kind of. From now on I'll be on reception.'

'Oh! Well, that's . . . that's wonderful! We are so proud of you.' Merrin could picture her mum's face, speaking in that way she did when she coated her words with gloss, trying to disguise the fact they came from a mouth contorted by tears. 'How I love you, little Merry.'

She nodded and closed her eyes, pushing the phone into her cheek, trying to get as close as possible to her mother across the miles, suddenly remembering again what it had felt like to be guided from the vestry and placed on the cart with Bella and Ruby holding her arms. *He's not coming* . . . The Reverend Pimm's words were as sharp and cutting now as they had been when she first heard them.

'I love you too, Mum. All of you. Will you tell Dad for me, about my new job?'

'Yep, 'course.' Heather Kellow caught her breath. 'Ruby's out with Jarvis, they're collecting firewood on the beach, but she'll be sad she missed you.'

Merrin wasn't so sure. Her mum did this too, tried to build bridges between her daughters. She took a beat to consider how to respond. It was no secret that things between her and Ruby had been a little fraught since she had left home. It seemed to have irked her sister that she had chosen to up sticks and leave, as if she took the fact that Merrin didn't need her help to heal or had rejected the life they lived personally. She had tried again only recently to explain it over the phone.

'I just can't be there, Ruby. I can't be in a place where I might bump into him or his mother on a daily basis.' She felt her mouth go dry at the prospect. 'And everyone else who might want to stare at me, whisper about me. It's more than I can stand to think about . . . and it hurts too much. Every place I look in Port Charles has a memory of Digby and me; I can't imagine being faced with that, and the thought of seeing him . . .' She'd shuddered.

'You're letting them win then!'

'I don't know about that.' She'd kept her cool. 'But I know it's me who has lost a lot.' *My home, daily contact with my mum and dad, walking barefoot on the beach, my beloved Cornwall . . .*

Even now, if she closed her eyes, she could smell the smoky fire in the parlour, and her mouth watered for the feel of hot tea sipped on the sofa, sitting with legs coiled beneath her, next to her beloved mum.

'I'd better crack on, Mum. Love you.'

'Love you too.'

She always took a minute at the end of a call to calm the syrupy loss that sloshed in her stomach. It was a strange thing: rather than make her feel closer to home, closer to those she loved, these calls with her parents or Bella, in fact any contact with home, had almost the opposite effect, like bringing a picture into focus, enabling her to see and feel all that she was missing, confirming how very far away she was.

But that was just how it had to be.

Merrin quickly got the hang of working on reception and more than liked her new position. And today it was a glorious morning. She sat at the French windows in her room and blinked, taking in the view from her bedroom, the beauty of which never failed to captivate her. The flat, manicured lawn beyond the patio was a constant wonder to her and she was thankful to those who worked hard to keep it looking just so. Having grown up on a wild and rocky outcrop, it amazed her that grass could be so neat, so vibrant, and not the spiky, untamed variety that sprouted between rocks, over the scrub land and on the cliff edge of Port Charles. This grass was entirely different, soft like nature's carpet, and when time and circumstance allowed and after a quick look around to make sure no one was watching, she loved nothing more than to slip off her shoes and run across it barefoot, feeling the soft yield of the verdant blades under her feet, connecting her to the earth in the way that she so loved.

Here, everything was flatter, calmer: the weather, the land and her life. It was a pleasant even keel of an existence and she found it comforting. Waking up in a castle every day was an amazing thing and her surroundings never failed to fascinate her. The high stone walls had been renovated and the original structure added to since it had first been built in the late 1500s, but always sympathetically and with grand style, befitting a once baronial family home such as this. The cathedral-ceilinged hallways and wood-panelled dining room were beyond stunning, with the scent of history and stories lingering in the air. And the library had a vast inglenook fireplace where, rumour had it, the finest ancient oak had been burnt to keep King Henry VIII and his entourage warm one day and night while he courted Anne Boleyn. Merrin liked to admire the walls and carved wood, wondering who else had done the same during their brief presence on this earth. It certainly wasn't a bad life, far from it, just not the one she had envisaged, and not the one she had wanted.

Lionel had recently found her running her fingers over the spines of the leather-bound books crammed on to the oak shelves of the library.

'I think it's a shame if they're not opened and appreciated. Like having an instrument that's never played or a vintage car that's never driven – quite pointless if these things are reduced to ornaments. So please' – he had gestured around the room – 'help yourself.'

'Thank you, but I'm not much of a reader.'

'Ah, that's the beauty of reading, it's never too late to start!'

She waited for him to leave before shyly reaching for a faded red spine that called to her. Taking the delicate book into her hands, she marvelled at its gold inlay title and the marbled pattern on the edge of the pages.

'*The Passionate Pilgrim – A Collection of Poetry by William Shakespeare*,' she read aloud. 'William Shakespeare. Might give the old dead bloke a go.' She swallowed the memory of her dad saying something similar, unable to stand the way she missed him, feeling it in her throat like a physical thing and longing for one of his hugs.

It had been only a week after her almost wedding when, quite by accident, Merrin had ended up in this fancy resort in a market town on the edge of Bristol. Having driven along the M5 in her battered, beloved Vera Wilma Brown with her heart and spirit in tatters, eyes swollen from sobbing and a pain in her chest, longing for the home she had only just turned away from, she saw a sign for Thornbury. Her little car, in need of fuel, slowed and she too had a fancy for a restorative cup of tea and so followed the signs to this place she had never heard of. Knowing it was vital she got back on her feet as quickly as possible, her intention was that after a quick rest stop, she would carry on to the bright lights of Bristol, find a job – *any* job – and go from there. She would show Digby Mortimer, she would show them all that she was not destroyed by the event that had rocked her world, but only thrown a little off course.

Thornbury was a pretty place with a traditional high street crammed with pubs, coffee shops, half-timber-framed buildings and double-fronted Victorian terraces painted in pinks, pale blues and the colour of clotted cream. She noted the groups of women chatting with a coffee in one hand while they rocked the handles of a buggy with the other, and how she envied them. Older men sat outside the pub nursing pints, having animated conversations. People raised their hands in greeting to friends and neighbours on the other side of the street and it felt nice to be among it, as if she could inhale the friendly atmosphere of the place and use it to help heal her broken self. What was it Reverend Pimm had said? '*Put yourself back together and that'll be your job for a while; take time to do it, let it be your preoccupation.*'

Well, Thornbury felt as good a place as any to do just that. A small market town where people seemed neighbourly, a bit like her beloved Port Charles, which had for her become tainted. Digby had done that. Taken it from her.

Merrin shook thoughts of home from her thoughts and considered what Ruby would say about the place.

'*Bloody boring!*'

And Bella?

'*Not a decent fella in sight.*'

‘Possibly, but it’s not you who is thinking about staying here, it’s me.’ Her whispered response.

At Milbury Court she had found her niche. Hard work, a no-nonsense attitude to any crisis and a warm manner had clearly made her stand out to the Milbury Fortescue family.

It had felt like a lucky happenstance when, sitting in a coffee shop on the high street, exhausted, the wind knocked from her sails and mentally frail, she had opened the local paper and spied an advertisement: ‘Staff Wanted. Accommodation provided’. On that day, still reeling from her loss and riven with humiliation, she had parked in the shadow of the grand and daunting castle façade and tidied her hair. Then, drawing on every bit of courage she could muster, she had raised her trembling fist and knocked on the office door.

The first person she had called was her sister.

‘I just got myself a job.’ Her words sounded surreal; here she was, building a new life out of the rubble that remained of her confidence, trying to forge on physically when her heart yearned to be in the place she loved.

‘Well.’ There had been a long and awkward pause. ‘That’s that then. You really are staying away.’

‘I think—’

‘We know what you think, Merry, that you can do better without us around reminding you.’

‘It’s not that I think I can do better, it’s about what I need.’ Her voice had cracked; her sister’s suggestion that this was a glorious life choice was wounding.

Ruby had spoken slowly, tearfully. ‘I told you, I promised you I’d help you, be there for you, me and Bella both did, but we can’t do it while you’re God only knows where!’

She heard the croak to her sister’s voice.

'I still need you and Bells, of course I do. In fact, I need you more . . .'

Hindsight helped her see that this was when the frost had formed on their conversations, not that being able to identify the moment made it hurt any less.

In some ways, the last six months had flown by, but when she thought of home it felt like years since she had been there. She was often invited to join in with the other live-in staff, who all seemed nice enough, and who socialised together after hours. But quiz nights and karaoke, five-a-side football and ten-pin-bowling leagues were not for her. Merrin was too bruised to join in, wanting to keep herself to herself and figure out how to put what had happened behind her. She was, in fact, uninterested in making new friends, not when she was yearning for the old ones she had in Port Charles. Plus, the idea of having to explain how it was she had come to be here and the circumstances that led to her packing up a bag and jumping in her trusty vehicle without too much of a plan was more than she could stand. If people didn't know what had happened, then she didn't have to face the daily shame of them judging or pitying her too.

And now here she was on this fine morning, walking briskly along the corridor towards the main reception, where she was to relieve Fred, the night porter, from his duties. Fred was nowhere to be seen and the main phone line was ringing. Merrin picked it up, raising her index finger and smiling apologetically to the man who walked up at that moment and now stood in front of her, tapping his room key and its overly large fob on the wooden reception desk. If it was an action designed to irritate, it was surely working.

'Sorry, one sec,' she mouthed, and smiled again, hoping for his understanding, as she tucked her short, bobbed hair behind her left ear and turned her attention to the phone.

'I am sorry to have kept you waiting. Thank you for calling Milbury Court. How may I help you?'

'Yes, hello.' The man spoke slowly, so slowly it was all she could do not to ask him to hurry. 'I'm, er . . . I'm, er, thinking of bringing the wife to stay at your establishment for a couple of days and I have a few questions.'

'I will certainly do my best to answer them, but can I remind you, sir, if I may, the best way to look at all we offer is to go on our website, and that's also where you will find the calendar with a list and description of all rooms, services and availability.'

'Yes, I have been on your website, but, well, the thing is' – the man drew a slow breath – 'my wife's cousin, Brenda, or Mrs Montgomery, as you would know her . . .'

'I do meet a lot of guests.' She found a smile, trying to ignore the key tapper, who had now taken to coughing occasionally, as if she were not already painfully aware of his presence.

'Yes, well, she came and stayed with you a few years ago and she remembers it was very cold. Cold rooms, cold lounge.'

'Well, I'm certainly sorry to hear that and I do hope it didn't spoil her stay. As I say, sir, we have a gallery on our website with images and details of all our rooms and availability. I think that might be your best bet.'

Key-fob man now subtly kicked the front of the reception desk and sighed. 'Be with you as soon as I can.' Again she smiled and whispered.

The man on the phone continued. 'That's all well and good, but I don't like websites. I prefer to talk to a person, a human person, none of this robot rubbish. Anyway, the wife has sciatica and likes an electric blanket.'

Key-fob guy huffed loudly and almost growled his dissatisfaction. Merrin had to make a split-second decision between a potential customer and a paying one standing in front of her who just might have an emergency.

'I am so sorry, sir, I just need to pop you on hold for one second.' She pushed the hold button and turned her attention to the man in front of her.

She smiled at him and joined her hands on the jotter. 'I am so sorry to have kept you waiting.'

This morning, despite her early start, all she'd done was apologise. They were short-staffed and each and every one of them was feeling the pinch. At that precise moment, Merrin should have been organising the staff rota for the next three weeks, writing a warning letter to the florist whose flower arrangements had been less than incredible for the third week running, and sending the new fabric samples for the re-covering of the vintage sofas in the reception area to Lionel's wife, who dealt with such matters.

'No worries. Can you recommend a good pizza delivery?'

'A pi—' Even saying the word within the confines of this high-end hotel with its award-winning haute cuisine and a wine list that she knew the sommelier anguished over, so keen was he to get the exact right pairings with the food, was difficult.

'A pizza joint? Somewhere that can rustle me up a stuffed-crust Margarita with a generous drizzle of chilli oil? You know what it's like when you are in a hotel, and all that truffle-infused whatnot and micro portions of grub leave you feeling a bit, meh.' He shrugged.

'And you want that right now? This morning?' She glanced at the clock and hesitated to recommend the breakfast buffet that would be in full swing in less than fifteen minutes.

'Yup. Jet lag. This is my night time.' He grinned.

'Yes, of course, let me find you a menu or at the very least a link to a website. Failing that, I will have the kitchen contact you directly and see what they can whip up. And I will have someone either bring it to your room or I will email you the link. Your room number, please?'

'One oh eight.'

'One oh eight. Consider it done.' She smiled sweetly.

'Thank you, and don't let me keep you. I know you put that guy on hold.' He winked at her and helped himself to a couple of the wrapped mints that sat on the desk in a natty glass bowl bearing the family crest.

'Thank you.' She immediately picked up the phone. 'I am so sorry to have kept you waiting, sir . . . hello?' But the line was dead. She felt the flare of guilt that she might at worst have lost a potential customer or at best offended one.

The front door opened and in walked a handsome man with dark hair and the gorgeous golden complexion that suggested he might be from the Mediterranean.

'Good morning, sir. Welcome to Milbury Court. How can I help you?'

'Hello!' He beamed, his accent a London one and his manner friendly. 'I don't know if I should have used another entrance.' He took in the grand reception. 'I'm the new restaurant manager.' He walked forward and held out his hand. 'Miguel. Miguel Rochas.'

Merrin shook it and felt a little shy, as the armour of her position slipped away and she was now aware of addressing a colleague.

'I'm Merrin.'

'Nice to meet you. Where're you from?'

This a standard question in this industry, where a team was, more often than not, international.

'Cornwall.'

'I went to Cornwall once.' He smiled at her.

'Did you like it?'

'No,' he answered sharply, and she laughed loudly. It was a laugh that came without hesitation, a reminder of the old Merrin who used to act with glorious spontaneity, before each movement and sound that left her body had to travel through a filter of hurt and second-guessing. He was funny. 'Of course I did! It was beautiful.'

'It is.' She pictured the view from the cobbles out over the cove and her heart danced at the image.

'What about you?'

'Kilburn, North London, not quite so beautiful, but it has its charms. People are often very disappointed when they meet me, given the name. I think they expect some charming Latino. I'm third generation Brit – my grandad's Spanish. You ever been to Spain?'

'No,' she answered sharply, and it was his turn to laugh. A couple walked through, making their way to breakfast. The woman's hair was wet and they were holding hands.

Merrin stood up straight. 'Good morning!'

'Morning.' They waved, barely noticing her, intently interested in each other. This she noted with a quiver of envy, despite her resolution not to allow love to cloud her judgement or damage her more than it already had.

'Is Lionel expecting you? Would you like me to let him know you are here?'

'Yes, please.' He rubbed his hands together. 'I'm a bit nervous!'

She lifted the phone to call her boss and smiled at Miguel. 'Don't be, he's lovely, and it's a great place to work.'

'What do you like to do? When you're not working?' he asked, his eyes not leaving hers.

In no particular order, I like fast cars, ice cream and tennis . . .

'Not much. I like to watch a bit of TV and walk on the grass.' She pressed the number and Lionel answered. 'Lionel, I have Miguel Rochas in reception for you.'

'Ah, splendid! He's early. I'll be down in a mo.'

'He's on his way.' She put down the phone.

'Thanks. Your hobbies are interesting,' he said in mock seriousness. 'What's the best grass you've walked on and where?'

'I didn't say they were hobbies!' she corrected. 'And actually, I do have some favourite grass. It's on a cliff edge, overlooking some pretty treacherous rocks.' She felt the swell of emotion in her throat as she remembered her last climb up to Reunion Point.

'I'm guessing it's in Cornwall?'

'You guess right.' She liked his manner.

'And great that you're only two or three hours away. Do you get back there much?'

'Erm . . .' As she tried to figure how best to answer she felt the pull of the tide and the lure of the salty breeze as it came off the sea and lifted her hair and her spirits, the feel of the cobbles beneath her bare feet . . . followed immediately by the image of Lizzie Lick. 'Not as often as I'd like.'

'The joy of working in the hospitality industry – long hours, little sleep and your time is rarely your own.'

'Yep.'

'Ah, Miguel! Welcome to Milbury Court!' Lionel shook his hand firmly and guided him away from the reception.

Merrin noted the way Miguel looked back over his shoulder at her before disappearing around the corner.

CHAPTER TEN

MERRIN

It was a year now since Merrin had arrived in Thornbury and yet there were still mornings when she woke and it took a second for her to remember where she was. The bed in her room was wide and comfortable, the carpet soft, the view lovely, and yet she would wake with a start, her breath coming quickly and tears trickling from her eyes.

It was almost instinctive, this mourning for the place she had lived her whole life. Especially on days like this when she had dreamt of Port Charles. She had been sitting on the embroidered cushion in the window seat, the sound of gulls filling the air while her dad whistled in the little bathroom at the back of the lean-to and her mum fried eggs on the range. It was revisiting this beloved normality in sleep that made waking hardest to bear. It wasn't that life here in Thornbury was desperate or that she was sad all the time, far from it, but still, to survive the day she had to shake thoughts of the harbourside from her mind and forge on.

Her telephone buzzed with an incoming call from Bella.

'Bit early for you?' she yawned.

'Bit late, actually, haven't been to bed yet!'

She could tell by her friend's excited tone that this fact was a cause for celebration.

'Hmm, so you've either got yourself a job with a nightshift or you met a man; let me guess . . .' If things were different and she was living happily in Kellow Cottages, then Bella would right about now be knocking on her front door and they would be sharing this news face to face and, more than likely, she would have been present when her best friend had actually met this man and would therefore be part of the story. And that really summed up what it was like to live away: she felt like she was no longer part of the story. Excluded. Written out.

'Oh, my God, Merry, he's gorgeous!'

She dug deep to find a smile, not wanting to taint her friend's lovely news with her own melancholy. 'Gorgeous-looking or gorgeous person?'

'Both! He's Dutch, tall, a yachtie. He crews on fancy boats for people with too much money and too little time, takes them from port to port and then hops off when the owner arrives. Travels all over the world. And right now, luckily for me, he's hopped off in Port Charles!' Bella squealed her excitement.

'Where did you meet him?' She wanted the detail.

'In the pub, where d'you think?'

Bella had a point.

'What's his name?'

'Luuk, and he's blonde and funny and laid back and—'

'Steady there, Bells, it sounds like you've got it bad.'

'I have! I've only known him for a few days, but you know when you meet someone and you just know it's more than a little fling or something insignificant? And you keep waiting for them to do or say something that really puts you off, but they don't! They just get more wonderful the more you know them. And you keep waiting for the bubble to burst, but it doesn't.'

'I do.'

She pictured the day Digby had asked her to marry him, how passionately they had kissed each other before going their separate ways to tell their parents the glorious news. Having run all the way home, she had paused at the open front door of the cottage, catching her breath, taking a moment to conjure confidence, wondering what she might say to her parents. It felt huge, an admission that she was no longer their little Merry, but a grown woman who had sex, was about to wear an engagement ring and sometime soon would be waltzing up the aisle of St Michael's. But nothing, nothing, could deter her from her course because what she had felt for Digby was an all-consuming, unconditional love.

''Course you do. Sorry, love.'

'Why are you sorry? Don't be! It's great news!'

'I just . . .' Bella paused. 'I feel awkward because, even though it's early days, I've met a bloke and I'm happy and I know you are still . . .'

'Yeah, I'm still . . . but that can't stop you from living, loving! I want you to be happy, Bells.'

'And me you. Wish I could give you a hug.'

Merrin closed her eyes and bit her cheek. 'I could do with one this morning.'

'I worry about you, Merry.' Bella's words were unexpected and sent a jolt of sadness through Merrin that made her shiver. She drew her knees up on the bed and pulled the duvet over them to feel cosy.

I worry about me, too, sometimes . . .

'Well, there's no need to worry, Bells. I'm fine. I work in a lovely place and my room's nice enough and if I have to be away from Port Charles, then it's as good a place to be as anywhere.'

'And *do* you have to be away from Port Charles? I miss you.' The note of hope in Bella's voice was heart-wrenching.

'I miss you too. But I do need to be away. I still can't stand the thought of everyone talking about me like they do Lizzie Lick.'

'Goodness, Merry, you are nothing like Lizzie, and if I were you, I wouldn't care so much what people say or think, love – let them talk. You can't live your life like that. You have to do what makes you happy.'

Her friend's words did little to reassure her. 'I *am* happier, getting there.'

She looked out of the window, watching the peacock strut on the lawn. She was yet to see him with his tail in full fan, but was more than content to watch him majestically saunter with his arrogant gait. The peahens stared in envy at his trailing skirt of teal and gold, his glossy blue body shimmering and his headdress crown that never slipped.

'Have you got a grand room in Thornbury? I can't imagine sleeping in a castle.'

'I don't exactly. I'm in an annex, but it's still quite grand, I suppose. Not much in it, but a nice double bed and a great view of the garden through the French doors. We have peacocks!'

'So? We have seagulls!' Bella retaliated.

'But peacocks are beautiful. Not that I've ever seen one with its tail up; I'd love to, mind.'

'Baby seagulls are cute!'

'A peacock doesn't try and nick your chips.'

'True, but when a sailor sees a seagull he knows land is close! And that's pretty awesome,' Bella added triumphantly. 'Sailors like Luuk, who might use them to help find their way back to me.'

'Bella, you are worrying me, coming over all poetical! It's not like you. Mind you, I can talk, I've been reading Shakespeare.'

'*Shakespeare?* As in *Romeo and Juliet*?'

'Yes. What other Shakespeare is there?' She laughed.

'And you like it?'

'I do, if I go slow and get into the rhythm of it. I used to think it was boring.'

'I still do.' Bella humphed. 'And for the record, I've never felt like this before, about anyone.'

'Wowsers! This is big news. How long is he staying?'

'Not long enough however long it is. Ruby reckons he looks shifty, but then she suspects everyone.'

'Sometimes with good reason.' She thought of her sister's dealings with her ex-fiancé. It was a painful truth. 'Not that she's that happy with me right now. She's still being off.' Merrin was wary of pulling their friend into the fray, knowing that when she and Ruby were out of sync it was Bella who felt the repercussions.

'She's . . . she's busy at the fishmonger's and goes out most nights.'

'Bella, I know you're trying to make me feel better, but it's a fact. She avoids talking to me.' It was hard to put into words, even to her best friend.

'I think she's painted herself into a corner, playing the part of the spiky, angry older sister for so long that she doesn't know how to reinvent herself.'

'I wish she'd try; we're sisters!'

'I know that. I think she's actually very sensitive, and in hiding that, she can come across as a bit brusque.'

'A bit?' Merrin laughed, before plucking up courage to ask the question that would not stay quiet in her brain, rattling around until she gave voice to it. 'Have you . . . have you seen Digby?'

She heard her friend's slow intake of breath, as if she were deciding whether or not to come clean. 'Yes. Once.'

Merrin sat up in the bed and pulled the pillow behind her, curling her toes inside her nightdress to warm them. This was how it worked: any snippet about him, a crumb of detail, was enough to reel her in like a fish on a hook – a fish that knew the bait was toxic, but was lured by a force of temptation too strong to resist.

'Where?' Her heart hammered in its desire for detail.

'He was up at Reunion Point.'

Our place! She felt both gladdened and saddened by the fact that he couldn't fail to think of her up there. But to what end?

'Me and Ruby and Jarv went up for a picnic. Well, not a picnic exactly.' Bella backtracked, as if aware of an unspoken sensitivity. 'You know, just to . . . just to get pissed.' She sounded flustered.

'Well, that sounds like a good idea.' Sarcasm wrapped her words. 'To get pissed on a clifftop. I mean, if you have to do it at all, then Reunion Point with the rocks below and a sheer drop is probably the best place.'

'I don't get that pissed!' Her friend laughed. 'Those two, however . . .' She let this trail and Merrin noted the use of the words 'those two' and felt a strange jolt of misplaced envy that her friend and her sister were having fun together, which of course she knew they would, and she wanted them to. But it was as if she had never been there, confirmation that life carried on regardless.

'If you say so. Anyway, come on, tell me about Digby.' To say his name out loud was not as painful as it once had been. If anything caused her immense sorrow, it was the memory of the night he had proposed, when, with wine and love sloshing in her veins, she had lain on her narrow mattress, kicking her heels with excitement, unable to believe that she had found true love and that her life was going to be rosy. Ruby had thrown a pillow at her face to make her shut up.

'Was he with anyone?'

'No.'

Aware that she had been holding her breath, she exhaled. This fact brought instant relief, although why it mattered to her that he was alone was frustrating. The thought of him with another girl was more than she could cope with. Instantly she pictured the posh girls who made up his gang.

'Did he say anything to you?'

Infuriatingly, Bella took her time. 'He said something like . . . "Sometimes you don't have an easy choice," or some such bollocks, I can't remember exactly. I might have had some cider. Quite a lot of cider, thinking about it.'

'So what did you say when he said that?' Merrin did her best to disguise her extreme interest. Not that she wanted him back or even hoped for reconciliation, not at all, but still she wanted to know, as if the exchange might finally throw some light into the corners of her mind that were very much in the dark when it came to understanding what had happened. She hoped Bella had said something that left him in no doubt that she was not bitter or hurt and was in fact thriving in his absence. It felt important that he think it, even if it wasn't strictly true.

'I didn't say anything, but Ruby told him that he was a prick and that if he ever spoke to any of us again she'd smash his face in.'

'Of course she did.' Merrin slumped down under the duvet and closed her eyes, hating the level of emotion that still hovered near the surface. And angry at herself that it was all based on no more than a fake emotion like unconditional love – how stupid must she have been to fall for the dream he peddled?

'Are you crying?' Bella asked across the divide as Merrin turned on her side and closed her eyes. 'It sounds like you are.'

'No.'

'Yeah, you are, darling, and I don't want you to cry.'

'I can't help it.'

'Well, you *need* to help it. You need to stop letting anything he did or said ruin things for you. You've already banished yourself to a castle and I bet you're letting it stop you finding a prince.'

'I don't want a bloody prince!'

'Oh, come on, you must have met someone in the last year who you thought was nice? Good-looking? Funny?'

Unbidden, the image of Miguel Rochas filled her mind and she opened her eyes. He was undoubtedly all three, but whether he was the kind of person she would take a risk on, as her mum suggested, was another question altogether.

'Maybe . . . but I doubt he'd be interested in an old misery guts like me.'

'You're not a misery guts. You've just been sad and you've needed time. And now you've had some time. *Now* what you need is a good kick up the arse. And to decide to let yourself live! So what if life isn't what you thought it would be. Is it ever? And what does it matter if you've taken a wrong turn? You've got to get on with it, Merry! Get out there! This ain't a rehearsal.'

'I know that. And I'm better than I was. Much better. I can get through a day without wanting to hide and I can even think about him without crying, so, progress.'

'I just miss you, Merry. We all do. Well, apart from old Ma Mortimer, who swans around the place with her sweet smile like butter wouldn't melt.'

'I can't stand the thought of seeing her or him.' *Go home, dear, go home to your family . . .*

'You'll have to at some point.'

'Not if I don't come home.'

'Brilliant, Merrin Mercy, that's the answer – never come home! What a thing to say!' Bella tutted.

'It's not that I don't want to. But can you imagine what it would be like to see him? When for him it's like I never existed? Like I might have dreamt the whole thing? To have him go from loving me so completely and grabbing my hand, not wanting to say goodbye for the night because he couldn't stand the idea of being apart from me, to . . . nothing! I'll never understand it, not really.' She closed her eyes to calm her thoughts; getting worked up was easy and served nothing positive.

'Me neither.' Bella gave a humph of laughter. 'But you gotta let it go!'

'Easy said. But it's like grief, and yet I can't legitimately grieve because he's not dead, he just doesn't want me.' It didn't get any easier saying it out loud, yet she was also glad of the opportunity to do so. Glancing at the window, she felt her gut shrink at the prospect that one day she might be within bumping-into distance of a Mortimer. Whether it be Loretta, Guthrie or Digby himself, she knew she wouldn't know what to say or how to act. The thought was enough to make the breath stutter in her throat with embarrassment. Far better to stay where she was and keep busy.

'You know, I think he must be a born fool to have thrown away such a lovely relationship.' Her mate sighed. 'But more than that, I feel he must be lacking or weak to let it go as far as he did if he had no intention of going through with it, and so I feel sorry for him, as well as being mad as hell at him.'

'You're kind, Bella, to consider him in that way.'

'I don't know about that, my lovely. And I know your sister certainly doesn't share my kindness.'

They both chuckled at the image, knowing Ruby would be as good as her word. Merrin took comfort from the fact that her sister still cared enough to defend her.

'So how long *is* gorgeous Luuk staying?'

'For ever, I hope!'

'Blimey! Don't tell him that; he'll run for the mountains.'

'They don't have a lot of mountains in Holland.'

'Good point, smart arse. Anyway, I've got to get ready for work. Love you.'

'Love you.'

After a restorative shower, and buoyed up by Bella's call, Merrin made her way across the front gravel to the main hotel.

'Hey, Merrin!' Miguel called after her. She slowed to allow him to catch up. 'Morning!'

'Morning.' She tucked her short bob behind her ears; the style was liberating not only in terms of the time it took her to get ready but also in freeing her of the memory of Digby running his fingers through her long locks.

'Glad I caught you. I wanted to ask you two things.' He smiled. She liked his open expression and his neat, white teeth.

'Fire away.' She carried on walking and they fell into step together.

'We're really short-staffed over the next two weeks: Sonja has gone down with the flu and I'd already told Gareth he could take a holiday, so he's in the Lake District – don't suppose you fancy some overtime in the restaurant? Nothing that would interfere with your shifts on reception, but if you could spare us the odd evening?'

'Sure.' It wasn't like she had anything else to occupy her evenings, and she couldn't deny the extra cash would come in handy.

'You are a lifesaver!' He joined his hands in prayer.

'What was the second thing?' She stood still on the winding path and stared at him.

'I was wondering if you fancied a drink?' he asked without any hesitation or nerves.

'Blimey, Miguel, it's a bit early, isn't it?' She glanced at her watch and drew breath through her teeth. 'How do you take it at this time of the morning? Gin on your cornflakes? Clean your teeth with Prosecco?'

'Very funny.' He ran his hand through his neat, dark hair. 'And actually, I meant beer, and later – tonight, as it's my night off, the only one I can see me getting for a while. Or another night, any night in fact, or day, if night's not possible.'

Now his nerves showed and she rather liked it, although she wasn't sure why. This was the first time someone had managed to put a crack in her protective shell for the longest time.

'So that's it. What I'm saying is: I think you need to go to the pub. And I think I need to come with you, if nothing else to see you safely home after you have consumed more beer than your legs are comfortable with carrying.'

'I don't like beer.'

'Ah.' He kicked at the gravel. 'So that's a no, is it?' He looked a little crestfallen and it gladdened her to know he wanted her company.

'No. It means I'll drink wine instead.' She felt warmed at the smile that split his face, remembering Bella's words that maybe it was time she let herself live. 'Tonight would be great.'

'Oh! Good!'

'You sound surprised.'

'I am.' He nodded. 'But glad! You don't really socialise with us, so I guess I thought you might prefer not to.' He met her gaze.

'I think . . .' She paused, wondering how best to explain the state of isolation in which she had chosen to live. 'I think I did prefer not to socialise, but now I might prefer *not* to do that. Does that make sense?' *Plus, my friend said I needed a kick up the arse and you might just be that very thing* . . . This she kept to herself.

'No. I literally have no clue what you're talking about. So, just to confirm, we are going for a drink tonight after work?'

'We are,' she confirmed, and liked the way his face lit up.

◆ ◆ ◆

At the end of her shift and having arranged to meet Miguel at the front gate, Merrin took her time getting ready, and it was nothing to do with slipping into her jeans and a shirt, cleaning her teeth and spritzing her perfume. Her preparation was more mental. She sat on the edge of her bed and took deep breaths.

'You can do this!' She glimpsed her reflection and tried not to see herself standing in front of the full-length mirror at home in a voluminous gown. With her heart racing and her palms a little sweaty, she trod the wide gravel path to the front gate, where she found Miguel kneeling on the grass, holding a sandwich crust in his outstretched arm.

'What are you doing?'

'Oh.' He jumped up and dropped the bread, dusting his hands on his jeans. 'I'm trying to lure the little wild rabbits from behind this bush with a bit of leftover afternoon tea.'

'Why?' She giggled, erasing the image of Digby proposing on the grass that had leapt into her mind. She didn't want to give him the satisfaction, not tonight.

'I just want to be friendly. Plus, I always wanted a rabbit, but I grew up in a flat on a main road and so it wasn't ideal. I thought I could rectify the fact by befriending the rabbits that run around here.'

'That's not going to happen. We have wild rabbits around the cottage at home and they're cute, but pests.' She laughed again. 'And trust me, it's a compliment I find you funny. I don't laugh half as much as I used to.'

'God, that's sad, why don't you?' He walked forward and she looked up at him, no longer worried about how the evening would begin and whether they might struggle to find common ground, as just like that and with no more than a few shared words, they had started. And it felt easy.

'I don't know.' She did know, of course, but figured it was better not to launch into the most depressing of stories before they had even left the hotel grounds. 'I guess I used to be the kind of person who thought that anything was possible and then one summer I realised that some things are not possible, and that sometimes life doesn't turn out how you think it will and there's not a lot you can do about it.'

'You sound wise, like Yoda.'

Again she felt her face break into a smile. 'Thank you. I think.'

The White Swan was their pub of choice and, in a cosy nook, Merrin drank three large glasses of wine, finding it easier to relax with each sip that passed her lips.

'It's nice, isn't it?' She beamed.

'What is?' He seemed to be concentrating and she knew then that her words might be a tad slurred.

'Being out!' She laughed, throwing her arms wide. 'Being out of our rooms and away from work!' The sensation reminded her of carefree nights on the beach with Bella, Ruby and Jarvis, and of running down the slipway with her shoes in her hands as the sun came up . . . glorious freedom in the most beautiful setting. How she missed it, but being out with Miguel in a pub felt like a small step on the road back to normality. Actually, no, it felt like a big step, and with it came a sense of pride that she had taken the step at all.

'You make it sound like a prison.'

'A prison I choose and where I read William Spakespeare! That's close enough!' She giggled. 'Me! Reading William Shh . . . akespeare. I used to think I couldn't do that; I used to think I couldn't do lots of things, but I can, Miguel. I can.'

'I think you can do anything you put your mind to. I also think we'd better get you home.' Miguel downed the remainder of his pint and helped her from her chair.

'Sorry, I'm a little out of practice; feel a bit tipsy.' She smiled and followed him out into the cooler night air, which hit her face and made her realise just how tipsy she was. 'You're my first friend here, Miguel.'

'I'm honoured.' He gave a mock bow. 'People talk about you a little bit; they wonder why you keep yourself to yourself so much. I mean, you are young, how old are you, thirty-four? Forty?' He laughed and she slapped his arm.

'Charming!' It was a moment that defused the hurt she felt that people talked about her here too. The very thing she had been trying to escape – the thought was sobering. 'What do they say?' Her voice was quiet, as if she didn't really want to know the answer.

'Nothing bad, nothing nasty; you're well liked. Everyone says you're sweet, friendly, hardworking, reliable, it's all good, Merrin, but that you seem a bit . . .'

'A bit what?' she pushed, as a lump grew in her throat.

'As you said earlier – sad, I guess.'

She nodded. Her head spun from too much booze and she hoped she wasn't going to be sick.

'There's a lady where I live, where I used to live, where I'm from in Cornwall.' She was gabbling a little. 'She's called Lizzie Lick.'

'Is that a common surname? Mr and Mrs Lick!' he called out, as if announcing them. His humour was like a balm; it lifted the moment.

'No. It's cruel, really. That's the name everyone has given her; I don't know why. I used to hide from her when I was a little girl; she has long, unbrushed hair and wide eyes.'

The two paused in Castle Street and Merrin rested on the porch of Epworth House, leaning on the oak beams as if she lived there. 'I remember seeing her coming towards me on the beach one winter morning. She was staring. I had my wellingtons on and we were collecting shells. I ran to my mum and gripped her hand and she bent down and whispered to me, "You don't need to be afraid of Liz, she's just sad. She won't hurt you. She's never hurt anyone." I wanted to know why she was sad and my mum told me that it was because the person she loved most in the whole wide world died and it was like Lizzie had fallen to the floor and couldn't get up again.' She looked up at Miguel, who didn't have a quip, but stared at her, as if taking in her words. 'I asked if it was her mummy that died? Because I loved my mum most in the whole wide world and I couldn't begin to imagine the loss of her.' She gripped the post as her legs swayed a little. 'But she told me it was her daughter she'd lost. It was the first time I understood that you didn't have to be a grown-up to die. I've never forgotten it.'

'No wonder Lizzie Lick is sad and doesn't brush her hair.' Miguel took her hand and prised her from the post, tucking her arm into the crook of his for the walk home. It felt nice to have human contact. She'd missed it.

'I understand now I'm older that what you see isn't her, it's not Lizzie, it's the shadow of her. And I know because that's been me for the last year or so. People are talking about me too, like they do her.'

He slowly formed his words. 'Did you . . . did you lose someone, Merrin? And don't feel you have to tell me. I don't want to pry.'

She leant into him, liking the support he offered as they ambled along the winding street lined with dainty cottages where lamplight shone from the windows and potted plants and hanging baskets graced the frontages. 'Have you ever owned something so beautiful that you can't quite believe it's yours and then through no fault of your own it gets broken, and you can't bear to look at it any more, because it's smashed and yet it used to be perfect, and even to glimpse it makes your heart break?' She looked up, almost having forgotten she was talking to him and not herself.

'I haven't, Merrin. I've never owned anything like that.'

'Well, I did.' She swallowed. 'I owned a lovely life in the most beautiful place you can imagine and I fell in love and got dressed up in a big, frothy wedding dress, and my dad covered the old cart with flowers and all the village came out to wave and then . . . and then it was all gone. All of it. And here I am.'

And just like that her tears had gathered and, suddenly weary, she rested her head on his shoulder.

'Well, for what it's worth, not that I would wish you a moment of sadness, I'm glad that you went through that because it brought you here, brought you to me.'

The two stopped and leant on the high stone wall of a garden. Merrin looked up at the man who she had trusted with her story. 'You are very good-looking.'

'Yes, I am,' he stated, and again she felt laughter erupt from her mouth without hesitation or self-consciousness. He moved in as if to kiss her and she pulled her head back.

'I want you to understand, Miguel, that I've been badly hurt and it's left a mark on me, changed me. And you are really kind and funny and good-looking.'

'Yes, I think we've established that.' He smiled and held both her hands in his.

'I'm sad that you will only ever know this new-shaped Merrin Mercy Kellow because I used to be different, better.'

Words raced around her head that felt at once presumptive and weighted. *I'm wary of any long-term commitment, suspicious of words of affection and I will never be able to love as freely as I did before because part of my heart has been boarded up, cut off, sealed . . .*

'I want to kiss you, Merrin, is that okay?' Again he leant in and, as he did so, she felt the rise of bitter wine in her throat.

'Oh God!' she shouted, before rushing to the kerb, bending over and throwing up into a drain, while Miguel palmed circles on her back.

'I gotta admit' – he pulled a handkerchief from his back pocket and handed it to her – 'this isn't quite how I pictured the evening ending.'

'Do you still want to kiss me?' She looked up at him from where she crouched on the pavement, a line of spit dangling from her mouth.

'I don't.' He grimaced and helped her up. 'I really, really don't.'

'I understand. I wouldn't want to kiss me either. What is it about me?' She stood up straight. 'Digby didn't want me, Ruby treats me badly and now you don't want to kiss me.'

'I . . .' He looked up and down the street. 'I don't know who Ruby is but I can't imagine anyone treating you badly. Digby, also a stranger to me, is a complete fool, and the reason I don't want to kiss you is because you have a little . . .' He touched his own mouth and she wiped her face on her sleeve.

'I need a shower and a nap.'

'Yup.'

Slipping off her shoes, she handed them to Miguel and wiggled her toes against the cool paving stones, then proceeded to walk along Castle Street. Barefoot.

Merrin woke before her alarm and sat up in bed, looking at her pale skin and bloodshot eyes in the mirror.

'Oh God!' She placed her head in her hands, partly to try to alleviate her thumping headache but also in shame at the memory of her evening with Miguel. 'He's never going to talk to me again!' she wailed. 'And he'll tell everyone what happened!' Picking up her phone, she fired off a text to Bella.

> This is all your fault. Headache. Hangover. Asked a man to kiss me after I'd been sick in a drain. You told me to get out there and this is what happened!

The reply came quickly.

Keeping it classy, I see. Nice! X

(but super proud of you, girl!)

Merrin jumped into the shower and took her time, letting the hot water pound her skin and restore her. She did a double shampoo, before lathering her face with soap and giving her teeth a good scrub. With a towel on her head, she caught sight of her reflection in the mirror. The effects of her hangover had lessened a little and the sickly smell of booze and sick had left her skin. In fact, she looked quite rosy and with more of a sparkle in her eye than she had seen for the longest time. Bella was right, this wasn't a rehearsal, it was her one life, and it felt good to have stepped out of her comfort zone. A strange sensation swirled in her stomach and she recognised it as excitement.

The knock on her door was quiet; in fact, she listened for the second knock to make sure she hadn't imagined it.

'Miguel!' Still in her dressing gown, she popped her head through the gap of the open door, hiding inside. It felt a little odd to be chatting to him like this on top of her behaviour last night. 'Are you still talking to me?' she asked with no small dollop of embarrassment.

'Don't worry, you didn't do anything to embarrass yourself.'

'Apart from be sick and then ask if you wanted to kiss me.' She closed one eye briefly; it felt easier not to look at him fully.

'Apart from that. Anyway, two things: first, I brought you this.' He lifted a small tray into her line of sight with a large glass of fresh orange juice with ice cubes bobbing on the top, a steaming mug of black coffee, a big, fat, flaky croissant and two Paracetamol.

‘Thought this might help you start your day, although I must say you don’t look too bad.’

‘Oh, thank you!’ Making sure her robe was secure, she opened the door. He walked in and placed the tray on the table. ‘That’s so kind.’

‘And I do, by the way.’

‘You do what?’ She wrinkled her nose, wondering how she had lost the thread.

‘Well, that’s the second thing. I wanted to kiss you. So I thought we should get it out of the way before it becomes one of those things that takes on more significance than it deserves and gets awkward.’

‘I don’t want that.’ She smiled and let the door close.

‘I don’t want that either.’ He took a step towards her and placed his hands either side of her face. The novelty of his handsome face was something she hoped would never wane. His kiss when it landed on her mouth was nice, soft and pleasant, promising even, but the fireworks of longing that had jumped in her gut at the mere touch from Digby . . . they were absent. But what did she expect? This was brand new and she was changed.

CHAPTER ELEVEN

Jarvis

No matter that the sky was grey and the cloud heavy over the water, Jarvis liked the routine of being back on dry land, liked to wander the familiar paths of Port Charles. Yes, he loved his job on the boat with Ben and Robin, loved the banter, but there were things he missed when he was at sea. He picked up the newspaper from the stand outside Everit's corner shop and went inside to hand the coins to Mrs Everit herself.

'You heard the sad news this morning, Jarvis?'

'No?' He held his breath. In a small place like this you most likely knew the family who bad things had befallen, but similarly he knew Mrs Everit had a tendency to gossip and so her interpretation of 'bad' or 'sad news' might be that the milk van was running late or the broadband was playing up.

'Old Guthrie Mortimer died. Very suddenly, apparently. In his sleep. Most unexpected.'

He nodded and breathed out, feeling a flicker of empathy for Digby, knowing what it was like to lose your dad from your life. 'But not that unexpected, really, Mrs Everit. He was getting on and I think I've seen him drunk more than I've seen him sober.'

'Not that we shall speak ill of the dead.' She fixed him with a hard stare that left him admonished.

''Course not. You have a nice day.'

He folded the paper under his arm and made his way down Fore Street towards Kellow Cottages, deciding not to mention it to Ruby. He didn't want to take the shine off their plans. The two had agreed to head up to St Austell for a spot of shopping and then grab a pasty in Mevagissey on the way home. He wasn't too chuffed at the prospect of shopping, but liked that she chose to spend her day off with him. Truth was, he liked her full stop. And on his latest fishing trip he had thought of her more often than not, missing her friendship, her humour, her warmth.

The roaring fire of passion and desire he had felt for Merrin was now no more than the smallest glow of an ember, but as long as it was there at all it was hard to see Merrin's sister as anything other than a good mate. So what that he and Ruby had kissed once up at Reunion Point? A good kiss, actually, a surprisingly good kiss, but one fuelled by cider and so surely it didn't really count. Scouring the headlines as he walked in the cold morning air, he stopped in his tracks at the sight of Ruby on the harbour wall, deep in conversation with Bella.

He combed his unruly hair with his fingers, as Ruby turned and called to him.

'Jarv!'

'All right?' he called back with his nerves jangling. Hoping he didn't blush or stare, he walked in a deliberate fashion towards the duo, who whispered in the way they always did, like witches plotting. He smiled, reminded in that moment of what it had been like to see the two of them with Merrin; the village was poorer for the loss of the atmosphere the trio had created. The last time he had seen them all together, Merrin had looked destroyed, lost, and Ruby had been distracted, prowling and incensed by the Mortimers' treatment of her sister. Not that he blamed her; that was what you did: stood by those you loved. His admiration for

Ruby had in fact grown because of how fiercely she loved and protected her family. It was still beyond him how a bloke like Digby the dickhead could throw away a woman like Merrin. But as his mother liked to remind him, 'Love can be fickle and your feelings for the object of your desire can turn on a sixpence into something a lot like loathing . . .'

He'd have to take her word for it. Walking towards the wall, he watched the two women, who, with furrowed brows, were once again deep in conversation. Maybe they had heard about old Guthrie Mortimer. As he approached, the sun punched a hole in the clouds and peeped its head through, showering light that lit the whole cove. He slowed and felt his heart give a little rhumba, recognising the feeling in his veins as one of longing. And all at no more than the sight of this girl . . . *This* girl, with the bright smile and her thick, long hair resting over her shoulder, was something else. *Ruby*, who had been under his nose his whole life, who had been by his side since they were kids and who had punched him in the mouth when he had dared laugh at her wonky haircut.

'Glad you're here, Jarv.' She smiled and her words warmed him. 'Gran's been taken ill.'

'Ellen? Oh no, she all right?'

'Not really.' Ruby ran her fingers across her forehead, suggesting a headache might be lurking there. 'She's been taken to Truro Hospital; she's proper poorly.'

'Is there anything I can do?' He folded the paper under his arm and reached for his van keys.

Ruby shook her head and Bella squeezed her hand.

'Don't think so.' She gave a grateful smile.

'Did they say what it might be or if it was serious?'

Ruby held his gaze, her eyes teary. 'She had a water infection and they thought she might just need antibiotics. Anyway, Dr Levington came out and she was very confused and had a high temperature and they've taken her in, more as a precaution, I think. Mum and Dad have gone with her. I'm just about to call Merrin and tell her.'

'She's one tough old bird is Ellen Kellow. Don't you worry.'

He liked how Bella tried to soothe her friend's anguish.

'You want me to drive you to the hospital?' He displayed the keys in his palm, knowing he would do anything for this girl who so loved her family.

She shook her head. 'Mum said it wouldn't do for us all to crowd the place when the nurses and whatnot are trying to do their job. I'm going to stay here.'

'I got to go,' Bella sighed. 'Who knows how much longer Luuk will be here before he gets the call and has to take off. Let me know how Granny Kellow is.'

Ruby nodded. ''Course.'

'Are you going to miss him?' Jarvis teased.

Her response, however, was anything but jovial. Bella hopped off the wall and stared at him with tears in her eyes. Then, putting her hand flat over her heart and with a voice shot through with emotion, she said, 'More than I can possibly say, Jarv.' Then she turned and walked briskly up the road.

'Reckon she's got it bad,' Ruby observed, as she, too, jumped down on to the cobbles.

'It happens. And often when you least expect it. Do you know what I mean?' He held her gaze as his heart thudded.

''Appen I do know what you mean.' The corners of her mouth lifted in a half-smile. Her question when it came was quiet. 'Will you . . . will you stay here with me today, Jarv? I don't want to be on my own.'

''Course I will.' He reached for her hand, which fitted nicely inside his own.

'We can go shopping another day.'

'We can that.'

As they stepped over the threshold of Kellow Cottages, he smiled at her; this loud-mouthed beauty stood out to him like something brightly painted in a world of sepia. It was in that moment he realised that he had been holding a candle for a memory, not a person. Merrin was an idea, but her sister . . . she was the real deal. It was true, there were many things he missed when he was on the water, but mainly, he now saw with clarity, what he missed was Ruby Mae.

CHAPTER TWELVE

MERRIN

'Oh, hey Mum, I'm glad you've called.' Merrin tried to keep the bubble of excitement from her voice, knowing it would only invite a barrage of questions that she would be unable to answer to her mother's satisfaction – *if*, that was, she confessed to one measly kiss received only an hour or so since.

Ooh! So, do you like him?

I don't really know yet . . .

Are you seeing him again?

I don't know, it's early days . . .

When can we meet him?

Not any time soon, Mum . . .

Although she had to admit, it had been a very good kiss, one with no small amount of promise. Smiling at the memory, she was still able to feel the soft bruise of contact on her lips, over which she now ran the pad of her index finger. It felt good to have a diversion like Miguel; a diversion that lit a small flame of hope inside her that she had thought was all but extinguished for good.

'I was going to call you. How's Gran? Ruby said you were with her. Please tell her I'm sending all my love and I hope she's feeling better. Does she need anything? Should I send a magazine or just flowers?'

'No, no, love . . .' Heather breathed deeply, cutting her off. 'That's what I'm calling to say, little Merry. I am so sorry, but she . . . she's gone, darlin', gone.'

Suddenly all the excitement of that one kiss was wiped out in an instant. 'What? What do you mean?' She sat down hard on the edge of the table in the staff canteen and let her breathing steady. The suit jacket of her uniform felt constricting around the armpits, and the neck of her blouse tight around her neck, where only moments before they had fitted perfectly. The sound of her mum trying to hide her tears was enough to twist Merrin's heart. It felt as if time slowed a little and the rest of the world fell silent as she listened to her mother's words.

'She passed away an hour ago; I've just left Dad with her. To say his goodbyes.'

'Oh no, Mum! No. But I thought . . .' Merrin closed her eyes and placed her palm over her face, wishing she were standing by her side, holding her close at a time when she knew that physical contact would make all the difference for them both. 'What happened? Ruby said she was only taken in as a precaution; I thought she was going to be fine!' Her voice was raised, not intentionally shouting at her mother, but as a means of venting her utter frustration that this was happening at all. Sadness rolled over her, covering her in a dark, sticky pulp that drew joy from her pores and seeped into her veins. In an instant, the sunshine seemed to have dulled and the air thickened.

'She just slipped away, Merry. No one was expecting it and, despite how horrible it is for us all, it really is quite wonderful that she left us mid-sleep. Peacefully.'

'It doesn't feel real, Mum. Or wonderful.'

'I know, darlin', I know. Everyone here at Truro Hospital has been amazing. Daddy is in shock, as you would expect; we both are, really, but I was just talking to the ward sister, who told me that even though it might not feel like it right now, the way Ellen went was the biggest gift to us all.'

'Doesn't feel much like a gift.' Merrin sniffed, aware of the juvenile tone to her response.

'Not right now, but when you process it all later, you might think so: no long-drawn-out illness, no galling treatment, no pain or violent accident, nothing like that.'

'It all feels . . .' She looked up through the little window and out over the treetops, which rustled in the breeze.

'I know, my love. I've got to go. I promised I'd call your sister. I'll call you again later.'

'Okay, Mum.' Ridiculously, she wished to keep talking to Heather – wished she could click her heels and be with her family – well, she half-wished that; the other half still felt queasy at the prospect of being anywhere near home.

'And, Merry, listen to me, I'd rather you didn't come rattling down the motorway and then back again, all tired. I'll only worry, and there's nothing to be done here. Not much will happen for a few days, and then it's going to be a very small funeral. Only us. No pomp or ceremony, in and out fast as we can. The least fuss. It's what she wanted. She made that clear often enough.' Her mum's voice broke. 'She'd say the same thing: don't you worry, little Merry, just do what you gotta do. And never forget, we love you so much. I know that you are here in heart, always. We're so proud of you.'

'I'm going to miss her.' She sniffed. 'But the thought of coming back . . .'

'I understand that, my love, I do. I told you already, no need to come. You're doing so well, Merrin, just keep your head up and keep feeling better. I need you to do that for me.'

'I will, Mum.'

Merrin held the phone long after the call had ended, feeling very far away. The thought of going home made her knees weak.

'You are a coward, Merrin,' she whispered under her breath, knowing that she would heed her mum's words and not go back to Port Charles. With this knowledge came nothing but the sweet, sweet relief that she was not going to have to face the demons that lurked around every corner, but this was followed immediately by the smack of guilt in her face.

'Good morning, Merrin!' Lionel said with his usual jollity. 'I'm looking for Vanya?'

'I haven't seen her yet, sorry, Lionel. But I'll go see if I can find her, if you like?' She looked up.

'Not at all. I can do that. Oh dear, are you upset? Have I interrupted you?' His face coloured and he wrung his hands, as though he might in some way be responsible for her distress. She wiped her tears and found a level of professionalism that would keep her sadness at bay, for now.

'I've just had a bit of sad news.' She raised the phone. 'My mum called to say my gran has passed away.' She bit down to stop her bottom lip from trembling as the words sunk in.

Lionel stepped forward and put his podgy hand on her arm. 'Merrin, I am so very sorry to hear that. Rotten news, entirely rotten. A certainty, and yet always a shock. Of course, take all the time you need. We'll manage.'

His kindness only served to encourage her tears. 'I think I'm better off working, to be honest. Keep my mind busy.' This had served her well in the past: head down, ploughing on . . .

'I understand that, a diversion.'

'Yes.' She gave a watery smile. 'A diversion.'

◆ ◆ ◆

Although Merrin remained distracted, with a dull echo of sadness belying her fixed smile, the day passed quickly, as they often did, with the hours blurring into each other, punctuated only by snatched coffee breaks and a foodless lunch hour spent crying quietly in her room at the loss of her beloved Granny Ellen. Heather texted to say that an initial call had been made to Mr Newcombe, the funeral director, and plans were afoot for a small, intimate send-off, as per her gran's explicit instructions.

Walking the grounds now at dusk, she gathered her thoughts and breathed deeply in an attempt to quell the disconcerting rise of unease that swelled inside her. Her mother's understanding of just how hard it was for her to return to Port Charles simultaneously eased her worry and fired arrows of remorse through her heart. The fact that she had missed the opportunity to see her Granny Ellen one last time filled her with a deep, unshakeable regret, which weighed heavily. It was yet another sorrow she lay at the Mortimers' door. Screwing her eyes shut, she pictured Loretta in her finery and felt the ache of distress in her gut. The Mortimers were the reason she lived away, they were the reason she hadn't got to sit and drink tea with her gran in what was to be her final year.

Her sister's phone number flashed up on her screen.

'Hey, Rubes.' Knowing she was in good company, her sadness came to the surface and Merrin welcomed the chance to talk about it. She sank down on to the carpet of soft grass beneath the low, broad boughs of the spreading cedar tree at the back of the garden and leant heavily against its trunk, taking comfort from it.

'Really? Is this a joke?'

Her sister's opener sent a spike of nervous adrenaline that lanced any boil of fatigue. Merrin was now wide awake, with her heart beating quickly.

'Why are you saying that?' She wondered if Ruby was intentionally addressing her, or whether her sister had misdialled.

'Mum's just told me you're not coming back for Gran's funeral! What the hell?'

'I . . . I can't, Ruby.' This was true. She was a mess at the thought of going back, enough to feel the rise of nausea at the idea. 'I *want* to.' This, too, was fact, she did, but even now a cold film of sweat covered her skin and her limbs shook.

'Well, you'd never know it; you haven't set foot back here since you left.' Her sister's reply was sharp and unexpected.

Merrin felt a flash of anger towards her. 'Are you being serious? You think I don't want to come home?'

'A whole year, Merrin!'

'I have a job, I work long—'

'Yeah, yeah, we *all* have jobs. We *all* work long shifts and we all have to squeeze in what's important around those jobs, and I would have thought what was important was getting back here to check on Mum and Dad, as Gran has just died! You're in Thornbury, not Guatemala.' The air crackled with the beginnings of a fight. Merrin hated the accusation, which was as unfair as it was hurtful.

'Check on them? What are you talking about? I call them all the time, chat to them and—'

'Right! Because that's the same as sitting at the table and having a cup of tea with them, giving them a hug. The odd phone call . . .' Ruby raised her voice.

'It's not the *odd* phone call! I call most days! Jesus, Ruby, the way you're having a go at me, and you wonder why I stay away?'

'So you *do* stay away? At least you admit it,' Ruby yelled.

'God, you are twisting what I said! Don't you think that things are hard enough for us today as it is?'

'Actually, Merrin, I *do* understand things are hard!'

'Why are you so mad at me? Because I escaped and you're still stuck there in Mum and Dad's back bedroom? You've always been jealous.' The words were hurtful and came from an ugly root of envy at the fact that Merrin did not get to wake up each day in the place she loved. No amount of peacocks on the lawn could make up for that, especially not today.

'Shut the fuck up.'

'You shut the fuck up, Ruby!' Merrin's heart beat a little too quickly and her hands shook as a lump of raw emotion stoppered her throat. The words would have been hurtful enough if shared with a stranger, but the fact that this was her sister, who she loved . . .

'Fucking hell, Merrin, you are clueless! You created a bloody tsunami with that Mortimer prick that swamped us all. Mum and Dad saved for months! Week after week of going without just to give you the perfect day – and all for nothing, and then you just sod off to your fancy castle and leave us to pick up the pieces!'

'Why are you saying that now?' she almost squeaked. 'You think I don't feel guilty enough about Mum and Dad paying out for a wedding that never happened? I'm paying them back each month! And you think I would have *chosen* to be left standing there like an idiot? You think that was a picnic for me? And yes, I went away, left everything and everyone I love. I couldn't stand to be the girl everyone was talking about, whispering about, pointing at and feeling sorry for! The new Lizzie Lick! Having to walk past the house I nearly lived in and seeing the man I nearly married! Can you imagine? And yes, I live in a castle, but it's just any other hotel. I don't lie around while people bring me grapes – I work hard, bloody hard! I fall into bed at night so tired—'

'Yeah, we know how hard you've had it,' Ruby tutted. 'Mum couldn't exactly go back to cleaning for old Ma Mortimer, could she? Not after that, and so she lost a big chunk of her monthly money and things have been tight. Really tight. And you might not have been able to stand people whispering about you, pointing at you, but do you think that stopped because you weren't here? Did it fuckery! It's always about poor Merry.' She swallowed. 'You created havoc and then swanned off into the sunset!'

'I did not!'

'You did, though!' Ruby shouted. 'You did! And people still whisper, Merrin. Our name is gossiped about, something funny or to be pitied, and what do you think that does to a man like Dad? A proud Port Charles man?'

Merrin felt her chest cave with sadness and guilt at the fact that this might be harming her dad, but equally that her worst fears were again confirmed.

Ruby wasn't done. 'Life has been shit here, while you wake up to peacocks! But it's bloody typical of you, like when you first met Digby and you all but dropped me and Bells.'

'I have never dropped you and Bells!'

'Yes, you did; you only wanted to be with him and now you've buggered off to Thornbury! I've been so bloody lonely. Thank God for Bella and Jarvis!'

'So what are you saying? That I'm not part of the gang because I fell in love with someone who shat on me from a great height and I had to move away? Instead of staying there and going completely mad?'

'No, that's not what I'm saying!' Ruby fired.

'Well, it bloody feels like it!' Merrin hated the catch to her voice.

There was a beat or two of silence while the girls regrouped.

'I think Gran deserves better,' Ruby said finally. 'I think we all do.'

'That's a low blow! I loved Gran and she knew it! Go to hell, Ruby!' Merrin sobbed.

After they'd ended the call, she lay slumped against the tree, spent and barely able to speak for the hollow shame that filled her gut at her inability to go home and honour her gran, combined with the adrenaline pumping in her system from the violent row. The simple truth was she couldn't face going to Port Charles and couldn't stand the idea of walking into the church. Even picturing it made her head swim. And now, on top of this, she had Ruby's words ringing in her ears, adding to her reluctance to venture home. For the first time in her life she did not want to come face to face with her own sister.

It was not a surprise to Merrin that a day which had started so beautifully could end with ugly tears and sadness seeping from her. It was, after all, not the first time she had encountered such a thing.

◆ ◆ ◆

On the day of the funeral, Merrin walked quietly into St Mary's Church in Thornbury and sat awhile, talking to her gran, confirming how much she loved and would miss her before placing a small bunch of yellow primroses by a lonely, unmarked grave and letting her tears flow as she uttered words of apology. In that moment she felt close to her beloved Granny Ellen, but a million miles from home.

CHAPTER THIRTEEN

MERRIN

Merrin woke to the sun coming through the French windows and the soft white curtains fluttering in the early-morning summer breeze. It would be inaccurate to say Miguel had entirely erased the hurt caused by Digby, but his lovely attention and the sheer beauty of him had certainly diluted it. Her gran's death, almost a year ago now, had reinforced what Bella had reminded her of: that life was not a rehearsal. And for her, this had certainly been a factor in slipping further into Miguel's arms. He made her laugh like no one else and understood the demands of her job: the long hours, the unsociable shift patterns and her utter exhaustion at the end of a trying day. He liked to pop a flower in a vase and leave it for her on reception, or he'd run her a bath when he knew she was due back. It was these little things that pepped up her day and reminded her how very lucky she was to have someone like him in her life.

They had forged their relationship slowly, kissing gently and walking in the fields on their days off. He had wielded his humour like a sword to cut away her reservations and over the last twelve months they had ended up here: a couple. She was in no doubt that they worked because she was away from the tittle-tattle of Port Charles, had shaken off her old skin and was free to exist in

Thornbury without leaving a trail of gossip and speculation in her wake.

That, and they shared an understanding. Their relationship was fun, frivolous and sometimes he spoke casually of a love she could not return, jesting in wine-filled moments: 'I could fall hard for you, Merry.'

'Don't you dare do that!' she'd answer with directness. 'Save your love and all about you that is fabulous – save it for someone who is not broken and disillusioned, Miguel. Don't waste it on a lost cause like me.'

His expression was crestfallen but, reaching for her hand, he rallied. 'I'll save it because I think you might change your mind. Who knows what's around the corner? Or how you might feel in six weeks? Six months?'

'None of us, I guess.'

Not that she ever gave him reason to think they should plan too far ahead. How would that even be possible when she lived her life one day at a time?

This weekend she was venturing home for the first time since leaving. *Home.* The thought of it was enough to make her stomach flip and her muscles clench. All at once she felt excited, nervous, happy and scared. How she longed to plant her feet on Cornish soil, but at the same time she felt the rise of sick nerves at what it might be like to return to the place of her humiliation. She would be lying if she said she wasn't wary of seeing Ruby, who was the reason for returning, as this was the weekend when her sister would waltz up the aisle to marry Jarvis Cardy.

Merrin was pleased that her sister had found happiness and delighted that it was with Jarvis who, as close to her parents as he had become, was already practically part of the family. It made sense to her. His kind and patient manner was the perfect complement to Ruby's fiery nature. Concentrating on her sister's marriage to such a smashing man kept her from submitting to the threat of nausea at the prospect of returning to St Michael's Church.

Miguel's arm was lying across her neck, clamping her to the mattress. She lay still, not wanting to disturb him, knowing he had come to bed late, his body heavy and his sigh weary. She understood the bone-aching fatigue that a busy day left you with, but at the same time she felt the pressing need to use the bathroom.

Her alarm sounded.

'Nooooo!' Miguel moved his arm and placed the pillow over his head.

'Go back to sleep,' she cooed, kissing his shoulder, as he rolled on to his side. 'I'm on an early.' She left the bed carefully, trying to cause him the least amount of disturbance, and hit the shower. Her uniform, laundered in-house, lay under plastic wrap and hung on the back of the bathroom door. The sight of it brought back a memory of when she was no more than eleven. It had stuck in her mind as it was the first time she heard the name Loretta, cast into the room from her dad's mouth in a torrent of anger. Mrs Mortimer had presented his wife with a uniform of starched cotton pinafore and a hat with a frill, which Heather had placed on the table, as if quite indifferent to them. Her dad, however, had raged at the mere sight of them.

'There's no way a wife of mine is wearing a get-up like that, and not for the likes of her! You can tell her to stick her job and her uniform where the sun don't shine!' he had yelled, and abandoned his supper of chicken pie and mashed potato, hitting the table with the flat of his palm so hard it caused the plate to jump. Thick gravy had spilled from the plate and run across the table on to the floor like a savoury, golden river. She and Ruby had been too shocked to move, staring at the little trickle and listening to the pleasing sound it made as it hit the wooden floor. 'Where does she think she lives?

Buckingham bloody Palace? She grew up in a caravan at the back of the bog! I won't 'ave it!'

Her mum had calmly held her ground and turned her attention to her sewing. 'I couldn't care less what I wear. I'll stick a turnip on my head if she likes. We need the money, Ben.'

This reminder of the fact that his fisherman's wages alone weren't enough to cover their living expenses did not help the cause. Her dad had grabbed the offending items and marched from the house. Merrin had no idea where they ended up, but suspected they were heaved into the fish-gut bin with a few choice words to send them on their way.

It was odd for her to think that Loretta, a woman who liked the finer things in life, had, according to local lore, spent a childhood without anything fine in it. Ben had always rather enjoyed telling the tale of how the woman with all the airs and graces had grown up living in a caravan, without running hot water and with only a shared compost toilet, at the back of Mellor Waters with her parents and siblings. Rumour had it that Guthrie Mortimer used to ride his horse in the area and took a fancy to the young Loretta, who, twenty-five years his junior, had been swimming in the lake one day. And according to those *same* rumours, she wasn't the kind of girl who owned a swimsuit. It was interesting to Merrin that seeing the Mortimers out and about, you would be pardoned for thinking it was *Mrs* Mortimer, with her shoulders draped in fur and her favoured pillbox hat sporting two curled pheasant tail feathers, who had been born with a silver spoon in her mouth and a biscuit fortune in the bank. And old Guthrie – the affable drunk who, before he spied young Loretta, had apparently spent a decade roaming the high seas on a yacht – who had grown up in a damp field.

Merrin felt a little sick at the thought of the woman, who even after all this time and without any contact, still had the power to make her feel anxious. They were on her mind, and no wonder when she was about to return to where a Mortimer might be within touching distance. The thought made her shiver. She had, of course, been sorry to hear about the passing of Guthrie, but mourned him little, as he had passed away at the same time as her beloved Granny Ellen.

And tomorrow she would set off for Port Charles. Excited and agitated thoughts about the weekend ahead raced around her mind and left her breathless with anxiety. She was nervous about taking Miguel home for the first time, hoping for the thumbs up of approval from her family, but aware that it was so much more than taking a new boyfriend home. It would be the first time she had been to a wedding, and the first time she had paraded around Port Charles, since *that* day, and the only thing that made the thought of it bearable was that she would be doing it with Miguel by her side; someone to cling to. With a man by her side no one was going to view her as pitiful – instead, if viewed through the right lens, she might be seen as triumphant, vindicated and happy! This felt important to her, especially if the Mortimers were within sight.

Of late, things were a little improved between her and her sister; they trod carefully, unpicking the fight that had fractured their bonds, both seemingly aware that those bonds were still a little brittle. There remained a thin film of awkwardness, rooted, Merrin was certain, in the fact that Ruby was about to become Mrs Jarvis Cardy – even though Merrin knew that what she and Jarvis had shared had been no more than a childhood fling with a bit of inept kissing thrown in for good measure.

It was Bella who had first told Merrin that her sister's trips with Jarvis up to Reunion Point to drink cider and their shopping days in St Austell had developed into something more, until there was no question that Ruby was dating the boy. And so, wanting to break the ugly stalemate, Merrin had plucked up the courage to call her sister to get the gossip and help patch up their wounds.

Still, she bitterly regretted the words that had left her mouth quite involuntarily. Words that she wished she could swallow back down and erase. Words that instead of putting a lid on the simmering stew of friction only served to put more heat under it.

'So come on then,' she had urged with a note of caution, treading carefully, badly wanting to erase the lingering sting of their row. 'Bella said you've been seeing *someone*? Tell me everything!'

Ruby had giggled. 'God, is nothing a secret around here?'

'Nope! So come on, spill.'

'It's Jarvis.'

'*My* Jarvis? I knew it! I could tell by the way you've always defended him that there was something there.'

The silence following her words was deafening. Merrin closed her eyes tightly and pulled a face, wishing she could rewind. When Ruby spoke her tone was cutting and her irritation apparent.

'First, he isn't *your* Jarvis.'

'I didn't mean—'

'And second,' her sister interrupted her, keen to make her point and clearly in no mood to hear any kind of justification, 'how many bloody Jarvises do you know, Merrin?'

She tried to smooth the waters. 'I'm . . . I'm happy for you both, I really am. You are two of my favourite people. I think it's brilliant. I really do!'

'You think I need your approval?'

'No! Of course not, I just . . . I'm trying, clumsily, to say congratulations and that he's a good catch. A good catch for you, that is, because you are made for each other!'

'A good catch for *me*?' Ruby snarled, her unspoken assumption that he was not, of course, good enough for Merrin. Merrin had rubbed her eyes. She couldn't win. But Ruby wasn't done. 'And what do you mean, a good catch? What is he, Merrin? A bloody cod?'

'No! I—'

'I've got to go, Mum's calling me.' Her sister had brazenly lied, and before Merrin had a chance to talk her way out of the situation, offering platitudes that might heal, Ruby had hung up the phone.

'Brilliant, Merrin!' She hid her face in her hands. 'Just bloody brilliant.'

These careless, ill-considered words, spoken without thought or agenda, were lodged in her mind so firmly that at every encounter with her sister she felt as though she were skirting around them. It felt like Ruby was slipping further and further out of reach. The dynamic of their relationship had uncomfortably shifted and it meant that even now, as Jarvis and Ruby prepared to wed, every conversation was bookended with a little awkwardness and reservation on both their parts. Merrin wished it were different, but was too busy in her new role as Front of House Manager of this five-star venue to allow such thoughts to cloud her mind today. It was, however, just another aspect that made the prospect of returning to Port Charles daunting, to say the least.

The day passed in a flash, as those worked hard often do, and before she knew it, Friday had dawned and she and Miguel were on the road. The car had been packed slowly and with trepidation as she considered the wisdom of returning at all. She paused often, looking at the little rust bucket that was to transport them, and at one point hoped it might break down and make travelling impossible. She even wondered how easy it would be to catch Vanya's nasty tummy upset, which would mean confinement to bed – anything that might give her a reason to legitimately bow out.

In the run-up to today, she had barely slept, tossing and turning as dreams wrenched her from rest, all with images of her in her wedding dress, the diamanté waistband glittering in the sunlight as she traipsed up the aisle after her sister, much to the amusement of the great and good of Port Charles. She figured the best way to get through it might be with the aid of Dutch courage. An image of a strong glass of gin being put in her hand formed in her head and how very, very happy she had been on her 'almost' wedding day . . . well, the first half of it anyway.

Not that she would be mentioning anything Dutch upon her return. It was not long after Granny Ellen's death that Bella had found herself single and pregnant. Abandoned by Luuk, her handsome Dutchman with whom she had enjoyed a short-lived but all-consuming fling. He was, it turned out, big on promises, but a little short on delivery. Merrin was proud of how her friend was coping as a single mum and couldn't wait to see her. It had been hard and isolating, offering advice and following her pregnancy remotely.

'I wish I could be with you . . .'

'Me too . . .'

And now she watched Miguel grip the passenger seat – this before they had even hit the motorway.

'You need to relax – you being a nervous passenger makes me a nervous driver.'

'Oh, great, that's all I need to know. As if it wasn't bad enough that I have to travel in this noisy old bone-shaker of a car!'

Merrin gasped and ran her hand over the dashboard. 'Don't listen to him, Vera Wilma Brown!'

'You are the only person I know whose car has a first, middle and last name.'

'Maybe you know the wrong kind of people,' she teased to cover her nerves, which she feared were obvious.

'Maybe I do.'

'I promise to deliver you safely if you apologise for calling her a bone-shaker. I can tell she's offended.' She pumped the accelerator to make the car jump a little.

'I really don't want to.' He folded his arms, his phone in his hand.

'Well, that's your choice, but it costs nothing to be nice, Miguel!'

'Jesus! I'm sorry,' he mumbled.

'Sorry, *Vera Wilma Brown*,' she enunciated, throwing him a hard look.

'Sorry, Vera Wilma Brown!' he yelled.

It made Merrin laugh. 'See, that wasn't so hard, was it? And now we're all happy!' She beamed.

'Are we all happy?' he asked gently.

She nodded. 'I'm painting on my happy face and hoping my guts catch up. I've got to do this. I *should* do this.' She was wary of letting on just how petrified she was. It was a big deal. She and Ruby needed to reknit their closeness and Merrin figured there was no better way to do so than with her sister's nuptials as their backdrop. Going home for the first time was nerve-wracking enough, but to attend a wedding? She shivered. On top of this she was taking home a boy, knowing that her parents would interpret this as a serious statement, whereas it was in fact anything but. Miguel was simply her handsome beau, on whom she could lean during this trying trip. She hoped that her family, or Miguel himself for that matter, would not get the wrong message, and was anxious about how she might manage that.

'Okay.' He squeezed her leg. 'Did we get journey snacks?' He sounded endearingly like a child.

'Journey snacks? You had a monstrous breakfast not an hour ago and we have only been going for minutes! You can't possibly need snacks!'

'Well, I don't right now, but I like to plan what I'm going to eat on the journey.'

'I have snacks,' she reassured. 'But if I didn't, I know Mum will have baked for us; wedding or not, she won't miss the opportunity to have you fawn over her chocolate brownies.' She felt a surge of excitement at the thought of seeing her mum. It had been too long.

Heather Kellow might only have been three hours away, but with work commitments, the fact that she didn't drive and was loath to leave Port Charles, where she had been in turn looking after Granny Ellen, supporting Ben after the death of his mother and then planning for Ruby's wedding, it had been hard to make a plan to travel to Thornbury. And that was before the cost of such an excursion was taken into consideration. Plus, with Merrin regularly promising to make the trip, no one, Merrin included, could have envisaged a whole two years passing before she jumped in Vera Wilma Brown and headed home.

'It's one of the only reasons I agreed to come. I love home cooking.'

'Charming! You mean you're not looking forward to seeing my sister get wed?'

'It's not that, it's more the sleeping arrangements I object to.' He sucked air through his teeth at the horror of it.

Merrin chuckled, having explained to him they would have to sleep in the tiny single beds on opposite sides of her childhood bedroom, where soft toys and boxes of Lego sat on the shelves and her parents slept on the other side of the wall. Her sister had moved into Granny Ellen's cottage next door not long after she had died and Jarvis had joined her almost immediately. Miguel had been informed in no uncertain terms that he was forbidden from crossing the gap between the two beds, as the slightest creak on the floorboard could almost guarantee her dad coming through the door with an axe. Okay, so she had made the axe bit up, but she hoped it served the purpose, encouraging him to stay put until daybreak.

'Two nights, Miguel,' she reminded him. 'Just two nights out of three hundred and sixty-five. I'm sure you'll manage.'

Both fell silent as the car trundled on to the motorway. Merrin felt a roll of nausea as she remembered where they were headed. The quiet was no good for her nervous musings.

'Penny for them?' she asked as he stared at her. 'What are you thinking? I can hear your cogs turning.'

'I was thinking how beautiful you always look and how I love the way you wear your hair and how lucky I am. I hope you know that, Merrin. We're always so busy at work, I guess I don't always take the time to tell you how amazing you are or to perform romantic gestures.'

'I don't need romantic gestures. I really, really don't.' She reached over and briefly found his hand, knowing how empty and hollow those gestures and words could be. Digby's words floated unbidden into her mind: *I'm happier sitting here on a patch of grass with this view than at any other time in my life . . . You make me happy because you love me no matter what . . .* 'But thank you, Miguel. You make me feel great.' This was the truth, but still she was able to maintain emotional distance, tucking a small part of her heart away for safekeeping.

'I hope I always do. I want your family to know that I will always look after you.'

She gave a brief nod and swallowed back the same old rhetoric that he was not to think too far ahead, not to rely on her emotionally; there were only so many times she could push the point. His was a statement that spoke of long-term intentions and caused her pulse to flutter. She was not at that point, not even close. 'I think they'd prefer to know that you support me while I look after myself.'

''Course, but I still think it's nice that I want to look after you. I love you.'

As ever, she found it hard to offer reciprocal words. 'Don't worry, it'll pass!' she laughed.

'I wouldn't be too sure about that.'

She could feel his gaze on the side of her face, but kept her eyes on the road. Merrin had never been anything other than honest with him, knowing how shitty it was when one of you thought you were heading in one direction while the other had an entirely different plan. The first time they had had such an earnest discussion, tears had accompanied her words as she explained how it had felt to be sitting in the vestry, knowing she was going to have to venture outside and face the music and how her heart broke as she drove away from the gossip, the scandal and her beloved Port Charles, which grew smaller and smaller in the rear-view mirror. How there were days when it felt easier not to think about the place and all that she might be missing, just to be able to function.

'I am happy to be going home, really excited to be seeing everyone, but I'm nervous too, and kind of looking forward to getting it over with and leaving again.'

'I think it's normal. Home has that unique pull to it, but it doesn't mean that's where you can live your best life. Sometimes you have to go far away to do that. Especially after what you went through.'

She nodded. 'I guess so. I've stayed away for so long, and even when I talk to my family on the phone, I kind of hold my breath, waiting for a comment or a word that will pull me back to that bloody day.'

'It's self-preservation, Merrin. Like going back to the scene of an accident. I think it's going to be painful for you, of course, but it'll get easier the more we do it.'

We . . . This word, uttered so easily, made her more than a little nervous. It felt like a pressure that she was at that moment ill equipped to handle.

'I'll be right by your side,' he tried to encourage.

'I don't want to dwell on it, Miguel, but . . .' She paused and swallowed, wary of raising the topic. 'People might, you know, want to talk about what happened to me.' She kept her eyes fixed ahead as her mouth went dry. 'What with my sister getting married and everything. It's bound to draw comparisons.'

'Will it make you sad, do you think? I can't stand the thought of you being unsettled or on edge, not on a rare weekend off.'

'I don't think I'll be sad, but I guess it'll be weird. I think I'm as prepared for it as I can be, and, I mean, I have to do it sometime, right? And at the end of the day, it's Ruby and Jarvis's time to shine. Plus, Port Charles now has an abandoned single mother to talk about.' She thought of her beloved Bella and shook her head at the tragedy of it all. 'So, hopefully, me getting ditched at the altar will be old news.' It was easy to joke but her throat constricted and her palms ran to sweat at her words.

'Good.' He reached out and touched his fingers to her cheek. 'Got to be honest, I'm still more concerned with trying to figure out how we have sex in your parents' cottage without your dad coming after me with a shotgun!'

'A shotgun? Hardly! I told you before, it's an axe.' She turned her head to kiss his fingers. Her stomach churned at the thought of what lay ahead: her sister's wedding preparations and walking up the road to the church. With the sting of tears at the back of her throat, she sniffed, and focused on the road ahead, doing her best to subdue the emotion that threatened, and ignoring the temptation to find the nearest exit and turn the car around.

CHAPTER FOURTEEN

Miguel

Miguel had fallen asleep, a miracle in his girlfriend's less than comfortable, ancient car, only to be woken by her excited shouts.

'Look, the sea! I can see the sea! God, it's so beautiful!' Merrin yelled with child-like energy.

He sat up straight, rubbing at the crick in his neck, and looked over at Merrin, who was bouncing up and down in the driver's seat. Her joy was infectious and a good thing to see, worried as he had been about her returning home for a wedding when the last one she attended was the disaster of her own. He was also aware of how he would be judged, eyed up and no doubt rated against the one that got away. But he could take it – especially when the prize was Merrin.

'Yes! It's the sea! But I don't want to end up in it. Please keep your eyes on the road.' He covered his own with his fingers as the car jumped down the lane. 'Tell me when it's safe to look.'

'Don't be such a baby; I know these roads like the back of my hand.' She threw her head back and laughed.

This, he figured, was the excited phase she had mentioned earlier. The car rounded the lane and they began the slow descent into the village of Port Charles. He looked over at her smiling face as she rolled down her window to let the atmosphere of the winding streets and narrow terraces fill the car. How he loved the way her short hair curled under her ear and showed off her heart-shaped face. A face he never grew tired of staring at. One of the things he loved most about her was how unaware of her beauty she was.

'Look, a rainbow!' He pointed at the house on the corner of a narrow junction with a rainbow painted in glorious colours.

She laughed. 'That's Nancy Cardy's house, Jarvis's mum and Ruby's future mother-in-law. She got so sick of the paint scrapes on the corner of her cottage that, a few years back, she decided to embrace them, adding to them with her own acrylics, and the result, as you can see, is a four-foot rainbow on the corner of her home. Jarvis told me the paint scrapes were probably worth more than the house itself when you take into account the fancy metallic finishes of the Porsches, Land Rovers and suchlike that flood the place at the first sniff of sunshine!'

'I love it!'

'Me too.'

A voice called out. 'All right, Merrin! Beautiful day!'

'All right, Mac! 'Tis that.' She waved her hand at a man who was carrying a crate of Coke bottles up the steep pavement. Turning, she smiled at him, almost in recognition that this greeting had been uneventful, nothing awkward about it, as if she had seen him only yesterday. She sat taller in the seat, as if it had given her confidence.

She had told him this, how everyone in the area knew everyone else. The Kellow family was, he had learnt, part of the fabric of the place and, as such, everyone knew not only Merrin's history, but her present too. He was looking forward to meeting the wider Kellow clan and wanted to make the best impression. It was important. He could see a future with this girl and knew that would be so much easier if her parents approved.

Merrin parked the car on a square of tarmac next to the cobbles and honked the horn. He took a moment, slowly unclipping the seat belt, flattening his hair and rolling up the window, wanting to give her a second or two to run into the arms of her squealing mother and the woman holding a baby – Bella, he assumed – who had run from the cottage. He could not have predicted Merrin's reaction. This girl who was always contained, efficient, quiet, mostly – it was as if her body concertinaed with loss, and she clung to her mother and friend as if they were her life support; great, gulping sobs left her body as she fought to catch a breath, as her face, instantly blotchy and twisted, spoke of such sadness it tore at his heart. Her dad, thankfully axe-free, came out of the house next door, where he knew Ruby had lived with her fiancé since their gran had passed away the year before. The man hesitated for a beat, as if he could barely cope with the intensity of emotion on display.

Miguel clambered out awkwardly, trying to give Merrin some privacy at what felt like the most intense of moments, concentrating on stretching his legs and breathing in the warm Cornish air. There was no doubt about it: this was a beautiful spot, picture-postcard perfect and right on the water; he couldn't imagine growing up somewhere so beautiful. He thought of his tiny bedroom in his parents' flat, which faced a main road. Growing up, his background noise had been honking horns and the wheeze of brakes, and the closest he had got to nature was when a hobbling pigeon landed on his grey window sill for a shit. But seeing this, he now properly understood her pain at having to leave it all behind.

When it seemed that Merrin had calmed a little, he turned to take in the family.

'Home at last!' Ben Kellow, a short, stocky man, rushed forward and folded Merrin in a tight hug. Both were a little overcome with emotion, and he understood; two years was a long time not to see your child. 'What a wonderful thing! My little Merrin Mercy.' Ben let her go and studied her, as if examining her face for change. 'How we've missed you. In't that right, Heather?'

Heather Kellow nodded as she held a handkerchief under her nose; it appeared she was a little too overwhelmed for words. She simply stared at her daughter's face before planting a kiss on her cheek.

'How long is it you're staying, little one?' her dad asked, with such excitement it was almost painful to watch.

'Give her a minute, Ben, she's only just arrived and already you're talking about her leaving!' Heather found her voice. 'Hello, my love.' She turned to him, her tone warm and kindly.

'Hello, Mrs Kellow.' He wasn't sure whether to shake her hand or hug her and so did neither, standing awkwardly with his hands on his hips.

'Call me Heather.' She winked at him and he liked her welcome.

'Just two nights, Dad.' Merrin spoke with a breathlessness that betrayed her nerves. 'And then back to work.'

'Two nights.' The man whispered the fact with no small echo of disappointment. His smile faltered, which rather took the joy from the moment. 'We shall make the most of it,' he rallied. 'A wedding!' He clapped his hands. 'Can you believe that someone wants to marry old Ruby?' He chuckled. Merrin had told him about this, the good-natured ribbing that flew back and forth.

Ben then turned his attention to Miguel and looked him straight in the eye. 'Hello there, boy! You must be Miguel.' He stepped forward and shook Miguel warmly by the hand. 'Good journey?'

'Not bad, considering Merrin was driving,' he whispered.

'I reckon you'll be needing a beer, am I right?'

'Now that sounds like a plan.'

The man nodded his head in approval. 'Plus, I want to give the girls a chance to catch up; her mother needs time with her littlest.' Ben's words were solemn.

'A beer is always a good idea.' Miguel had heard enough about Merrin's father to know that when he offered a beer it was because he wanted one himself and to refuse was not the way to ingratiate himself with him.

'I'm taking the lad to the pub! He's had a traumatic journey! Come on out, Jarv!' he called to the groom, who came lumbering from the cottage with his boots in his hand.

'Traumatic journey?' Merrin wiped her face and called over her shoulder as she made her way inside the cottage. 'He's eaten snacks and slept most of the way!'

He caught the smile she flashed him, though her eyes were swollen and her face streaked with tears, and felt the swell of longing for her in his veins. A longing that he would have to bury until they were back in Thornbury, where they could share a bed without the tell-tale creak of an old floorboard giving him away.

'Good to meet you, Jarvis!' He fell in step with the man who had come out of the cottage next door and was tying his dusty work boots loosely on to his feet.

'And you.' Jarvis slapped his back.

'Looking forward to the big day?'

'Be glad when it's all over, truth be told.' He kept his voice low. 'But don't tell Ruby I said that.' He looked over his shoulder as if checking she was out of earshot.

'Your secret is safe with us!' Ben laughed loudly. 'He's had enough of it, haven't you, Jarv? Nothing but wedding talk for months now! Everyone all of a dither over every little detail. He's been happy to get out to sea, where we talk about fish and football, not frocks and flowers!'

'I wouldn't go that far.' Jarvis rolled his eyes at Miguel.

'I'll just be bloody glad if he turns up at the church! We've got our Bella left high and dry with a little 'un to look after now the bloody Dutchman's done a flit, and before that our Merrin abandoned!' Ben spoke from the side of his mouth as they walked towards the slipway with the pub in sight. 'That was a rum old business, make no mistake.' He addressed Miguel for the first time on the subject, and it made him wonder how many people would feel the need to remind Merrin of that one disastrous day – which was apparently lodged in the memory of Port Charles and the people in it – and for how long. He looked back towards the cottage and considered how this must feel for her, especially as they were here to celebrate a wedding. His heart flexed with concern for her.

'I can't imagine.' He spoke sincerely.

'Terrible business,' Jarvis concurred, shaking his head, as if remembering. 'Reckon if I didn't turn up tomorrow, Ruby would have my balls made into earrings.'

'Ouch!' Miguel cringed at the thought.

'I'll go get the beers in; Robin will be waiting for us at the bar, so you lads make your way up and grab a table.' Ben broke into a small jog while he and Jarvis took their time. It was nice to be by the sea and away from work, and to feel the sun on his skin.

'Ben jokes about it, but what happened to Merrin wasn't funny. It changed things for the whole family.'

'In what way?' Miguel was keen to gain any insight into the life of the woman he loved.

'Well, it's why she moved away, for starters.'

This he knew. 'Port Charles's loss is my gain then,' he joked, but his words seemed to fall flat, as Jarvis didn't laugh.

'And she and Ruby aren't as close as they once were, not really, and I know Heather misses her. Ben, too, but he'd never say as much – doesn't want to hold her back. But yeah, it changed the family. Folk still talk about it.'

So I'd noticed . . .

'And that can't be easy for any of them.'

'I can't imagine any bloke letting a girl like Merrin slip through his fingers. I know I never would.'

'Well, I can't imagine a life without Ruby. Truth is, no matter what Ben says, I'm excited to turn up tomorrow, seal the deal!' Jarvis took his time, as if wanting to get the words right. 'I consider myself very lucky to be marrying Ruby. I feel like the luckiest man alive.'

Miguel punched him playfully on the arm, his relief instant. 'You old softie, Jarvis! She must be some girl.'

'For sure.'

'How did you know Ruby was the one you wanted to marry?' It interested him, the certainty with which Jarvis was willing to make such a commitment.

Jarvis looked out to sea. 'I think . . . I think you can love more than one person, and I think you can love different people in different ways. Love can be fickle, your heart and your mind can play tricks' – he tapped his temple as his mouth lifted in a wry smile – 'and then, one day, you realise that the thing you've been waiting for, searching for, has been right under your nose all the time and it can make you feel a bit stupid that you'd spent the longest time looking in the wrong place – do you know what I mean?'

Miguel nodded, even though he didn't know, not really. He thought about his ex, Christina, who he had been with for just over a year. She was a nice enough girl – no, that was unfair, she was a *great* girl – who would make most men happy for life. But after they had finished and he moved to Thornbury, he had met Merrin and knew what it was like to be in her company, the way her nose twitched when she was making a choice and how happy she was to go barefoot . . . so many little things that made the fantastic whole of her.

'And I know that it might have taken me a moment to catch up, but Ruby is . . .' He smiled. 'She's everything.'

Miguel liked the phrase; it pretty much summed up how he felt about Merrin, who was at the heart of his every decision and every action. He couldn't imagine his life trundling on without her. He knew that his deep love might not be reciprocated but was certain that, given time and when she was ready, it would grow.

'Oi! Ladies!' Ben called from the rear terrace of the pub. Three pints of beer sat in a triangle within his wide grip. 'When you've quite finished putting the world to rights, there's beer going warm up here!'

The two ambled up Fore Street towards the pub.

'And of course, when you marry a Kellow girl, you marry the whole bloody clan.' Jarvis laughed and Miguel got the impression that, far from being a negative, this was a thought Jarvis relished.

CHAPTER FIFTEEN

Merrin

With her heart pounding, Merrin stepped into the parlour and could feel her mum staring at her. It was all she could do not to fall to the floor and sob again, for so many competing reasons. The loss of the last two years, the memory of the days after her wedding spent utterly broken by grief, and also in deep sadness that her beloved gran was not going to heft the back door open with her bottom and tell her that she needed to eat something. And in that moment, as she thought of her Milbury Court quarters, which consisted of just a bedroom and a bathroom, she realised how much she had missed this homely space.

At the same time, she looked with nervous regularity at the back and front doors, her spine stiff, prepared for someone to walk in and make a comment, reminding her of the day she was left at the altar. That, and she was fearful of reuniting with Ruby. The frank and hostile words exchanged between the two of them were lodged in her skin like thorns. There was a small part of her that worried her parents might take her sister's part, especially as they saw Ruby every day and Merrin was not around to put her side or fight her corner. Telephone calls that spilt love down the wire as if it were liquid gave her some reassurance, but she knew that until she sat in the parlour and was handed tea, this thought would not quieten.

'What is it, Mum?' She turned towards her with eyes brimming.

'I just can't get over your hair!' Heather shook her head as if coming to terms with a tragedy.

'I cut it ages ago!'

'I know you did, but because I don't see you every day,' she said pointedly, 'I imagine you to look like you used to, with your lovely long, thick hair, and it's a shock to see you with that little short bob thing going on.'

'I really like it.' Bella voiced her opinion, and she was grateful.

Merrin stared lovingly at Bella as she undid her blouse and helped little Glynn latch on. It was no wonder her baby boy was growing so fast with his constant desire to feed. Merrin was so proud of her best friend; she seemed a natural at this mothering lark, and was coping well with the fact she was doing it alone. But as Ruby had said on Skype when he was born, 'They say it takes a whole village to raise a child and, in my opinion, there ain't no better village than Port Charles.'

The memory of the words touched Merrin as she now stared at the crumpled face of the newborn; she used to think the same and had planned on it for the kids she and Digby would have, picturing them making the beach their playground as they ran across the sand barefoot.

Horatio? You have got to be kidding me! She had laughed at the suggested name. It had felt so close she could almost touch it: motherhood and all that came with it. She realised that not having kids would be the consequence of her aversion to a lifelong commitment and she was, most days, fine with that.

'Whose heap of junk is that parked outside?' Ruby yelled. Her tone was jovial and it broke the ice under which Merrin had been sitting, holding her breath.

'Don't let her hear you, she has feelings, does that Vera Wilma Brown!' She hesitated for a beat, then turned and ran to her sister, holding her close and hoping it spoke of love and reconnection.

'My big sister is getting hitched,' she whispered.

'She sure is,' Ruby replied. 'Wouldn't have done it without you here, Merry.'

Merrin closed her eyes. This meant the world. She felt some of the tension leave her shoulders.

'Flippin' 'eck!' Heather put her hands on her hips. 'You two being nice to each other? Hugging each other? What's going on here?'

The two girls sprang apart.

'And if you think you can come back and take my side of the room as well as your own, you've got another think coming,' Ruby said. 'I might have left home, but I'm not moving my old shit off the shelves for no one!'

'Aaaand normal service is resumed,' Heather clucked.

'You look really well, Rubes. Happy.' Merry threw the verbal olive branch towards her sister as they sat at the table.

'I am. It's good to see you, Miss Shorty-hair. It suits you.'

'It's good to see you too.' Merrin stared at her sister's luscious locks, feeling the echo of her mother's words and more than a pang of regret at having taken the nail scissors and hacked off her mane.

'It's funny, really. I've been so stressed over the last few weeks, fretting about all the little things that need doing and worrying about how it would all come together, but right now, with everything pretty much organised, I don't feel that nervous at all. Plus, I mean, it's Jarv, he's my best mate. There's no wondering if it's the right thing to do or any second-guessing or doubt – easy.'

'I guess that's how it should be.' Merrin thought of Digby and remembered a time when she had taken his words of love as gospel, letting them fill her head with crazy, misplaced notions of a future spent in harmony. Lies, no doubt, but how she had fallen for them and the promise he offered. It had felt like the right thing to do, no second-guessing or doubt in her mind – easy . . .

'Absolutely.' Her mum walked to the stove. 'It's exactly how it should be. I've made a Bakewell tart and some walnut-and-apple cakes. Or there's fresh bread if you want some with jam?'

'Ooh, I'll have a cup of tea and a bit of Bakewell tart, please.' Her mouth watered and again her tears fell at this most simple gesture that she had missed.

'Coming up!' Her mum's face broke into a look of sheer delight. 'And don't you cry, my darling. You're home!'

'I can't help it, Mum.' She sniffed. 'It's so good to be here in this room, the way it smells . . . the furniture . . . everything . . .' It was a little overwhelming.

Her mum nodded and wiped at her own tears.

'You and Miguel still going strong?' Bella called from the sofa, doing what she did best, lightening the mood, steering the conversation. 'He seemed happy to run off to the pub with your dad – that'll earn him plus points with Ben!'

'Yup.' She looked towards the window and hoped he was having a nice time. She swallowed the uncomfortable thought that it was pointless for her family to get too involved with him, but this was not the time or place to say that.

'He's a gorgeous-looking lad.' Bella jostled baby Glynn into a comfier position. 'I bet you just stare at him all day.'

'I do, Bells. I don't actually do any work, I just follow him around, staring at his face.'

'It's not only his face I'd stare at,' Ruby joined in. 'From what I saw of him walking up the slipway with Jarv, he's got a peachy little bum 'n' all.'

'Ruby Mae! And there's you about to be a married woman!' her mum called from the stove.

'I can still look! 'Tain't nothing in vows about lookin'!'

The women laughed and the sound filled the room, wrapping them in a cocoon of love, the warmth of which Merrin had quite forgotten. She bottled the moment and buried it deep inside.

With a mug of tea now nestling in her palm, she sat back on the sofa. Her mum's smile was so wide she thought it could only make her cheeks ache. She had almost forgotten what it felt like to arrive somewhere and be so welcomed.

'I still can't believe you're here.' Heather Kellow bit her lip and continued to stare at her. 'I've cooked a proper tea.'

'I've only just had some tart!' She took a sip of tea. 'But what have you cooked, out of interest?' Merrin's mouth watered at the thought of her mum's home cooking.

'I've made a big steak-and-ale pie with butter-mashed potatoes and peppered greens, followed by apple crumble with home-made vanilla custard.'

'Sweet Jesus, Mum, that's a feast!'

'You know your dad likes a good supper after being at the pub and I wanted to make a good impression with Miguel.'

'You'll do that right enough, he's a gannet.' She laughed.

'We've missed you so much.' Her mum fidgeted with the hem of her shirt. 'I can't even tell you.'

'And me you.' Merrin admitted, taking another sip of tea to avoid having to voice her loneliness or her guilt.

'I wish Gran was here.' Ruby looked towards the shelf, where a photo of Ellen and Arthur on their wedding day lived.

'Me too,' Merrin mused. She and her sister exchanged a look and Merrin knew the row that had flared about her not returning for Granny Ellen's funeral was likely fresh in Ruby's mind too.

'Well, I reckon what she'd want is for us to enjoy the weekend. I mean, I'm not married yet. There's still time for me to get out there and have some fun!' Ruby grabbed a mug of tea from the range and took a sip.

'What are you talking about? Me and Bells are planning on having lots of fun! It's only you that's going to be an old married woman.'

'I'm not old!' This, apparently, was where Ruby's objection lay.

'I've got to be honest, Merry, *I'm* not having that much fun.' Bella pulled a face. 'I mean, I love being Glynn's mamma, of course I do, but the chances of me finding a man who's looking for a skint single mum with sore nipples and a baby who's yet to understand that night time means sleepy time . . . I think it's fair to say that type of bloke is in quite short supply. But you know what? It's his loss. Whoever he is!'

'What's the latest from Luuk?' Merrin liked to be up to speed with the state of affairs with the 'Flying Dutchman', as they had nicknamed him, because, despite finding out that Bella was pregnant, he had flown.

'He says he's still coming to terms with the situation.' She rolled her eyes. 'Says he's in *shock*, the poor love, and thinking about what he wants to do with his future. I told him that having an actual human the size of a large melon pop out of your tuppence was also quite shocking, but . . .'

Ruby spat out her tea. Merrin shouted her laughter and she remembered what was so wonderful about being in this little house with the women she loved and who loved her in return. The familiar ache at living so far away rolled in her stomach.

'Tuppence!' Ruby howled.

'Honestly, you girls!' Her mum delivered the tea and cake to the table. 'Right, come on, Ruby. Sit down, my love, the curling tongs are hot. This is our last rehearsal; we'll be doing it for real tomorrow.'

There was a moment of awkward silence as the women all shared uncomfortable glances, until Merrin decided to take the lead.

'A rehearsal, now that's smart.' She ran her fingers through her own fringe. 'Don't want any burnt-hair disasters on the day!' She felt the weight of tension leave the room.

Ruby sat down and put her head forward. 'Like we practised, Mum: demi-wave curls, a sharp part to the left and then the big hair comb put in nice and tight – pulling the one side back up off my face. Okay?'

'Okay, lovely.' Her mum grimaced over her head. 'Don't know who she thinks I am, but I'm not a professional hairdresser, I can only do my best.'

'You'll do fine, Heather!' Bella called out her encouragement. 'This must be a bit weird for you, Merry? Remind you of Digby the shit?'

Merry gave a snort of laughter at this nickname and was thankful in a way that Bella had mentioned him, glad of the opportunity to let off some of the tension that bound her insides tight.

'I suppose I've thought about it a bit more than I usually do.' She played it down. 'But it's not like I'm traumatised at having to relive the whole thing or anything like that. I still feel embarrassed if I think about it, though.' She stared at her lap, her quick blinking and the redness that crept over her neck and face suggesting it was not quite the breeze she suggested.

'You have nothing to feel embarrassed about. His loss.' Bella used this for the second time in as many minutes.

'It's not even about him.' She preferred not to say his name. 'It's how daft it made me feel. I was so sure, so confident, that I could rely on him. I still think about the surprise of it, his face and the way he looked at me differently . . .'

'No one's seen him, apart from that one time up at Reunion Point.' Bella laughed. 'I think he hides away in Bristol with his biscuits, or I think Mrs Everit said he might be in London. Anyway, who cares as long as he's not in Port Charles?'

'I think Jarvis saw him once up at the petrol station on the way up to St Austell. Said he was in a Porsche.'

'Well, lucky old him!' She bit the inside of her cheek and sipped her tea. It bothered her how the mention of news about him so piqued her interest. 'So how are you getting to the church, Rubes? Want me to take you in Vera Wilma Brown?'

'Christ, I'd rather not!' She giggled. 'I think Nancy's coming here and we're all going to walk up together. I thought, what with Jarv not having a big family, it would be better if we all went in one group, rather than Nancy arrive alone.'

'Is his dad coming?' Bella asked the question Merrin was about to.

'Yes, apparently.' Ruby sighed. 'Jarvis is determined not to make a fuss of him, but I said to him, he may be a waste of space, but it will take courage for him to come back to Port Charles and be among his old friends, who all hold him in the same low regard, and so we need to make him feel welcome.'

Merrin understood this more than most.

Her sister's voice faltered. 'I just don't want anything to go wrong. I want it to be perfect. I can't be doing with falling out and bickering or even telling stories of all the bloody things that can and might go wrong!'

She and Bella shared a knowing look, the one they did when Ruby was on the verge of losing it and interventive action was required.

'Now, Rubes,' Merrin began, 'we must turn to the matter in hand; it's a rite of passage that you now have the "wiggle and tuppence" talk – time you knew what to expect on your wedding night. I'm sure we all have some good advice to give. Over to you, Bells.'

'For the love of God, don't make me part of this!' Bella yelled. 'I am the last person to give any advice on that particular subject. Aren't I, babby?' She leant forward and kissed her boy's tiny hand.

'Oh, I don't know, Bells.' Her mum spoke, as she kept her eyes firmly on Ruby's locks. 'I'd say you are probably the best person to give advice!'

'If I must. What I *can* tell you is this: if you're on the pill and you drink too much wine and throw up, you might also throw up your contraceptive, and that makes you more likely to get up the duff. Oh, and if a tall, handsome Dutchman tells you he can see a future with you, he might actually just be saying that to get into your knick-knacks and not mean it at all. Oh! And if for the briefest moment you think that what you're feeling might be the dizzying first effects of love, remind yourself that, most likely, it is in fact the dizzying effect of the white wine you have necked – the same white wine that will make you sick and ultimately get you pregnant!' On cue, baby Glynn cried and Bella jostled him into a new position so he could feed on the other side.

'I can't wait.' Ruby looked up and reached out, taking the mug of tea from Merrin's hand. 'I can't wait to become a mum.'

Bella nodded. 'I joke, Rubes, and you know things have been shit for me, but' – she stared at the face of her baby boy – 'the way I love him: it's like nothing on earth.'

'And it doesn't fade, Bella,' her mum added, taking in both of her girls. 'It never fades.'

Merrin felt a flush of guilt, knowing her mum missed her on a daily basis and wishing things weren't so complicated.

'And what about how you feel towards Dad. Has that ever faded?' How had her mother felt reassured enough to take the leap?

Ruby, too. Merrin was intrigued, having seen first-hand how very wrong it could go and how damaging it could be.

'Oh, goodness.' Her mum held the curling tongs still and looked towards the sea, gently shaking her head. 'Your dad is . . . well, he's part of me. I loved him completely from the beginning and something that's complete is, I think, perfect. God knows it's not always an easy life.'

They all laughed.

'But it's the only life I'd choose. I can't imagine not being his wife and I can't imagine any sort of happy life without him in it.'

Merrin felt the pull of tears, sick at just how wrong she had got it with Digby.

Suddenly the door to the cottage flew open, and there stood her dad in his underpants and t-shirt with a pint glass in his hand.

'For the love of God, Ben! Where's your trousers?' Heather barked at her grinning husband.

'I lost 'em. Long story!' He turned back to the cobbles to catch the eye of Jarvis, Miguel and Robin, who had collapsed on to each other in fits of laughter. 'You ladies carry on! I'm not staying, just come back for some fresh clothes.' He winked at his wife and ran up the stairs.

'I take it all back.' Her mum sighed, as she again picked up a section of Ruby's hair. 'The man's an idiot!'

Once the men were again secreted back inside the pub, Merrin rocked baby Glynn to sleep. It felt lovely to hold the little one as he slept trustingly in her arms, comforting in a way she hadn't expected. Feelings of loss bubbled to the surface; this should have been her, at home with a baby, married and living up the hill at the Old Rectory. Her level of fragility floored her even after all this time.

'I'd better get him home.' Bella took the sleeping bundle from her friend and placed him snugly inside the sling now placed around her body.

'Will we see you later, Bells?' Ruby asked from the chair, where she was admiring her fancy hair-do in a hand-held mirror.

'No, I don't think so. But I'll be here bright and early in the morning. Mum's going to have the little 'un and I'll express milk so she can feed him. Then she'll bring him to the church.'

'Smashing.' Her mum smiled. 'It's so exciting! See you in the morning, Bells, and night-night, baby boy!' She blew a kiss.

'Merrin, if you fancy a walk, love, we're nearly out of tea bags.' Her mum nodded her head matter-of-factly towards the larder.

'Oh.' The thought of heading out into the village was almost paralysing. 'Did . . . did you want to go, Rubes – get some fresh air? I could stay and chat to Mum?'

'I ain't going out! Don't want Jarv or anyone else seeing my hair! Plus, Mum's going to paint my nails now.'

Heather gave a false grin.

'I'll walk up with you, Merry, as far as I can?' Bella held her eye.

Feeling a little bit cornered and a whole lot anxious, Merry closed the door behind the two of them, stopping by the gate to take in the view of the bay. It was more beautiful in person. Her memory had not done it justice or, more accurately, her memory could not perfectly capture how it felt to look at it. There was something about the landscape that she knew would always affect her like no other because this was where her heritage lay.

Dusk was falling as they strolled slowly up the coastal path. Merrin breathed in the fragrant sea air and felt it help soothe her troubled mind. She might not wake here every day, might be living far away, but Port Charles would always, always, be her home.

'Do you know how lovely it is just to see your face here?' Bella called over her shoulder, drawing her from her thoughts. 'It's like, now you're back, all is right with the world.' She cradled Glynn's head against her. 'I've missed you.'

'And me you.' Merrin pushed her hands into her pockets to stop them shaking and looked up over the path to check no one was coming.

'So what's the deal with you and Miguel?' Bella asked casually.

'What d'you mean?'

Bella stopped. 'I mean, I can't put my finger on it, but I don't think you're . . .'

'Don't think I'm what?' Merrin felt the blush on her cheeks as if being accused of something heinous.

Bella took her time. 'I know you, Merry Mercy Kellow. I've known you my whole life and I know when something is making you fizz with happiness, and I know when you're going through the motions.'

'You think I'm going through the motions?' She couldn't disguise her discomfort at the topic or the whiff of truth that went with it, feeling her face colour.

'Not exactly, but I can see that he doesn't light that fire inside you and I worry you might be treading water.'

'What does that even *mean*?' She looked at the sleeping Glynn, conscious of having raised her voice and not wanting to wake the baby.

'You know what it means.' Bella reached out and took her friend's hand. 'I love you, Merry. You and Rubes are my sisters, even if you are a Cornwall-fleeing traitor.' She made as if to spit on the path and Merrin laughed. 'And I want the best for us all and this is the last time I'll mention it, but when you were with Digby the dickhead' – this, too, made Merrin chuckle, despite a rising sadness – 'you were glowing! And it was wonderful to see, but since then, whenever I've seen you, it's like you're a little diluted, a little turned down, as though you're afraid to fully grab life or love in case you get it thrown back at you again. And the way you hide away in Thornbury . . . I mean, I can't believe you're being brave enough to go to the shop. You! The girl who runs barefoot over rocks. My fearless Merry.'

'God, that's so sad.' Merrin felt the sting of tears at the back of her throat. 'I don't want that to be how I'm viewed. But I know it's the truth. Trust me, Bells, I'm so much better than I was; coming here is such a big deal, and I figured going to the shop would be a good rehearsal for tomorrow.'

'I get it. And I think it *is* sad. And I only say it because I want the best for you. I want you to glow like you have this incredible secret; I want you to be *that* happy!'

'I do like Miguel.'

'I know you do, and you don't have to justify yourself to me or anyone, but the fact is, I like salt-and-vinegar Pringles, doesn't mean I want to spend my life with them.'

'Are you honestly comparing beautiful Miguel to a salt-and-vinegar Pringle?'

'I actually am.'

Merrin turned and looked out over the bay, where the streetlights were starting to flicker on. It was always her favourite time, as the stays on the masts of boats in the harbour knocked in the gentle swell of the tide, and the sky turned pink and orange with the promise of warmth tomorrow. Gulls took to the cliffs to bed down for the night and lamps in windows were clicked to life, sending beams of honey-coloured light to pool on the pavements and walkways. It was beautiful, cosy, and the place she had walked happily for the first two decades of her life.

'I know you love me, Bells, and the feeling is entirely mutual.' She squeezed her friend's fingers. 'And I know what you're getting at. I think . . . I think it's hard to go through what happened to me and not be a little bit damaged by it, even if you do your very best not to be. And I also think that the kind of crazy, full-on, all-encompassing, firecracker love is something that's easy when you haven't seen the other side. But as you get older and live a bit more . . .'

'The cynicism sets in?'

'Something like that.' Merrin smiled at her friend, whose face fell, confirming that Bella knew it as well as she. 'The good thing is, Miguel and I are on the same page. We're happy and things are plodding along nicely.'

'Yaaay!' Bella did a mini fist pump. 'The phrase that all romantics the world over hope to hear: "plodding along nicely" – just so lovely, passionate.'

'Okay, now I know you're taking the piss and I need to get to the shop before it closes. Can you imagine Kellow Cottages without tea bags in it?'

'God, no. I think the whole place might fall down! Like the ravens leaving the Tower.'

'Exactly.'

The girls continued their march along the path until Merrin stopped in her tracks and looked back towards the cottage, picturing the safety of her mother's parlour.

'You can do this, Merry.'

'Okay.' She closed her eyes and briefly gripped her friend as tightly as she was able without squishing the sleeping Glynn, before they peeled off in different directions.

'Can you pick me up some Pringles, salt and vinegar?' Bella called over her shoulder.

Merrin stuck her tongue out at her friend's back.

'I know what you're doing,' Bella tutted.

◆ ◆ ◆

Merrin rounded her shoulders, as if this might offer some small disguise as she waited by the step of Everit's for the tourist family to come out with their booty. A standard haul, by the looks of things: an ice cream each for the kids, a large bag of toffee popcorn, no doubt for movie night, a bottle of white, a slab of Cornish Blue cheese, a jar of The Cornish Larder chutney and Popti crackers. She knew that no matter how old she got, this place would always take her back to her childhood, when, with warm pennies gripped tightly in her palm, she and Ruby would scan the sweetie counter and agonise over which to choose. Even right now in her early twenties, the temptation to march in and ask Mrs Everit for a quarter of pineapple cubes or a slack handful of fizzy shrimps was strong. She took a deep breath and walked in.

'Oh Lord! Oh, Merrin!'

She heard the shock in Mrs Everit's tone and was a little confused, having expected the woman to rush forward with a deep hug, or at the very least to go into verbal overdrive, telling her how she and Mr Everit had fared since her last visit. But this greeting sounded almost panicked. It was hard not to think about the last time she had seen her, running back from her devastating encounter with Digby, her heart broken and with her pretty wedding make-up streaking her tear-soaked face. It was only when Merrin let her eyes settle on the woman with her back to her in front of the counter that the reason for Mrs Everit's tone registered.

Merrin felt the breath catch in her throat and knew beyond a doubt that if the shopkeeper hadn't given her away, she would have quietly taken the three steps backwards and left the shop as discreetly as she had entered. The slender legs in jeans, riding boots and a neat, pale-blue shirt, tucked in, belonged to none other than Digby's mother.

The woman turned sharply, her eyes narrowed, as if it took a second to place her, though that could have been down to the fact that Merrin was far skinnier now than she had been in those days, and also the loss of her long hair. Merrin felt her legs shake and was convinced her tremble would be apparent to anyone looking. She forced her limbs rigid as if this might hide her nerves. The blood ran from her head, leaving her feeling simultaneously faint and icy cold.

'Hello.' Loretta's tone was clipped and her manner that of someone addressing a stranger.

'Hello.' Despite the sinking feeling in her stomach, Merrin was not going to look away or blink or cower in front of this woman. Merrin, knowing her husband, old Mr Guthrie Mortimer, had passed away around the same time as Granny Ellen, was wondering how or whether to offer her condolences, when the woman, who looked remarkably together for one who had only a year since been widowed, spoke calmly and steered the conversation.

'I believe congratulations are in order. Your sister's getting married, isn't she?' Her fingers flexed ever so slightly around her handbag.

'That's right.' Merrin held her ground. *Why, Loretta? Why were you so foul? What did I ever do to you?* Many was the night she had imagined this meeting and this conversation, picturing how she would stand firm and demand answers from the woman who had so nearly become her mother-in-law. But when it came to it, Merrin realised she wasn't up for the fight, didn't want to dredge the murky waters of her misery and wanted nothing more than to be as far away from the woman as possible. Loretta Mortimer was toxic and the less she had to do with her, the better chance she had of coming away unscathed. Merrin looked briefly towards the door, her head jerking involuntarily as she calculated whether she might get to it before she was sick.

'Lovely.' Her one-word response, but with an expression that suggested she thought it was anything but.

'Merrin's got a smashing job; she's a manager at a fancy castle hotel just outside of Bristol, in't that right, Merrin? Heather is very proud, and rightly so. We all are.'

Sweet Mrs Everit was all of a dither, her face puce, as she tried to present Merrin's life as a success to this woman who everyone in Port Charles knew had played a part in her downfall.

'That's right, Mrs Everit.' She smiled at the woman, who was inadvertently giving the other woman information she would rather wasn't shared. With her hand on the bread rack, she did her best to steady her legs, which now felt rooted to the spot.

'How charming. Well, shan't keep you!' Mrs Mortimer plucked her wicker shopping basket from the countertop and fixed her smile. 'I do hope the weather holds for your sister. They say there might be a storm coming in.'

'They say a lotta things,' Merrin countered, 'but I don't pay no attention to none of it.' It was deliberate, her double negative and her slide into an accent stronger than she was used to. She watched the woman sweep past without so much as a sideways glance, before the little bell tinkled, as if to herald her departure. She turned to face the kindly shopkeeper who was as much a fixture of the place as the brick itself, and let out a long, slow exhale as she blinked, feeling giddy, but also a little proud that she had not buckled, not entirely.

'Oh, Merrin.' Mrs Everit took a deep breath. 'It is lovely to see you. I didn't know what to say, my love. Sorry you had to encounter her.'

'It's okay, Mrs Everit.' Merrin smiled, placing her hand on her stomach, trying to quell the ache in her gut.

'You did very well, little lamb. And I think it's fair to say, that woman is a proper fucking cow!'

Merrin's intake of breath was sharp and fuelled the burst of laugher that spilled from her. 'Mrs Everit!' She grabbed the countertop and hung from it, laughing so hard her sides hurt.

'Well, I'm sorry, Merrin, but she is!' She flattened her tabard against her chest. 'Now, what can I get you, lovey?'

CHAPTER SIXTEEN

Miguel

Ben slept with his head thrown back in the old leather chair and his arms folded across his ample tum. Robin sat next to him in the other, snoring like billy-o and curled like a baby. He and Jarvis sat on the floor nursing cold bottles of beer and looking out of the loft, watching the sun go down.

'Do you know, I've been all around the world, mainly for work, been to some incredible hotels, some insane resorts and I've seen some beautiful sunsets, but I don't think any of them are as incredible as this view right here.' Miguel, too sloshed to recognise his drunken haze, but loving the moment, made the bold statement.

'Thank you, my friend, you've just saved me a king's ransom!' Jarvis chuckled.

'How come?'

'Well, I might have spent thousands travelling all over trying to look at a sunset prettier than this, but now I don't need to if I know I'm not going to get any better. No need to take Rubes on any expensive honeymoon next year when we've saved up. I shall instead invest my money in one of them all-singing and all-dancing gas barbecues that she keeps on about for the backyard.'

'Cheers to that!' Miguel raised his bottle. 'So what do you think it'll be like, Jarvis, being a married man?'

'Not much different, I don't think; we already share a home and have a joint loan on the van. I reckon she'll like being the only married Kellow daughter, though, like it's an achievement.' He breathed out. 'There's more than a bit of sisterly rivalry there, and Ruby will like the win.'

'Why is there rivalry?'

'God knows.' Jarvis took a swig of his drink. 'Sisters!' He shook his head.

'Where did you propose? Was it the grand gesture, rose petals, champagne on ice? The whole nine yards?' Miguel tried to picture the big man on one knee.

'Not quite.' Jarvis laughed. 'I asked her in the queue at the chip shop in Mevagissey. We'd stopped off to pick up supper and it was raining hard and I looked at her with her little hood up, the string drawn around her face so she was all squished, and I knew it was the right time and so I said, "Will you marry me, Rubes?" And she said, "Do you want your sausage battered or plain?" I told her, "Plain, obviously, I'm not too fond of batter," and then she said, "And yes, I'll marry you, Jarv!" And that was that.'

'Wow!' Miguel, encouraged by the beer that swilled in his blood, found his story strangely moving. 'I've got to be honest, Jarv, I get why you want to be a part of this family. They are good people.'

'They are that.' Jarvis took a deep breath. 'My own dad is worse than useless and Ben . . . he's been good to me.'

'And now he's going to be your father-in-law.'

'I am indeed!' Ben hollered from the chair. 'And thank God you was only saying nice things, cos I'd have your innards for fish bait! You're good lads, both of you,' he announced, before falling straight back to sleep.

He and Jarvis laughed quietly.

'My dad's great, I just, I just don't really know him.' Miguel whispered this truth. 'He was always working when I was a kid and, now I'm an adult, he's still always working.'

'No shame in a man grafting to earn an honest living.'

'No, none at all,' Miguel agreed. 'But I think if I ever have kids I'll do it differently. I want more balance; I want to have a relationship with them.'

'I can't wait to be a dad. I'll make sure I'm always around and give them the best I can.'

Miguel felt the embarrassing sting of emotion at the back of his nose, which quickly turned to laughter, as Jarvis swiped his own tears and the two chuckled. He realised for the first time that day that he might be a whole lot drunker than he had thought.

CHAPTER SEVENTEEN

Merrin

Merrin woke with something that felt a lot like relief at the fact that she was in the place she loved where the sounds and smells were familiar and comforting. Running her hand over the wall she had faced on more nights than she cared to count, she pictured the little girl she had been, casting wishes that she hoped would scamper up the wallpaper and leap out of the open window, shooting up into the night sky. As a big girl, too, all the things she had hoped for her and Digby had been pictured clearly with her eyes screwed shut and a smile on her face while her sister snored in the bed opposite. The thought of Digby stirred the sediment of anxiety at what the day might hold; the thought of what lay ahead: seeing people for the first time, attending a wedding! *I need to get through this, I need not to crumple and I want to be invisible* . . . One more wish that she hoped would come true.

She looked across the room at the beautiful shape of Miguel, asleep under the quilt in the space that used to be occupied by her big sister. It felt strange to have Ruby living next door, where their gran had lived all her life. And the pang in her chest was one of longing: how she would like, just for a while, to go back to when the Kellow girls had lived a simple life with their gran and gramps next door and the whole family meeting for endless cups of tea and supper wherever it was being dished up. This in the time when everything was funny and she, Bella and Ruby would regularly collapse in tears of laughter over the smallest thing or innuendo. A time before she had even been aware of Digby.

Closing her eyes briefly, she tried to imagine coming home for good. What would that life look like? The way it had felt to see Loretta had floored her, briefly, but she had survived her once and she could survive her again. Mrs Everit's unwavering support meant more than she could possibly say. It spoke of community and was the very thing Merrin loved most about living in Port Charles. Did it matter that at some level she felt like an outsider, aware of how things had trundled on without her, and that her being here felt like something special, unusual, a novelty, as if she had lost her place as a local and lost her confidence in her ability to fit in?

'And where would I live?' she whispered into the ether, knowing now that the world was big and she was yet to find her place in it. Gone was her dream of having a husband and a family in this little fishing village and so she had forged another life. It was supposedly a temporary life, but it had become her only life, her permanent life with work at the heart of it; working hard to keep distracted from all she missed in this little cove.

'Oh, my God!' Miguel wailed from under the covers. 'I have the worst headache in the world. I feel like your dad might have actually put that axe in my head.'

'Well, I can't think why you feel so bad, love? Do you think it was that bag of chips you brought home with you last night; maybe they had some dodgy vinegar on them?'

'I'd forgotten we got chips!' he admitted.

'Or . . . could it be the endless pints of beer you sank on an empty stomach yesterday?'

'I don't know what happened!' He sat up, his whole demeanour riddled with regret, and she felt the smallest amount of pity as she looked at his pale face and bloodshot eyes.

'You got Kellowed is what happened – my dad's specialty. He kidnapped you and robbed you of an afternoon. But don't worry, I shall protect you from him today and you don't need to think about alcohol until much, much later, when we'll no doubt raise a glass in toast to the newly-weds.'

'Oh, my God! Merrin, please don't even mention alcohol.' He lay his head back on the pillow and pulled the duvet over his face. This was where she left him, as she tiptoed down the creaky stairs and into the parlour.

'Morning, my little one.' Her mum was sitting by the range with a cup of tea. 'Oh, Merrin! How lovely it is to see your face as you walk down the stairs. You have no idea how wonderful it is to have you here!'

I think I might . . .

'Morning, Mum. Excited?' She walked over and kissed her mother on the cheek, and took the mug of tea from her hands, sipping it gratefully as she thought of her wedding morning and the pure joy that had coursed through her veins at the prospect of meeting Digby in the church.

'So excited! I've been up since silly o'clock!' Heather tutted. 'It's all well and good getting an early start, but I'll pay for it at the other end of the day. I'll be ready for my bed by eight tonight. And how are you, my lovely? I can't imagine what it must feel like for you today.'

'I'm fine.' Merrin's answer was brisk, a shutter going up to stop any further enquiry into the very thing she was trying not to dwell on. 'Dad still asleep?'

'Yep, sleeping it off. I'll give him a few more minutes and then I'll take him up a cuppa. Where are you going?'

'Just outside.'

Opening the cottage door, Merrin stood barefoot on the uneven cobbles, liking the way they fitted inside the high arch of her instep as she curled her toes around them. It was still her favourite place to stand, and how she had missed it, this little ritual that anchored her to the ground she so loved. She breathed out long and slow and closed her eyes briefly, feeling instantly better, calmed. This was the perfect spot with the widest view. Looking out over the purple bruise of sky where clouds hung low over the ocean, she offered up a silent prayer: *Please don't rain! Not on my sister's wedding day . . .*

She inhaled the salt-tinged breeze and closed her eyes. How she loved this little corner of the wild Cornish coast, where her roots still ran deep, despite her absence.

'So what will you do, Merrin? Visit often? Stay away?' she asked herself, and she was just pondering the response when a voice called from above.

'Oi! Merry, you dozy mare – do I have to fetch my own tea today of all days? You're my bridesmaid, you're supposed to be waiting on me – catering to my every whim!'

She turned and looked up at Ruby, who was smiling and hanging out of the little upstairs window. It was what she needed, this jovial, loving familiarity that meant she and Ruby were at peace and Merrin would get through the day.

'Is that right? Good morning, bride! How you feeling?'

'Bloody parched!'

Merrin laughed. 'Does Jarvis want one?' She figured, as she was making.

'Jarvis? Don't be ridiculous. He in't here! It's bad luck to see the bride the night before the wedding; you should know that!'

Merrin swept the cobbles with her toes; good luck or bad hadn't come into it with someone like Ma Mortimer pulling strings in the background.

'I made him sleep at Nancy's.' Ruby yawned. 'I thought she could deal with his hangover. Anyway, I'll be down in five!'

'Is that Ruby?' her mum called from the parlour.

'Yep, she wants tea!'

'On it! But tell her not to dawdle; I've got the curling tongs on!'

Merrin felt an unwelcome pang of envy that this had once been her . . . her day . . . her future. She swallowed the bitter reminder of how it had ended.

The rain, thankfully, held off and it was now a big, bright, summer-blue day. One where the sky and ocean were of a similar hue and to look out over the vast expanse made the world beyond the harbour wall and all its glorious possibilities seem infinite. She and Miguel stood with the throng on the apron in front of the cottages; the atmosphere was electric and everyone was laughing.

She and Bella wore tea dresses in a delicate shade of rose pink, with pin-tuck fronts, sheer blouson sleeves and three-quarter-length pleated skirts. They had tortoiseshell combs in their hair, and ivory T-bar shoes that were perfect for dancing in later.

'You look gorgeous,' Miguel whispered in her ear, his words enough to partly fill the gaps of doubt inside her with the dust of confidence. Her heart felt like it rattled in her ribs as she fought to suppress the image of walking out of the cottage with her dad and her first sight of the cart in all its floral glory. It had been . . . perfect. And her girls waiting to escort her to the church, the photographer clicking away and her gran about as proud as she could be . . .

She hated that tears now gathered at the back of her throat; it was way too early in the day to give in to tears. This was the first taster of her sister's wedding day and Merrin knew she was going to have to fight hard to keep her high emotions tamped down. Her plan was to think only about the moment, nothing further ahead, and to remember that this time yesterday felt only a blink away, as it would this time tomorrow . . . She was grateful that her trembling hand sat inside Miguel's.

Her dad and Robin were in smart, navy pinstripe suits with large pink carnations on their lapels. She thought they looked like Port Charles's answer to Al Capone, but kept this to herself. Jarvis's dad stood awkwardly on the periphery, smoking, as if not quite sure of his place. Merrin watched him taking in the view and wondered if he mourned it as much as she did. For this alone she felt a pang of empathy for the man. Nancy Cardy looked so happy, beaming in her finery, her arms linked with her sister's. It was lovely for the Kellows and the Cardys, as the two were officially becoming family. She couldn't help but think briefly of Digby's mother, who had kept her and her loved ones at such a distance, which hadn't made any sense to her, until it did.

Encountering the woman in the village shop had unnerved her. How Merrin wished she'd had the guts to stand up to her directly, to question her meanness and the calculated way she had gone about destroying a young couple. She cursed the naivety with which she had waltzed into the whole affair. It sat like a thorn in her shoe, a noise in her brain, the legacy of which she still hadn't fully processed, even after all this time.

Her thoughts were interrupted when, without fanfare, Ruby appeared at the doorway of the cottage with her mum fussing over her short veil.

'Oh, my goodness! Look at her. She's absolutely stunning!' Merrin felt a tightening in her throat and wished her gran and gramps could see their oldest granddaughter today of all days. How proud they would be! Her sister had opted for a sleeveless ivory gown that was gathered in at the waist and sat in a slinky knot on her hip. Her frock was set off with a champagne-coloured faux fur stole draped around her shoulders and the wide gold-and-pearl brooch that held it together sparkled where the sun caught it. Her make-up was thankfully minimal, save for the pillar-box-red lipstick that highlighted her full lips. The wedding theme was very vintage/wartime and her sister had nailed it.

'Wowsers!' She heard Miguel gasp and smiled for her sister.

'Ruby Mae!' Her dad stepped forward and her sister slipped her arm through his. 'You look beautiful.' He beamed and Ruby looked out over them all with an uncharacteristic softness to her expression that only added to her beauty.

Merrin's bottom lip trembled; the way her dad looked at his oldest daughter took her back to the moment she had descended the stairs.

'Thought you might have rigged up the old cart!' Ruby looked around, although it was unclear whether her expression was one of disappointment or relief.

Merrin followed her eyes, hoping this was not the case; anything that might have mirrored her disastrous day was not a thought she relished. She painted on a smile, aware that this statement had encouraged people to turn and look at her as if seeking out her response. Keeping her eyes fixed on her sister and gripping Miguel as if her life depended on it, she beamed.

'Better than that, Rubes!' He turned towards the slipway and called out, 'All right, lads, when you're ready!' And on cue music floated up over the wall.

'What the . . . ?' Ruby craned her neck, as they all did, turning towards the unmistakable sound of a jazz band, who walked in perfect formation from the slipway and around to the front of the cottages. They were playing an upbeat, catchy tune more likely to be heard in New Orleans than Port Charles and the effect was electrifying. Everyone, as if rehearsed, either broke into a little jig, moved their shoulders, waved their hands or shuffled their feet. It was genius; a band to lead the procession up to the church, meaning the party started the moment the first note was played.

Merrin ran forward and gripped her sister in a hug, whipped up like the rest of the revellers into a state of pure excitement that made her feel like anything was possible. 'Isn't this wonderful?'

'It is!' Her sister was breathless and uncharacteristically short of words, clearly swept up in the moment.

'Have the best day, darling!' Merrin looked steadily into her eyes, willing her sister to see only love. 'You look out of this world! Enjoy every second!'

'I will. I love you, sis. Always have, always will.'

Ruby held her gaze as the band got closer and the music got louder. Merrin took the words and sewed them beneath her heart. They were forgiveness for that terrible row that lived in her memory and the conversation that had threatened to damage them. No matter how far away Merrin might stray, she was bound to this woman and this place: a Kellow.

Finding her way back to Miguel, she slipped her hand inside his again. It might have been her imagination, but Merrin felt sure that as the noisy, dancing troupe made their way past the slipway, along Fore Street and up towards the church, all eyes were on her sister before they sought *her* out, as if she were a separate spectacle entirely. Miguel's hand was where she found comfort, holding it tightly as they meandered slowly, waving to tourists and the friends and residents of Port Charles who were not already inside the church.

Don't be stupid, Merrin, no one cares. No one is thinking about that day . . . She swallowed to try and relieve her dry mouth, watching as Miguel moved ahead in the churchyard, turning to wave at her as he and the rest of the group disappeared inside St Michael's. She felt the absence of him and smiled at Bella.

'You okay, doll?' her friend asked.

'Yep.' Her voice was steady; her legs, however, shook.

The jazz band played their encore and peeled off to a waiting van, revelling in their triumph. She, Bella, Ruby and her dad hung back and formed a neat square on the patch of tarmac outside of the main church door.

'Nearly off!' Her dad raised Ruby's fingers and kissed them. 'You look smashing, and God knows I'm fond of Jarvis. This is a wonderful day for an old dad to see.'

Merrin swallowed, thinking of how her day had cost her parents a pretty penny and had come to nothing. Her stomach bunched and she felt the throb of sorrow in her chest.

The church doors were flung open and the breath caught in her throat, but no, there was no sign of the Reverend Pimm with an anxious look and a nervous stutter, no hurried ushering of the bridal party into the vestry. Instead, the dizzy notes of 'At Last' floated from the church and Ruby, with an air of calm, confidence and poise, walked on her dad's arm into the building where her beloved waited for her at the end of the aisle.

It was the first time Merrin had walked up an aisle since her wedding rehearsal. Her limbs felt leaden and her seat so very far away. There were the usual smiles and winks of appreciation for the stunning bride, and nods of congratulation for her dad, but it was obvious by the hushed whispers behind cupped palms and the surreptitious glances and narrow-eyed expressions of pity cast in her direction that the assembled, silently or otherwise, compared the moment to the last time a Kellow girl had donned a wedding dress and trundled up the hill to St Michael's. Even Reverend Pimm held her with a lingering stare that sent a spread of crimson embarrassment over her neck.

Squeezing into the pew next to Miguel, she arranged her skirt over her knees. The hurt was tangible, as was the sad and humiliating hum that rang in her ears, but there was something else: anger. As her limbs shook, she felt angry that she had been led to that point outside the church only to be so humiliated by Digby's absence. Who did he think he was that made it okay to treat her like that? Who did his mother think she was, able to offer such calm advice? *Trust me, Merrin, go home, dear. Go home to your family . . .* How dare they!

Merrin closed her eyes and tried to get a grip. Her dad sidled into position next to his wife, who passed him a pressed handkerchief, with which he immediately dabbed his eyes and blew his nose.

The Reverend Pimm did a fine job, setting the right tone for the ceremony that was amusingly anecdotal and not too solemn.

When he asked: 'If any person present knows of any lawful impediment to this marriage you should declare it now . . .' The congregation concentrated on his words before he comically looked skyward and mouthed his thanks at the lack of response. This drew laughter from everyone except Merrin, her dad, who mumbled a response using words that were usually reserved for outside of church, and Ruby, who looked back over her shoulder and fixed her with a look that bordered on fury.

Merrin's jaw tensed, as she sensed every pair of eyes behind her homing in on her back. She concentrated on keeping her head held high, realising that no matter how hard she tried to pretend, how much she perfected her sweet laugh of indifference, this was how it would always be: she was the jilted girl of Port Charles, and no matter what her future held, she doubted she would ever be able to leave it behind her. In this church and this village, it seemed others were loath to forget or let her move forward. It was a bitter blow. She looked at the dark-tiled floor and wished she could drop right through it.

◆ ◆ ◆

Darkness was falling as Merrin realised she had not managed to secure a minute alone with her sister during the whole exhausting day, although her parents had, throughout the celebrations, felt the need to check on her constantly.

'If you are finding things tricky, my little love, no one would think any less of you for slipping away . . .' her mum had whispered in her ear as they queued for the ladies.

'I'm fine, Mum, really.'

And, 'Merrin, don't feel sad today, darling, you *will* have your day. I am sure of it . . .' Her dad had squeezed her arm when she bumped into him at the buffet table.

'I don't need "my day", Dad! God, I'm fine!'

''Course you are, my little one.' Maddeningly, he had ruffled her hair.

Judging from the wide smiles on their faces at the end of the evening, Ruby and Jarvis had, thankfully, had the day they wanted. As Merrin and Bella prepared to leave, the newly-weds were falling against each other on the dance floor at the back of the pub and had barely noticed any of their guests exiting.

'Look at her face.' Bella leant on her as the two watched the slow dance. 'Reckon she's the happiest I've ever seen her.'

'Me too.'

'I'm glad she's stopped punching things; reckon we've got Jarvis to thank for that.'

'Good old Jarv.' Merrin knew he was the kindest soul.

'Yep, good old Jarv,' Bella concurred. 'Seeing as he's now married your sister when he was once so sweet on you, is it weird at all?'

'Is what weird?' Miguel bounded over and overheard the tail end of the conversation.

'Having a sister who is a married woman!' Bella replied as quick as a flash and rubbed briskly under her nose with her finger.

Miguel grabbed Merrin's hand and twirled her around, before pulling her in for a kiss.

'Oh, get a room, you two!' Bella mimed retching.

'We have got a room, but it's got two single beds in it and a selection of dolls staring at us, not to mention Ben within five feet with an axe close to hand . . .' Miguel pulled a face.

'Half your luck, I share a room with a fidgety baby who snores like a drunk and who wakes up demanding food every couple of hours!'

'Sounds a lot like Miguel.' Merrin laughed, her eyes fixed on the newly-weds, as Miguel went to grab his jacket so they could leave. 'And no, Bells, don't be so bloody stupid! Me and Jarv were just kids; I never had feelings for him and I don't want it mentioned again. But then there's lots I don't want mentioning, which seems like too much to ask in Port bloody Charles!'

Bella stared at her, as if a little taken aback and a whole lot lost for words. This kind of outburst was rare for her and Merrin felt sapped by it, as if the emotionally tiring day was finally catching up with her.

Bella stepped forward and placed her hand on her arm. 'Are you all right, my love?'

'God! For the last time today! I'm fine! Absolutely fine!'

Bella leant in and kissed her cheek. 'You're not the only one who's found today tough. I thought Luuk and I might get married, and look how that's turned out. I miss him.' She bit her bottom lip and swiped the tears that filled her eyes. 'But life goes on, Merry, it has to.'

'It does, my darlin'.' She regretted snapping at her wonderful friend, who had her own shit to deal with. 'And for what it's worth, if the Flying Dutchman doesn't know how fabulous you are, then he isn't worth losing a moment's sleep over. Love you.'

'I know. Love you too.' Bella wiped the remainder of her lipstick from her mouth on the back of her hand.

Merrin turned on her heel, keen to get some fresh air. It had been a pretty wedding, a fabulous day and Ruby was in her element, but in truth she couldn't wait to get in the car and drive back to Thornbury, away from the Port Charles gossip, the sharp winds that blew inland, her family's well-meaning, challenging stares and Miguel's apparent inability to pace his booze intake. His overindulgence had, according to reports from her dad and Robin, led to him vomiting over the harbour wall on his way home from the Old Boat Shed the previous night. She cringed at this image of him. It was not the Miguel she knew and loved, preferring the sedate version of him who turned up to work every day looking sharp.

She thought about Bella's words and considered the possibility that she might indeed be treading water. If there was the smallest chance it was true, it threw up two questions – first, what did that say about her? And second, what the hell was she going to do about it?

CHAPTER EIGHTEEN

Miguel

Vera Wilma Brown was loaded up and ready to head off. Miguel slammed the boot shut and watched Merrin hold her mum tight in a drawn-out goodbye that felt like an intrusion to watch, before kissing her sister briefly on the cheek. It warmed him to see the displays of love so freely offered and put a pang of regret in his stomach that his own family was not that close or that demonstrative. He would have liked it.

'Goodbye from me, Mrs Cardy!' Ruby shouted, giggling at the novelty, and Bella howled her laughter as she stood with baby Glynn in her arms. He watched as she and Merrin, who was, if anything, a little subdued, held each other tearfully – this despite the lingering party atmosphere from the previous day's wedding.

Ben walked forward and reached for Miguel's hand, shaking it vigorously. 'What a weekend, eh? One we won't forget in a hurry!'

'My liver certainly won't!' He winced at the memory of the hangover, one of the worst he'd ever had. 'Thank you for your hospitality, it's been incredible.'

'You take good care of her.' Ben pointed at him, smiling, but his finger was ramrod straight and almost in his chest.

'I will. Although she's keen to remind me that she can look after herself.'

'Don't make me get that axe now!'

Miguel laughed, wondering who had let him in on the joke.

'And don't always believe her, Miguel. She thinks she can look after herself but she's made of glass as well as steel.' Ben held his eyeline.

With Merrin preoccupied in goodbyes, Miguel coughed to clear his throat and did his best to control the tremor in his voice. 'I do . . . I . . .'

'Spit it out, boy!' Ben slapped his back.

'I guess I just wanted to say, to reassure you . . .' His gut flipped with nerves.

'Sweet Lord.' Ben patted his pockets, as if looking for his wallet. 'It's not money you're after, is it? Because I'm a little short after this weekend's knees-up!'

Miguel ignored the joke.

'I . . . I love . . . I love Merrin,' he stuttered. 'That's all I wanted to say. So you don't need to get your axe, because I do, I love and respect her.'

'Well, that makes two of us.' Ben smiled at him. 'All I can say is that she's got a good head on her shoulders, always has had. But she's not as strong as she thinks she is.' He paused and looked over at Merrin, who was crouching low and kissing baby Glynn on the cheek. 'I'd prefer to keep her close; she's my little girl. Always will be. But I like to think she can rely on you, Miguel. But make no mistake, she's her own person and knows her own mind. I just want her to be happy, that's all I've ever wanted.'

'What are you two plotting?' Merrin walked over with the car keys in her hand, her sunglasses on her head and dark rings of sadness and fatigue beneath her eyes.

'Best route home,' Miguel answered.

'No.' Ben shook his head and fixed him with a stare. 'She *is* home; you mean best route out of here.'

Miguel saw the crush of sadness on Merrin's face at Ben's words and wondered what it must feel like to want to be in one place, but be based in another. He decided there and then to make more effort with their room at Milbury Court – make it more homey, maybe he'd get a plant – until they could make proper plans. He took one long look around the cove and had to admit that if she wanted to come here and build a life, he would not be against it. He'd go wherever made her happy, because, like he'd said to Ben, he loved her.

'Love you, Dad!' She wrapped him in a tight, brief hug and kissed her mother once more before jumping into the car and starting the engine.

'I don't want to go. I never wanted to go. And yet I can't wait to be gone. How do I reconcile that?' she whispered, and he wondered for a minute if she'd forgotten he was there.

'Have we got snacks?' he asked, trying to lighten the mood. She looked at him sharply and smiled, exactly as if his question had reminded her of his presence.

'I haven't taken the handbrake off and already you're after snacks!' She shook her head and waved to her parents, who held each other close as they waved back. Ben winked at him as the car pulled away. Ruby, with her arms wrapped around Jarvis's waist, gave a nod, her lips almost pursed. Miguel looked out over the wide expanse of sea where the sun shone high in the sky; there was no doubt about it, this was a little slice of heaven right here.

'Mr and Mrs Cardy,' he said aloud.

'Yep, Mr and Mrs Cardy.' She beamed, while sniffing the tears that threatened. 'They did it!'

'They sure did. I love you, Merrin.'

She reached into the back seat and grabbed an old lidded ice-cream tub. 'All right, flattery will get you everywhere! Here's some left-over sausage rolls from the buffet and a slice of wedding cake.'

As they rounded the bend by the pub a woman walked out in front of the car, as if not caring less whether it hit her or not. Merrin touched the brakes and slowed until the woman had time to reach the pavement safely.

'Bit weird!' He stared at the woman with the wild, white hair and staring eyes.

'That's poor old Lizzie Lick. I've told you about her.' Merrin spoke solemnly.

'Yes, you have, and you know, every town, village or postcode has one.'

'One what?' she asked.

'You know, someone that everyone else talks about, that person whose reputation goes before them and who trails their tale in their wake. Someone who can't escape what others say about them, a history that gets embellished until they don't stand a chance. It's sad.'

'It is sad, Miguel. Fucking sad.' She spoke with a quaver to her voice.

'Oh God, Merrin, I didn't mean . . .' He felt a little sick that she might think he had meant her. *You idiot!*

'Forget it.'

As she put her foot down, he replayed his words and wished he could take them back.

CHAPTER NINETEEN

MERRIN

Merrin had thrown herself into her work, trying to block out the feelings of longing not only for Port Charles, but also for the life she had lived there before she became a marked woman. It had taken all this time for her to realise just how much she had lost, and all through no fault of her own. She was still angry.

And now it was Valentine's Day. Merrin wondered how Ruby and Jarvis might celebrate their first Valentine's as a married couple, six months after they had wed. But she was too busy to think too hard about it, intent as she was on giving their guests the best possible experience, even though she herself thought the whole thing a little ridiculous, unable to get into the swing of celebrating the deep love that she knew for most to be a temporary state.

It was always a popular event at Milbury Court. The private dining rooms were fully booked, vases of red roses adorned every table and the spa was chock-a-block with lucky couples enjoying being pampered. Merrin hardly had time to come up for air, as her to-do list seemed only to grow in length. She stared at the rather corny card with a rabbit on the front holding a large heart – hardly romantic, and grabbed in a hurry from the Tesco garage. It now nestled under the reception desk, while she wondered what to write to Miguel. As she reached for a pen she decided to go with something comic, still keen to avoid the romantic, mushy stuff, which had no real currency and could fade as quickly as the ink dried. She had just started to write when the hotel door opened and a mane of tawny blonde hair appeared. Putting the lid back on the pen, she rested it on the card and painted on her greeting smile.

The woman was about her age, but beautiful. Shiny and polished in a way that made Merrin wish she wasn't always in a navy wool trouser suit, white shirt and the gold-and-navy cravat favoured by the hotel chain that issued her uniform.

'Hello! Hello! God, it's cold out there.' The woman dumped two large leather overnight bags on the floor and rubbed the tops of her arms. 'I should warn you to prepare for chaos!' she said lightly, as she trod the two shallow steps and swept further into the reception.

Merrin liked her on sight. This was how it worked when dealing with the public all day, every day: she very quickly decided whom she liked and would go the extra mile for and whom she would not. And it was a decision largely predicated on how the person entering the hotel treated her. She thought 'prepare for chaos' an odd choice of phrase for someone with the poise of this woman in her tailored jeans, high heels and with a large mustard-coloured handbag hanging from her slender forearm; chaos didn't seem like her natural bedfellow. That was until two adorable, shiny-haired twin boys ran in directly after her and, with arms wide like aeroplanes, whizzed around the reception like a couple of Spitfires mid dog-fight. They matched in chinos and mini blue Oxford button-downs beneath woollen tank tops, and Merrin wondered if she had inadvertently wandered into a Gap ad.

The woman smiled at them lovingly and shook her head. Merrin could see that far from their antics troubling her, the blonde lady clearly adored the chaos that these little scamps brought with them.

'Freddie! Noah! Don't touch anything. I mean it – nothing! And don't go too far,' she called out. Her accent was pure cut-glass and Merrin thought she'd make a lovely newsreader.

The boys, chubby little babies who teetered on fat legs, as if walking were still a novelty, ignored their mother and disappeared on to the deep sofa. She could hear them burbling sweet baby talk.

'They're lovely.' She smiled at the woman who now rested her stunning Birkin bag on the countertop.

'Yes, they *are* lovely, most of the time, but my God, don't be fooled by their sweet faces; they can be absolute monsters. And they gang up on me, you know. There are many days when the time I love them most is when they are sound asleep and I get a big fat gin as a reward for surviving the day!' She ran her hand through her hair, a large, square diamond sparkling in the chandelier's light. Merrin wondered if it were baubles like that which kept the woman happy, maintained the illusion of love.

'Well, we have a wide selection of gins and so I hope you enjoy your stay here. Would you like to check in?' Whilst not wanting to hurry the woman, she had a million chores awaiting her attention.

'Yes, please! Let's do that. My husband's parking the car and probably secretly smoking somewhere, which is why he's taking so long. He thinks a handful of Polos can disguise the smell, the poor love.'

Merrin laughed, liking the woman's easy manner. She understood. It was this quiet tolerance that kept the wheels oiled for her and Miguel too, turning a blind eye to his penchant for eating in bed, showering the clean bed linen with crumbs, and his love of the trashiest pop music her ears had ever endured. He, too, could no doubt give a dozen examples of habits of hers that drove him to distraction, but the two of them worked. They were mates who had good sex. That was it. He told her he loved her and, whilst she would not exactly call it love, she knew her life was better with him in it and was happy to have a partner in this sometimes transient environment, where they could close their door and play at families on a rare day off. But as for the future? Merrin wondered where she might venture next when she had a little more experience under her belt – a warm country, maybe? And if Miguel wanted to come along, that would be fine, but if he didn't, she would miss the beautiful man, but that would be fine too.

'We're here for two nights and please tell me your swimming pool is open. I can't function without my morning swim. My mother-in-law is treating us for Valentine's and I want to make the absolute most of it.'

'Well, how lovely!'

'Oh, she really is.' The woman crinkled her eyes in fondness.

'Good news: the indoor pool *is* open in the spa and we have wetsuits if you fancy a dip in the outdoor pool.'

'Really?' The woman sounded amazed.

'No, not really, it's beyond freezing, you'd have to chip the ice off.'

'Oh, my God! You're *hilarious*!' the woman yelled, throwing her head back to reveal her shiny, white teeth.

'I have my moments.' Merrin liked that this fancy-pants woman found her funny. 'Have you travelled far today?'

'From London. Thought we'd grab a couple of days away either side of this treat. We are actually en route to Cornwall for a flying visit.'

'Oh, Cornwall! That's where I'm from.' She pictured the bay of Port Charles and felt the familiar pang of loss. She missed her mum's cooking, sleeping in her childhood bed, walking barefoot over the cobbles, all the way down to the water's edge, and even her fat sister. Wasting no time, Ruby was nearly five months pregnant and Heather had gone into knitting and crochet overdrive – the little babby had a whole wardrobe of impractical and beribboned items waiting in a drawer. Merrin felt strangely removed from her sister's pregnancy, not only by the fact that she was physically absent, but also because becoming a mother was so far out of her sphere it felt very much as if Ruby, like Bella, was leaving her behind.

'But you're sensibly living away from the hordes during the holiday invasion?' the woman asked.

'Something like that.' She smiled. 'Can I take your name, please?'

Merrin opened up the computer screen to check the woman in and it felt as if the three things happened simultaneously. First, the little toddlers tumbled playfully from the sofa and came careering back to the reception desk, chattering and laughing loudly as they ran and shoved each other, before crashing into their mum's long legs. Second, the woman spoke her name, clearly, audibly and without hesitation, but to Merrin's ears it arrived as a garbled message that took a second to decode, and third, the door opened and in walked Digby Mortimer.

'That's Mortimer. M.O.R.T.I.M.E.R.' The woman turned at the sound of the door opening. 'Hello, darling, there you are! Just checking in. The boys nearly escaped and I am in need of a large gin! This lovely lady has been making me laugh. I'm sorry, I'm so rude, I didn't ask *your* name?'

Weakened, she felt her body slide forward a little until her legs made contact with the back of the unit. It kept her upright. Aware that she was staring, but unable to look away, her stomach flipped and she found it hard to take a full breath. Her mouth was dry and she could feel the twitch of discomfort under her left eye, as beads of nervous perspiration gathered on her top lip.

There he was, right in front of her. She had imagined this moment many times and it was never like this. It was the first time she had seen him since she abandoned him on Reunion Point, where he sat holding the thin engagement ring that with shaking fingers and a shredded heart she had placed in his palm.

'Merrin.' She answered the woman's question.

Her voice so quiet, no more than a squeak, as the woman leant forward, craning her neck.

'Sorry, what? Did you say Mary?'

She shook her head and swallowed. 'It's Merrin,' she managed, and coughed.

'Merrin! I've not heard that name before, it's lovely!'

The woman's words were confirmation that Digby had never mentioned her to his wife, and knowing that the whole episode that had so shaped her life and had such an impact on her self-esteem was not even worthy of discussion was devastating.

'Have you heard of it, Digs?'

Digs . . .

'Is it common in Cornwall?' She turned to look at her husband, who stood by the door, transfixed and awfully pale.

Merrin took the opportunity to stare at him. He looked horror-struck and clammy, suggesting he was just as surprised as her. His hair had thinned a little and his eyes were smaller than she remembered. The navy linen shirt that hung outside of his jeans was the same item that he used to wear, and as much as she tried to douse it, a familiar flame of longing rose in her gut for him, the cowardly, cowardly pig.

Eventually he gathered himself and it was a shock to hear his voice, as clear and as lovely as it lived in her memory. 'I-it's n-not that common, but I have . . . I have . . . I did hear it before. Once. It reminded me of the sea.' His voice carried the rasp of emotion and he swallowed. Like her, he seemed unable to look away and, judging by his searching expression, she was convinced she was the last person he had expected to see.

'Are you okay, darling?' The nice lady walked over and placed her manicured hand on his crumpled sleeve.

He nodded and tried out a smile, before pulling out his handkerchief and wiping his sweaty forehead. 'Actually, I feel a bit . . . a bit sick.'

'Oh, you poor love!' His wife ran her hand over his chest. 'Wonder what's brought that on?'

A bit sick? Merrin thought. *I know that feeling. Like your stomach has dropped down into your boots and your brain is fogged with shock and people are looking at you as if trying to figure out what to say or what to do, but you can't tell them because you don't have the words . . . because your world is spinning and you are wearing a wide and fancy wedding dress that feels like it weighs tons and the bodice is so tight you can't breathe . . . Yes, it can indeed make you feel a bit sick . . .*

'Sorry, Merrin, I got stuck with a delivery, would you like me to take over here?' Vanya offered sweetly and Merrin nodded.

'Thank you, erm . . . thank you, Vanya, can you check in Mr and Mrs—' She tried to say the word but it stuck in her throat.

'Mortimer,' Mrs Mortimer offered helpfully. 'It's Mr and Mrs Mortimer.'

'Yes.' She forced a smile. 'Vanya will get you checked in.'

Merrin slid from behind the reception desk and, without looking at Digby again, walked briskly along the corridor, seeking solace in the wide laundry cupboard. Deciding against turning on the light, she closed the heavy door behind her and slipped off her shoes, before sitting on a large white bag full of tablecloths and placing her bare feet on the cold tiled floor.

'Oh, my God!' Leaning forward, she buried her face in her hands and tried to slow her pulse. 'Oh, my God, he's here! He's right here! He's here!' she whispered into the darkness. 'What am I going to do?'

Her phone rang in the dark and she jumped. 'Jesus! You scared me!' she cried out.

'That was my intention,' Bella responded. 'To scare you from afar and not to see how you are doing?'

'Oh, Bells!' Merrin sighed and again flopped forward. 'Oh, my God, I can't believe it!'

'What's the matter? And where are you? It sounds like you're in a loo?'

'No, not a loo. I've shut myself in a cupboard in the dark.'

'Ok-aay. And can I ask why? Are the police after you? Do you *need* the police? Give me the code word and I'll leap into action.'

'Do we have a code word?' She tried to remember.

'No, but we definitely should for situations like this. I'll give it some thought. Anyhoo, more to the point, why are you in a cupboard in the dark?'

'You're not going to believe it.' Her breath came in short bursts.

'Try me.'

'He's here . . . he . . . he just walked in.' She hated the tremor to her voice. 'I was on reception and his *wife* came in, really pretty, wearing decent clothes and holding one of those bags that Victoria Beckham has, and her hair was all, you know, neat and shiny. I was looking at her and thinking how good she looked and how nice she seemed and he just . . . he just walked in behind her.' She let out a deep breath.

'Merry, I need you to go back a few paces. Who walked in? I don't know what's going on.'

'*You* don't know what's going on? *I* don't know what's going on!' She raised her voice. 'Digby! Digby is here!'

She heard Bella gasp. 'Digby Mortimer?'

'Yes! How many bloody Digbys do we know?'

'Oh, my God!' Bella screamed.

'Exactly. I don't know what to do! I can't hide in here until they leave!'

'How long are they staying?'

'Two days.'

'No, you definitely can't. Although I could send snacks and a Portaloo.'

'It's not funny, Bella!' Merrin felt like crying, her distress gathered in her throat like a physical blockage. 'I haven't seen him since . . . since . . . and I thought I was going to faint or throw up. It's like it happened yesterday – just the sight of him's enough to take me right back to that moment when Reverend Pimm came and got me and everything unravelled . . .'

'Right, Merrin' – Bella spoke with force – 'you listen to me. That was a lifetime ago. You are a grown-ass woman with a lovely life; a lovely future ahead of you and a lovely Miguel. And Digby is a shit. He was a shit then and he will be a shit now. He did you a favour. You might have been saddled for life with him and that would have been so miserable.'

She swallowed the thought that Mrs Mortimer hadn't looked miserable – quite the opposite.

'Did he recognise you?' Bella's question drew her thoughts.

'Yes, of course he did – it's only two and a half years since he last saw me!'

'What did he say? "Can I have my room key and, by the way, sorry about all those sausage rolls that must have gone to waste when I did a runner and left you standing like a tit in the vestry!"' Bella's anger was still very close to the surface.

'We weren't having sausage rolls, it was a three-course, sit-down meal with little chocolates served with the coffee with our initials piped on them . . .' She pictured the very things; they had looked . . . exquisite.

'Listen to yourself, woman! He ditched you at the altar, and don't you dare think one nice thing about him! Your face that day, Merrin. You looked . . . you looked broken.'

I was broken.

'And I shall never forget it. And if it wasn't for the whole bloody fiasco, you might have stayed closer to home and right now be sitting opposite me instead of hiding in a cupboard with the lights off.'

Merrin gripped the phone and closed her eyes; her friend's accurate assessment was like a punch to the throat.

'I don't like him being here, Bells. It's made me think about it all over again. And you don't have to remind me of how terrible it was – I don't want any part of him.' She whispered the truth. 'I know it sounds stupid, but seeing him, it's . . . it's scared me.' There was a crack in her voice, as if further evidence were needed.

'You don't need to be scared, Merry. You are safe and happy; this is just like peering off the edge of a cliff – a bit unnerving, but it doesn't mean you're going to fall. You are safe, you're on solid ground.'

Merrin nodded. 'It's taken me a long time to . . . to feel less shaky . . .' she admitted.

'I know, I know, babby. And you have given that man more thought and more minutes of your time than I think is right; he was a blip and you need to make the decision not to give him a minute more. He doesn't deserve you, he never did.'

'Thanks, Bells.'

'S'okay, mate. I miss you.'

Merrin cursed the pull of tears that would smudge her make-up when she needed to get back to work. 'I miss you too.'

'You have a lovely life, Merry – you live in a castle! You get to have sex with the gorgeous Miguel! While I sit here with my scruffy son, who usually needs his bum changing, hanging around my feet.'

'Would you swap your scruffy son with a dirty bum for a life in a castle?'

'Merrin, you know I would, in a heartbeat; wouldn't even stop to pack,' Bella joked. 'I mean, literally the first this baby boy and my mother would know I was missing was when they ran out of milk and needed the TV turning on, as I'm the only one who can work the remote. Anyway, I gotta go. Love you, and please, please, leave the cupboard!'

'I will, love you too.'

It was amazing how much better she felt after just one chat with her friend. Sitting up, she tucked her hair behind her ears and took a deep breath, trying to steady her pulse. Bella was right, she had to go outside, plus the Mortimers would no doubt be ensconced in their adjoining rooms and the chances of her running into Digby were slim. Her limbs trembled and she did her best to get the shakes under control. She felt torn, desperately keen to avoid him and yet also knowing this might be her only chance to tell him just how much he had destroyed for her.

After a few more seconds of sitting on the laundry bag with her feet on the cold floor, she slipped her pumps back on and stood up, straightening the waistband on her trousers and retying her cravat. She tucked her hair behind her ears again, wiped her top lip, opened the door with a flourish, and with her head down, walked into the corridor and slap bang into Digby.

'Oh! Oh, shit!'

She never swore at work and looked over her shoulder, partly to check that her boss wasn't around or that Mrs Lovely Mortimer wasn't bringing up the rear with her gorgeous boys, before practically jumping out of Digby's path and standing as flat as she could against the cupboard door, trying to put as much distance between them as possible. Her stomach lurched and she feared she might be sick, as was her MO. She felt a fine film of sweat break out over her skin and her thoughts were scrambled.

'Merrin!' He placed his hand on his chest.

'Well, that's going to be awkward, I'm Merrin too.' She hadn't meant to let the nostalgia float from her lips, didn't want him to feel a moment of warmth or joy or comfort in her presence. But there they were.

They stared at each other for what felt like an age. His face and all the promises he had made still with the power to lure her. It was confusing because she hated him. His smile lifted one corner of his mouth, but his eyes looked downcast, sad even. And in truth she was glad to see some semblance of regret; it was all she had ever really wanted, to know that he was sorry, that there had been more reason behind his actions than the promise of a credit card.

'I . . . I had no idea, I am so sorry . . . Mother suggested it and booked it and . . .' He sounded sincere, his expression one of excruciating self-consciousness.

I bet she bloody did. Merrin remembered Mrs Everit giving the woman enough of the details about her place of work when she had bumped into her in the village shop.

She nodded, believing him. Not that it made this encounter any less devastating. For either of them, it would seem.

'How . . . how have you been?' he asked softly.

'How have I *been*?' She stared at him, almost at a loss as to how to begin. 'I don't even know how to answer that. How far do you want me to go back? And surely you're not interested in my welfare now; I mean, you weren't interested back then when you cut me loose.' She pulled back her shoulders, emboldened a little at having found her voice, no matter that it shook with nerves. She might have looked together, sounded it almost, but inside, nerves sloshed in her stomach.

'Oh God!' He looked up and exhaled, rubbing his face in the way he did and showing her the smooth underside of his wrist, which still for some reason held an unfathomable allure. 'I've always wondered when I would bump into you. I knew I would. But I thought it would be in Port Charles.'

'In that heaving metropolis? Highly unlikely.' She released her grip on the wall and put her hands in her trouser pockets to stop them from shaking.

'I never go back, not really. I didn't feel comfortable being there after . . .' He let this hang. 'It's like everyone was pointing a finger at me or had something to say.'

'Really? I can't imagine,' she fired.

He gave a low snort of laughter. 'It was always your place, your home, and I've only been back when I've had to.'

'It's changed massively; we have a casino now, a ten-screen cinema, an ice rink, department store, bowling alley, a Tesco.' Merrin rattled out the funny to ease the atmosphere and helped hide what she really wanted to say, which was, *Why? Why did you leave me like that? I loved you! I loved you!*

He nodded and gave a brief laugh. 'So I've heard.'

'I was sorry to hear your dad passed away.' Guthrie had only ever been kind to her, or at least indifferent.

'Yep. Your gran too, Ellen?'

'Yes, they died within twenty-four hours of each other. Strange.'

'Yep.'

There was a beat of silence where she looked along the corridor, knowing there was no reason to linger, and yet the pull of a shared history and the awareness that this encounter might never be repeated kept her fast. What did she want from him? An apology?

'Your boys look lovely.' She spoke without malice, hiding her hurt that it was his very betrayal that meant the darling little boys belonged to another woman who in another lifetime might have been her, and that he had clearly wasted no time in creating this new life with his new wife.

'They are.' He gave her his first open, proper smile. 'A handful, but brilliant.'

'And you decided against Horatio? Noah and Freddie, much better.'

Again that chuckle. 'Actually, it's Noah Columbus and Freddie Horatio.' He widened his eyes and held her stare.

'Poor little sods.'

'Lydia drew the line at having them as first names.'

'She seems like a nice lady.' Merrin was not surprised that he had settled for a well-spoken Lydia, she was far more in keeping with what Ma Mortimer would expect.

He nodded and again his smile faltered, as if this were straying into territory that was less than comfortable.

'I want to say . . .' He paused, and reached out almost, but she folded her arms. 'I've wanted to say for the longest time that I'm sorry, Merry.'

She felt her spine soften and her lungs fill with something close to relief. 'For what?'

'What do you mean for what?' His expression was nonplussed.

'I mean' – she looked along the corridor, checking she was still able to talk freely – 'there's so much for me to feel . . .' She bit her lip, *Come on, Merrin, you have had years to plan this conversation in your head, what do you want to say?* 'Shitty about.' *For the love of God, is that the best you've got?*

'I can imagine.'

'No.' She took a small step towards him, emboldened and picturing herself in her wedding dress being helped up on to the cart driven by Jarvis, as thick clouds gathered overhead and she didn't care if she lived or died. 'I don't think you can imagine. It's not only what you did, Digby. It's how you did it.' She let this hang.

'You had every right to change your mind, defer our wedding, even finish things, those were all possibilities and none of those decisions would have hurt me any less.' She paused, allowing this admission of pain to permeate. 'But did you need to humiliate me like that? I'm a Port Charles girl and it's a small place. Far, far smaller than it looks and feels. And not only did you throw me away like a thing you didn't want any more, but you changed the way Port Charles sees me. I used to be Merrin Kellow, Ben's girl, the one with the hair.' She ran her fingers over her short bob. 'But since that day, I am the one Digby Mortimer left at the altar, the one in the big dress with the fancy cart, all the trimmings.'

'Merrin, I—'

'No, let me finish! I moved away because I didn't know how to live with the new shape you carved for me, the new version of me, and the worst thing was, I hadn't changed! Not one bit! I still wanted to run barefoot, to sit on the harbour wall outside the cottage and drink tea as the sun came up and went down – that was all I wanted! Yes, I liked the idea of spending time in the big city with you sometimes and stretching my boundaries, but I always thought I'd travel on my terms and then go home. *Home* to settle down for good. But . . .' She cursed the tears that pooled, wiping her eyes and sniffing. 'What you did to me, it changed things for me. You broke my heart. You broke my heart, Digby.' It felt hard to say out loud; her voice was thin. 'It never healed quite the same, you know?'

'I do know,' he whispered, looking like he, too, might be close to tears, and for this she was strangely thankful.

She placed her palm on her chest. 'It's like I have a little fault line running through it of which I am overly aware. I doubt it would survive being dropped again.'

'I'm sorry, Merrin. I was conflicted, and my mother—'

'Merrin!' Vanya called from the end of the corridor. 'So sorry to interrupt you, but I'm swamped!' She held up a clutch of room keys. 'Could you help me with check-ins?'

'Of course, Vanya, on my way.' She let her eyes lock with his and smoothed her jacket, before tucking her hair behind her ears.

'I am sorry, Merrin.' He searched her face, almost imploringly.

Standing straight, she took a moment, before speaking clearly. '"Words are easy like the wind, faithful friends are hard to find." William Shakespeare said that.'

He smiled at her. 'Did he? I'll have to take your word for it.'

'Goodbye, Digby.'

As she walked away, Merrin felt surprisingly calm. It felt good to have had her say, and to see the look of anguish in his eyes was a reward of sorts. Not that she wanted him to hurt, but she did want him to acknowledge the hurt he had caused. It had been strangely healing and today, on Valentine's Day, as tears snaked down the back of her throat, she felt his eyes on her back and knew he was watching her walk away.

CHAPTER TWENTY

Digby

Digby sat at the small, leather-inlaid desk positioned at the bedroom window with a lovely view of the large cedar tree that grew outside. He thought this must be the perfect spot at Christmas, especially if they were lucky enough for snow.

'Darling, I'm going to take the boys for a little amble in the grounds, wear them out a bit before supper. Do you want to come?' His wife leant forward and kissed his scalp.

He reached up and touched her face, the smell of her as intoxicating as ever. 'I think I'll stay here, if you don't mind. I have some correspondence to catch up on, and then I'll shower. Really looking forward to supper.' He smiled warmly at the woman he loved.

'Me too!' She kissed him again and turned to her sons, who sat side by side on the wide double bed, glued to a cartoon, the noise from which was infernal.

'Daddy!' Noah called, as Lydia grabbed their padded coats from where they rested on top of the overnight bag.

'No, Daddy is hiding up here and will probably nap for twenty minutes and then make out he hasn't so he doesn't feel too guilty that I am in a permanent state of knackeredness and he is unfairly refreshed.'

Digby laughed. 'Am I that transparent?'

'Always.' She beamed. 'But I wouldn't have you any other way. I like your transparency. I like knowing everything about you.' He felt the cold bolt of deceit fire through his core, knowing this was not quite true; she didn't know about Merrin Mercy Kellow, the girl he almost married. She blew him a kiss and trundled out of the room with the boys rushing ahead.

He opened up his leather folder and placed it open on the desktop before taking the fountain pen from its natty little holder against the central spine of the file and twisting off the lid. Next he turned the pad to an angle and stared at the blank white sheet of paper. It was hard to start, but strangely, once he did, his hand danced across the page with speed and a rare fluidity of communication.

> Dear Mother,
>
> I can't remember the last time I wrote to you – from school, possibly, when we had to pen the obligatory monthly note home to reassure you that we were being well fed and that your fees were being wisely spent. Matron used to check every letter before it was sealed and so even if we had been living off gruel, among cold punishments and misery, it would have been hard to tell you. We weren't, by the way; I was very happy at school. I liked almost every aspect of it.
>
> I guess it feels easier to write to you rather than try and have this long-overdue conversation face to face, and so here we are. What was it Dad always said? A straightforward question deserves a straightforward answer? And so here goes.
>
> I've asked myself what I want from this communiqué. What outcome? And the rather

inadequate answer is: I'm not sure. Do I want a different life? No, not at all. So, what then? Maybe a little understanding? An acknowledgement that the decisions you have made on my behalf have not been without consequence? Recognition that every stone you have cast out in order to achieve your aims or to satisfy your drive has always caused ripples that I suspect you are quite unaware of?

This is also probably a good place to tell you that I love you. I do and I always will, but love and like are two very different things, Mother. And so, do I like you? Again, the rather inadequate answer is: most of the time.

I want to talk to you about Merrin. That name that has not passed our lips in conversation from that day to this. Merrin Kellow.

I think back to that summer, less than three years ago, but a lifetime too. I was a naïve kid, but who isn't at twenty-two? I did, however, feel old enough to make good choices. That was another thing Dad always told me: make good choices – and I did. I chose Merrin. She was sweet and made me laugh and she made me happy. She made me really happy. And now whatever I write with regard to her makes me feel disloyal to Lydia. Darling Lydia, whom I adore and who is the best mum to Noah and Freddie, but life with Merrin would also have been good. Life with Merrin *was* good! Did you know she was at this hotel? I can't believe you did, not even you would be that cruel, surely?

I feel again, it's important to say that I love Lydia. And ours is a good, strong, solid love, but I loved Merrin, too, and she loved me, and you know, Mother, she made me so very happy when I was discovering who I was. She didn't want anything from me, from us, despite your warnings to the contrary. You were wrong about her, and the way I let her down, guided, encouraged and coerced by you, is something that will haunt me. She deserved better, we both did.

The love that I had for her might have waned, might have dried up or might have bloomed into a whole lifetime of love – who can possibly know? Not me and not you. But you know that feeling, that love that is so all-encompassing it's like a drunken madness, obsessive and singular – when the prospect of not being with that person is a thought that's almost unbearable. Well, it was like that. It was everything, and I desperately wanted to find out what came next, but you took that opportunity from us. Should I be thanking you? Because if you hadn't intervened I might not have met Lydia and my Noah and Freddie would be different or not at all, and those thoughts are as desperate as they are unimaginable to me. But good God, Mum, it was a hard lesson.

I've seen Merrin and she is still the same, sweet person; a little shy, but smart and with a warmth and honesty that shines from her. It's funny, I always think of Port Charles with her in it and yet apparently she has stayed away, away from her home, and all because of what happened. This is a bitter pill for me to swallow because I know that the place is her home far more than it will ever be mine. I guess that's it. This is what I wanted to say, and a different relationship between us might mean I did not have to write to you, but again, here we are. The whole episode caged us in a thin sheet of awkwardness that I find hard to break out of. If it were easy, I think I would have done so a long, long time ago.

I have decided to leave this letter for you to find after we say goodbye at the end of our stay – and I leave it up to you as to whether you want to discuss it further or, if you prefer, do what the Mortimers are so good at: sweep it under the carpet or tear it into a million pieces and pop it in the fire as if it was never written and as if you had never read it. As dad to Noah and Freddie, I can tell you that I would never meddle in their lives as you have in my mine; would never want to exert such control that it impairs their freedom to think, their freedom to explore, their freedom to choose . . . I want them to choose whomever and whatever they want, Mother, because I think that is real love, love without conditions.

I could go on, but what's the point? Merrin is still sweet and holds understandable anger, but little malice; she still has so much about her that drew me to her. Our time, our opportunity has of course passed and we both, I am sure, have happy and productive lives, but seeing her has made me ask certain questions: what if? What if I had gone ahead in spite of your dire ultimatum? What if I had packed a bag, married her and moved in with Ben and Heather Kellow? What if I'd chosen to follow my heart and not my head? What if I had chosen her? What then?

All hypothetical, of course, as we will never know, but I want you to know that you did me a great disservice, and her too, and that is a great shame, which I will have to carry always. I hate coming back to Port Charles and rarely do, not only because of the understandable disdain in which the locals hold me, but also because it reminds me of that, the saddest episode I have ever had – it really was – when I was hurting more than I knew was possible and I hurt the girl I loved; because be in no doubt, I loved her. I loved her.

Digby x

CHAPTER TWENTY-ONE

MERRIN

It was the end of a long and exhausting day. With a muddled head and wanting to avoid the corridors and guests, or more specifically, certain guests, Merrin decided to walk the long way to their quarters. She trod the woodland path where damp leaves gathered and the stone flagstones grew a little slippery when rained on. To walk among nature helped still the torrent of intrusive thoughts.

'Merrin! I've not heard that name before, it's lovely!'

'I-it's n-not that common, but I have . . . I have . . . I did hear it before. Once. It reminded me of the sea.'

The branches of the oak and horse chestnut trees formed a canopy that in autumn, with an array of burnished leaves in shades of red through to the palest yellow, was something to behold. It was one of her favourite things: to take her time, idling along and looking up through the branches as the sun peeked through where it could and the leaves moved in the wind to sing to her a rustling sonata. Tonight, she stood at the end of the path and slipped off her shoes and, holding them in her fingers, she placed first one foot and then the other on the cold, damp path, feeling the stresses and worries of the day travel down her legs and disappear through the soles of her feet, worming their way into this little patch of garden behind the castle wall.

Her phone buzzed in her pocket. She pulled it out and was delighted to see it was Bella's number.

'You're up late.' It was nearly midnight.

'It's Valentine's! Of course I'm up late – there are chocolates to eat and champagne to sip! Oh no, wait a minute, that's just my fantasy life; I'm up because Glynn has diarrhoea and I've had to change several leaky nappies. Welcome to my world in all its glamour!'

Merrin laughed. 'Poor little thing.'

'Me or the babby?'

'Both.'

'I wanted to see if you were okay, after the whole Digby episode. I can't believe he just turned up like that.'

'Me neither. I spoke to him,' she whispered, looking around, checking she was alone.

'What? How? Where? Oh, my God! What happened?' All traces of fatigue had gone from her tone and Bella now sounded wide awake.

'I came out of the cupboard and he was just there in the corridor, alone.'

'Fuck! Did he try it on?'

'What? God, no, of course not!' she tutted. 'What do you think we are, fifteen?'

'In my head, yes.'

'No, it was nothing like that, Bells, it was . . .' She took her time, picking her way along the path, lit only by the uplights that the gardeners had artfully placed to highlight the magnificent trees. 'It was strange and surreal. I need to think about it more to see how it's left me, but right now? It feels like it's over, done. I don't have to fear bumping into him, do I? And that's huge.'

'What does that mean, it's over, done? Weren't you done a long time ago?'

'Yes, of course. I don't know, I guess it was a chance to . . . to say goodbye.' A lump rose in her throat at this truth.

'That's sad.'

'Is it? A bit, I guess. I think it's closure and, whether I've admitted it to myself or not, a chance for me to let it go – properly put it behind me and start my next chapter.' Her mouth twitched into a small smile. 'Yes, my next chapter.'

'I'm happy for you and I'm proud of you, but you know that, right?'

'I do.'

As Merrin rounded the bend in the path she saw the French window of her and Miguel's room and it seemed to be glowing. *A fire?* Her heart leapt at the prospect. It was only as she picked up pace and got closer that she realised the light came from candles, lots of candles, which were burning brightly. She felt conflicted: irritated that he had gone full Valentine, yet happy that she was not alone, pleased she had someone waiting for her, someone who cared enough to do this. Especially as Digby and his lovely wife and kids were at that very moment enjoying a luxury suite in this hotel.

'Gotta go, Bells.'

She ended the call and gripped her phone. Guilt edged her thoughts as she pictured the heart-holding rabbit on the front of the crappy card she had left propped up in front of Miguel's computer on his desk earlier.

Clearly he was looking out for her, as the French doors flew open as she approached. He had showered and looked devastatingly handsome in his jeans and a denim shirt. She always found him most attractive with the curls of his short, dark hair damp against his neck and his beautiful face glowing.

'Welcome home!' He ushered her in and helped remove her suit jacket, before pushing her shoulders until she sat in the soft armchair located just inside the door, next to the large plant he had installed. Miguel dropped to his knees and reached for a large fluffy towel in which he wrapped first one foot and then the other, gently wiping her damp, cold feet on the soft fabric. The perfect welcome home for a barefoot enthusiast such as her.

'Oh, my goodness! That feels so lovely. Thank you.' It took a while for her to take it all in. In addition to the many candles that were on the floor, the bookshelf and the TV unit, there was a generous spread of rose petals on the bed cover and the room was scented with lavender oil. A fancy silver ice bucket, purloined no doubt from the restaurant, sat brimming with ice and the foil-wrapped neck of a bottle of bubbly poked from the top.

'Miguel! This is all very posh!' She felt a little overwhelmed, knowing how hard his shift would have been today and still he had found the time for this. 'Thank you.'

'You're welcome.' He placed her feet on the floor still wrapped in the warm towel and reached for a large, flat, red box, tied with a red ribbon.

'Chocolates! Well, now you're talking. Forget the petals – give me the candy! Do I have to share them?' She laughed, trying to lighten the atmosphere, to make it funny, to hide the painful recollection of having seen Digby and the barrage of uncomfortable memories that he had awoken.

Again he sank down on to the floor and held the box in his hands; the candlelight lit up his handsome face.

'It's not chocolates,' he began. His fingers pulled on the red bow and she silently hoped it wasn't lingerie, knowing that tonight she was running on empty, tired from running around all day, and the encounter with Digby had been more than a little draining. Their exchange and the shock of it all had taken its toll. All she longed for was sleep. The thought of having to slip into something slinky when what she really wanted was the feel of her fleecy pj's against her skin and to put her head on her pillow . . .

'I love you, Merrin.'

He held her eyeline and spoke slowly, earnestly, and she felt the flicker of recognition at what was to come and with it came a sinking feeling in her stomach, reminded by her encounter with Digby of just how differently she felt about Miguel. She adored him, of that there was no doubt, but love – big, real, grown-up, happily-ever-after love – no, no, that was not how she felt. And if he proposed, she knew she would have to refuse him. It was almost more than she could stand, to look at his beautiful face lit by candlelight knowing she was going to hurt him.

'Thank you.' Her voice was small as she sat forward in the chair. 'Miguel, I—'

'Merrin Mercy Kellow,' he began, ignoring her, his voice steady, as if the words he was about to say were well practised and he needed to get them out. 'I think you are the most amazing person I've ever met. I remember the day I arrived here and I was happy enough to be starting the job, but then I saw you and—' He broke into a big smile, as if the thought of that day was enough to make him happy. He removed a smaller red box from the larger one – ring-sized.

Sweet, sweet, beautiful Miguel . . .

'You were so warm and kind and funny and beautiful, and then when I plucked up the courage to ask you for a drink and you threw up in the drain . . .'

'Miguel, please, I need to say—'

'No, you don't get to interrupt this time, this is my moment, and yours comes in a minute.' He gripped her hand. 'I love you. And I know I will love you for the rest of my life. And it's a life that would be poorer if you weren't by my side.' He jostled the little red box and was about to open it when her phone rang in her pocket.

'Ignore it,' he implored. 'Please.'

She looked at the screen, a little relieved that a call had come in for her at that moment. She could stall, think!

'I can't. It's Ruby. She never calls, and never this late.'

'Ruby?' She held the phone to her ear and struggled to make out any words between the unmistakable sound of her sister crying and trying to catch her breath. 'Ruby, what's the matter? Ruby!' She sat forward, calling with some urgency, as her heart thudded in her throat and her chest filled with a rising sense of panic. Had something happened to the baby? To Jarvis?

'Come . . . come home, Merry. You need . . . you need to come home!'

'What's happened?' she pressed, wanting and not wanting to hear whatever it was that had reduced her sister to this. 'What's the matter?'

'Dad—' she began, and Merrin felt the first bite of shock.

'Is he okay? Ruby, please, take a breath and tell me what's happened!'

Miguel came closer, his expression alarmed and the red box nowhere in sight.

'He's dead, Merry! Oh, my God!' her sister wailed. 'He died! My dad died!'

Merrin felt the air leave her lungs and her throat almost close. She didn't remember ending the call or explaining to Miguel what had happened, but was aware that he had crouched down in front of her and had taken her hands into his own.

'Don't worry, Merrin. Don't worry. You are in shock, love. I'll drive you home. I'll drive you to the front door. It's all going to be okay.' She remembered offering her sister a similar lie when Gramps had died. 'We'll go in my car. Take your time, it's all going to be okay,' he repeated. 'I'm taking you home, my love. I'll take you home.' He kissed her forehead as one might a child's and she sat back in the chair. His words echoed around her, surreal and almost comical in their absurdity. *Her dad . . . not her dad!* She felt swamped by exhaustion but at the same time wired, on high alert, trying to make sense of what Ruby had told her. It didn't feel true.

Without waiting for her response, Miguel pulled the small suitcase from the bottom of the wardrobe and she watched in silence as he packed her jeans, trainers, sweatshirt, nightclothes, toiletries and her black dress and shoes – thinking ahead, helping her in her dire time of need, this marvellous man.

'My dad, he, erm . . .' She couldn't say the words.

'I know, my love, I know. You already told me. Don't try to speak. Just sit tight and we'll be on our way in no time. Just sit tight.' Again he kissed her forehead.

'You don't have to do that. You're working tomorrow, I can get a cab and then get a . . . erm . . . a . . . on the tracks.' Ridiculously, the word 'train' eluded her. On the tail end of his double shift, and in light of their horrendous and emotional evening, Miguel insisted and she felt a wave of gratitude towards him.

'No, I'll take you to Port Charles. Of course I will! I'll always be right here when you need me, Merrin. Always. That's the deal. It's what your dad would have wanted: for me to see you safely home.'

She stared at him with her head cocked to one side and felt the embarrassing temptation to giggle because it was at once shocking and funny that he had used the past tense . . . as if . . . as if . . . But it couldn't be real, it couldn't . . . not her daddy.

'You're in shock.' He grabbed the duvet from the bed, scattering petals as he did so and blowing out the rest of the candles. 'I'm right here. And I'll get you home safely. You can sleep in the car on the way down.'

His kindness left her tearful.

'Thank you, Miguel.' She reached out and gripped his forearm.

He nodded and placed his hand over hers. 'I love you. I wish I could make all the hurt go away.'

And if her brain hadn't been full of the loss of her dad and the way Ruby had sounded on the phone – utterly, utterly broken – she would have explained that there was so much hurt inside her she was worried that if you removed it all there might be nothing left. Energy and coherence were for her in short supply. Her body and mind were numb, as if suspended and waiting, waiting to get back to Port Charles, where her heart resided. She shook violently, as if freezing cold.

Guided now by his hand on the small of her back, and wrapped in the double duvet that did little to stop her shaking, he steered her towards the car park.

'Good evening, sir.'

She turned to look at the person Miguel addressed and saw Digby leaning on a car, smoking. Her stomach bunched and it felt unreal; she had temporarily forgotten that he was here.

'Good evening,' he replied to Miguel.

She locked eyes with him.

'All okay?' He put the cigarette on the floor and crushed it with the heel of his brogue, staring at her wrapped up in the car park at this ungodly hour.

'I'm . . . I'm going home,' she managed, wanting to tell Digby, who knew her dad and who was part of her life, her history.

'Has something happened?' He stepped out of the shadows.

'My dad . . . my dad died.' She felt her gut fold with the punch of her words as realisation dawned that this is what had happened. *Her dad had died . . .*

'Oh God, no! Not Ben! Oh, your poor mum. Is Ruby with her? Is there anything I can do?'

Miguel seemed to stagger back a step or two as if sideswiped.

'What the fuck is going on here?'

Merrin stared at him and then looked back at Digby, as her tears trickled down her cheeks.

'This is . . . this is the guy, the one who . . . who, you know, from home. I told you once about having something perfect and that it got broken – well, this is him, the person who broke it.' She cried now, great, breath-stealing sobs that left her spent.

'Get out of my fucking way!' Miguel spat, and she watched as Digby stumbled back into the shadows.

Neither of them spoke until they reached the motorway. Merrin was too busy trying to make sense of Ruby's terrible news. The surreal addition of Digby into the equation was just another strange thing for her to deal with on this momentous night.

'Digby.' He kept his voice low, respectful and yet still with an urgency to understand what was going on. 'The rich kid from Port Charles . . .'

'Yes.' She managed to scramble the word from a throat full of grit.

'Why is he in our hotel? Did you know he was here?' He gripped the steering wheel.

Merrin wanted him to be quiet to let her think, to try to understand what had happened to her dad, but was also vaguely aware that she was in his car and he was going out of his way to help her.

'Yes,' she whispered.

'Did you arrange for him to be here on Valentine's?' he asked quietly, as if he couldn't quite bear to hear the answer.

'No. No. Of course not!' She pulled the duvet around her form for warmth. 'He turned up with his wife and kids. I had no idea. It was awful to see him walk in. Awful.' She let her head fall on to her chest, as if the effort of holding it up was more than she could manage right now.

'Go to sleep, Merrin.' He sounded kindly, but also as if this might be his preference.

◆ ◆ ◆

It was in the early hours, a little before dawn, that she felt the cobbles beneath the car bump them along. She sat upright, and in that glorious second before she remembered what had happened, wondered why and indeed how she was home! She smiled at the sight of Kellow Cottages all lit up like Christmas trees against the dark of night, as if it were not the time when most people were asleep. Miguel left the engine running and came around to her side of the car and, gently opening her door, he removed the quilt to ease her movement. The weather was foul, wet and windy, as he helped her from the car, holding her close for a beat and kissing her face as she hugged him.

'Thank you for driving me home. Thank you,' she whispered, laying her head on his chest. 'Are you . . . are you going to come in?' she asked weakly.

'No.' He shook his head. 'I need to get back and I think it's only right I leave you with your family to come to terms with this, but give your mum and Ruby my condolences. I'll call you tomorrow and if you need me at any time of the day or night you just pick up that phone and I'll be here. I love you. I really do.' His voice cracked.

'Thank you. Drive safely.'

Miguel held her tightly and kissed her tenderly once more, before climbing back into the driver's seat. She felt his love and knew she would never forget his actions on this night, knowing it was one of the kindest things anyone had ever done for her. As she watched the tail lights of his car trundle back up the road, as if creeping quietly in the dead of night, the door to the cottage opened and out came Ruby, beautifully swollen with pregnancy, but her face red and contorted as she cried from eyes that were now no more than narrow slits.

'Merry!' Ruby's voice was no more than a rasp and her face tortured as her fingers gripped Merrin's arms.

'Oh Ruby!' Merrin fell against her, the two clinging on to each other as if their lives depended on it. Silently they held each other on the slippery cobbles in the dark, as rain fell and the wind rushed at them, carrying salty, sea-laden sheets that soaked their skin and the fabric of their clothes. It was as if this wild corner of Cornwall was roaring at the loss of its son, and she understood, wanting to roar too.

'He's gone!' Ruby gasped.

Again Merrin's tears broke their banks, as her heart felt like it might dissolve. The sight of her sister and the fact her dad was not running outside with arms wide to welcome her home told her that it was true.

Making their way inside, she rushed up the stairs of the cottage and knocked gently, before walking into her parents' room. The sight was something she knew she would never forget.

Heather Kellow had got old, just like that and almost overnight. She had lost her shine, her sparkle, her plump face, her laughter and her joy; replaced by a dull, slender imitation of the woman, but one with a vacant expression, sallow cheeks and eyes that wordlessly spoke of pure sorrow. She barely shifted in the bed, but with great effort, raised her head a little from the pillow and said her daughter's name, her voice, barely audible, one of sadness and gravel.

'Merrin . . .'

'Oh Mum! Mummy!' Merrin climbed on to the rickety brass bed next to her mother and wrapped her arms around her. It was as if her spirit had fled and she now gripped the shell of Ben's wife.

There was no welcome smile, no offer of tea or baked goods, no interest in anything other than lying very still and hoping the minutes might pass, or that they might all wake in a time where either they hurt a little less or they smiled, realising that the whole horrible thing had been no more than the very worst kind of dream.

'He's gone,' she mouthed, as tears sprang from her bloodshot eyes and ran down her face. 'He's gone . . .' This followed by a sound, a whimper that was animal-like and wounded.

'It's okay, Mummy. I've got you.' She grasped at words, anything that might help her mother heal.

'Ben,' Heather murmured, pushing her face once again into the pillow, her call a low moan. 'Ben!' As if she might be able to summon him if she tried hard enough.

To see her mother like this added an unimaginable layer of distress to her own grief. Merrin didn't know what to do, didn't know how to make things better. Her first instinct was to call for her dad – he'd know what to do. And this thought was enough to rip a hole in her heart, as she sank down next to her mother on the pillow and inhaled the scent of the man who was no more.

CHAPTER TWENTY-TWO

MERRIN

It was early morning. Merrin sat on the soft, embroidered cushion that had, for as long as she could recall, lived in the window seat. She took as much comfort from running her fingertips over the abundance of raised, brightly sewn flowers as she always had. It was something soft and pretty to distract her broken heart. With her legs raised and her chin on her knees, she stared out of the window of the cottage. It was raining and the sky was a dark, brooding grey, which suited her just fine.

On a day such as this, it was hard to remember how different the place looked in the sunshine; hard to remember sunshine at all. It was, however, hardest to imagine a life here in Port Charles without her dad. He was always around. *Had* always been around. Whether he was in the house, sitting in the chair by the fire, leaning on a wall chatting to someone, down by the quayside in his rubber waders getting ready to go out to sea with Robin and Jarvis, or going in or coming out of the pub – singing, if it was the latter. One of the most prominent sounds of her childhood was lying in her little bed with the window cracked open and listening to his whistled song growing louder as he drew nearer home and then his booming voice greeting her mum as he finally came through the door after any time away. And, of course, his legendary snoring that escaped from beneath the bedroom door. He was a short man, but a noisy giant, larger than life with a presence that made him tall.

And now, even if she returned to Port Charles, she knew it would never be the same, because her dad would not be here. Running her hand over her chest, she felt where a deep ache of discomfort grumbled, and pinched her nose to stop her tears – a neat trick she had learnt that enabled her to sit here and hold in the sadness that would, if released, certainly upset her mum.

She had been home for three days and in all that time her mum had barely left the bedroom. Three days that could have been an hour or a month. The clock was relegated to those with a regular routine; those whose entire lives had not been fractured by an all-consuming loss that distorted time.

Miguel had called often, offering in his sweet way to do whatever might help take away her pain, but she knew there was nothing to be done. Pain like this had to be lived, endured and, if you were lucky, you might, in time, come out the other side. This she knew more than most.

Ruby arrived and proceeded to fill the kettle. The sight of her sister's beautifully rounded bump was enough to solicit the smallest of smiles; it was a good, good thing in this, the worst of times.

'She still asleep?' Ruby took the chair opposite the sofa.

'Still in bed, but I don't think she's sleeping. She just lies there.'

Ruby nodded. 'I don't blame her. I wish I could just go to bed, but this little one has other ideas.' She ran her hand over her stomach. 'And Jarvis is in a bad way too, so I'm keeping an eye on him. We're taking it in turns to fall apart – it's like there's some grief rota. And when one of us sinks the other goes into responsible adult mode until the buzzer goes and we switch. I feel like I've either been sleeping or crying for days.'

'You have.'

'Yep.' Ruby let the next bout of tears trickle down her face and rubbed at her eyes. 'I'm exhausted.'

Merrin nodded her understanding; they all were.

'Tell me again, was Jarvis with him at the end?' She wanted to know the details.

Ruby picked at a loose thread on the hem of her sweatshirt. 'Yes. They'd only been in for an hour or so, everything on the boat was packed away and Jarv was washing the deck down, and he heard a . . . a thud, and when he looked up towards the rear deck, Dad was . . . he was lying on the nets. Jarvis thought he was mucking about, but then when he didn't move, he called him and ran over, he could see something wasn't right.' Ruby stopped to catch her breath. 'Robin was on the quayside and Jarv yelled to him and Robin called the ambulance. They got here as soon as they could and while they were waiting, Mac and Mr Everit, who are on the lifeboats, both came running down. I think they'd been in the pub, and they're both trained, obviously. They did CPR but it . . .' Her sob was loud and raw. 'It was too late, Merrin! He'd already died.'

She felt hot tears fall down her face where her skin was already sore from crying. 'I can't believe it.'

'*I* can't believe it; none of us can!'

'Do you think it will ever feel true?' She didn't expect a response and Ruby's answer floored her.

'I think one day it will and I dread that day more than this one, because at the moment while my brain is catching up, at some level I think it might all be a mistake and there is the smallest chance he might walk through the door, but once I know it's true, then that door is closed forever, and that scares me, Merry. That really, really scares me.'

'What are we going to do, Rubes?'

A voice came from the doorway as their friend parked the pram at the bottom of the stairs. 'Same as we always do, girls, we are going to hold each other close and get through it together.'

'Oh, Bella.' Both she and Ruby lumbered to the open doorway and held her close, as the three stood in the doorway with the rain at their backs.

'I need a dry-off with a towel, a cup of tea and a chat with my girls. In that order.'

In spite of the circumstances, Merrin smiled at her best friend, whose mood was, as always, infectious; just the sight of the girl enough to lodge a sliver of happy into the dark crevices of her grief.

◆ ◆ ◆

Jarvis had lost weight. Merrin stared at him now as he pulled on his boots and prepared to meet up with Robin and the others in the pub.

'You all right, Jarv?' She hated to see him so low when he was about to become a dad and this was supposed to be the happiest time.

'Truth is, I don't know really, Merry. It hasn't sunk in yet, but I guess that's what funerals are for.'

'They are that, Jarv.' Bella smiled at him. 'Things will look a lot different this time tomorrow night.'

'I'm dreading it,' Ruby announced.

'We all are,' she agreed.

'Is Miguel coming back down? I was looking forward to seeing him.'

'No, Jarv. He has to work.' She thought again of his incredible selfless act of kindness: delivering her home when she had needed him to, remembering for the first time the trouble he had gone to for Valentine's and certain now that he had been about to propose.

It was a funny thing, she was adamant she would have said no, letting him down as gently and as honestly as possible, but the way he had behaved in light of this tragedy, how he had given Digby short shrift . . . it made her think. Not that she had much spare capacity for these thoughts right now.

'Shame. I like him. He's a good bloke.' He walked over and kissed Ruby on the forehead. 'See you later, love. If you need me, just text and I'll be straight back.'

'I will.' Ruby gripped his hand and kissed the back of his fingers. He loped slowly from the parlour and closed the door behind him. 'I'm glad he's gone out.' Ruby swallowed. 'It's desperate with him sitting in the house all day, just staring out of the window.'

'He loved Dad.'

'Yes, he did. Talk about state the bloody obvious, thank you for that, Merrin,' Ruby snapped.

She stared at her sister, who stared back. Bella subtly shook her head and closed her eyes briefly; code for *ignore her.* It was like this sometimes, as if she inadvertently pushed Ruby's buttons that took her from calm to furious in seconds. She took Bella's advice and the atmosphere settled a little.

With baby Glynn sleeping soundly in his pram in the corner, Merrin, Bella and Ruby settled back into their seats around the hearth with large mugs of tea, warming their toes in front of the fire. It was just like old times, except they were solemn and thoughtful. Merrin knew without doubt that they, like her, took solace from the proximity of the others.

'Shall I take Heather up some toast or something?' Bella looked towards the ceiling.

'She won't eat it, Bells,' Ruby sighed. 'We've tried, ain't we, Merry?'

She nodded. This, too, was her sister's MO – to throw a verbal olive branch after snapping at her.

'Jarvis is right, Miguel is a good bloke.' She pictured the effort he had gone to, the petals on the bed, the smell of lavender oil, the candles . . .

'Yes, I thought he was lovely,' Bella added.

'He is lovely.' She smiled at her friend. 'I think he might propose . . .' She let this trail.

'God!' Bella sat forward in her seat. 'That's big news. And what would you say?'

'I don't know.' She rubbed her sore eyes. 'I'm thinking that he's got a lot of qualities that make for a good life partner.'

'But is that enough, Merry? Don't you want that glow of real love?' Bella, she knew, had reservations about the two of them.

'I don't think that happens for most people, if it exists at all, and so why would I hold out for it?' she surmised. 'Besides, I'm honestly too muddle-headed right now to think about anything. I don't know if he's what I'm looking for.'

'What *are* you looking for exactly?' Ruby sipped her tea.

'I don't know,' she mused. 'And I guess that's half the problem. But I do know what it felt like to *believe* in love – so much so that the thought of a marriage proposal filled me with joy, not dread, but I won't feel that again because I know it's not real. I think there are some exceptions: what Mum and Dad had was real, rare and special.' This admission was a big deal, hinting at a recovery of her heart, but was lost among the next wave of sadness that hit hard.

'Dad really liked him after spending time with him at my wedding,' her sister added. These words were enough to make all three girls cry harder, with thoughts of Ben on that proud, proud day. They foraged for tissues and wiped their faces.

'I can't believe that was the last time I saw him. Why didn't I come home again? I feel as if I've let him down,' Merrin cried.

'Oh, don't worry, *that* wasn't why you let Dad down, Merry.'

She and Bella looked towards Ruby, whose words had been cutting, and Merrin felt her pulse quicken.

'What d'you mean by that?' She sat up straight and turned towards her sister. This barb was too deep and painful to ignore.

'Nothing.' Ruby twisted in the chair to get comfortable.

'Ruby! You can't say something like that and just expect me to drop it!' She was aware of Ruby and Bella sharing a knowing look, and this only added fuel to the twin flames of intrigue and unease. 'How did I let Dad down?' she pushed. Even asking the question was enough to make her throat close with distress and for tears to form and slip down the back of her nose.

'By up and leaving, by not being here.'

'Stop, Ruby! Just bloody stop!' Merrin's voice was strong. 'You told me once before what a rubbish daughter I was in going away, and it hurt me more than you know. But Mum and Dad seemed to understand a lot more than you do that it was about my survival! I did what I had to do to grow, to get over what Digby did to me! And so don't you dare, just don't!' She raised her voice a little, wary of waking Glynn. 'In fact, it's not about Mum and Dad, Ruby, is it? It's about you and some stupid jealousy that has always hung around you like a bad smell. It needs to stop, it just needs to stop! I've had enough.'

'*You've* had enough? And don't even start me on Jarvis. *My Jarvis!*' she enunciated. '*My Jarvis*? That's what you said!'

'That was a fucking lifetime ago!' Merrin felt her heart hammer in exasperation, as she punched her thighs. 'I didn't mean to say it, I didn't mean it! And I've already apologised. I can't keep apologising!' She shook her head and rubbed her face, wanting silence, wanting Ruby to shut up.

'Not for me; it wasn't a lifetime ago for me! And how dare you say that? Even on my bloody wedding day, half the talk was about how *you* were coping with the day and how strange it must all be for Merrin, the poor lamb. *My* wedding day! People were coming up to me all day and I thought they were going to congratulate me but instead they looked me in the eye and said, "Oh, this must be so tough for little Merrin . . ."'

'And what do you think that was like for me? I can't shake it off! The girl who got jilted, "poor little Merrin!"'

'And even now, your little comments like, "Oh, Jarvis loved Dad . . ." Don't tell me about my husband, you don't know him, you have no idea what goes on in his head.'

'I never said I did! I don't know him like you do, of course I don't, and sometimes, Ruby, I wonder if I know you!'

'Enough! Enough now!' a desperate voice boomed.

Merrin turned to see her mother leaning on the wall, pale and listing, as if the strength might at any moment leave her legs. She and Ruby jumped up from their chairs and rushed towards her. They each lifted an arm and walked her to the seat Ruby had just vacated, helping to lower her into it. Bella went to fill the kettle, as if knowing if ever there was a need for tea, it was now. Merry's heart raced, still raging at her sister's words, sad beyond reason for her loss and now guilty, too, that she had caused her grieving mother one second of further anguish.

Heather spoke softly but with uncharacteristic anger. 'I never say this, I never think it, but I am bloody ashamed of you both. We are waiting to bury your father and yet you two see fit to fight like children before he's even cold? What the hell is wrong with you?'

Merrin looked down, ashamed and belittled. Ruby chewed the inside of her cheek.

But Heather wasn't done. 'This world is full of strangers who couldn't give a rat's arse about your health and happiness, and you can count on one hand the number of people who've got your back. We are Kellows; we stick together! We help each other. I will not allow you to fight, not today, not any day. It's selfish and an indulgence you can't be afforded. Do you understand me, both of you?' She looked from one to the other, her words flat and direct, but her meaning razor sharp.

'Yes, Mum,' Merrin offered first, admonished like a child and awash with the shame that came with it.

'Sorry, Mum,' Ruby seconded.

Heather pulled her shawl around her shoulders and stared at the fire. Her hair was matted and stuck up at the back of her head, her skin had taken on a greyish hue and she had lost so much weight in the shortest time.

'I've lost Ben.' Her tears fell silently and she did nothing to remove them, as if it were her normal state. 'And you've lost your dad. And my whole world is torn apart. I feel . . .' She struggled to find the words. 'I feel as if I'm hanging on by a single thread. One single thread, and I don't mind admitting that it wouldn't take much for me to snip it and fall.' She let this sink in. 'In fact, over the last few days, that thought has been attractive.'

Ruby whimpered and Merrin followed; it was a thought too hard to bear.

'I'm sorry, Mum.' Ruby spoke through her tears.

'You don't have to say sorry to me.' Heather slowly levered herself into a standing position, making her way across the room, reaching for pieces of furniture as if they were handrails as she headed back to the stairs and the comfort of her bed. 'You have to say sorry to your sister.'

'I'm going home.' Ruby grabbed her jacket from the dining table and slipped her arms into it.

'Don't go home, Rubes.' Bella said the words Merrin had been considering.

'I'm knackered.' Ruby rubbed her lower back. 'I'll see you girls tomorrow.'

'We love you!' Bella called from the stove as the front door closed and Ruby walked out into the driving rain.

Despite her fatigue, Merrin knew she wouldn't sleep well tonight. Not now. Instead, she would lie awake, trying to digest the words that filled her throat, their taste bitter and their effect poisonous. The little parlour was usually a haven, but now, with the echo of their fight still bouncing off the walls, it had never felt so small.

'She didn't mean it.' Bella did what she did best and tried to stitch the tear back together.

'I think she did,' Merrin whispered. 'But Mum's right. We've all got enough on our plate right now without Ruby and me falling out. I'm exhausted with it all and I need this petty jealousy to stop. It used to be funny when we were little, arguing over a bit of cake, a toy we both wanted to play with or who had the lion's share of floor space in our bedroom, but now' – she rubbed her tired eyes, thinking of the nights she had replayed the words of their big row and knowing that she had neither the energy nor the inclination to do it again – 'I can't be doing with it, Bells. Can't live waiting for the next flare of aggression to fill my head for months on end. It's not fair.'

'Everyone's tired. Everyone's grieving and everyone is on edge. Things will calm down, Merry.' Bella offered the voice of reason. 'I'm glad you are getting on well with Miguel. You seemed happy enough at Ruby's wedding, and even though I had my doubts about you guys long term, everyone seems to really like him. And I don't want you to be on your own.' Bella spoke softly, as she tucked a blanket around the sleeping Glynn in his pram.

'*You're* on your own and you're doing okay.' She admired her friend more than she could say.

'I'm not, though, am I? I've got this little munchkin. Although I can't pretend I wouldn't rather be raising him with Luuk, but what you gonna do?'

'I hear ya, Bells.' She got up and hugged her friend.

'But we all know it needs more than good looks to make it work. There needs to be love. That brilliant, magical spark.'

'Did you think that's what you had with Luuk: love?' His absence was for her another example of the unreliable nature of those strong feelings.

Bella nodded. 'I do love him. And as daft as it sounds, I know he loves me. His calls are never nasty, he's always kind; he's trying to figure things out and, in a way, I don't want him to sell me a false promise.'

'We all know how that ends,' Merrin quipped.

'It's true; in some ways I admire his honesty. He's only ever been completely open with me. And I him.'

'But he *left* you, Bells. How can you say you love him?'

'Because I do! It's that simple: I love him! And he didn't leave me, he went back to work, jumped on that big old yacht and headed off to Costa Rica, and after he'd gone, I found out I was pregnant.'

'But he should have come back!'

'Maybe.' Bella looked towards the pram, where her heart lay sleeping. 'But I'd rather he didn't if it was only to tell me we have no future and then for me to watch him go again. Glynn is a happy babby who is doing great, and that's all that matters, isn't it?'

'I guess. You're the best mum, Bella. I'm proud of you.' Merrin nodded as she sank down on the sofa. 'And I agree in not complicating matters. Miguel and I are happy, but marriage?' She shook her head.

'You'll figure it out, my girlie, you always do. But don't make any decisions now, not when your brain is fuddled.' Bella smiled at her. 'And I'm proud of you. Look how far you've come.'

There was a knock on the door. This in itself was unusual, as every regular visitor knew the door was unlocked and you only had to open it and pop your head inside to call out your arrival.

'Might be someone dropping off another card.' Bella went to the door.

Merrin looked at the row of 'In sympathy' cards that now lined the shelves and the mantel, feeling grateful for and hating them in equal measure. She yawned and, when she opened her eyes, Bella was standing back to allow none other than Loretta Mortimer into their little home.

It was such a shock to see her there with rain lacing her hair that Merrin couldn't find any words. Instead she stared at the woman, as if glued to the seat.

Digby's mother's manner was uncharacteristically hesitant and she looked down, running her fingers over the heads of the roses and ferns in her hand.

'I was very sorry to hear about your father.' She addressed Merrin directly. 'I brought these for Heather.' She held them out and it was Bella who took them and walked to the sink where a vase lived on the shelf above it.

Merrin felt rooted to the spot.

'I saw Digby.' She hadn't intended on saying anything, but this came out almost instinctively, knowing it was Mrs Mortimer who had sent him.

Loretta nodded. 'Yes. I thought . . . I thought . . .'

'You thought what?' Her voice was surprisingly clear and steady. Gone was the quiet, pleading tone that had wrapped her words that day in the vestry.

'I thought it might do Digby good to have a conversation with you, to lay some ghosts to rest. For you to see him settled and move on and for him to do the same.'

'I am not a ghost, Loretta. I am a *person*: a living, breathing person with feelings!'

'I know.' The woman held her gaze. 'Digby and his family left yesterday and he . . . he wrote to me. I don't think I've ever mulled over any correspondence in such a way.' She looked close to tears. 'I know it by heart.'

'And you are telling me this *why*?' Merrin folded her arms across her chest as her whole body shook. How she hated that this woman was in her home at all, especially at a time like this.

'Because years on the planet gives one a certain perspective that is sometimes hard to see when you are young.' There was the smallest smile to her mouth, as if picturing her young self. 'It's only age and experience that allow you to see the big picture. Helps you understand the ripples of actions that reverberate for a lifetime. And that was why I acted . . . why I intervened.'

'You let me get dressed up and go to the church with the whole of Port Charles watching. You did that to me!' Despite her new-found strength, Merrin's voice cracked at the memory of her dad walking her into the vestry.

'I didn't do it *to* you . . . I just pointed out the facts. Gave him options; the fact that he chose to act how he did confirms I was right all along. He wasn't ready and I knew he wasn't. I tried to see a happy future as we planned your day, but I knew that in the long run I was saving you from a whole lot of heartache, both of you.'

'You know nothing of the sort. You *caused* the heartache! You meddled, pulling strings like we were puppets!'

'For the right reasons!' Loretta looked up with a hint of tears in her eyes and her bottom lip trembled. 'I know what it's like to marry in haste and to live a life feeling sidelined ever after.'

Merrin shot Bella a look, wondering if she was hearing this too. Bella widened her eyes and pulled a face that in any other circumstances would have seen the two rolling about with laughter, but not today.

Loretta straightened and wiped her eyes. 'I might have acted inappropriately, but I did so with the very best intentions.'

Merrin shook her head. There was nothing the woman could say, nothing she could do to make amends.

'Those weren't your choices to make.'

'You're right.' The woman jutted her chin and tidied her hair from her face. 'But trust me when I tell you that a bad marriage, a marriage made in haste, a mistake – can ruin a life. It can *utterly* ruin a life, even if it's a life you thought you wanted. Imagine if you married a drunk, or worse, someone who could never love you because they loved someone else! Imagine becoming the person everyone talks about.' Loretta gasped as if she had spoken too freely.

'Digby's not a drunk, he didn't love someone else!'

'*Digby?*' The woman looked at her quizzically, as if confused.

'Yes! And I did become the person everyone talked about.' Heat rose in her flushed cheeks.

'For a while,' Digby's mother whispered. 'Only for a while. Imagine it for a lifetime.'

'Is that you, Loretta?' Heather called softly from the top of the stairs. 'Come up.'

Merrin felt flustered by her mother's invitation, knowing her dad would have thrown the woman out, just as he had the uniform she had presented to his wife. It was another reminder that he was gone and his absence left them a little exposed, vulnerable even. She heard the creak of floorboards overhead as her mother made her way back to the bed. Loretta turned slowly, and quietly trod the stairs.

Falling back into the chair, weakened by the exchange, Merrin felt her heart clatter in her chest.

'Did that just happen?' she whispered to her friend, who placed the vase of flowers in the middle of the table.

'She's in your house!' Bella looked up as if she, too, could not quite believe the turn of events.

Merrin again thought about the uniform debacle. *Where does she think she lives? Buckingham bloody Palace? She grew up in a caravan at the back of the bog! I won't 'ave it!'*

She wondered what her lovely dad would make of the fact that old Loretta from Mellor Waters was in his bedroom. The thought of him was enough to signal a fresh bout of tears.

CHAPTER TWENTY-THREE

MERRIN

Merrin sat up straight at the table and stared out to sea. It was what her dad would have described as a 'golden day'. Cold, but with a blue sky and that magical bright-after-the-rain feeling that was as fresh as it was hopeful.

'Gallop home, little ones,' she whispered.

'Who you talking to?'

Her mum, sitting to her right, pulled her from her thoughts, but her gaze stayed resolutely on the water. 'The little horses.'

'Little horses,' Heather whispered under her breath. 'He had lots of daft little sayings, didn't he?'

Merrin nodded and pushed the plate with the remainder of her toast across the table.

'Not that hungry, love?'

She shook her head. Her eyes were drawn to Loretta's flowers, which sat in pride of place in the middle of the table.

'Did Loretta tell you we had words?' Merrin felt shy raising it, knowing it was not the main topic, today of all days.

'No, but I heard a bit of it floating up through the floorboards. She was proper cut up, sat on my bed and was quite teary. Not that I was in any state to comfort her.'

Merrin patted her mum's arm. 'It felt good to say things I've wanted to for a while, but I never wanted to upset her.'

'Wasn't only your words, love. She's mournful – often got that way when I was cleaning for her over the years. Everyone has a story, Merrin.'

'I guess so.' She wondered what Loretta's story was.

'Do you mind if I go out for a little walk before the service, Mum? I know Ruby and Jarvis are coming through in a bit and we'll all go to the church together like we've planned, but I need a bit of fresh air. I'll wait right here until they arrive. You won't be on your own.'

'Avoiding your sister?' Heather asked wearily.

'Maybe, but mostly I don't want to make a show of myself in front of everyone and I know if I can take a minute to order my thoughts, I can walk in and do Dad proud.' Her voice caught.

'Your dad was proud, always. So very proud of both of you.'

Merrin reached across and took her mum's hand inside her own. 'Would you like me to do your hair?' She avoided looking at the back of Heather's head, which needed a decent brush through it.

'My hair?' Her mum stared at her as if her words were in a foreign tongue.

'Just so you look nice for the funeral? I could pop the curling tongs on?'

Heather let her head fall forward and reached for the toilet tissue in front of her. 'I only ever bothered about looking nice for Ben, only ever cared what he thought. I can't be bothered with anything, Merrin, not anything. Not if he isn't here! What's the point?' Her sob was loud and unrestrained.

'You won't always feel that way, Mum. I promise.' She hoped this was the truth, as much for her mum's sake as her own. Heather made her arms into a cradle and placed her head on them, again lost to the wearying pull of grief and ignoring her daughter's words of comfort.

Merrin had for the longest time doubted the validity of true love, knowing it could change and be fleeting, proving there was nothing 'true' about it. But to see her mother so broken, so adrift without her Ben by her side . . . it was proof that a deep, true love existed, and to lose it was like losing part of yourself. Her heart ached for her mother, but at the same time swelled with joy that she and Ben had been lucky enough to know such a thing.

The service was at eleven thirty in the morning and by the time Merrin made it up the hill in the black dress and shoes that Miguel had so kindly and thoughtfully packed for her, a borrowed scarf and her coat, the blue sky had taken on a grey bruise. It was the colour only the Cornish coast knew: a special dull, mink grey that filled the big sky, conveying not only the damp chill in the air, but also the misery.

Of course, she hated arguing with Ruby at any time, but especially right now, with so many other upsetting and intrusive thoughts jostling for position in her head. She made the decision to apologise to her sister when the opportunity arose, whether justified or not, but still she was pleased at how she had stood up for herself, not only to Ruby, but to Loretta too. It was all about clearing the air and making things as smooth as possible for her mother. Plus, Ruby was pregnant and any added stress could not be good for her or the baby.

Kicking off her shoes, she found a spot on the verge overlooking the church in the centre of the village and squatted down out of sight, resting on gorse and hidden by the trunk of the great oak tree, on which she rested her palm, taking some small measure of comfort from the history of the place in which she had been born and bred. Leaning against the tree, she pulled the scarf into her neck, not that it stopped her shaking – nothing could. Her cold went all the way to her marrow. She didn't cry. She couldn't. Today her sadness went way beyond tears. Her bare feet anchored her to the spot and helped clear her muddled head in the way that they did. Her heart hurt as much as her head and she felt a little otherworldly.

'I can't believe this is happening, Dad. Can't believe I won't see you . . .' She had learnt over the last few days that a lack of response did not stop her chatting to him.

With a clear view of the neat flint walls surrounding St Michael's, she watched as people began to arrive early. Mrs Everit from the shop with Mr Everit in tow. Dr Levington, his wife and their two children. Mac and Mrs Mac from the pub, and Mr and Mrs Higgins from the butcher's, Robin. Everyone was there. And still they kept coming. Faces she recognised from school and other businesses around Port Charles, neighbours near and far, the vet – everyone, that was, except her own family, who she knew were waiting until the last minute before having to step inside the church, delaying the moment they had to say goodbye to the man they so loved.

A shiny Range Rover pulled up and out popped Loretta. Merrin held her breath and peered at the woman, paying close attention to her and the very red lipstick on her thin lips. And something occurred to her: while she would never be fond of the woman and most likely would never forgive her, gone was the intense hatred she had felt towards her, and more importantly, gone was much of her fear. It was a wonderful realisation that she could bump into her in the street or even the shop without anger and dread in her stomach. In fact, there was no one in the whole town she felt the need to avoid, not any more. She was a Kellow and it was here in Port Charles, a place she had missed so much and where everyone had now turned out to show love for her dad, that she would always belong.

She looked up at the sky and noticed how very still the clouds were, as if not a whiff of breeze dared stir the solemnity of the moment. There were no birds flying overhead; even the resident gulls were silent. And the ocean appeared to have lost its roar. Life was on hold and to Merrin this made sense, as for her, too, time had almost stood still. A quick glance at the church clock told her it was ten minutes past eleven; time to go. She wiped the bottom of her feet and slipped her shoes back on before making her way to the path and walking down the hill, just as her mum, Jarvis and Ruby came alongside the slipway and into view. Their arms were linked, like a depressed cabaret act, all in textures of black and staring down the street with heads that looked heavy as they waited for the hearse, which they would, as agreed, walk behind. Merrin rushed over and stood behind Ruby, before reaching forward and holding her sister close to her in a tight hug.

'I love you, Ruby Mae,' she whispered. 'My big sister.'

Ruby turned her head and smiled through her sore, swollen eyes.

Merrin kissed her cheek and walked to the end of the chain, linking an arm with her mother, who squeezed it against her waist with love.

The car moved slowly into view. It was long, black, shiny and imposing, quite out of place in their little village. It pulled over a little way down the lane and out climbed a man in a black frock coat and a black hat. He nodded ceremoniously at them and moved to the middle of the road, where he walked with solemnity, and the car followed.

The family held each other tight as the vehicle passed them and there in the back lay a pale-wood coffin with shiny handles and a large fish made of flowers lying on the top, perfect for their man of the sea, a son of Cornwall.

With almost perfect choreography, they fell into step behind the car, not crying, not wailing, but leaking their sadness and wiping at eyes that in recent days might have wondered if this was their new permanent state: releasing tears and swelling in response. Heather was strangely silent, walking like a drunk and being held up by those who loved her.

As they started the slow procession, accompanying Ben on his final trip through the place he loved, a sound so mournful and beautiful cracked open the stillness. It was the voice of a male choir, lined up on the terrace of the pub and all with eyes closed and faces turned towards the heavens, singing 'I Am Sailing' – loudly, proudly and beautifully, their deep voices carrying the words higher and higher all the way up to Heaven and out over the sea. There wasn't a soul present who could fail to be moved by the soulful melody, sung in perfect time.

'Did you do this, Jarv?' Heather asked, looking from her son-in-law to the men singing them along their passage.

Jarvis nodded through his tears.

'I thought he'd like it,' he managed.

'Oh, Jarv.' She smiled at him with a hint of life behind her eyes that had been missing for days. 'He'd bloody love it.'

And so they walked together, with the song falling and rising around them, carrying them forward like the tide itself.

◆ ◆ ◆

'Where are you going, Merry?'

'Just for a walk on the beach. I want to get the last of the light.' She grabbed her dad's old yellow oilskin jacket and popped it on, letting the sleeves hang over her hands and liking the scent of him that lingered on it still.

'How are you feeling?' her mum asked softly, her expression tortured, her eyes tired.

'Glad today's nearly over. I'm sad, Mum, a bit numb. I don't really know how to feel.'

Heather nodded, suggesting it was the same for her.

'I'm going to close my eyes in the chair for a minute or two. I know it's early, but I'm done.' Her mum bit her lip and wiped her face with trembling fingers.

'I shan't be long,' she said over her shoulder as she quietly closed the cottage door behind her.

Merrin walked the cobbles and let the cold air of early evening sharpen her thoughts. The moon was full and the sea calm. The sounds of celebration and remembrance and hoots of laughter drifted from the back room of the pub, where Ben's wake was still in full swing for those who had decided to make a night of it. And for the briefest moment in the foggy confusion of grief, she pictured her dad inside, propping up the bar and laughing at whatever merriment was occurring, before the hard lance of realisation made him fade from the picture. The irony was he would have loved today: the singing, the beer, being the centre of attention . . .

At the edge of the coastal path where the steps veered to the left, she began her descent to the beach, treading them with caution as she looked out over the darkening landscape. About halfway down the steps, she sat, running her hand through the air, and reaching back to feel the sandy soil, trod by those whose bloodline she shared.

Home . . .

She drew breath and spoke aloud. 'It's not been my home for a long time now, and yet part of me lives here, always will.'

Her eyes swept over the cove where fragments of her heart and every memory of her beloved dad were lodged in the rocks along the shoreline, the bark of the full and ancient trees that stood proudly on the clifftops, and where his laughter would carry as faint whispers on the summer breeze. She could see him now on the deck of the *Sally-Mae* with his head thrown back and eyes closed, laughing loudly in abandon.

'I wish I could have one more day, Dad. Just one more to tell you that I love you, and that I hope Ruby was speaking in grief and frustration, because the thought of letting you down—' She gulped the sob that built in her chest. 'I want the life you had, Dad: solid, happy, and even one filled with love.' She closed her eyes and thought about Miguel. Her thoughts flew to the night of her engagement to Digby and her dad's words: 'I wish . . . I wish for you both a long and happy marriage like the one we share. Cos I know that without Heather by my side there's no point. She's everythin'. My good mate, my great love and all my happiness.' Her mum's eyes had misted as she wiped her face with a tea towel. That was what Merrin had hoped for. But maybe it was unrealistic; maybe making Miguel happy, even though her feelings were a little muted, would be enough.

CHAPTER TWENTY-FOUR

Jarvis

The bar was full of drunks in their darkest finery, black blazers and suit jackets hung on the backs of chairs like the saddest of skins shed for the purpose of drinking and remembering. Black ties sat askew against throats that were hoarse from singing and shouting as they reminisced about the man they loved and had lost. The windows were steamed up and the floor sticky with booze slopped from unsteady hands. One such pair of hands now made their way to the little corner table where Ben had held court on many a night. The oak tabletop still pulsed with the touch of his hand and the legs were scuffed where his steel-toed boot had kicked as his leg jumped in excitement, as the fisherman's tales grew more elaborate and the jokes more raucous with each sip.

Jarvis felt a bit third party – here but not here; everything had a dream-like quality. When he found himself to be having a good time he'd look around for Ben and his brain would remind him sharply that this was his wake, the news landing like a jab to his gut.

'Here we go, mate.' Robin placed the full pint of beer in front of him on the table.

'Cheers.' Jarvis took a sip. 'It don't seem real.'

'It don't.' Robin stared at him.

There they were, the two survivors of the glorious trio who had sailed the seas, propped up this table and sat for more hours than they cared to recall in the loft of the Old Boat Shed.

'I'm worried about Ruby. It's a lot for her to deal with, what with the babby on the way.'

Robin smiled. 'You have a lot to look forward to, Jarv.' He sipped his pint. 'And I remember your face on the day Merrin was supposed to marry that waste of space – what's his name?'

'Mortimer.'

'That's the one. Good lord, you looked like a ghost of yourself. Ben and I were worried about you.'

''S funny, Robin, I remember how I felt.' He shook his head. 'Like my heart had been pulled out through my chest and replaced with a rock. I couldn't sleep, couldn't eat.'

'I know what that feels like.' His friend nodded. 'You was in a bad way, that's for sure.'

'I was.' Jarvis nodded, recalling that intense level of hurt. 'Looking back, it all feels a bit daft. I think I'd never really got upset or angry over my dad leaving, and then to have Merrin, my first kind of girlfriend, marry someone else . . . it was all too much. All of my sadness and all of my rejection came out in one big gulp and it was hard. But Merrin, even though she's a sweet, lovely girl, she was never for me. We were kids when we knocked about together and I think she was one of the only people to be kind and take an interest in me back then, but nothing happened, really. It was a non-event and I overthought it. It felt like the end of the bloody world, which is more than a little embarrassing. My mum said at the time, "Love can be fickle," and I didn't know what that meant, but she was right. When I started spending time with Ruby, it's like I saw her for the first time, despite having known her for years, and that was it: I loved her – properly, properly loved her.'

'You old softie, Jarv!'

'No shame in that.' He sipped his pint. 'Not that I'm talking to my mother at the moment.'

'Not talking to Nancy? What's she done to deserve that?'

'She's rented out my bloody room! Got herself a lodger.'

'Well, why not? It's money in the bank and there's plenty of folk who want a room with a view like yours.'

'Yes, but that's the point – it's *my* room. Supposing I want to leave Ruby for a night in protest if we have a row.'

'Jarv, mate, have you met your mother? She'd march you straight back to Ruby's doorstep with a thick ear!'

'You're probably right, but I dunno, I don't like the idea of some stranger sleeping up there. It was my space. The place Ben built for me.'

He pictured his teenage self mid-renovation, with Ben barking orders that kept him occupied, gave him purpose. And there it was again, that punch to the gut.

'And now you don't need it, cos you are a grown-ass man,' Robin teased.

'Suppose so, but it still don't feel right. I'm glad Ben knew we were having a babby, he was excited right enough; used to talk about all the things he was going to do with the boy. Take him fishing, of course, and to the stands at Truro FC.'

'You know it's a boy then?' Robin asked.

'No! That was just Ben's intuition.' The mention of him was enough to fire a bolt of grief that speared him. Jarvis looked towards the door. 'I keep expecting him to walk in. I keep looking for him down at the harbour or in here.'

'Me too.' Robin looked down and, to Jarvis's surprise, big, fat tears rolled from the man's chin. 'I miss him, Jarv! I miss the old bastard!'

'I know, mate. I know.' Jarvis placed his hand on the man's shoulder and let his own tears fall. 'I miss him too.'

CHAPTER TWENTY-FIVE

Merrin

Merrin's eyes were fixed on the slowly rising sun, captivated as ever by the spectacle. It was two days after the funeral and that afternoon she was heading back to Thornbury, her train ticket booked. She catalogued the view, knowing she would be walking away from it soon enough.

'Merrin?' The call was low yet firm. She looked around from where she stood on the cobbles, surprised to see Heather up and out of bed and standing in front of the cottage, although she was still in her long, white nightdress with her dressing gown wrapped tightly around her and thick socks on her feet to ward off the chill. Her complexion looked a little brighter, her eyes a little clearer. It was a start, no more.

'You okay, Mum?'

'I am, but I need to speak to you and your sister. Can you go fetch her and both come inside?' Without waiting for a reply, she turned and made her way into the cottage.

Merrin looked up to the bedroom that used to be Granny Ellen's, as Ruby looked out and opened the window.

'Mum wants to talk to us both,' she called up. 'Now.'

'Bit early, isn't it?' Ruby rubbed at her face and yawned.

Merrin shrugged and splayed her hands to indicate she didn't know what was going on.

'Close the door, please,' her mum instructed as she settled into the chair in front of the blazing fire. Merrin did as she was asked and sat on the sofa. Ruby came in, still in her pyjamas and thick socks, and sat next to her. They both arranged one of the woollen blankets that lived on the arms of the chairs over their knees and sat like kids, awaiting further instruction. The air crackled with anticipation.

'Jarv just told me Loretta came here.' Ruby glanced at her, her tone carrying the vaguest hint that she was aggrieved Merrin hadn't told her.

'She did.' Heather spoke softly, but unapologetically. 'I worked for her for the longest time and we used to talk. I think she saw me as her friend, believe it or not.'

Merrin shifted in her seat. 'And did you see her as a friend?' She knew the answer might be conflicting: how could anyone treat a friend's daughter in the way she had treated Merrin?

Heather drew breath. 'I felt sorry for her; I don't think she had many people to talk to, still doesn't.' She took her time. 'She's a foolish woman, a vain one, a snob too, but I don't think she's evil. Your dad never liked us being friends, but yes, I think we were. Think we are,' she corrected. 'She used to talk openly to me while I cleaned. And I never made too much comment, just got on with the job, which I think suited her too.'

'I didn't know that, Mum.' It felt strange to see their relationship in this new light and she suspected Heather had played down their friendship, because she was right, her dad would have had a strong opinion on it.

'There are things, Merry, that . . .' – her mum paused and looked to the fire, as if that was where the words might lurk – '. . .

that happened a long time ago that reflect on her and on us in some ways. *Things* that maybe Digby is unaware of and that a woman like Loretta, for whom reputation is everything, might have felt too difficult to face.'

'Could you be any more vague?' Merrin was curious.

'Why are you defending her? What kind of things?' Ruby was, as ever, more direct, but still asked with a respectful softness in recognition of their situation, when on any other day, Merrin guessed, she would have yelled.

'I'm not defending her, Ruby, just trying to explain. And as for what things, it's not my story to tell, but know that for Loretta Mortimer one of the worst things in the world would be the feeling that she was second choice, second best. She's spent her whole life trying to run from that very thing.'

'Because she was born in a swamp?' Ruby asked without sarcasm, but rather with emotion to her tone, as if her mother's words had resonated.

'Something like that.' Heather smiled sweetly at her girls. 'Anyway, I didn't ask you both to come in to talk about Loretta; there's something I need to do.' She shook her head and slowly reached for her glasses and a folded piece of paper that lay on the table. The clock ticked loudly on the wall.

'This . . . this is a little bit odd, but I've been given my instructions.' She managed a small smile that didn't quite reach her eyes. 'I have a letter to read to you, so pop another log on the fire and both get comfy. And don't speak until I've finished – that's part of my instruction: "Don't let them speak until you've finished." It says it right here.' She pointed at the sheet of paper now nestling in her hands.

'A letter from who?' Ruby asked the question Merrin had wanted to, before putting a cushion behind her back on the sofa while Merrin did as she was asked and jumped up and retrieved a log from the wicker basket with the frayed edge and tossed it into the grate, before settling back under the blanket.

Heather held her gaze and answered slowly. 'It's . . . it's from your dad. A letter from your dad.'

'Oh!' Merrin felt her stomach fold with loss and didn't know if she could bear to listen. Ruby whimpered softly and buried her face in her hands.

Heather Kellow cleared her throat and began.

> Bloody doctors! I told them this heart has faced storms, the wildest seas you can imagine, and even the wrath of my missus when I've come home late and dinner is spoilt! It's seen me right every day of my life and now they're telling me it's failing? Load of old baloney! But just in case, I figured I'd better get some stuff down on paper and send a copy off to our shark of a solicitor!

Heather paused to catch her breath, and looked briefly at her and Ruby sitting close together as she smoothed the letter in her palm. The wood in the grate flared into life. Merrin, like her sister, was in tears before her mother read another word. The ache to see her dad was physical.

> My Girls, this is a letter I don't want to write; in fact, I hate writing all letters, as you know, and I ain't too keen on receiving them, neither. But such is my love for you all I will give it my best. First thing to say, that Dr Levington is a born idiot! I need to put that in writing so that when I might find these sheets of paper tucked away in my bedside drawer as I wait for me telegram

> from our trusty monarch, I can rightfully say, 'I told you so!' But that aside, Levington reckons me old ticker is on the blink. I did suggest a good old squirt of WD40, as in my experience it fixes most things, but he looked at me like *I* was the idiot, if you can believe that!

Heather shook her head and took a moment, as if to let a chirp of happiness form in her breast. Ruby let out a half-laugh and Merrin joined her. It was some skill that Ben had: the ability to make them laugh in this, the saddest of moments, to raise their spirits and offer some small relief when they needed it the most.

> All joking aside. What will be will be, my loves. I been doing a lot of thinking recently and I know I would be hard pushed to say which was the prettiest sunset I've ever seen, the best day of fishing, the best roast potato or the sweetest pint in the pub – all of these things I love! But I can, without a moment of hesitation, tell you when I am the happiest: and it's when I am sat at our little table with a fire in the grate and your three faces in front of me.

Merrin looked towards the table and saw her dad sitting there, smiling at them all. Her loss spilt from her – a pure and all-consuming thing that left her feeling wretched. Ruby reached for her hand and they sat, hand in hand, while their mother continued to read aloud.

> Heather, my girl and my love, what did I do right to get you, eh? Something, that's for sure. Marrying you has meant a blessed life and the

> truth is, if I lived from now until the end of time and told you every second of every day how much I loved you, it would still not come close to conveying just how much. But I do, Heather. I love you beyond words, beyond life and I always will. Thank you for loving me. It is surely the greatest gift you can bestow upon one another: to love and be loved.

Her voice caught and she coughed to clear her throat, speaking through her tears.

This, this was the glorious love that Merrin wanted to wait for. The words were honest and moving: *he would love her beyond life . . .* It was beautiful and he was right: to give and receive such love was the greatest gift.

> Ruby Mae – my feisty little Ruby Mae. How I love you, my firstborn. You have been a bundle of delight since the moment you landed in our lives! You amaze me. You're strong and sharp and I don't think there is a situation in the whole world that can get you down for long. You have made me laugh on more days than you haven't, and what a gift is that. Always there to keep an eye on your mum and sister – I know you are going to be the best mum to your little 'un. What a lucky little babby to choose you and that great lump Jarvis. He's a good man; I love him like my own and I must admit I'll rest a little easier knowing he's holding your hand. I've left him *Sally-Mae* in my will so he can build up the business into the fleet he dreams of and do his best to keep the

> Kellows and the Cardys in fish for generations to come! And to you, Rubes, I leave the number two cottage, your home. Yours on paper now too. Official.

'Oh, my God!' Ruby's hand flew over her mouth as she took great gulps of air to fuel her sob. 'I can't believe it!'

'You deserve it, Ruby. Jarv, too. It's wonderful.' Merrin gripped her sister's hand.

'Thank you, Dad!' Ruby sobbed.

Her mum smiled at Ruby, and Merry wondered what he might have to say to her and braced herself as Heather continued.

> And Merrin Mercy, my littlest. I love you, Merry. I love you to the big old moon and back again. I'll keep this short: I've left you the Old Boat Shed with planning permission to turn it into a house.'

The news was shocking and thrilling all at once and she gasped. 'Really? Oh, Dad! I can't believe it! Mum, I . . . I don't know what to say!'

It was Ruby's turn to squeeze her fingers. Heather looked lovingly at her daughters, unified in joy and sorrow, then she shook the paper and recommenced reading.

> When you're ready and you've done enough adventuring and figuring out, come home, Merrin. Come back to Port Charles, this little place where your spirit lingers even after you've driven off in Vera Wilma Brown. Walk the beach barefoot in all weathers, my little wanderin' maid,

and let yourself be. Be open to what is right in front of your very eyes and let yourself be happy.

Merrin smiled through her tears. *I will, my daddy, I will . . .*

That's it, my girls. Look after each other. Hold each other close. Drink tea. Sit in the sunshine. Celebrate the good. Don't dwell on the bad. Know that you girls made me a king. A bloody king! And Rubes, don't punch anything, ever again.

Your dad. Your husband.

Ben Kellow. X

There was a moment of weighted silence during which Heather smiled in spite of herself, ignoring the tears that pooled in her eyes, just as Merrin and her sister did the same, snuffling and laughing and shaking their heads as if still not quite able to believe what they had been gifted. Their father's words were like a soft, gentle broom, starting to sweep away the sadness of his loss, starting to help them heal.

'Poor old Dr Levington!' Heather tutted, wiping her nose on her handkerchief. 'Your dad's right, though: we can miss him, mourn him, but we mustn't let guilt or bickering be his legacy. Do you understand me?'

Her words were pointed and firm as she looked between her daughters. Merrin nodded and felt Ruby do likewise.

'Now.' She sighed deeply, rubbing at the deep furrows etched across her brow, a reminder that she, like them, was still in the first stages of deep grief. 'I want to go back to my bed.' Heather stood slowly and walked to the door, then, gripping the frame, she turned to face her daughters. 'Your dad isn't the only one who loves you fiercely. I do too. My flesh and blood. My girls. I'm quite sure you've both got a lot to talk about.' Her words were gently spoken, but felt very much like an instruction.

Merrin and Ruby stared at each other a little sheepishly and let go of each other's hand. Her parents were right: they had to draw a roadmap of how to go forward without the bickering or negativity that had the power to slay the other's confidence. The fact that it happened at all was as ridiculous as it was damaging.

'Shall we go sit outside for a bit?' Merrin asked tentatively, knowing the view and the fine sea air would be lost to her once she jumped on that train – that and it was easier to talk looking straight ahead.

Ruby nodded and they grabbed coats and hats from the rack by the front door and carried the thick blankets to place over their legs. They sat on the wide, low wall with the best view of the bay in the whole of Port Charles. Side by side, just as they had been doing since they were toddlers while their mum cut their hair or their dad stood alongside telling them tales of the big old ocean.

The golden winter sun loomed large in the morning sky, splintering the moody clouds with its rays as the white foam of the waves broke against the rocks along the foreshore. The two girls pulled their coats about their shoulders and Merrin wiggled her toes inside the knitted socks on her feet. The air was still and salty and even the gulls were subdued, as if acknowledging that life would never be the same again.

'You're very quiet.' Her sister nudged her with her elbow.

'Yeah, for the first time since the day I was supposed to marry I don't think I want to leave. I don't feel scared of the place, the gossip, the rumour, like I did.'

'So don't then.'

'I have to, really, Rubes. I have a job, responsibilities, and all my things are in Thornbury. Plus, I need to talk to Miguel. And what would I do here?'

'I don't know, build that house?' They both looked over towards the Old Boat Shed.

'Can't believe it's mine. And the cottage is yours. All that lovely history of Gran and Gramps and now you and Jarv and the babby.'

'Property owners – us? It's wonderful, isn't it?' Ruby looked over her shoulder at the bricks and mortar that made up her home.

'It really is.' The glorious fact was still sinking in.

'I love the little place.' Her sister beamed.

'I know you do.'

'And Jarv gets the boat – he will be made up; more than made up. Can't wait to tell him.' Ruby stared at the little trawler moored against the harbour wall. 'He loved me, didn't he?'

'Dad?'

Ruby straightened and nodded, her expression one of embarrassment, as if she hadn't intended to say the words out loud.

'Of course he did. He loved you so much!' Merrin hoped that this message had finally sunk in and that her sister would go forward without the snarky chip on her shoulder.

Ruby's smile was wide and softened her pretty face.

'I guess what I meant when I said I don't want to leave is that I don't want to leave you and Mum,' said Merrin.

'We'll be fine. She's got me and I've got Jarv.'

Merrin dug deep and found the confidence to speak. 'I don't want you to ever feel jealous about me and Jarvis: it's nuts and unnecessary and hurtful. I swear to—'

'I know, Merry.' Ruby interrupted her and held her gaze. 'I know. I think it might be my hormones and—'

'And what?' She pulled the blanket around her legs and turned to face her sister, wanting to have this conversation, no matter how painful, knowing it was open communication that would take them forward. Her dad had paved the way with his beautiful letter. 'What is it you were going to say?'

Ruby looked into the middle distance. 'I don't want to say it,' she said slowly.

'Come on, whatever it is, it's better out of your mouth than sticking in your throat, where it'll only go bad until you *have* no choice but to spit it out!'

Ruby took a deep breath. 'When you left Port Charles, after Digby—'

'Yep.' It was Merrin's turn to interrupt, with no desire to go over the details of that day again.

'Mum and I gave nearly all the presents back to the people who had sent them, apart from a bottle of champagne from someone at the Rotary Club, which we drank when we ran out of blackberry wine.'

'That's fair enough.' Merrin let her mouth twitch in the beginnings of a smile.

'There were a load of cards, all unopened, and there was one in a shiny gold envelope. It was from Jarvis.'

'Right. Yes.' She vaguely remembered him dropping one off and the girls ribbing her.

'I don't know why,' Ruby began, 'but I opened it.'

'What did it say?' Her curiosity surged along with her fear; did she really want to know if Jarvis had made some misplaced declaration? She knew it could only make her feel awkward in his company and stoke the fires of her sister's ire.

'It said' – Ruby swallowed – 'something along the lines of, "Have a nice day, but if things with Digby don't work out, then I will always be there for you."'

'Well, that was kind. He *is* kind. Maybe he had a sixth sense.' She felt more than a little bit uncomfortable, but figured it could have been worse.

'It felt like . . .' Ruby chose her words slowly. 'It felt like he was saying, "*Pick me, Merry! Pick me!*"'

'Don't be ridiculous! Of course he wasn't! That's nuts. He was just being a good friend, being funny. Don't forget he wrote it thinking Digby and I were going to open it together; he'd hardly have written that if he was being serious, would he?' she reasoned.

'I guess not. It just hurts me, because I always liked him, loved him even, and the thought that he might have had deep feelings for you—'

'He didn't.' She spoke sharply. 'We were kids, and if Digby and I had opened that card you would never have seen it and never have had those crackers thoughts. Have you asked Jarvis about it?'

'Yes. He said he doesn't even remember writing it.'

'There we go!'

'I think about it a lot,' Ruby confessed.

'Well, don't. Stop it! It's stupid and destructive and we've just lost our dad – our family's got a little bit smaller, and Dad's right: we need to be tight and close and supportive. We have never needed each other more than we do right now. We need to look after each other, hold each other close, celebrate the good and not dwell on the bad. That's what he said.'

'You're right.' Ruby nodded. 'I'm tired of feeling mad at you because of my own stupid insecurity. It's like it's built up. It started as a joke when we were kids, but then I didn't know how to stop it, how to be different. I do love you, Merry.'

'And I love you.' She felt a lightness to her being as Ruby's posture softened and she and her sister sat quietly in an atmosphere of calm.

'I wish my babby had met Dad.' Her lips trembled.

Merrin reached for her hand and held it, mitten to mitten. 'I remember saying once to him that I wished Gramps was here, and he told me he was, and I think the same. I think Dad's here with us, and so are Gran and Gramps; I think they always will be.'

'I think so too.' Ruby wiped her nose on her sleeve. 'We're going to be okay, aren't we, Merry?'

'We sure are. We're Kellow girls.'

'Kellow girls,' Ruby repeated.

'Oi!' Bella shouted from the top of Fore Street, waving from the other side of the slipway as she pushed baby Glynn in his pram in the early-morning sun.

'She's got some gob on her,' Ruby noted.

'She has. I sometimes hear her yell when I'm in Thornbury.'

They both laughed a little, as much as their sadness would allow.

Bella came close and jumped up on to the wall with baby Glynn snug as a bug, asleep and swaddled warmly in his pram.

'Look at us all up and out like early birds!' Merrin commented.

'Actually, I haven't been to bed,' Bella corrected her. 'Not in the way we used to in the olden days when I didn't have to be a responsible adult and we danced till dawn, but in the way that I got drinking tea, and then before I knew it, the sun was coming up, and here I am. I thought the funeral was the best it could be.' Bella smiled. 'I think we did Ben proud and Jarv did so good with them singers.'

'He really did.' Ruby beamed with a pride that was heartening.

'And you're heading back to Thornbury and Miguel this afternoon?' Bella pulled a sad face.

'I am; need to find a way to hide my eyes that I've cried into little puffy slits and my sore nose that won't stop running. I look a right state.'

'Didn't your mother ever tell you it is what's inside that counts?'

'Oh, Bells! Says the girl who won't go out to the doorstep to collect the milk if she hasn't got her push-up bra in place,' Ruby tutted.

'I wasn't talking about what *my* mother told me, I was talking about what *her* mother told *her*!' Her friend gave the thin defence.

'Do you really believe that, Bells? That the outside wrapping doesn't matter?' Ruby snorted her laughter. 'Cos you sure used to spend a lot of time making sure you were nicely wrapped!'

'Truthfully?' Bella seemed to consider this. 'I think men want the whole package. They want you to be funny, smart and sexy.'

'What about what we want?' Merrin asked a little sheepishly.

'The same, I think, and why not?' Bella stood her ground.

'Agree.' Ruby looked up to the bedroom window where her husband slept. 'I guess I got lucky with my Jarv.'

She and Bella looked from one to another, as if not quite seeing the same level of appeal, but knowing what voicing it would mean, even in jest.

'You sure did.' Merrin snuggled up to her sister.

'I can't see myself dating any time soon.' Bella checked on Glynn. 'It's not the dating that bothers me as much as the idea of stripping off in front of a stranger . . .' She exhaled. 'Sure, I can glam up the outside, but I caught sight of myself in the mirror yesterday and I've got this bulge of tummy that now hangs over my knickers and stretch marks that have destroyed my once immaculate boobs. Honestly, my chest looks like a map of the Nile Delta. I can't imagine any man finding me remotely attractive. I think I might have to face the fact that the Flying Dutchman might actually be the last man to see me naked and dancing in the candlelight.'

Merrin and Ruby stared at her, and then at each other. Merrin wondered if her sister, like her, was thinking she'd never had the confidence to dance naked in the candlelight, stretch marks or not.

'And there's no chance of anything happening with him?' Ruby asked gently. 'I know you really liked him. We all did, but I can't say I'm so keen now after how he's treated you, just running off like that.'

'I did. I do.' Bella smiled warmly at her baby boy. 'And in his defence—'

'There is no defence!' Ruby asserted.

'*In* his defence,' Bella carried on regardless, 'it was not meant to be any more than a fling and, as I told Merry, he didn't know about the baby until he was back at sea on the other side of the world. But that ship has definitely, metaphorically and physically, sailed. I hear from him, he sends money for Glynn and we get the odd text and call, but . . .' She shook her head.

'You could always find a man with failing sight, or better still, one that lives in a dark cave and only wears gloves. That way he won't be able to feel your saggy skin or see it.'

'You are not making me feel any better, Rubes,' Bella tutted.

'Oh, you should have said!' Ruby laughed. 'If it's reassurance you're after, then, Bells, you absolute goddess, you have the body of a supermodel and skin like peaches! In fact, scrap that, I don't want you to think I am referring to your top-lip fuzz.' She touched her finger to her own top lip.

'Top-lip fuzz?' Bella squealed, running her finger around her mouth. 'Do I have top-lip fuzz? Did you know about the top-lip thing?' she asked Merrin directly, who shook her head, but looked away.

'For the love of God! Well, that's that then: dark-cave-dwelling, glove-wearing man it is . . . And you can laugh, Ruby Mae, but in a few short months you too will be pushing a small human from your tuppence and then we'll see who's laughing!'

'I hate you,' Ruby spat.

'I know, but you are stuck with me.' Bella grinned. 'You both are.'

'Digby Mortimer turned up at Milbury Court. On the night Dad died.' Merrin let this drop like it was incidental.

'You're actually kidding me right now?' Ruby stared at her.

'I'm not.'

'When?' her sister practically yelled, 'Jesus! You didn't think that was worth sharing?'

'Believe it or not, I've had one or two things on my mind,' Merrin shot back.

'What did he want, pitching up after all this time? The prick,' Ruby added for good measure.

'He didn't want anything! He didn't know I was working there.' She pictured his lovely wife, smiling and chatting, and then his ashen face when he'd walked in . . .

'And actually, I think it did you good, don't you, Merry? It sounds like you laid some old ghosts to rest,' Bella added.

'Oh, and of course you *knew* about this?' Ruby snapped, but with humour and not spite; it felt good to be able to speak this freely.

'She answered the phone from the cupboard!' Bella yelled in her own defence, pointing at Merrin as if whatever was amiss were her fault. They laughed and Merry realised this was just like old times, the three of them chatting the morning away without the shadow of bitterness from one of her and Ruby's squabbles falling over them. It felt like progress, it felt like love, it felt like home. And if she closed her eyes, she could kid herself that her dad was inside, upstairs with her mum, and that Digby Mortimer hadn't nearly succeeded in throwing her so wildly off course. This was the truth: he had not succeeded, because here she was, a little adrift and in mourning, but undoubtedly stronger than she had been. Like a house rebuilt after a flood or a tornado – rebuilt stronger than before, able to withstand whatever life threw at her because she had come through the storm.

'A home.' She looked out over the boat shed.

'What did you say?' Bella cocked her ear to better hear.

'My home. The Old Boat Shed. It's mine.' She beamed, as a plan took shape in her mind.

◆ ◆ ◆

Miguel met her from the train station, placed her small suitcase on the back seat and drove her out to Thornbury.

'I'm so glad you're back.' He kept glancing at her as he navigated the lanes, as if almost unable to believe she had returned, but also something else – possibly a sixth sense that she carried news he might not want to hear. 'I had a word with Lionel and you've got today and tomorrow to get yourself together and aren't on the rota until Friday.'

'Thank you.' She meant it, as ever, truly grateful for his thoughtfulness.

'I thought this afternoon you could just nap and I'll bring you a nice supper and you can settle back in.'

She nodded, not able to deny that a nap sounded tempting, but knowing there were more pressing things to attend to. The castle looked a little gloomy in the winter light and was without a peacock in sight as she kicked off her shoes and lay on the bed. Her heart suddenly filled with longing for her dad. Her grief did this: hit her like a wave that could knock her off her feet with only the smallest of provocations.

'Hey, don't cry!' Miguel dropped down by the side of the bed and knelt on the floor, smoothing her forehead. 'I am so sad for you, for your whole family. I wish I could make it better.'

She stared at the sweet man and sat up straight, her tears contained. For now.

'The night you left, I had plans that went horribly wrong. It was one of the worst nights I can remember, but I know it was much, much worse for you, Merrin. First that creep turning up, and then your dad . . .'

'Miguel, we need to talk,' she began.

'I know.' He gave a half-smile but his eyes spoke of sorrow.

She placed her hand over her mouth and sat very still, while trying to order the words that had been forming in her mind since that very night.

'Miguel, you are the most wonderful human being. I love you in my own way. I do! But . . .'

'I don't want there to be a "but",' he whispered.

'But, I don't want to marry you and I know that's what you were thinking of.' She knew that straight talking would make all the difference when he looked back on it.

'I was. *I am*,' he corrected. 'So what about what *I* want?' He looked up at her and her heart broke at the sadness that dressed his face. 'Everything is always on your terms, Merrin, but what about what *I* want?' he repeated.

She hated that she was hurting this lovely man because she could not give him what he wanted. An image of Digby floated into her mind and she wondered if he had felt similar. It was both revealing and distressing how easy it was to harm another when one person's emotions were out of sync with the other's.

'I want *you*.' He swallowed his tears.

She spoke without hesitation. 'I've had the brakes on for so long, emotionally, and that's made it impossible for me to fall in love. I haven't liked who I've become, Miguel; I haven't liked this half-life, hiding away here and pretending at happiness. And I know any woman would be so lucky to be asked by you, it's me who's—'

'Don't!' He held up his hand, his tone sharper than she was used to. 'Just don't, Merrin.'

Curling her hand into her lap, she stopped speaking. He was right, he deserved more than an old platitude dredged from the book of what to say when you want out. They sat in silence for a beat or two, the atmosphere weighted with acute embarrassment, shock and, on her part, a gnawing feeling of guilt.

'I think you're wonderful and you deserve to be with someone who loves you in the way you need them to. I care about you, Miguel. I have loved spending time with you and your kindness is something I will always treasure, but I need to go home and I came back to tell you goodbye and to hand in my notice.'

'Do you know, I think it's kind of worse.' He jumped up from the floor and paced. 'It is. It's shit to know you would have been happy to let us drift, working our shifts, having sex at the weekends and eating warmed-up leftovers in front of the television, for how long? *For ever?* While I thought we had a destination, a plan, marriage, kids, the lot . . . I feel so bloody stupid!'

'I don't want you to feel stupid. That's the last thing I want. You are nothing but kindness. And in the long run . . .' She wanted to make things, if not better, then as easy as possible. 'I think too much of you to let you linger on in hope, or worse, receive some flimsy excuse over the phone as to why we are not suited. That would be cowardly, and I'm not a coward. Trust me that it's better we talk this way. No matter how hard.'

Miguel kept his eyes on the floor. 'I'm so disappointed. Gutted.'

'I take it as nothing but the most incredible compliment that you could even consider feeling the way you do about me. Because you are wonderful.'

'And good-looking.' He looked up at her as his tears pooled, despite his crack at humour.

'You are, Miguel. Incredibly good-looking.' She felt the creep of tears at the fact that she was cutting loose from this human who was beautiful both inside and out.

'What are you going to do now?' he asked, coughing to clear his throat.

Merrin looked out through the French windows and gasped as a peacock strutted into view, his tail spread to reveal a stunning broad fan of teal and gold, shimmering in all its glory. It was breathtakingly beautiful. A fine farewell to this chapter of her life.

'I'm going to pack up and go home.' She smiled softly with the joy surging through the rocks of her grief. 'I'm going home.'

CHAPTER TWENTY-SIX

Merrin

Merrin stood on the wooden balcony with her wool pashmina about her shoulders, taking a minute before she whacked on the radio and picked up the paintbrush for the evening. She closed her eyes, feeling the last of the day's sun warm her spirit as surely as the cup of tea in her hands. How she loved this house; she was happy they had managed to retain the original footprint and the rugged features that showed its age. But more than how it looked was how it felt: the peace of it, particularly this little spot looking out over the cove. The renovation was nearly complete and then she could start thinking about furniture, plants and cushions – all the exciting finishing touches that, when funds allowed, would make this place perfect.

She had started the project a little over a year ago with Jarvis, Robin, Mac and others providing the labour in their spare time for the love of Ben. Merrin knew she would be forever grateful to this community, *her* community. Between her job on reception at the Port Charles Hotel and the odd cleaning shift Nancy offered, she too had picked up tools. Physical labour, she found, was the perfect distraction from her mourning, diverting her sadness through the hauling of lumber, the sawing of wood, the hammering of nails and the laying of the floor. It felt good to take out her frustrations and sense of loss on joists, lumps of metal and vigorously mixed buckets of plaster.

'I tell you something, Jarv,' she had stated one afternoon, as they smashed out wood to put in a window. 'Doing this kind of thing makes me feel better, helps me forget. Do you know what I mean?'

He had laughed and wiped his eyes. 'I know exactly what you mean.'

'I'm glad we're mates, Jarv. Always have been, haven't we?' The fondness she felt for her brother-in-law was in no small part down to the way he treated her sister and his beautiful baby girl, Katie-Ellen Kellow-Cardy.

'We have, Merry. Always will be.'

'Yeah, but he picked the best sister, didn't you, Jarv?' Ruby yelled comically from the leather chair in which she rocked her little one.

'I did, my love.' He winked at Merrin. 'I certainly did.'

Ruby beamed, wrapped in the bubble of love that had surrounded her, Jarvis and Katie-Ellen since the baby had arrived with much fanfare in the middle of the night some eleven months ago.

Merrin had laughed, happy how they could talk freely, jest freely, without repercussions. Looking after each other. Holding each other close. Just as their dad had asked.

It was still unbelievable and incredible to her that the Old Boat Shed was hers. The plans had been drawn for an 'upside down' house with the living room and kitchen on the first floor to take full advantage of the unrivalled view, with bedrooms and a bathroom below. It had the potential to become a home beyond her wildest dreams. And during construction, Heather had been more than happy to have her ensconced back in her old bedroom. Merrin remembered her saying how she only slept well when everyone she loved was under her roof. And even when she moved out, at least she could still see the front door of the cottage from the side of this balcony and Ruby, Jarvis and baby Katie-Ellen were only on the other side of Heather's wall.

She closed her eyes and felt the pull of fatigue, but shook it off, knowing the newly plastered walls were not going to paint themselves. All she needed to do was tear herself away from the view that was all hers.

The sharp ring of her phone roused her.

'Can't believe Glynn's going to be two soon.' This Bella's opener.

'Me either,' she yawned. 'This last year has flown by, hasn't it?'

'Sure has. Where are you?'

'Where do you think I am?'

'Yeah, stupid question. How long till you move in? And more importantly, how long before the house-warming?' Bella asked eagerly.

'I reckon another couple of months and one day. It's going to be beautiful.'

'It is. Your mum seemed on good form today. I saw her in the shop.'

'I think it's harder for her to feel low with Katie-Ellen around.' It was true, the baby girl had given Heather a wonderful, much-needed lift, though even the little latest addition could not entirely fill the void left by Ben. 'And I know I'm biased, Bells, but she is the sweetest little thing ever.'

'She is that.'

'Ruby said last week that she's planning for her and Glynn to marry. Jarvis shot us a look that made me think he wasn't quite so on board with the idea.' Merrin laughed.

'She'll marry who she chooses. Maybe she won't marry at all.'

She thought of Digby and his face in the corridor, his apology, and now she was able to consider it with time passed, it meant the world. And this in turn led to an image of Miguel, beautiful, kind Miguel . . . she wished him well.

'I liked Miguel.' Bella read her thoughts.

'*I* liked Miguel! It was never about not liking him, it was about not *loving* him.'

'He loved you,' Bella stated.

'Yep, I think he did, but I guess that kind of sums it up.'

'What do you mean?' She heard Bella reach for a crisp and cram it in her mouth, speaking through the crunch.

'I mean, the idea that he was happy loving me without digging deep, without truly understanding how I felt about him. I get the impression that the way he loved me was enough for him.'

'Wasn't it like that for you and Digby? Wouldn't you have waltzed back to him had he welcomed you with open arms when you went to meet him up at Reunion Point?'

'That's different.' She blinked.

'How?' Bella crunched another crisp.

'Because he sold me the dream! He *told* me he loved me deeply, unconditionally, and I fell for it. With Miguel I never told him that. I thought I was straight with him.'

'But he hoped for something different.'

'I guess, and how can we account for someone's hope? How are we supposed to modify our behaviour to take that into account?' She wondered if her friend was thinking about Luuk.

'I guess you can't.' Bella paused. 'Lots of women would jump at the chance to marry a guy like Miguel: good-looking, kind, sociable . . .'

'I know all of that, but loving someone is so much more than that, isn't it? It's about that magic ingredient that you can't define, something that sets a person apart from everyone else you know – to the point where no one else exists or could exist for you romantically.'

'And you didn't feel that for him?' Bella's tone was soft, as if she understood that feeling.

Merrin shook her head. 'Not even close, and I wish I had, because on paper . . .'

'Oh, on paper!' Bella interrupted sharply. 'On paper I should be living in domestic bliss with my handsome yachtsman and our beautiful boy, but in reality, he's sunning himself in warmer climes and I'm sat here, sleep deprived and eating cheese-and-onion crisps. Life sucks sometimes!'

'Sometimes it does.' Merrin drew a slow breath. 'It's not logical, love, is it? You can't really define it and you can't really explain it. You can't chase it or hold on to it and yet sometimes you can't let it go.'

'And you can't know when it will come knocking at your door and pull you into its web.'

'If it comes knocking at all,' Merrin asserted.

There was a loud knock at the door, so loud that even Merrin heard it down the line, and they both laughed.

'Does it make you broody? Spending time with your little niece?'

'Nah, too busy to be broody.'

'Is that right?' Bella tutted, before her tone suddenly changed. 'Oh, shit! Oh, my God!'

'You all right, Bells?' She stood still, suddenly alert and wondering what she could do from this distance, should there be an incident at Bella's mum's house.

'Yeah, it's . . . he's on the path, by the front door! I just looked out. It looks like . . . Oh, my . . . oh, my God . . .' Bella gasped.

'Bella! You're scaring me. What's going on? Are you okay? Do you want me to come up? I can be there in minutes?'

'He's . . . he's at the window. He's . . . he's here . . .'

'Who is, love? Who? Bella, talk to me. Shall I call Jarvis, or the police? Where's your mum?' She wished they had figured out that code once mentioned, the one to use in an emergency.

'Oh, my God, Merry! It's the Flying Dutchman! Luuk's here! I gotta go.' Bella, almost breathless, spoke with such excitement it was electrifying.

'Letmeknowwhathappens!' she managed to squeeze in before the phone went dead. 'Oh, my God!' Merrin placed her hand on her beating heart. 'Please don't mess her around . . . she deserves better. She deserves to be loved by someone as much as we love her.' She threw her thoughts out into the ether and hoped the universe was listening.

An hour passed and Merrin stood back to admire the old-white colour she had chosen for much of the interior, a lovely contrast to the exposed brickwork and worn timbers it sat against.

'Hello?'

She heard the woman's call from the bottom of the open staircase, but with the radio on couldn't quite work out who it was, wondering if it was her mum with food, Ruby with wine or, better still, Bella with news!

The head that popped up and into the space was a surprise, to say the least.

'Loretta!' Merrin stood still, holding the paintbrush, letting the shock settle before turning off the radio and plopping the brush into an old jar of water to soak.

'Come in!' She felt a sense of pride in welcoming the woman into her home; the terrible anxiety that used to bookend any interaction was now no more than a mere flutter of nerves.

'Heather said the place was really coming along and so I thought I'd bring you these.' With a slightly shaky hand, she held out a bunch of wildflowers, whose subtle colours and delicate green fronds were beautiful.

'Oh! The first flowers in my new house. Thank you.' Merrin, genuinely touched, took them from her and laid them gently on the floor in the shade, planning to find a bucket to put them in when Loretta had gone. 'Would you . . . would you like to sit down?' She indicated the two beaten old leather chairs that had been there for as long as she could remember, now facing out over the wide balcony and the view of the cove beyond.

'I don't want to keep you.'

Merrin noted the creep of age over the woman's once well-oiled vowels.

'Not at all. The light's fading and I was just about to make a cuppa.'

'Well, if you're making.' Loretta sat in one of the chairs and was quiet, taking in the view. Merrin gripped the mugs of tea in her palms, made on the floor with the kettle plugged into an extension lead. 'I can't wait to have a proper kitchen.'

'I think if you have to wait for something you tend to appreciate it all the more, don't you?'

Merrin nodded and wondered if she, too, were thinking of love . . . She handed Loretta a hot mug of tea and took the seat next to her.

'This really is some spot.' Loretta seemed a little transfixed by the view. 'I brought you something else too, something I've wanted to give to you for a while, but I wasn't sure.' She hesitated, displaying uncharacteristic nerves as she pulled an envelope from her pocket. Merrin was curious and wary in equal measure.

'What is it?' She took the envelope from her.

'Open it,' Loretta urged, keeping her eyes on her face.

Peeling open the gummy flap, Merrin pulled out a black-and-white photograph.

'Oh, my goodness! Will you look at that!' She felt tears gather as, holding it close, she examined the beaming faces of Bella, Ruby and her mum, her beloved gran, Jarvis with a face like thunder and her dad, laughing so hard with his head tipped back and looking like a proper gent in his morning suit. The cart on which they all sat was abundant with flowers. Her gran had her stick in the air and Bella was brandishing a big, fat bacon sandwich. The sun shone overhead and Merrin herself looked full of joy. In the background, boats were dotted on the blue sea and it was in truth the most beautiful picture she had ever seen. 'Look at my dad! And my gran!' She sniffed, making no attempt to hide the tears that fell. 'This is . . .' Emotion robbed her of eloquence. 'This is fantastic, thank you!'

'The photographer sent me all the pictures. I got rid of them. It didn't feel right somehow to keep them, but that one, I couldn't throw away.'

'Do you know, I never gave them any thought, but I'm glad you kept this. I shall treasure it.' It was a snapshot of love and happiness and a reminder that life turns on a penny.

'And you can look at this day without pain?'

'I can.' She swallowed. 'Not that it makes the pain I've been through any easier to reconcile.' To say so felt bold, but this was the person she was now, emerged from a chrysalis of timidity.

'I understand.' Loretta looked into her lap. 'I'm getting old, Merrin. There's not much to recommend it, but it gives you clarity, I'll say that.'

Merrin stared at her over the rim of her mug, suspecting that Ma Mortimer wanted her to listen rather than comment.

'I wasn't born rich. I'm sure you have heard that – I know my story goes before me,' she huffed with a wry smile. 'I never had pretensions, and despite what folk say, I was never ashamed of my background or my family; quite the opposite. I think my parents were remarkable to raise six healthy kids in such adversity. That takes some doing, doesn't it?'

'It really does.' Merrin spoke sincerely and was fascinated by the woman's words, her candid admission.

'But Port Charles was determined to paint me in a certain way and, after some years of hiding away up at the Old Rectory, running off to Bristol whenever possible and crying myself to sleep, I embraced it. Sod the lot of them! I thought. I even bought a hat with two curled pheasant tails and my pearls' – she ran her fingers over the double string that sat over the silk collar of her shirt – 'and I cocked a snook at them all. Still do.' She took a sip of her tea. 'Guthrie,' she began, pausing to lick her dry lips and take a breath. 'Guthrie was a couple of decades older than me, and rich. I found both of these aspects fascinating and I remember the first time I walked into that big old house.' She looked again at the view as if lost in a memory. 'It was like a dream, to think I could live in a place like that!'

Merrin was rapt, the atmosphere silent, allowing every nuance to be heard and savoured from this woman who wanted to tell her story, revealing her inner self.

'I loved him. Contrary to popular belief, it wasn't only the trappings that appealed. I loved him. He read Shakespeare, he knew about wine and art and he had travelled. Can you imagine what it felt like to have someone like him interested in a girl from Mellor Waters? It was intoxicating.'

'I *can* imagine.' She spoke softly.

'Our wedding was modest; I was giddy with happiness and for the first month or so things were wonderful. Until I realised that they were only wonderful for me and that Guthrie, despite my every effort, was not happy, not at all. He was either sad or drunk.' She nodded and sipped her tea. 'And that was pretty much how he stayed until the day he died.'

'Why was he so sad?' Merrin asked without hesitation, swept up in the tale and unaware now of any reason to feel nervous when addressing Loretta.

'Because he loved someone else.' Her lip quivered and the hurt at this admission, even after all this time, was clear. 'He loved someone else very much and they had planned to marry, but his parents intervened and made a deal. They sent Guthrie around the world on his yacht for a few years and the girl – a local girl – they paid off her parents and the parents of a local boy whom she was encouraged to marry. And marry they did. Beneficial to all except dear Guthrie, who, broken-hearted, went off the rails.'

'God, that's—' She fumbled mentally for the word – what was it? Sad? Horrific? Cruel?

'It is.' Loretta finished her tea and placed the mug on the floor. 'He told me that on the day he was supposed to marry the girl he loved, his mother, Eunice, came into the room and presented him with a note saying the girl had changed her mind. His mother was furious, of course, shouting around the corridors "How *dare* she? A local girl! The daughter of a fisherman? A bloody fisherman!"'

'A fisherman?'

'Yes. A fisherman.' Loretta held her gaze. 'But it was all a ruse. It was the very next day that he set sail on his big life adventure, away for seven years. He was never able to forget her, but found escape in the bottom of a bottle. He saw her from time to time over the years, his would-be bride, but never spoke to her again. On the odd occasion when interaction was unavoidable, whether I was there or not, she looked through him like he was a ghost, and many was the time I wondered if he might be. So thin was his heart, so transparent his body that ached his whole life for the girl he lost.'

'So, you . . . you saw her? She was a Port Charles girl?'

'Oh yes. Guthrie died without ever knowing the cost of the transaction on what should have been his wedding day. But I've unearthed the documents since.'

'What was the transaction?' Merrin asked quietly with her pulse racing and her mouth dry. Outside, dusk drew its blind on the day as the sun sank beyond the window and the two women sat in the cocoon of her new home, transfixed by their conversation.

'It was a gift of the Old Boat Shed and a fancy trawler, given to the Kellows on the condition that their oldest boy, Arthur, marry Ellen Bligh. A fine vessel and one on which Ellen's husband worked happily until the day he died. And then I believe your father, too, and now Jarvis. The boat, *Sally-Mae*, a combination of Arthur's mother's name and Ellen's mother's name, is that right?'

'Yes.' Merrin's voice was no more than a murmur. *Granny Ellen and Guthrie* . . . It was a lot to comprehend, shocking, and she wondered how she had never questioned how humble fishermen had come to be the owners of this lovely building and the little trawler that had no debt.

'Ellen – the girl who married a Kellow, who gave birth to Ben and never left Port Charles,' Loretta surmised.

'I . . . I don't know what to say.' Her thoughts came thick and fast.

'Guthrie never forgot his first love and when he died I found this in a book of verse by his bed.' She reached again into her pocket and produced a small black-and-white photograph that she handed to Merrin. It was of her gran, Ellen Bligh; she was smiling with eyes lit up in a way Merrin had never seen before, beautiful.

'Look at the back,' Loretta instructed. Merrin turned it over and read the calligraphy.

'I would not wish any companion in the world but you.' William Shakespeare.

'So was it revenge, Loretta?' Her tone was kindly despite the nature of her question. 'Did you want to spoil Ellen's granddaughter's life because Ellen seemed instrumental in destroying Guthrie's?'

'Maybe a little bit at first.' The woman's eyes misted. 'But then I realised you two were in love and I did my best to make things perfect.'

'But then?' Merrin asked with emotion.

'I could see that my son wasn't ready. Was too young, immature, and so I asked him which he would choose: you or our money. It was a test. Guthrie would have given up every penny he owned for Ellen.'

'But Digby chose the money.' Merrin spoke with a crack to her voice, her distress not at the loss of him, not any more, but at the whole bloody mess and all the heartache that their love affair had caused.

The two women sat in silence with their thoughts.

'Is there anything else you want to say, Loretta?' Merrin braced herself for more revelations.

'Yes.' She sat up in the chair and straightened her pearls. 'Do you have any wine?'

'Oh! I do, somewhere.' She walked to the cardboard box in the corner and fished out a bottle of red, rinsed the mugs in the bucket and gave Mrs Mortimer a slug of warm red in an old tea mug before lighting a candle and sitting down with her own.

'So what now, Loretta? Do I need to give you this place back? Is it rightfully yours? Is that what you're saying? How about the *Sally-Mae*?' Her jaw was tense, her tone firm, and she decided in that moment that if that were the case, she would do it and she would survive. After all, she'd been through worse.

Loretta laughed out loud. 'Good God, no! Of course not! They're yours, of course they are yours! They were never mine. None of it is mine. Not a penny. Guthrie's parents made sure of that. Everything passed from Guthrie to Digby. I don't own a thing. Which is odd, really, as even my parents owned their caravan and the one hundred and fifty prime acres it sat on.' She winked at Merrin and lifted the mug to her lips. 'Cheers!'

She felt a loosening in her shoulders and neck and raised her own mug. 'Cheers, Loretta.'

The woman stood and wiped her mouth, and Merrin followed, ready to see her out. It was a surprise when she walked forward and held her in a tight hug, talking over her shoulder.

'I meant what I said that day: let yourself live, Merrin. Grab life and run with it because it's short.'

Having stood on the slipway and watched Ma Mortimer make her way up Fore Street, Merrin decided to sit on the steps that led down to the beach and try to make sense of the evening they had shared. As the cool night air bit, she looked towards the cottages, where lamplight glowed from the windows and her beloved family awaited her return. Sitting still, she looked out over the water.

'Oh, Gran, how I would love to chat to you right now . . .'

Turning her eyes towards movement, she saw the silhouette of a figure walking briskly up from the shoreline, as if newly sprung from the sea itself. A silhouette she didn't recognise, but a man, certainly. Tall and broad, he appeared to be heading straight towards her, his stride purposeful. Her mouth went a little dry with nerves. It was one thing to be alone out here in the environment she knew back to front, but with a stranger? She looked back at the lights along the quayside and took comfort from them, halfway between home and the pub, where family and friends were within shouting distance.

'Oh! Hi!' His voice was friendly and his manner confident as he lifted his hand in a wave and came closer.

As he approached she recognised the shape of him as someone she had seen jogging once or twice at a distance or had opened the door of Everit's for to let him pass. 'I thought I saw someone coming down to the beach; made me quite self-conscious, and then you disappeared. Didn't realise you'd taken a pew there in the shadows.' He wasn't from around here, no Cornish accent.

'Ha! I don't take a pew often,' she retorted.

'What?'

'Church, I . . . I don't often go to church.' She didn't know why she shared this.

'Ah, just the usual then? Weddings and funerals?'

'You don't know how accurate that is!' She laughed.

'I keep meaning to pop into St Michael's there on the hill.' He pointed over her head. 'It looks lovely, but I haven't been inside.'

'It is . . . Last time I went in was for my dad's funeral. He died.' She didn't know why she felt the need to tell the stranger, but did so anyway.

'It's probably best.'

'What is?'

'That he'd died, if you had a funeral for him.' He drew breath. 'Sorry, that's my idea of humour, which I can see by your expression is entirely the wrong thing to do at the moment. I do that when I get nervous, and death makes me nervous.'

'I think it makes everyone nervous.' She stared at the stranger, his manner odd.

'I'm sorry for your loss.' He let the sentiment settle.

'Thank you. It was a little while ago now, but still feels like yesterday in some ways.'

'Yep, I know that feeling. It gets you here.' He thumped his chest, where his heart lurked. 'It's awful, isn't it, when your dad dies? I lost mine five years ago and it's . . . awful. Yes, that's the best word.'

Merrin felt the spring of tears.

'Oh no, you look like you might cry! That's really bad! Worse than my joke.' He took a step towards her and stared, as if figuring what to do or say that might help. He had a kind face, crinkly eyes and a nice mouth. His hair was quite long.

'No, it's not; I mean, it *is* bad, but it's not you. I can usually control it. But tonight has been quite emotional and sometimes any mention of him or any thought of him and it's like flicking a switch, and that's terrible because when I saw him in real life, I never felt like crying, just smiling.'

'Well, the good news is that it stops. I can promise you that.' He spoke with authority.

'Which bit?'

'The sudden crying. Although I still cry – not all the time, but if I see someone in a coat similar to his, because I think it might actually *be* him and the disappointment is overwhelming. And I cry if I hear his voice on a message or a video. I cry when my mum or my brother cries about him; it sets off a sort of chain reaction.'

'You still seem to cry a lot.' She sniffed. 'After five years.'

He looked up towards the darkened night sky. 'Not really, maybe twice a month, and I think that's okay. But that switch thing you were talking about, that resets.'

'So it'll keep getting easier?' she asked with a note of hope that was too much to be putting in the direction of a stranger.

'Easier?' He put his hands in his pockets and looked out to sea. 'Not easier, no; it gets different.'

'Different?'

'Yeah, it's like it hurts just as much, but you've lived with it for so long you don't notice it quite as much, and you still miss him like crazy, but you learn to talk to him in your head and hear his answers too, if you're smart about it.'

'I do that already.'

'Then you are way ahead of the game.' He nodded in her direction, his expression kind.

She looked over at the *Sally-Mae*, moored against the harbour wall. 'My dad was my guy, my person. I knew that, no matter what, he would be there – not always sober, not always with the best advice. Some of his ideas were hare-brained!' She smiled. 'But he was my guy.'

'Well, I think you were very lucky.'

'Lucky?'

'Yes, I think so. Some people have terrible fathers and they would give their left nut to be sat here today feeling an overwhelming love and gratitude for a dad who's gone.'

'I guess you're right.' She looked down and noticed he was barefoot on the cold, wet sand. 'Where are your shoes?' She sat up straight, a little aghast.

'Behind you.' He pointed. 'That's why I was coming over here, to retrieve them.'

'Oh, I thought . . .'

'You thought?'

Merrin sounded it out and thought it ridiculous to say, '*I thought you were coming over to me* . . .' 'I thought you had shoes on!'

'Oh, no. It's my thing. It's odd, I know, but since I was little I like being barefoot. There's something about walking on the sand or the grass or dirt and feeling it beneath your feet, it sort of connects you to the planet. I know that sounds a bit—' He pulled a face.

'No.' She smiled. 'No, it doesn't.'

'You should try it.'

'Maybe I will.' She tucked her hands inside the sleeves of her pashmina; a chill was starting to bite.

'So are you from Port Charles? I think I may have seen you once or twice before.' He reached behind her and gathered his trainers and socks, which she hadn't spotted, into his hands, leaning close enough for her to inhale the scent of him: a clean, lemony scent, fresh with a hint of sea salt.

'Maybe. And yes, I'm from Port Charles.'

'Oh, right, and you like it?' he asked as he balanced, popping on his socks and shoes.

'I love it. It's my home. I have a memory lurking behind every pebble and every grain of sand.'

'I get that. But for me, swap grains of sand for blades of grass. My family is in Herefordshire – farmers. My brother runs the business now, and I like knowing everything is as I left it. And I love going home to see my mum, but when you're more than a phone call away . . .' He exhaled. 'It can be tough.'

'So where do you live now, if not Herefordshire?'

'I currently live with Nancy Cardy. Up on the corner of Fore Street and Lamp Hill. Do you know her?'

'Yes. Yes, I know her.' She smiled.

'I'm the head teacher at St Endellion's School and I'm lodging with her until I find a house.'

'My dad converted that room; it used to be loft space and he made it into that brilliant room with the view.'

'Oh! So you're related to Nancy! Are you Jarvis's sister? I've met him once, seen him around. Don't think he's that keen on me.'

She let out a small laugh. 'No, no, I'm not Jarvis's sister. But I am his sister-in-law.'

'Is everyone in Port Charles either related or feuding?'

'Yes. That's about the sum of it.'

She looked over her shoulder towards the lights coming from the cottage and felt the worry that her mum might be waiting for her to come and eat supper.

'I should probably be getting home.'

'Yes, of course, it was nice talking to you . . . sorry, I don't know your name?'

'Merrin. Merrin Kellow.'

'And I'm Alex, Alex Morgan.'

Merrin jumped up from the damp step, wiped the back of her jeans and slowly climbed the steps up to the path. Alex followed and fell into step beside her and she noted that he was really very tall, and his hair was curly and sat below his ears and brushed the top of his turtleneck collar. Her dad would say it was too long. He had rolled his jeans down and now zipped up his navy hoodie.

'You're going to be okay, Merrin.' He forced his hands into his pockets, as the wind picked up.

'I know.' She nodded. 'I am okay.'

'When you have a great dad, everything he does and everything he says throughout his life is subtle instruction for times just as these. And so you will be okay because he has made sure of it.'

Looking at him now, she felt the grumble of longing in her stomach, ridiculously wishing that he didn't have to go. It had been a while since she had felt this . . . this firecracker of anticipation in her gut.

'So, will I see you again, do you think? What are the chances of us bumping into each other in a huge place like Port Charles?'

Alex looked over her head. 'I think the chances are very high.' He smiled. 'I'm actually thinking I might be here at the same time tomorrow, just on the off chance.'

'Right.'

'Right. But today is what's important right now. Because we've met, put a stake in the ground. Our first step.'

'Yes.' She stared at him. 'Our first step. I like that.'

He leant forward and she thought for one glorious, scary, horrifying, heart-stopping moment that he might kiss her, but he didn't. Instead, he ran his thumb over her cheek and looked into her eyes. He pulled away and she saw the paint on his thumb. She wiped at the blobs of emulsion on her skin, of which she had been unaware.

What she was aware of, however, was how his touch had pulsed through her very being, warming a place deep inside her that for the longest time had been cold.

'I'll see you tomorrow, Merrin Kellow.'

She nodded, hardly able to respond due to the bubble of happiness that stoppered her throat. Minutes. That was all it had taken, mere minutes in his company and it was as if she were lit from within, aglow with an incredible optimism.

'Now I have to run.' He sighed. 'I've left Frank Ferdinand Falkenstok in a rather precarious spot.'

'Who's Frank Ferdinand Falkenstok?' She was curious.

'My car!' he yelled over his shoulder. 'A Fancy Ford Focus – what else was I going to call him?'

She laughed and looked over at Vera Wilma Brown parked on the cobbles outside Kellow Cottages, wondering how the two might get along . . .

EPILOGUE

'Morning, Merry! Beautiful day for it!' Robin called from the quayside, where he walked hand in hand with his partner, John, who waved back. John had moved to Port Charles nearly eighteen months ago. According to Jarvis, they'd been in the pub watching football on the big screen when in walked a group of townies. John had made a beeline for Robin and the two had chatted and laughed until closing time, when, at the ringing of the bell for last orders, John had simply taken his hand and *out* they had walked . . . John had opened up a coffee shop, which was thriving. Folk went for his coffee, the glorious fresh-baked patisserie and his banter, which was loud and welcoming. The first person he had employed, on Merrin's strong recommendation, was the lady she had become friendly with since her return – Lizzie, who washed the dishes and kept the place as neat as a pin. With her new haircut, a steady routine and no more than human kindness, the woman had blossomed, bringing shame to all those who had not similarly embraced her over the years.

'It really is, Robin.' She blew him a kiss. 'A beautiful day!'

Merrin stood on the broad balcony that sat along the front of her fine chalet home. She ran her hand over the steel ridge of the handrail and down on to the tempered glass below, marvelling at how she was now able to sit out on this solid terrace in all weathers. Modern and open-plan on the inside, yet using local stone and weathered timbers that sat on the original footprint, the Old Boat Shed in its present form looked as if it had always been here. Standing proud and grand on the quayside, its half-timbered walls supported the wide smoked-glass gable end that made it seem as if their sitting room were floating on the sea itself. A beautiful house, sprung from the ashes of her loss.

Turns out her dad had been right when he wrote:

> When you're ready and you've done enough adventuring and figuring out, come home, Merrin. Come back to Port Charles, this little place where your spirit lingers even after you have driven off in Vera Wilma Brown. Walk the beach barefoot in all weathers, my little maid, and let yourself be. Be open to what is right in front of your very eyes and let yourself be happy.

It was good advice from the man who loved her and had bestowed upon her the greatest gift.

'How I miss you, Dad.' She let the words carry on the wind out over the sea.

Currently, she and Alex were sleeping on a mattress on the floor of the master bedroom, waiting on delivery of their brand-new bed. Heather was doing well, excited to cook for Alex, whose appetite was legendary. It gave her the incentive to start cooking again. And in the process she had regained a little of her spark.

Ruby had admired the finished place, but followed it with a barbed comment. 'It's nice enough, Merry, but you can't beat an old cottage for character, can you?'

It made her chuckle now to think of it. The Kellow cottage was worth more financially, but of course, Ruby was cursed with a demeanour that believed the grass was always a little bit greener on the other side. But how they loved each other, always would. *Kellow girls.*

'Silly moo,' she whispered affectionately, with one eye on her sister's home from this vantage point.

Luuk and Alex were standing on the slipway, chatting. Alex caught her eye and waved, before laying his hand on his mate's broad shoulder and jogging away. It was nice for everyone that they were mates. And along with Jarvis, they had been christened the Three Amigos and were pretty much inseparable. It certainly made it easier for her, Ruby and Bella to hang out. Luuk was still proving himself in her eyes, but she had to admit, the devotion he showed to Bella and Glynn was warming – and about time too.

Her bare feet gripped the cold, slate floor. The wind kicked up and whipped her long skirt around her legs as she looked out over the coastal path, towards Reunion Point. It was a place she liked to visit from time to time, taking comfort from the thud of her heart inside her ribcage as she stared out over the untamed, ever-moving sea and behind her, nothing but the slow roll of green fields. She liked to be still there and close her eyes, letting her fingers comb the salty air of this place where her heritage lurked beneath her feet and her own story had taken two twists. A proposal and a goodbye, both of which had shaped her in ways she could never have foreseen.

It might have been six years since she had been abandoned in the vestry, but still the thought of that day could, on occasion, make her wince, causing the breath to stop in her throat and forcing her to swallow the sickening embarrassment that was like a toxic sediment lining her throat and sitting in her gut. And being there on the cliff edge sometimes stirred it up and swirled it in her blood like a fresh disease. And it was for this precise reason that she went there. It was *good* to remember. It helped her appreciate all she now had and how far she had come. And here she was, back in Port Charles for good. Home. And a happily married woman.

The Reverend Pimm had agreed to their rather unusual demands and had married them in secret – no guests, no flowers, no music, no frock and no disaster. Just a solemn exchange of vows with hands grasped, eyes locked and a shoeless walk on the beach to follow.

Three days it had taken, *three days*, before Heather noticed the shiny gold band on her daughter's finger.

'What in Judas's name?' She had grabbed Merrin's hand and studied the little gold circle.

'Is this what I think it is?' she had asked with her hand at her throat.

'Oh yes, did we not say?' She beamed. 'We got married. I am now officially Mrs Alex Morgan!'

'Oh, Merry! Oh, my Lord!' Her mum had held her in the longest, warmest hug and they had both cried. She was in no doubt that her mum, like herself, wondered what Ben would have made of the news. Merrin guessed he'd have been happy and would most likely have cracked open a bottle of Bella's dad's blackberry wine.

Now, in the cool morning light, she looked down into the water, where the fat wooden stumps of an ancient jetty were still visible when the tide was out. Some larger stones, too, that had once been part of the harbour walls, littered the wet sand, and to her they summed up life in Port Charles: things withered, evolved, collapsed and aged, but if you looked hard enough, you could see they never truly disappeared.

She heard the front door downstairs shut and turned to watch her husband lope up the open-plan stairs, using the thick rope bannister for support before coming into view. The sight of him was still a wonder to her, this man who had sprung from the sea on the day Loretta and she had built a bridge. She smiled and waved.

Alex opened the sliding glass door and came to stand behind her. He slipped his arms around her waist and placed them on the large mound of her stomach.

'So, what's going to arrive first, do you reckon?' He kissed the back of her neck. 'Our new baby or our new bed?'

'I don't know.' She placed her hands over the back of his palms. 'And it doesn't matter too much; what will be will be.'

'True that.' He reached forward and took the mug of tea from her hands, sipping it. He had learnt that in Kellow homes, tea was communal.

'I was just saying to Jarvis, I've heard juicy gossip today. Some of the staff were talking about Loretta Mortimer, who's the chair of the board of governors. They reckon she was born in a field on the outskirts of town and that old Guthrie Mortimer only married her because his father made him marry *someone*, and that he drank because he never got over his one true love, Helen. No wonder she's so spiky! What do you think of that?'

She turned to face him, the man who held her hand across the mattress at night. The man she loved beyond words and would love beyond life.

'I think that it's a shame folk still find the need to talk about someone at all, sad that she should be the brunt of gossip and tittle-tattle for all these years. And I think you'll find the girl Guthrie loved and who loved him in return was called Ellen, not Helen.'

'Hah! Your gran was called Ellen.' Alex smiled at the coincidence.

'Yes she was, my love, yes she was.'

ABOUT THE AUTHOR

Photo © 2012 Paul Smith
www.paulsmithphotography.info

Amanda Prowse is an international bestselling author of twenty-eight novels published in dozens of languages. Her chart-topping titles *What Have I Done?*, *Perfect Daughter*, *My Husband's Wife*, *The Coordinates of Loss*, *The Girl in the Corner* and *The Things I Know* have sold millions of copies around the world.

Other novels by Amanda Prowse include *A Mother's Story*, which won the coveted Sainsbury's eBook of the Year Award. *Perfect Daughter* was selected as a World Book Night title in 2016. She has been described by the *Daily Mail* as 'the queen of family drama'.

Amanda is the most prolific writer of bestselling contemporary fiction in the UK today. Her titles consistently score the highest online review approval ratings across several genres.

A popular TV and radio personality, Amanda is a regular panellist on Channel 5's *Jeremy Vine* show, as well as featuring on numerous daytime ITV programmes. She also makes countless guest appearances on national and independent radio stations, including LBC and talkRADIO, where she is well known for her insightful observations and infectious humour.

Amanda's ambition is to create stories that keep people from turning off the bedside lamp at night, that ensure you walk every step with her great characters, and tales that fill your head so you can't possibly read another book until the memory fades . . .